BLEED THROUGH

ALEX GRECO
ADA SERIES BOOK 2

BY
ROGER CANAFF

BROOKLYN
WRITERS PRESS

Bleed Through
By Roger Canaff

BROOKLYN WRITERS PRESS
BROOKLYN, NY

ISBN: 978-0-9997903-7-3 (e-book)
ISBN: 978-0-9997903-8-0 (paperback)
ISBN: 978-0-9997903-9-7 (hardback)

Library of Congress Catalog Card Number: 2019913320

Cover Design by: Mark Thwaites

www.brooklynwriterspress.com

www.rogercanaff.com

For Kristi

"Cut off as I am, it is inevitable that I should sometimes feel like a shadow walking in a shadowy world. When this happens I ask to be taken to New York City. Always I return home weary but I have the comforting certainty that mankind is real flesh and I myself am not a dream."
Hellen Keller

"Persistence. It's that certain little spirit that compels you to continue just when you're at your most tired. It's that quality that forces you to persevere, find the route around the stone wall. It's the immovable stubbornness that will not allow you to cave in when everyone says give up."
Estée Lauder

"We know what we are,
but know not what we may become."
Ophelia, from *Hamlet*, Act 4, Scene 5

ALSO BY ROGER CANAFF

COPPERHEAD ROAD

AMONG THE DEAD
Alex Greco Series Book 1

ONE

After 9/11, the cameras went up. New York City, like everywhere else, was on its way to becoming a full-time surveil-
lance environment anyway, but the nightmare of that day
accelerated the trend. In addition to the multitude the NYPD
monitored, they were attached to every business, school
and residential building–unblinking, 24/7 observers of endless ATM transactions, street traffic, and quiet opulence in
the right apartment lobby.

The last one to capture the slender, coiffed image of
Kimberly Hadley in the final moments before her life was
shattered was from such a lobby. The building, called The
Vernon, was in SoHo, on a quiet, brick-paved section of
Wooster Street. Fastened on the wall across from the
doorman's desk, the camera recorded the small but sleek,
dark accented lobby, with its black marble floor gleaming
beneath the polished mahogany desk.

Passing in front of it at 10:54 p.m., with their backs to
the camera, were Kim Hadley and Kevin Dunaway, her dinner companion. Dunaway lived in the building and paused

momentarily at the desk to ask for an expected envelope. The doorman, a friendly, perpetually smiling man named Gavin, dug it out from somewhere on the desk and handed it to him. Kim and Kevin then disappeared around a corner toward the elevators. Kevin led the way, with Kim following close behind.

The next camera to capture Kim Hadley, crawling and bleeding profusely from her mouth and nose, an eye-socket nearly fractured and her skirt torn at the waist, was mounted outside and pointed toward a narrow, time-beaten alley to the left (if someone were looking out) of the building's glass front doors. Another doorman, Luis, had relieved Gavin at 11:00 p.m. Luis monitored a group of four cameras that recorded different areas in and around The Vernon. He was watching the Mets game on his iPhone with half a hoagie in his mouth when movement on the alley camera caught his eye. At first, he thought he was seeing an animal, a dog maybe, hobbling along on a bad leg. Then he spit out his sandwich, dropped his phone on the desk and sprinted out the door.

TWO

"Miss?" she heard. Still on her hands and knees, she turned toward the voice, one eye open. *Another doorman,* she thought. *Not the first one.* She saw his eyes widen in shock and horror. "Miss, can you hear me?"

"Yeah," she said, a guttural croak. "I'm okay. I just ... need a cab." She was dragging her bag behind her with her left arm. Her right hand was gripping the pavement, moving in time with her knees as she edged herself toward the curb. Her hands were small and delicate, and immaculately manicured.

"I think you need an ambulance. Do you think you can walk? I'll have you wait in the lobby while I call one. We should call the police."

"No police," she said, lifting her right hand painfully in the air as if warding something off. "Please. No police. No ambulance. I just need a taxi."

"Miss, I really can't do that. Please ... if I can just help you up, I'll ..."

"I called 9-1-1 already," another man called out from across the street. He was huffing and puffing, striding across the street toward them. Kim saw him with the one eye she could see out of and grimaced. He was older, maybe fifty-five or sixty, white-haired and stately looking, and holding his cell phone. Like the doorman, he wore a look of horror and disgust. "They should be here any minute. I don't think she should try to move."

"I need to leave here," she said, still garbled but a little clearer. She was forcing clarity into her voice the same way she was forcing it back into her thoughts. She had hoped the alley would be a good way to get out of the building unseen. Apparently not. "No police. No ambulance. Please."

"She's probably in shock," the older man said to the doorman, as if she wasn't in their presence. He was dressed in slacks and a fine silk sweater with a collared shirt underneath. Kim recognized the make of shirt from the pattern—a top-of-the-line British brand.

"No, I'm not," she said, finally getting to her feet. She was maybe five-foot-three, thin with narrow shoulders. "Not in shock. I'm okay. Now please, if you want to help me, hail a cab."

"Absolutely not," the old man said with an air of authority she found unsurprising. "Young lady, just stay where you are." Then she heard them. Sirens. At least two cars, coming around the corner at Spring Street, from the west. Kim summoned the remainder of her strength, now upright on wobbly legs, clutching her skirt with one hand to keep it from sliding off her frame. She could see a few other people, drawn from Spring Street by the ruckus but keeping their distance. No one appeared to be filming or snapping photos of her yet. But all of them, as far as she could see, were holding smart phones and staring at her intently. It was only a matter of time.

She turned and stared back down the alley, past the

side door she had stumbled out of after her escape from Kevin. New construction had opened the alley temporarily through to West Broadway. She hadn't wanted to go that way as West Broadway was lined with high-end shops, bars and restaurants and was likely to have more foot traffic, especially around midnight on a cool and pleasant Friday night. In this moment, though, she simply couldn't stay where she was. As the first blue lights strafed the building tops on Wooster Street and the sirens screamed louder, Kim turned and bolted down the alley and out of sight.

THREE

"Don't touch it," the older cop said to his partner, who had only a few months on the job. The younger one shined his flashlight on it–a balled up, bloody piece of cloth with someone's initials on one corner. They were in the alley beside The Vernon, awaiting squad detectives for what was proving to be a very strange case. It was an assault of some kind, maybe even a rape. Two guys saw a nicely dressed Caucasian woman, bleeding badly and crawling out of the alley like a dog after a fight. But the woman had taken off like a rocket as two First Precinct squad cars approached. As far as anyone knew, she just disappeared on West Broadway. Maybe into a cab, or another building.

"The victim ran," the younger one said with a shrug. "They tried to help her and she took off."

"They'll find her. Or she'll come back."

"Why'd she run, though?"

"Who the fuck knows? Maybe she panicked. Or maybe she was illegal or a pros or something, I don't know. But leave it. Let the dicks bag it up. It's not our problem. Besides, the second you touch it, you're in the chain."

"Chain?"

"Of custody, dickhead. You don't want that, trust me.

Just keep your Maglite trained on it, they'll be here any minute. I'll take statements from the doorman and that old douchebag in the meantime."

***

Around the time police discovered the bloody handkerchief, Kim was just realizing she dropped it back in the alley. She was in a cab, moving slowly but steadily through late-night Manhattan traffic toward the apartment she shared with her younger sister Emily. Her face was aching, the pain finally encroaching where shock had numbed things earlier. But she was grateful to be away from whatever shit show was going on back at Kevin's building, between responding police officers, the nosy old man and the poor, freaked-out doorman. They meant well, she supposed. The cops, even. But she was not their problem. Thankfully none of the revelers and passers-by on West Broadway had seemed to look at her twice, and her cabbie hadn't even looked in the rear-view mirror since she'd climbed in. There were advantages to life in New York City. Anonymity was one of them.

Wanting something to hold over her bad eye, she remembered the handkerchief, the one she carried around and cleaned her disabled sister with after one mess or another. Then she cursed as she realized she had used it already to pad the bleeding from her mouth while she searched for an alternate exit from Kevin's building. She had eventually found such an exit, a side door in a trash collection room, and had burst out into the alley. The handkerchief was probably clutched in her hand, but then she had collapsed.

The cab turned north onto Third Avenue and Kim found some old coffee napkins in her bag to use instead, folding them and holding them gingerly against her face. She could barely touch the area without wanting to scream in pain. She sensed she was probably in for more than a black eye. She had had plenty of those, but this was going to be worse. She sighed as she contemplated what limits *that* would put on her in public—a badly bruised or broken eye socket. Neither was an easy thing to explain away. Traffic was thin on Third Avenue, and the cab rounded her corner a minute or so later.

There were things that might have given it away, she thought. *What he wanted from me. All night long, there were signals. But I ignored them. Because I hoped.*

The cab slowed to a stop in front of her building and she glanced up at her fifth-floor window. She wasn't sure if her sister was awake or if she'd wake her coming in. Generally, Emily didn't ask a lot of questions. But the sight of Kim, she knew, might freak her out. One more thing to deal with.

Fuck Me. I hoped.

That, in a nutshell, was Kim Hadley's biggest problem.

FOUR

Friday, September 15 (earlier), 11:00 p.m.

"You look like you're made of glass," Kevin Dunaway said, gently taking Kim's wrist and turning it so that his thumb was just below her palm. He moved it back and forth a little. She pretended like she was blushing, not sure how else to react. She had heard rumors about Kevin. So far, they were all spot-on. "So delicate. And your skin? My God. You're a perfect spokesperson for your own product, I hope you know that."

"Thank you," she said. "I'm proud to say my products work. I'm not a model, though. Just a businesswoman."

"You could be," he said. "I know, I know, it sounds like a line. But it's true." They were seated in Kevin's spacious living room, she on the couch and he on a leather ottoman across from her. He had poured them both champagne after insisting she come up for a nightcap. That was a little worrisome. For one, Kevin had had a great deal to drink over dinner, more than she expected. And of course, it put her further into a quandary faced by so many women–that of being stuck in a situation where the line between professional and personal was blurring.

"Well, you're great for my ego," she said, smiling. Things had been okay so far, but she was looking for a way to end the encounter on a nice, pleasant note.

Kevin was a partner at the venture capital firm that was considering making an investment in Kim's skincare line, named "Emily" after her younger sister. It was a move that would make her instantly and solidly wealthy. He had been polite if not shamelessly flirty at their dinner, which had doubled as a business meeting. But now he was bordering on pushy.

"But I've got to get going. Really, thank you for everything, Kevin. Having you and CIG behind Emily means everything to me. I won't let you down."

"Tomorrow is Saturday," he said, giving her an admonishing, raised-eyebrow look. "Relax, Kimberly. You can sleep in."

"I generally don't. And honestly, I've got to get going." At this, he feigned a wounded look.

"Boyfriend?"

"No. My sister. She's an adult, but ... I take care of her."

"Ah. I'm sorry. Is she ..."

"Mildly disabled, yes. She's great. I don't mind at all. But I do need to get back."

"Oh, I'm sorry. Does she need medication, or ..."

"No, nothing like that. She's probably asleep. It's just better for me to be there."

"Well, it's 11:15," he said, filling her glass. "My guess is, you're right, she's in bed. Stay a little longer. I'll get you a car home, of course." He winked at her. Kevin was handsome, square-headed with dark eyes, a heavy brow and a sturdy chip for a chin. He wore a beautiful, gleaming white French-cuff shirt and a power-red tie, now casually loosened. Kim assumed he normally got what he wanted from women. This, too, was a rumor about him. But the darker rumor was that he could be persistent. And that was putting it lightly.

"She's unpredictable," Kim said, sighing. She slid her wrist out from under from his hand and smiled at him. Kevin was right that Kim was both beautiful and delicate looking, with doll-like features and small, elegant limbs. "So really, I should be there."

"Twenty minutes," Kevin said, putting his hands in prayer formation around his champagne flute. "That's all I ask. I know about your brand. I love it. We're going to back you. But I'd like to know more about you."

"About me?"

"Sure. You're a beautiful young woman. You're brilliant, and you work your ass off. That's all obvious. But I make it a point to know about my investments, professionally and personally."

"Okay," she said with a shrug. Inside, she tensed. *Not the past. Please.*

"You're from Virginia, right? Originally I mean?"

"I am," she said, hoping a shadow didn't cross her face. "From a very small place, though. It was in Tolland County. Not many people know of it."

"You know I'm from Maryland," he said. "Annapolis. My father was a defense contractor. I grew up there and went to college in D.C."

"Oh wow, D.C.," she said. "I guess technically I'm from the D.C. suburbs, but it was pretty far out. We didn't make it to the city much."

"Well, you have to admit, it's nice to be connected with someone who reminds you of home."

"A little," she said, suppressing a dark grin. That was a whopper of a lie, probably the biggest she'd told all night. "But New York is home now."

"Yes, for you and your sister, I guess. Anyone else?"

"No, no one else."

"Your family. Are they still in Virginia?"

"No," she said, dropping her eyes unconsciously. "They're gone. It's just me and Emily. But that's okay. It's how we like it."

"Ah yes, your brand's namesake," he said. "Well, she's going to be rich also." His eyes now rested on hers. There was a mask of relaxation in his look, but underneath it was something intense. Something heated, and focused. "Whatever challenges she has, you'll be able to give her the very best. That's got to feel good." Carefully, as if he was about to place it on an uncertain surface, he set his flute down on a side table, and took hers as well. Then he took her small hand in both of his. They were warm, heavy, and dry.

"It does, of course," she said, her heart beating more forcefully now, and not in a good way. "Thank you."

"You *have* thanked me," he said. "Just ... relax. Stay with me a while." He slid from the ottoman over to the couch and sat beside her. In front of them was a floor-to-ceiling window with a beautiful view of the Hudson River and the lights of Hoboken on the other side.

"Kevin, really. You're sweet. This apartment is beautiful. But I've got to go."

"I'm going to make you rich, Kim Hadley. There isn't much I ask in return. Let this happen." His arm went over her shoulder, dwarfing her underneath it. Kim weighed barely one hundred five pounds.

"It can't happen," she said, putting a little bit of steel

into her voice while trying, desperately, not to offend him. "I'm sorry, but it really can't." He sat back against the couch, folding his arms.

"I told you I'm not a man who takes 'no' for an answer. I wouldn't be where I am if I was."

"You don't seem like it," she said, swallowing something dry in her throat. "But I have to go. Thank you for a wonderful evening. No need to call a car. I'll just get a cab downstairs." His left hand now went to her knee, bare just below the hem of her skirt. She made a move to rise, but his hand moved up just slightly, keeping her on the couch.

"It's not that simple, Kim," he said. She could hear it now, the meanness under the charm. It was coming through like a bell over water. "You don't just walk out on this. On me. No one does."

"Kevin, please."

"I'll ask you the same thing. *Please.* Will that work?"

"What? No, I told you, I have to go."

"Not. Yet." The big hand moved up to her mid-thigh under her skirt. Her heart was a hammering thing in her chest. His hand felt like hot lead.

"What exactly are you telling me to do?"

"Nothing you won't do on your own volition. Now relax and let me kiss you."

"I won't. Please let me leave. Now." She tried to push up from the couch, but the big hand on her thigh pushed her back down. She felt pain for the first time that evening. He pivoted so that he was almost facing her, placing his right hand on her left knee, edging her skirt up from that side.

"Stop it! I'll scream, I swear to God."

"No, you won't," he said, staring at her, his eyes alive with excitement. This, she knew in that instant, was what

Kevin craved. Not sex. Capitulation. "You're not a scream-er." Then she used the heel of her hand, a trick she had learned years before as a child, to strike him as hard as she could in the shoulder. She could have gone for his chin or his nose, but she was still trying not to really hurt him. The blow must have been harder than Kevin expected; he fell back on the couch and his hands came off of her body. She stood up quickly and reached for her bag.

"I'm leaving now," she said, and turned away from him toward the door. He said nothing but leaned forward and grabbed her skirt at the waist, pulling her back toward him. The zipper tore; his hand felt like a steam shovel. For a terrible second, she felt complete control leave her body. He was going to pull her onto his lap, or just tear the skirt off of her altogether. Then she saw the two delicate champagne flute glasses on the side table. She reached for one and swung it backward at him, still clutched in her hand. Reflexively he put up a hand to stop the glass, and it shattered against his right palm.

"A*uggh*! God damn it, you bitch!" He was bleeding badly from his right palm and gripped it with his left hand. Then he looked up at her as she was backing away from him. She could feel the rush coming off of him now, a glee mixed with rage and blunt resolve. And then, with diz-zying speed, he launched himself up from the couch and punched her with his bleeding hand, square in the eye. He pulled back and jabbed at her again, hitting the right side of her mouth. Blood seemed everywhere, a mixture of hers and his. She felt the flesh of her mouth mash and tear over her teeth. It was a pain she knew well from a long time before. The pain in her eye, though, was worse. It was like he shattered something. Instinctively, she turned away from him. He reached for her left ankle and grabbed it, sending her flying forward, almost face-planting on his hardwood floor. Her palms broke her fall, but not without sending shooting pains up each arm.

"Fuck-whore," he breathed behind her. He grunted and grabbed for her right ankle, this time with his bleeding hand. She could feel him, pulling her legs apart and simultaneously drawing her toward him. She felt his right hand moving up the inside of her leg, gripping every few inches. She felt his fingers brush her underwear, at the crotch panel between her legs. She heard his voice, like a snake's rattle. "I've got you now."

Then she screamed, kicking backward with her right leg, pouring into it every last ounce of energy she had. She had on Louboutin Mary Jane pumps, the ones with the red soles, and hoped the heel would find his eye. Instead it seemed to have found his chest, the same place she had struck him earlier. It was enough to cause him to bellow and let go with his left hand.

This is it, she thought with bitter clarity. She had been in a place like this before. Feeling his grip loosen, she scrambled to her feet and caught sight of the now empty champagne bottle, next to the one remaining flute on the little table. She smashed it on the side table and held the remainder of it out in front of her, a jagged, dark-green bottle neck. She couldn't see herself in this moment, but she imagined a bloody apparition. A doll, maybe, from a nightmare.

"Come on, motherfucker," she said, the last word sliding out of her mouth like a well-practiced slur. Her voice took on a throaty edge. This was yet another battle in a miserable series, but she was ready. Kevin didn't make a move, though. Instead, after a few seconds, he started laughing, still clutching his shoulder.

"Your accent. I can hear it now. The one you tried to bury all night. White trash. That's all you are. And you just blew your only chance to at least pass for something else."

"You're gonna regret this," she said, backing away toward the door. "You have no idea what I'm made of."

"Bullshit," he said, spitting the words at her as she tossed the bottle neck onto the floor. "You're made out of glass. And you'll shatter just like it, you stupid cunt."

FIVE

Tolland County, Virginia, 2001

The song on the radio that was perched on the scarred dresser among the tubes and little jars in front of the mirror was "Shattered Dreams," by Johnny Hates Jazz. Outside it had been raining, seemingly for days, but the girl in the mirror didn't care. The girl in the mirror was pretty, and happy. She could ignore the rain. She could ignore the loneliness, the constant fear, the stomachache that never really went away. She could even ignore the chemical stench from what passed as the family kitchen, that horrid smell which poor Emily was too young and broken to even notice. To Emily, the girl supposed, that's just how houses smelled.

She smacked her lips to make the pink shade even, brushed a little bit of powder on her cheeks, and then made a kissy-face in the mirror. She smoothed her top, a frilly blouse that exposed a little of her midriff above a bright skirt with deep, soft pockets. She drooped her shoulders and then turned, lifting one in a vampy pose, and smiled. It was wonderful, in the mirror. Her eyes fell to the collection of beauty products on the dresser. She loved just spreading it all out on the surface from the hidden box in the closet, like it was hers. Someday she wanted a real make-up mirror and vanity, with a little chair that went with it and a million things to try on. She looked over the products, searching for one last, perfect thing to apply. Then her eyes caught movement in the mirror, and her breath stopped dead in her throat.

He was supposed to have been out, until at least ten o'clock.

"You wanna go to school?" her father said in a drunken slur. He had pushed the door open and now sauntered in, taking wide, uncertain steps. His eyes met hers in the looking glass. Her mouth opened and closed, but nothing came out. She turned away from the mirror; her father's image in it was somehow worse than seeing it in front of her. He came closer as she braced herself against the dresser.

"Dad, please. I was just playing."

"You wanna go to school? Like a regular fuckin' kid?!" He let a beer bottle fly from his right hand, barely more than a flick of his wrist, and it shattered against the wall just above her bed.

"I ... I don't mind homeschool," she said. She pasted a trembling smile on her lips, and then swiped a hand savagely across them, remembering she had lipstick on.

"Oh, that's not what I hear," he said, his voice lower. He seemed suddenly calm, but she knew better. Her father was thin and slight, not unlike she was, but he was leather tough, sinewy, and all muscle. He leered at her through reddened eyes, set deep below thin, black eyebrows and a high forehead. "You love to talk, don't you? You talk about wantin' to go to school. Real school. So how the fuck is that supposed to work? Huh?! Whaddam I supposed to do? Send you to school like this? Like a fuckin' whore?!" In time with his voice reaching a crescendo, he backhanded her in the face with his right hand. She saw bright, white spots of light for a moment, then went sprawling across the bed, face-down. Then she panicked as she realized that was probably what he intended.

"Dad, please," she said, close to tears but not daring to cry for fear of more of his wrath. Her father hated cryba-bies. And then, as if the worst couldn't wait to arrive, she could feel him, leaning over her, his left hand in the small of her back. "Please. Please let me go clean up. I'll throw it all away, I promise ..."

"Shhh," he hissed into her ear. "You wanna be a whore? Dress like a whore? Make yourself up like a goddam fuckin' whore? Then I'm gonna treat you like a whore."

"No, no ... Please!" She couldn't help it anymore. She hadn't wanted to scream for fear of waking Emily, which could get the child killed if she walked in in a moment like this, but still she shrieked as she heard him unbuckling the old, cracked leather belt with the rebel flag buckle. She had felt the buckle. She preferred it to what was coming next. She had had that, too.

"You make it easy, dontcha?" he said, digging under the skirt and reaching for her underwear. "But that's what you get, see? Dressin' like this."

There was a window beside the bed, covered with a faded blue shade about three-quarters of the way down. Underneath it, she could see the rain against the window, and shadows of the bleak trash-strewn yard beyond it. It should have been dusky, but the weather darkened things early. Mostly she could see her own reflection in the win-dow—the smeared lipstick and running mascara—and she stared beyond it as her father grunted behind her. His right hand, always the stronger one, was dug into her hip as he

27

thrusted. She gritted her teeth and waited for it to be over.

And then she saw something else in the window. It wasn't her reflection. It was on the other side, corpuscular and shrouded. It was a face, staring back at her. The eyes, red-rimmed and haunted, were familiar. Not quite a reflection. But perhaps, as close as it got. She squeezed her eyes shut, willing the face in the window to leave her.

SIX

When Kim opened her good eye, the nightmare releasing her like hands from a grave, Emily was standing over her bed in the dark, staring down at her. For a split-second Kim almost screamed anew, and then realized where she was. Where *they* were. They were in New York City, in her safe, comfortable luxury building in Kips Bay.

"You had a nightmare again, Kimmy," Emily said. She spoke slowly, and in a mournful, lumbering tone. Kim grunted and sat up with difficulty. A *nightmare, yes. But really a memory.* She ached, and in more places than just her face, which was still throbbing at her eye and her mouth. Despite an ice pack she had put on before bed, her eye was a cauldron of pain. She still couldn't see out of it, and it was excruciating to try to open it.

"Yeah," she said. "What time is it?"

"It was a bad one," Emily said, as if she hadn't heard the question about the clock. "You were moaning. Something awful." At this, Kim just nodded. Emily had a tendency to watch her while she slept. Whether a catnap during the day or deep in the middle of the night, Kim would often wake up with her little sister, twenty-four-years-old in less than a month, staring at her, sometimes from a chair she'd pulled up. Or sometimes from a standing position, towering over her.

"Go back to bed, Honey. I'm okay now."

"You're not okay," Emily said, in the same sad tone. "You got hurt. Who did that to you? A boy?"

"Yeah," she said, sighing. "A boy. A bad boy, named Kevin. But it's okay, Em. It won't happen again, I promise."

"You sure?"

"I'm positive. I made a mistake tonight. I went to a meeting and a bad thing happened with the guy I was meeting with. But I got home just fine, you can see that."

"You need a doctor, maybe."

"Maybe, yeah. I'll walk down to City MD tomorrow. Please. Go to bed. We'll talk about it in the morning. Okay?" Emily's gray eyes, wide and perpetually staring, seemed to roam over her sister's face in the dark. She was heavy-set, taller than Kim, and had a rat's nest of dirty blonde hair that went in ten different directions around her head. Kim could keep her clean most of the time. She could even get Emily to wear some fine skin products, and once in a while, make-up for fun. But her hair was a lost cause.

"I missed you tonight," Emily said, an uncertain grin finally appearing on her face. Emily didn't have Kim's fine, almost bird-like features. Hers were more blunt, rounded and ruddy. A scar from childhood, the one that had given her the traumatic brain injury that now labeled her in terms of her condition—"TBI"— crawled pink and wiry across her forehead and down behind her right ear.

"I missed you too," Kim said, smiling. "I love you, Em. Now go to bed."

"Okay. Kimmy?"

"Yeah?" Emily's face suddenly lit up.

"Trump's a fuckwad!" she said. Kim wrinkled her nose for a moment, then just smiled. Emily liked to parrot things she heard, anywhere from the subway to what was on TV. So maybe that's what it was. Or, maybe, the sentiment about Donald Trump was genuinely hers. Who knew?

"You're a pip, Em. I love you."

Kim's nightmares were usually gauzy abstractions of things she was afraid of. But sometimes, like the one she just had, they were super-charged memories, played out again in her subconscious with some garish addition of color or sound. She laid still for a long time after Emily padded off to bed, her heart pounding. Thankfully, she was schooled at calming herself, and also very self-aware. The dream and the memory were no surprise, and almost certainly a product of what Kevin had tried to do to her a few hours before.

She had diagnosed herself with Post-Traumatic Stress Disorder years before, and she knew Emily suffered from it also. In Emily's case, the diagnosis was official; she saw a therapist in Manhattan regularly as part of her treatment regimen for the brain injury that also caused her to suffer mood swings, apparently low intelligence, and sometimes uncontainable rage. The PTSD, the therapist told Kim, made everything worse.

Yeah, no shit.

Kim sighed in the dark and clutched a pillow. After everything else—the terror, the shock, the agony—there was the bitter taste of disappointment. She had started, in her own kitchen, a line of organic skincare products that she had, in five short years, built into a multi-million-dollar online business. The pace of her success thus far had been dizzying. She was very lucky in the beginning. Crucial help from crowdsourcing and two angel investors had allowed her to go from formulating the product in her kitchen to her first manufacturing contract. Steady sales allowed her to work full-time on production and web marketing from home. Then suddenly she had a buzz going—a couple of key shout-outs in *Glamour* and *Cosmopolitan* magazines, followed by interviews. Before she knew it, she was managing a nationwide supply chain. She picked up an assistant, then another one, and a PR rep. Her team was fielding orders feverishly and selling enough online to where Kim found herself in need of an accountant to keep track of it all and help shelter her money. It was enough, by 2015, to set up a trust for Emily, and then to move both of them to a two-bedroom apartment on Manhattan's East Side.

It was a grind, but it was lucrative. She could keep doing it, and she could care for herself and her sister in comfort and style. But the goal, always and ultimately, was a venture capital buyout. That meant real money in the bank and the opportunity, after a difficult and treacherous life, for permanent stability. Moving to New York had been about that most of all. She could do what she did from anywhere, and God knew Emily didn't care where they were as long as they were together. But being in Manhattan put her in the game, where the biggest cosmetic companies had headquarters and the biggest shows were debuted, and it added cachet to her brand.

Callisto Investing Group, "CIG" for short, would have been the perfect venture capital partner. They specialized in beauty and wellness brands and had launched several wildly successful projects. Kim could barely contain her excitement when the friendly inquiries from CIG repre-sentatives started at cosmetics shows, and then became serious ones. There were a couple of key meetings at the firm. The idea would be for CIG to acquire her line and seek to sell it to an industry giant like L'Oréal or Estée Lauder.

After consultation with a few trusted colleagues, she was ready to allow CIG to take over the brand for the right amount of money. She loved what she invented, but she loved being free, rich and caring for Emily more. Dinner with Kevin Dunaway, a general partner at CIG, should have sealed it. Next step, get the rest of the partners to sign on, then call in the lawyers and draw up the papers.

God, I was so close.

But then Kevin wanted to "wrap things up" over a cele-bratory dinner, and now she had a fat lip and an eye inju-ry. She also had a dead deal with Callisto, however Kevin chose to explain that to his partners. She could tell her-self, as her friends in the business would surely tell her, that Callisto wasn't the only big fish in the sea. Sure, but what was Kevin going to say to the rest of the partner group? She had met most of them, and they seemed to like her. She supposed that, if he said anything, it would be that the brand wasn't as promising as it had seemed, Kim seemed unwilling to cede control, etc. That was bad, but it was still a best-case scenario. The worst case was she was blackballed, assigned a reputation within the venture capital world as a crazy person or some kind of freak. That haunted her more than anything.

For the time being, she had to mend her body before she could schedule further meetings, and she had exactly one card to play with regard to putting Kevin Dunaway behind her. That card was the one she'd been playing since she had escaped his clutches to begin with: Say nothing, talk to no one and bury it.

Like the past.

SEVEN

Saturday, September 16
1:30 p.m.

"Jane Doe," Alex Greco said as he held up the photo. With his feet on his desk, he stretched out in khaki shorts and a dark blue T-shirt with the Bronx Homicide Unit emblem on the chest. It was the afternoon after the incident at The Vernon, and Alex had stopped at his new office on the way back from a long bike ride down to Battery Park to see what had come in overnight. He handed the photo back to Judy Levin, the victim-witness specialist who had showed it to him. "I heard about this when I got here. But I don't think it's going anywhere, Jude."

"There's something about it," she said, examining the photo as he handed it back. Judy was about sixty, youthful, with jet black hair and bright green eyes. The photo, the only known one of the victim was transferred from a witness's cell phone shortly after the woman, whoever she was, fled the scene. It was a decent photo, but it showed almost nothing of her face, as she was turning away from the camera when it was snapped. What could be seen was her hair, dark, and pulled back sleekly into a bun, and her left earring. The cords on her neck stood out. She looked petite. She wore a black suit jacket and matching skirt. With one hand, she was actually holding up the skirt, clearly torn open down the back where the zipper was. In her other hand was a stylish handbag. She was in expensive-looking pumps. Judy frowned at the photo and said, "I think we can find her."

"Maybe," Alex said, sitting up in his chair. He was a big man, broad-shouldered and handsome, with an old-school haircut that gave him a little bit of a Robert F. Kennedy look. Usually he tried to sweep it back, but a little shock of it nevertheless tended to flop down in a half-moon shape over his forehead. "But that begs the question of whether she wants to be found. She clearly didn't want to stick around last night."

"True. But I think she'll respond to us, if we can find her." She gave Alex a leveling look. "We should try."

"This is what I get for coming in on a Saturday," he said, scratching his head. "Guys from the First took a full report, right?" The First Precinct covered SoHo and the financial district.

"Yep. They're probably assuming nothing will happen with it, but squad detectives responded. They collected a piece of evidence. It was a handkerchief. Lots of blood on it. They packaged it for the lab. I can get you the fives." *Fives* meant DD-5's, which were standard NYPD detective reports.

"No worries, I'll call someone over there and get them." He took the photo back from her and looked it over. "Weird. From what I understand, cops assumed she ran because she's a pros, or a call girl or something. But I don't really get that from the photo."

"You mean a woman used in prostitution," Judy said, and Alex offered an apologetic look. Judy didn't define anyone as a 'prostitute,' or, as Alex had stated it in cop parlance, a 'pros.' In Judy's mind, people referred to as "prostitutes" were almost always used in the trade by someone more powerful.

"You're right, I'm sorry."

"Just keeping you on your toes and in the twenty-first century," she said, smiling at him. Judy liked Alex a great deal. Like him, she had been recently invited into the same pilot program that combined an elite group of ADAs, detectives and victim-witness specialists from the city's five boroughs into a centralized special victims office. It had been titled the Specialized Crimes Unit, or SCU. Its task was to investigate and prosecute serial cases, some high-profile matters, and things that seemed to exceed the resources of the individual DA's offices and detective units. They dealt with cases from all over the city but were housed with detectives and victim-witness staff in the same building that held Chelsea Market on Manhattan's West Side. Judy had spent many years working with crime victims, especially rape victims. Most of her career had been in Brooklyn. Alex had come from the Bronx DA's Office, where he still had a desk.

"Well, she doesn't look like a woman used in prostitution," Alex said, "but it wouldn't matter to me if she was. And anyway, looks can be deceiving. The bigger question is, why are we looking for her when she obviously didn't want to be found when it happened?"

"You know the dynamics," she said. "She might have panicked or been disoriented."

"Sure. But it's now fourteen hours later and, to my

knowledge at least, she hasn't come forward. Although that could mean she's badly hurt. Or worse."

"That's another reason to look for her, then."

"Judy, you're preaching to the choir. I have no problem with trying to find her. I can find a detective who won't, either. But we both know I'll get questions as to why I'm pursuing this case, given that she ran." Judy frowned at this.

"You mean Ramos," she said. Gerry Ramos was the chief of the new unit, a respected, veteran ADA from Manhattan who had been brought in to get things going. It was a high-profile job, and Ramos, with ties to the mayor's office and boundless ambition, planned on making it more so. That was fine with Alex. He could deal with press and politics. But Ramos, for reasons that still mystified him, just didn't seem to like him. It seemed personal, and it was irritating at least, troubling at most.

"Yeah, Gerry. He looks for things to second-guess me on. This will look like one of those things."

"Gerry will allow us to investigate this. Trust me."

"Why?" At this, Judy held the photo up for him again.

"Because she's a well-dressed white woman in a white neighborhood. You may not have noticed, but the bag she's carrying is expensive, and I'm guessing the shoes and the suit are also. I have to pick my battles, too. I'm ashamed to say it, but no one would follow up if the victim was poor and black, and in the Bronx or Bed-Stuy. But with these circumstances, he'll let you go after it. We might as well take advantage of that."

"Fair enough," he said with a shrug. "But if we do find her, we should respect her choices. That's what you'd tell me, anyway."

"Correct," she said. "But after thirty years of doing this, you get feelings about things. I have a feeling about this woman." She studied the photo more closely, speaking to it at a low volume. "Who are you, Honey? And what the hell happened to you?"

EIGHT

Monday, September 18
9:15 a.m.

"Can you see out of it?" Evelyn Robinson asked. Her face, smooth and dark brown, was inches from Kim's, and a little pen light in her hand played over Kim's eye injury. The slightest contact with the area was still painful, but thankfully Evelyn had an astonishingly gentle touch. The scent of her body lotion, something with vanilla and sandalwood, was calming. Kim sniffed and wondered about the ingredients. She and Evelyn were in Evelyn's only treatment room, which also doubled as her office. She lived and worked in a small but well-appointed brownstone apartment in the Park Slope area of Brooklyn.

"I can now, yeah," Kim said. "Still hurts."

"But less than yesterday, right?"

"Yes. I can touch it now, at least. Without screaming."

"Any double vision?"

"No."

"Does your vision jump around when you move the eye? I know it hurts but try moving it."

"No, nothing jumps."

"Okay," Evelyn said, clicking the light off. She looked closely at Kim, her dark eyes moving in circles around her small, heart-shaped face.

"Girl, what did this man do to you?" she asked, a little above a whisper. Kim could only shrug.

"He was an asshole."

Kim had told Emily she was going to City MD, an urgent care clinic where she sometimes took her sister after a scrape or a fall. But she had no desire to walk into a clinic on Third Avenue looking like she'd been the obvious victim of an assault. Of course, she should have had her own doctor by now; she had been in New York for almost two years. She had good insurance and excellent care in place for Emily, but her own health was an afterthought. Kim had never suffered serious health issues and had received little medical care as a child, so finding her own doctor just hadn't been on her mind.

She did, however, have Evelyn, who was a homeopathic practitioner in Brooklyn and not a medical doctor. Her treating license in New York was as an acupuncturist, but her real passion was in natural healing and holistic medicine. She and Kim connected after Evelyn first tried—and was wowed with—Kim's premier product, her facial scrub. One of her first steady customers, Evelyn reached out to Kim on a lark through Kim's new website. The two became friendly online, and Kim made an appointment to see Evelyn when she got to New York. She had never visited a homeopath, but had heard good things, and in particular wanted to get strategies for Emily's diet, which she suspected was often related to her emotional state.

It wasn't long before Kim herself became a patient of Evelyn's, and since then she had been a godsend. Evelyn was kind, trustworthy, and also great with Emily. She was a Brooklyn native, savvy about New York City and its various pitfalls, whether the subject was dating, mass transit, conflicts with landlords, or any other issue. Kim didn't see Evelyn outside of her appointments, but Evelyn tended to schedule them during slow periods so they could spend time talking. This often amounted to therapy as far as Kim was concerned, something she felt self-conscious about because she didn't want to take advantage of Evelyn's time. But Evelyn seemed to love her company and was a fantastic listener. As a result, Evelyn knew more about Kim's horrific back story than anyone other than Emily, and of course Emily wasn't quite all there. Kim had surprised herself by opening up to Evelyn, something she had done with no one else, but she didn't regret it. For now, where medical care was concerned, Evelyn was all Kim figured she needed. And especially now, she was the best possible person to turn to.

"I think you're lucky," Evelyn said. She sat down on a three-wheeled stool in front of the exam table.

"I don't feel lucky."

"I know. But I don't think you have a blowout fracture. Just a bad bruise. Guy must have had a big hand, and he landed a good one on you. But you really need to see a doctor. A *real* doctor, Kim. You need to be sure. Get an X-ray."

"You're smarter than a real doctor."

"Yeah, well ... I can't replace an X-ray machine."

"I'll keep an eye on it, I promise. So to speak." Evelyn smiled wryly.

"I stay in my lane, Honey. That's the agreement we have. I'll always take care of you the best way I know how. But I won't see you suffer more because of some condition that a licensed M.D. could identify and treat."

"I know. I'm grateful, believe me. Let's wait a couple of days. I swear to you, if it's clearly more than a shiner by then, I'll find someone. Emily has a doctor I can see." Another thing Kim loved about Evelyn was the almost cryptic way she just accepted everything that was placed before her. She never seemed shocked or judgmental at anything Kim told her. Evelyn, Kim suspected, also had a difficult past. Really, there was no other way she could seem so unsurprised about what Kim shared with her, and yet also be so empathic and concerned at the same time. But Evelyn had shared very little of her own story with Kim so far, whatever it was.

"How is Emily?" Evelyn asked. "Did she ask you what happened?"

"Yes. I told her it was a guy. She's worried, of course. But she'll be okay. We've both been through it before. Sad to say it's not altogether shocking."

"It might be more shocking for her *now*, though," Evelyn said quietly, as if she knew she was treading on a sensitive subject. She was, but Kim trusted her more than even Evelyn knew. "You've been in a safe place now for a while. A stable place. This kind of violence hasn't intruded on it until now. I'm not blaming you, please understand. Just be in tune to the effect of this on Emily."

"You're right," Kim said, feeling suddenly guilty. "It's selfish, I'm sorry. Whatever rolls off my back or not, it's not fair to her."

"It's not selfish. It's just what you're used to. And it's not your fault. It's the bastard who did it. Do you want to talk about it? We don't have to. But if we don't, I'd suggest a therapist. I can hook you up with someone I know."

"You're the only therapist I need for now, Ev. Thank

you." Evelyn smiled, the crinkles around her eyes deepening. There was a sadness to them that Kim could see clearly. But Evelyn seemed to mask her own pain the same way she did her age. Kim knew Evelyn was fifty-five, but she looked far younger, except for that nest of sadness.

"Okay. Lie down and let me take a look at the rest of you."

NINE

Standing in front of The Vernon, the scene of the strange and so far "victimless" crime she was investigating with Alex Greco from SCU, Detective Angie Keegan could see straight south, down Wooster Street to the new, gleaming Freedom Tower in the financial district. As always, her heart both swelled and sank when it came into view. The towers there before, One and Two World Trade Center, had been her father's ticket to the United States as a sheet metal worker from Belfast in the late 60's. Angie herself, on September 11, 2001, was almost killed as they tumbled down around her. She had been at a meeting on a federal case just across the street. It turned out to be the longest day of her life.

"Ang?" Alex asked. She looked over at him, snapped back to the present by his voice. He was standing just inside the alley beside the building.

"Hey, sorry. Daydreaming."

"Check this out. The victim was seen crawling out of this alley, the same one she ran back into. But it goes all the way through, look. There's an opening in the fence back there, where the construction is. So, she could have come from West Broadway to begin with."

"Yeah, but why run in the same direction you just came from? Especially when you got fucked up back there?" Angie walked into the shadowy alley. Barely twenty feet wide, it was freshly swept and neat. Porters and doormen took out trash here and brought in deliveries through the alley's side door. But beyond the end of the building, the pathway disintegrated into a rough and narrow rubble-strewn space toward the construction zone. It was the construction that allowed, temporarily, for the opening onto West Broadway. "Plus, that end is a mess. It's a good place to trip and fall on a nail or broken glass or something." Her eyes, light blue, scanned the surroundings. "Shit, before this construction, that alley probably didn't go all the way through for a hundred years. Maybe more." Angie was tall for a woman, with a sturdy but athletic build and particularly large breasts, an attribute she found more annoying than anything. She had naturally blond hair, short, and almost always pulled tight to her head. Her skin was reddened and freckled, something she assumed was inevitable given a combination of being Northern Irish and loving the beach. It kept her close with her dermatologist.

"True, but maybe that's why she was crawling," Alex said. "Maybe she tripped on a brick or something, then ended up crawling the rest of the way. That might explain an injury or two."

"Mm-mmm, I don't think so," Angie said, shaking her head after a moment's thought. Her voice was higher than one would expect, almost girlish. It contrasted with an attractive but tough exterior. "I'm thinking she came from inside the building."

"This building? Where the doorman was who found her?"

"Yeah, why not? Look." She walked down the alley toward where the handkerchief had been found. She consulted a crime scene photo in a file to get a sense of exactly where it had been. "Side door," she said, kneeling down and looking over at him. She spoke with a tone of both satisfaction and budding stubbornness. This was true even though Alex wasn't really challenging her. When Angie believed she was right, about anything, she was unmovable. The trait was a net positive in her life, as she had good instincts. But it had also burned her. She pointed to the door. "It's right near where they found the bloody rag."

"Yeah, but that's a door they use for trash and deliveries."

"I'm telling you. She bolted out this door."

"Patrol went through there, though," he said. "They went through the lobby and out that door with the building super. No blood was found leading out the door."

"Okay. But if she was using the rag, maybe that caught it." Alex seemed to consider this.

"Maybe. Yeah."

"And the doorman who found her," she said. "He had only come on a few minutes before seeing her on camera, right?"

"Right. Maybe fifteen minutes. I think he came on at 11:00."

"Okay. So, there's no reason to believe he would have seen her walk into the building if she came in earlier than that. Either alone or with someone."

"Yeah, right. So..."

"So, we need to look at their security tapes from Friday

night," she said. "You got the super's number?" He nodded and scribbled it on a pad from the initial police report. Angie would soon receive a full file for herself, but she had just been assigned the case, and had come down to the scene to get an initial sense of the layout. Alex had come along mostly for the hell of it; it was a slow morning so far, and he was curious about the situation. Most ADAs didn't go out to the scenes, at least not this early in a case. But part of the mission of the new SCU was to get responders to work more closely together. Alex also wasn't most ADAs.

"You know, you might be onto something," he said. "They didn't talk to any of the residents, it was too late to knock on doors."

"Yeah, I thought about that, too. I'll call this guy and review their tapes." She looked down the ragged alley and then back at Alex. "How did you get me assigned to this case anyway? I'm surprised we're on it at all, since she took off like that."

"Normally it would have died with patrol, but Judy Levin convinced Ramos it was worth running down, at least for now. I'm sure it wasn't said to Gerry, but Judy was fairly certain he'd let us go after it because the victim is white and well-dressed. And hey, we're in SoHo."

"Whatever works," Angie said with a shrug. The two scanned the alley for a few more seconds while Angie scribbled some notes on a pad. Neither one of them noticed a gaunt-looking, middle-aged man in khakis and a golf shirt, watching them casually but steadily from the shadows of a storefront awning across the street. The man was making a few notations of his own, and just before walking away, snapped photos of both of them as well.

TEN

"I guess that's Kim," Kevin Dunaway said as Angie and Danny Lopez, a younger detective also assigned to her unit, sat silently in front of his desk after handing him the still photo from the security camera. It was the one that showed him with Kim at the front desk of The Vernon lobby the previous Friday night. He had been staring at it for several seconds, his brow knitted. While he did so, Angie glanced around his office and the busy open area beyond it. Almost everything around them at Callisto Investing, on the forty-first floor of a gleaming building in midtown, was see-through. There were floor-to-ceiling windows with an airy, panoramic view of Central Park to the north. Kevin's corner office had a heavy-looking glass desk and minimal furniture, just his chair and two smaller ones in front of it.

"Kim," Angie said, jotting the name down. "Do you know the last name, sir?"

"Uh ... Hadley. Kim Hadley."

"Hadley, like H-A-D-L-Y?"

"With an "E," Kevin said. She noticed him watching as she crossed out the first thing she'd written and replaced with it with the second. "I'm sorry, I don't know what this is about. Is she okay?"

"We really don't know," Danny said. "A woman fitting her description was attacked outside of the building you live in on Friday the fifteenth. We're trying to determine if the woman in the photo we showed you is the person who was victimized."

"Victimized?" Kevin asked, his eyes widening. "Wait a minute. I heard something about this. A woman who was seen coming out of the alley next to my building?"

"That's right," Angie said. "She had been assaulted, as far as we can tell. Unfortunately, she fled the scene before she could be attended to by police. We're trying to track her down."

"Oh boy," he said. His eyes fell to his desk and moved in circles around some papers there. Angie and Danny glanced at each other.

"Is there something you know about that?" Angie asked. "Anything at all?"

"Her being attacked?" he asked, looking back up at them, one to the other. "No, not at all."

"But the woman you're with in this camera shot," she said, a little slower, "Kim Hadley, if that's who she is, she closely fits the description of the woman who was assaulted. Can you tell us when this woman left your apartment?"

"Maybe...fifteen or twenty minutes after she got there," Kevin said. "She wasn't at my apartment very long. But..."

"But?"

"But...look. I don't know how to say this, but I guess I have to." He spread his hands out on his desk like he was smoothing out a map. "I would not be surprised if Kim got into some trouble after she left my apartment that night."

"Okay. Can you explain?"

"Kim was a potential client of ours." Kevin spoke calmly and made eye contact easily with both Angie and Danny. "The business details of that are confidential. But suffice to say, she's an entrepreneur. She developed a product and a company around it called Emily. This is a venture capital firm, as you may know. We invest in the kinds of products Kim developed. There was a strong possibility we would have invested in her company."

"But you didn't."

"No, we didn't. Unfortunately, Kim's numbers didn't add up. And when I met with her that evening…"

"You mean, Friday, the evening in question?" Angie cut in.

"Yes, exactly. When I met with her that evening, she seemed…off. Strung out. Almost disoriented. It was subtle at first, but it got worse as the night went on."

"What was the purpose of the meeting?"

"It was a dinner meeting," Kevin said, leaning back, his hands still on the desk. "I'm going to be honest. She almost had us locked in. Our firm, I mean, as an investor. A couple of my partners got to know her during the process. Staff also. You're welcome to talk to them. We had high hopes. But then I did a little more digging and found some things that didn't add up the way they had seemed to before. Again, the details of that are confidential. But the point is, I found out about some of this stuff the day or so before we were scheduled to have dinner."

"But you proceeded with dinner anyway," Danny said, not really a question.

"Sure. I figured there was probably a discrepancy she

could explain. It happens. But when I brought it up, Kim got very defensive. And again, she seemed a little out of it from the get-go."

"What was the name of the restaurant?" Angie asked.

"Abbey, off of Seventh Avenue South," he said. "It's small. Quiet."

"I know it," Angie said. "Pricey. Not easy to get into, either."

"Like I said, we were serious about Kim. I saw no reason to cancel the reservation just because I had some questions to ask. I didn't expect her reaction."

"Was she shouting in the restaurant, or aggressive? Anything another patron would have observed, or a waiter?"

"No, nothing like that. Kim is petite and very soft-spoken, at least in my experience. It was more like she took on a sarcastic, almost mocking tone with me. It was just off-putting. Anyway, we didn't get anywhere with my questions."

"You mentioned that she seemed 'off.' Was she drinking alcohol? Were you?"

"We both were," he said, with a shrug. "But nothing out of the ordinary. She didn't drink that much. It was more like she was out of it, or getting there, when she arrived. I suspected pills, to be honest. Or something like that."

"Did you point it out?"

"No, I didn't think it was my place. I just thought we needed to end the evening at that point. I should have put her in a cab at the restaurant, right then and there."

"Tell us how she ended up at your apartment," Angie said. Kevin seemed to search himself, then sighed.

"She told me there was an idea she wanted to share

with me. A branding idea, like a marketing strategy or the like. It was on her computer, which she had with her. It was a MacBook Air—one of the really compact ones. Anyway, we shared a cab back to my apartment on Wooster. I told her I could give her a few minutes, tops, but that it was getting late. It was a Friday night, but it had been a hell of a long week. We stopped at the desk, which is what you see in the photo. I picked up a FedEx envelope. Then we went upstairs to my apartment."

"Please continue."

"She asked if I had any champagne," Kevin said. "That seemed a little weird. We really didn't have anything to celebrate at that point. But some people like a nightcap, so ..."

"So, the champagne was her idea?" Danny asked.

"It was. And I had some in the fridge, so I popped it. We both had a little, and I asked her to show me her idea. She opened the computer and showed me a few sketches she had done in a PDF file. It was rough. Really, it didn't mean much to me. Then, she got up to go to the bathroom. I showed her where it was. It was when she came back that things got strange."

"Okay."

"She must have snorted something in the bathroom, okay? I have no idea what, but I'm sure of it. She came back, you know, sniffing a little, and within a minute or two, she was like a different person. Talking a mile a minute. Going on and on about plans she had. Money she needed. At that point, I suggested we call it an evening, and that I had some thinking to do."

"How did she react?"

"Badly," Kevin said, lowering his eyes and staring straight ahead, as if seeing it again. "She sat down. Filled her glass again, then mine. That's when she started getting aggressive. Physically, I mean."

"Aggressive like violent?" Angie asked.

"No, more like...sexually. She put her hand on my thigh. She started saying something about how she knew how the game was played. She said she'd do anything to land an investment with my firm. I was getting pretty uncomfortable at that point, as you can imagine. I told her she needed to leave."

"Okay. And then?"

"She asked if I had any cocaine," Kevin said, again looking from Angie to Danny and back. "She said she was out. Anyway, I told her I didn't. I said again it was getting late, but she just kind of ignored me. She took her phone out and started texting someone. Then I got up to go to the bathroom, to just sort of collect myself."

"Were you worried about something happening at that point?" Angie asked.

"Uh, yeah, it was starting to look like I had a crazy woman in my apartment. I'm sorry for how this sounds, but this is the truth. I'm a big guy. I have a nice apartment. I'm sure it looks like I have a lot of money. Suddenly there's a woman in my place, acting strangely, snorting coke or God knows what in my bathroom and refusing to leave. I didn't know what to do. Call the cops? How would that look? I didn't want to do that. So, I figured I'd just take a minute, let things settle."

"Okay. How long were you gone?"

"Barely a minute. When I came back, I acted like nothing had happened. I was polite. I was quiet. I asked her if I could call her a car."

"What did she say?"

"She was still texting. Finally, she stopped and put her phone in her bag."

"Did she tell you who she was texting with?"

"I didn't ask who. I really didn't care. I asked if she was calling an Uber or something. She shook her head and gave me this weird look. She said it was a 'connection.' That's how she put it. A dealer, I guess. She said she would meet him around the block in about ten or fifteen minutes, because he was at a party in the neighborhood. She asked if she could come back after she'd met him."

"She wanted to go buy drugs of some kind and return to your apartment?" Danny asked. "That's the impression you got?"

"Yes, exactly. What she told me was she didn't want to go home. She told me she lives with her sister. I think the sister is disabled. So, she wanted to run out and come back up, presumably with something illegal. Of course, I wasn't about to allow that. I told her I'd call her a car, and that it was time to get going."

"And then?"

"Then she snapped," he said, sighing. "She had a champagne flute in her hand. I tried to get it from her, you know, just trying to get her up and out the door with her purse. But instead of just handing it over, she slammed it against my palm and it broke. I'm lucky, I guess. It could have been a lot worse. Still, she cut me pretty good." At this, he lifted his right hand, palm exposed. There was reddish-purple spot with stitches almost dead center. "After that, she took the bottle itself and broke it over an end table in the living room. Then she turned around and left. Slammed the door behind her. I bandaged myself up and cleaned the place. That was it."

"You didn't call the police?"

"No. I didn't think there was any reason. She was gone. She cut me with a champagne flute, so what? I was just happy she was gone. I really didn't want the attention. Would you?" The question was aimed at Danny, who just shrugged. Angie noticed that, while Kevin was polite to both of them, he seemed particularly deferential to Danny, who like Kevin was handsome, athletic looking and charming. Danny was younger with plenty of tattoos and a generally edgier look, but Kevin seemed to identify with him.

Then Danny asked, "Was that the last you saw of her?"

"The very last. By Monday I decided the firm couldn't work with her. There were too many unanswered questions, and then that...performance. I explained the situation to my partners. Again, you can talk to them. But that was it."

"Did you tell anyone at the firm about what happened?" he asked. "About getting injured by her?"

"No, I probably should have, but...I don't know. It didn't seem worth it, and I really didn't want to get into it. My hand was bandaged for a couple of days. One or two people asked about it. My admin person, at least. I said I cut myself on broken glass. It wasn't really a lie."

"Did anyone reach out to her?" Angie asked, "about the deal being off, or whatever?"

"Well, there wasn't a deal. We were close to one, that's all. Everything still needed to be finalized. Look, things happen quickly in this business. Nothing matters until paperwork is drawn up and signed. We have a lot of paperwork on Kim's company, for sure. But there were no legal agreements. I suppose I should have had an assistant draw up a letter or something, informing her we were passing on the deal. But to be honest? I wasn't happy about how she acted. And I'm not just talking about cutting my hand with a glass. As far as I'm concerned, she portrayed herself and her company in a light that wasn't completely genuine. Again, I really can't get into business details, but it's enough to say I was glad to see her go. But listen, if she was hurt, or attacked, after she left my apartment? Jesus, I don't know what to say. That's awful. No one deserves that."

"Well, we can't be positive it was her," Angie said, handing him a business card. "But this gives us a starting point. Thanks for your time, Mr. Dunaway. If anything else occurs to you, please let me know."

"Sure," he said. He stood up and offered his hand, first his right one. But then he pulled that hand back and offered the left, shaking his head and offering a quick apology about the right one being stitched. Angie also noticed that he winced when he reached over the desk and twisted to switch hands.

"Were you injured otherwise, Mr. Dunaway?" she asked. She tapped herself just below her right collar bone. "Something happen there?"

"Oh, that," he said, glancing down. "No, that's an old injury. It acts up sometimes. Again, I'm sorry for what might have happened to Kim. I keep my ear to the ground in this business, and I haven't heard anything from her lately. I don't mean personally, I mean announcements, things like whether she'll be at a trade show. My guess is she's in trouble. If she got hurt that night and she ran from the police, I'd say that explains it. It's sad. She's a smart young woman, but I think she's got a lot of problems."

ELEVEN

"What do you think?" Danny asked as the two stepped off the elevator at street level. Danny was young for his position in the police department and Alex, who had worked with him in the Bronx, was mostly responsible for getting him added to the elite SCU squad. Despite him having less years on the job than most of the squad, Angie liked him from the start and enjoyed working with him. He had good instincts and was great with victims, especially women and children. The fact that he was both handsome and dangerously charming tended to help him in that regard, but he was genuinely good-hearted as well, if a little irreverent and a fountain of inappropriate jokes. Today he wore khaki slacks, a dark shirt and a loosened tie, his usual outfit. Angie dressed as she almost always did in the field, in a slate-gray, tailored pants suit with a tunic collar. Her hair, as always, was pulled tight and slicked back. Around them, professionally dressed men and women toting coffee cups and file folders scurried past the reception desk and waved security badges before the turnstiles at the elevator banks.

"He's wrong," Angie said. "You see it, right?"

"I can believe it, sure," he said. "But he talks a good game."

"He's been doing that for a while, I'll bet. Talking a good game. That guy could sell shit to a shit salesman."

"Doesn't mean he's lying, though, Ang," Danny said. "I don't really like him either, but..."

"She stomped out, right?" Angie said, turning to him on the street and lighting a cigarette. They were under a large street sign that said, "Avenue of the Americas," the correct name for Sixth Avenue since 1945, and one that every New Yorker had ignored for over seventy years. "Left to go meet her dealer."

"That's his story, yeah."

"Right. That could've happened. But why the hell didn't she go out the front door, the way she came in? I sat and went through the security video, from the time I spotted her until after she was seen on the other camera. She never walks out the entrance she walked in."

"So, she must have gone out some other way. Like that side door you saw."

"Yeah, exactly. But why?"

"I don't know," Danny said, shaking his head. "Maybe the guy—the dealer—told her to meet him in the alley next door to the building?"

"So what, did he tell her to go through the trash room and out a side door? Of a building she's never been in before, as far as we know?"

"No," he said, and paused for a moment. "You're right, that's fucked up."

"She got out. Out of his apartment, I mean. But then—" Angie slowed her speech, punctuating each word— "she avoided walking past a doorman."

"Yeah. And then she ran when patrol showed up. Maybe those two decisions are related. First, we gotta ask why she avoided a doorman going out. Then we gotta ask why she ran."

"Running from the scene or the cops I can accept," she said. "That could be shock, or something like it. She freaked out. Took off. Then maybe she figures it's too late to report, so now she's just laying low."

"Agreed. But finding another way out of that building? After whatever the hell happened up there? That was a decision she was able to make before patrol got there. She was looking for a quiet way out even before she saw cops were coming."

"True," Angie said, watching the traffic along the avenue. "So, she's jammed up for some reason. Let's find out why. I still think it comes back to that S.O.B. up there somehow. At least we've got a name."

TWELVE

For Kim, the concern was not that there were police at her door, wanting to speak to her. She wasn't sure if the NYPD would eventually track her down somehow, but she was prepared for it. The issue was that Emily, watching TV in the living room, was the one closest to the door when they knocked. Their doorman, Josh, had called up to Kim to let her know they were on the way, but by that time the officers were almost at her door.

"Emily!" she called, rushing to the living room and smoothing her hair, "let me get the..." Too late. The doorbell chimed and Emily was up in a flash to answer it. She was somewhat dog-like that way, Kim had noticed over the years. It was almost like she could sense when someone was at the door. And for a big girl, she could move fast.

"Good evening," Kim heard a male voice say as Emily stood before the open door. "Kim Hadley?"

"That's me," Kim called. The two-bedroom apartment was decent-sized by Manhattan standards, and it look

Kim a few seconds to reach the door and place herself between Emily and the officers.

"They're police," Emily said, drawing out the word "police" and taking a step back.

"Yes, Emily, they're police," Kim said, pasting a smile on her face and focusing on them. There were two, a male and a female, both in uniform. Both were staring a little warily at Emily, who as usual looked unkempt, her hair a frizzy mess.

"Why're they here?" Emily asked, demanded really, as Kim identified herself.

"Emily, they're just here to talk to me for a minute, okay? Go back and watch TV. Everything is fine." And to the officers, "I'm sorry, just give me one moment with her, please."

"Sure," the male one said. He was older, jowly with a reddish face and heavy eyelids. He kept his eyes on Emily. The female looked much younger, maybe mid-twenties. She looked Hispanic, and was plump and short, but solid-looking.

"There shouldn't be cops here," Emily said, her voice a little higher, her eyes wide and fixed on them. "We haven't done anything wrong."

"Of course not, Honey," Kim said in a low purr. "It's okay. This is a big city. Police come to talk to a lot of people. Go back and sit down, okay?" Finally, Emily's eyes shifted to Kim, and then she turned sullenly away. She plopped down on the sofa with a loud huff and turned up the volume on her DVR'd show, *American Ninja Warrior*, as high as it would go. Kim stepped into the quiet hallway and closed the door behind her. Thankfully no neighbors were coming or going.

"I'm sorry," she said. "My sister is disabled. Police tend to frighten her. Can I help you?"

"We were asked to come to this residence, miss," the male cop said. His last name, on a brass plate below the badge, was Ornouski. "You're Kimberly Hadley, correct?"

"I am."

"Ms. Hadley, there was an incident in another part of the borough that involved a woman matching your description. This happened last Friday night. She appeared to be roughed up."

"This was in SoHo," the female officer said. Her name was Milagros. She was about Kim's height, although much heavier. Unlike the male officer, whose eyes seemed to go almost blank after Emily's reaction, the female seemed much more concerned. Her eyes settled into Kim's when they made contact. "Do you know anything about this ma'am?"

"I assume I'm not a suspect in anything, is that right?" Kim asked after a moment's pause. Her mouth had gone dry. She wanted to cast her eyes downward but resisted the urge. She made eye contact with both of them.

"No, of course not," the female officer said. "We're actually looking to see if *you* were victimized."

"Well, I'm fine," Kim said. "But I appreciate the concern."

"Miss Hadley," the male cop spoke up, "are you the person who was involved in the incident we're describing? Or another one like it?"

"I don't mean to be disrespectful," Kim said, slowly and carefully. "But am I obligated to answer these questions? I just want to be clear."

"Nope," he said with a shrug. "You're not. We're here on orders to follow up on a possible assault. You don't have to talk to us. Sounds like you don't want to."

"That's correct," Kim said. "But I appreciate your coming by to check on me. May I go back inside?"

"Of course," the female, Milagros, said. The other one—Ornouski—had already turned away and was sauntering back toward the elevator. Milagros kept her eyes on Kim. Kim could almost feel them glowing now, the obvious bruises on her face and discoloration around her eye. Milagros reached into her back pocket and produced a business card.

"If you change your mind and want to talk," she said, "you can reach me at this number. There's also information there for services." A pause. "For battered women." The elevator dinged behind them; Ornouski had hit the button.

"Gina? You coming?"

"Yeah," she said, her eyes still on Kim. The cop's eyes were dark and intense. But not accusatory. It was more like the opposite of that. "Take care, Ms. Hadley. Okay?"

"I will, thank you."

***

"Fuck their questions," Emily grumbled as Kim tried to slow her own heartbeat, mixing herself a bourbon and Diet Coke at the little teak bar she had installed next to the entrance to the kitchen. Emily had finally turned down the television, but she remained agitated, hugging one of the sofa pillows tightly into her bulk.

"Em, please. They were here for less than a minute. Everything is fine."

"No fuckin' cop is taking us away!"

"Of course not," Kim said, softening her tone and

forcing the same calm into her voice she had used with the cops. She was upset also, but it did no good for Emily to sense that. "No one is ever taking us away, Emily. We're completely safe. Okay?"

"I guess you should tell that to the mirror," Emily said, half into the pillow. Her head remained pointed at the TV, but now her eyes, almost devilish, swept over to Kim at the bar. Kim opened her mouth to say something critical, and then shut it. Emily, usually blunt and simple, was at times almost quick-witted. Occasionally eerily so. Anyway, there was nothing productive Kim could offer in retort.

"You're a pip, Em," Kim said, steadying her hand before taking a drink. "I'll give you that."

THIRTEEN

Thursday, September 21
3:30 p.m.

"But...we know her name," Alex said. He was sitting across from Gerry Ramos, his unit chief, in Gerry's large and well-appointed office. On the first day of fall, the weather in New York was unusually hot but otherwise gorgeous, and sunshine poured in through Gerry's windows. Shelly Burris, the deputy chief, was present also, on a small leather couch against the wall. Gerry had just told Alex, with no fanfare or animosity, that the case involving the woman in the alley wasn't one Gerry's unit would be concentrating on. "It's Kim..."

"Hadley, I know," Gerry said, his hands folded comfortably in his lap. One of the most striking and intimidating features about Gerry were his eyes. Dark brown with flecks of yellow, they were bright, alive and could bore into the person he was staring at, as if the act might set them on fire. But for now, they were dulcet. Almost sleepy.

"Do we know she's okay?" Alex asked. He glanced over at Shelly, who looked back at him evenly, then tilted her head just slightly back toward the boss. "She's a crime victim, I mean, I thought we were clear to investigate this one. Angie and Danny interviewed a suspect yesterday."

"Actually, *he* looks more like a victim at this point," Gerry said. He was dark-haired and olive-skinned, handsome with a solid build. He had a naturally commanding presence as Alex did, but also a politician's air of entitlement. When he spoke, his words seemed to erase any other sound in the room. "Ms. Hadley is really the suspect in a would-be assault case. And to answer your first question, she's fine. Mostly healed up, as far as the officers could tell."

"Officers? You mean someone's reached out to her? I know it wasn't Angie…"

"Thirteenth Precinct," Gerry said. "Her apartment is in Kips Bay, off Third Avenue. They sent two officers, one a female, over to check on her, yesterday evening."

"Okay. Was she interviewed?"

"She declined to be interviewed," Gerry said. "She didn't want to speak to them. They ascertained she was otherwise alright, and they left."

"I don't understand," Alex said. "Did they take photos of the injuries? Did they call in special victims?"

"No," Gerry said, still controlled but forceful; the word coming forth like a hammer. "It's not a special victims case. It's not a case at all."

"She was injured. Witnesses were clear on how bad she looked, crawling out of the alley. We found blood."

"Patrol found blood," Gerry said, correcting him. "Yes, I know she was probably banged up. That's unfortunate, and it appears to be at least partially of her own making. As for the blood, for all we know it was from *her* victim, Kevin Dunaway."

"Wait," Alex said, putting a thumb and finger to his forehead. "This is about Kevin Dunaway?"

"It's not *about* anyone," Gerry said. His eyes were starting to narrow, just enough to let Alex know how serious he was. Alex glanced over at Shelly again, whom he genuinely liked, and then instantly regretted it. It was obvious to Gerry that Alex and Shelly got along well. Now it looked like Alex was appealing to her like a child going from one parent to another. "Alex, there is no case here," Gerry went on. "That's mostly because Mr. Dunaway doesn't wish to press charges against Ms. Hadley."

"I didn't know Dunaway was thinking about pressing charges," Alex said. "Angie and Danny Lopez interviewed him. Nothing like that was mentioned as a possibility."

"Dunaway's attorney talked to a sergeant at the First Precinct earlier this week. It's all above board and I was consulted on it. He reached out because he believes Dunaway was really the victim of whatever happened between them but wanted to make sure there wasn't something that would take them by surprise. Like an over-zealous pair of detectives, or an enterprising ADA."

"I don't think asking questions about a woman who was brutally beaten is unfair," Alex said. He kept his eyes locked on Gerry's now. He had learned the hard way, years before, that he had to pick his battles, and it was far from clear whether this one was worth it. But for now at least, he wasn't planning on backing down.

"I agree. But I think you're going too quickly from questions to assumptions, and without context. Look, whatever she went through? It's unfortunate. No one deserves to be found on the street like that. But we don't know what happened to her, and she won't tell us. On the other side of this is a well-respected guy without a blemish who's been forthcoming and cooperative, and who gave a believable account of what transpired with Kim Hadley. He's also got a row of stitches in his hand. You don't have a scintilla of evidence to dispute what he's saying."

"I don't yet," Alex said. He could feel the tension in his muscles stiffening down his back, but he forced calm into his voice and measured the pace of his speech. "But that's why I'd like to investigate it further. Angie and Danny got a bad feeling from their interview with Dunaway. And they've got good instincts."

"Their instincts don't equal evidence. We're going to let this go."

"She should be approached once more," Alex said, quietly but firmly. Now he looked intentionally over at Shelly. As far as he was concerned, this was for both Gerry and her, as the management team of the unit. "I understand she declined to be interviewed, but that fact shouldn't be confirmed by two patrol officers checking a box. She should be approached by an investigator, a good one from special victims. Whatever happened to her should be fleshed out. If there's a connection between her injuries and Dunaway, that should be fleshed out also." At this, Gerry looked up at the ceiling, and then back to Alex. The fire in his eyes was now gone, carefully put away, Alex figured. Gerry, in Alex's estimation, wasn't about to get heated up over a disagreement with a subordinate. That would just lend credibility to Alex's point. And to Alex in general.

"I don't have time to pursue your theories, Alex. You've made your points. This case is closed. As far as I know, NYPD's closing it also. You can go, thank you." Alex gave a clipped nod, stood up and walked out, shutting the door gently behind him.

FOURTEEN

When he had gone, Shelly stood up and moved over to the chair Alex had just vacated. Shelly was Gerry's hand-picked deputy, also from the Manhattan DA's office. African-American, she was tall and graceful–elegant, with a naturally calming presence. She was an excellent manager and could have easily filled Gerry's chair, but she had neither his burning ambition nor his apparent zest for brass-knuckle politicking. Shelly cared about her attorneys and her cases, but all matters professional came after her husband and family. She worked to live, not the other way around.

"I respect our relative positions in this office," she said, her voice light and clear as always. "But I'm also about a year from being eligible to retire, so don't bullshit me, Gerry. Really, what's your issue with this guy?"

"Alex? Personally, nothing. He's a likable guy."

"But ..."

"But what? I gave him some news he didn't like. He pushed. I pushed back. And my word counts. What's this about?"

"You're the one who wanted me to be present for that," she said. "That's fine. It's a part of my job. But it's also part of my job to check your darker side. And I've been seeing it with him long before this case came up."

"Well, I didn't hire him," Gerry said. That was true. The new unit was staffed with experienced ADAs from every borough, and the choices had been made by attorneys in one of the deputy mayor's offices before Gerry and Shelly had been brought in to head things up.

"Of course not, we didn't hire anyone. But he's well-liked. He works hard. He's cheerful, for God's sake. That alone is unusual in this business."

"It isn't personal," Gerry said, his tone softening in a way Shelly figured was on purpose. "But the fact is, I don't like the way he thinks as a prosecutor. I don't particularly trust his instincts. And you know that."

"Yes," she said, nodding slowly. "I know how you view him. But I don't think he was off-base here."

"Come on, Shel, there's nothing to see here other than an out-of-control, violent woman who, I'm sorry to say, might actually have gotten something that was coming to her."

"That could be," she said. "But that's what he was trying to figure out. Isn't that kind of our mission? To get into the tough cases? To spend time on the stuff most offices can't or won't deal with?"

"Sure. We take tough cases. But that doesn't mean we go down every rabbit hole looking for things that probably aren't there. Our job is also to put up stats. That makes the mayor's office happy. That keeps us around."

"We're doing that pretty well."

"Yes, because you and I set the priorities and measure out our resources. You know what Alex does, left to his own devices? He looks for crusades. And I don't like it."

"So, it is personal," Shelly said. "I mean at least a little bit." She broke a tiny grin. She could push Gerry, to a point, and she hadn't reached that point yet.

"Ugh," he said, tossing his hands in the air. "Okay, you win. No, I don't particularly like the guy. I know you do, though. And you know what? I don't get it. He's a showboater. Yeah, he's a swell guy. Southern charm, all that bullshit. The judges love it. But he's out of his element. Particularly in this unit. What I remember hearing about his interview for this job is that he didn't even want these cases until maybe a year ago."

"Correct," she said. "Until after that child homicide case he tried..."

"And lost," Gerry said, as if seizing on a point.

"That's not fair. He indicted the wrong guy, he figured it out, and he saw justice done. He did the right thing. He received a commendation for it. And apparently it got him interested in these cases again. He handled them very well when he was down south. I checked."

"Yeah, yeah, out in the sticks, I know."

"It was Alexandria, outside of D.C. It's like Westchester, not the sticks. As for how he fits in up here, I'd say he's made a very good transition. He had an impressive conviction rate in the Bronx outside of the Ruiz case. That's not an easy place to try cases on behalf of the government, especially when you're a handsome white boy like he is."

"Something's not right, though," Gerry said, much quieter now. It was a tone that, agreeing or not, Shelly sensed was genuine.

"What?"

"Something," Gerry said, as if he was honestly frustrated at not having figured it out. His eyes moved around his office, and then back to Shelly. "For one thing, I don't like how he got up here. To the city, I mean."

"Did you ever talk to Tony Washington about it?" she asked. Washington was the District Attorney of Bronx County, where Alex had his start in New York City.

"Only enough to know it wasn't Tony's idea," he said. "It was a rich developer named Jonah Schwartz who splits his time between here and D.C. Alex used to be married to Schwartz's daughter. It didn't end well."

"I know about that," Shelly said, nodding. "And how it ended. It sounds like the marriage couldn't take the death of their son. That's not uncommon. So, he needed a new start. He found one here."

"Yeah, and he found one fast," Gerry said. "You know he has deep roots down there, right? His father's a lawyer and he was like a favorite son or something, moving up the small-town ladder. Then there was his toddler's death, and from what I understand a rushed investigation. And then, within a few weeks, after ten years in an office he probably could have run someday, Alex wanted out. So, Schwartz made the call to Tony Washington. He got fast-tracked through the bar and he was up there as a senior line prosecutor, real quick."

"So, grief drove him to something new? So what?"

"It's not the grief," he said, and his eyes told Shelly he knew he was starting to sound like an asshole and didn't want to. Shelly could always get to him. It had been that way since they flirted—and more—in criminal court as rookies in the early 90's when they were both single. She sensed he both admired and feared her for it. "It's the circumstances. First, Schwartz is dirty. He has a reputation for greasing palms to get what he wants. The AG and the city have been on him for years about payoffs to bend the rules for developing in places he has no business being."

"Places where the Democratic party has interested constituents, I gather," she said, a little wryly.

"Sure, that's how I know about it. But it doesn't change things. Schwartz has spent more time in court than he has on construction sites. He's been able to buy himself out of trouble on a few other things also. He's something of a philanthropist, and his money goes a lot further down there than it does here. So does his influence."

"So, he's a rich developer who isn't squeaky clean," she said, her arms folded.

"Yes. And one who provided a really quick exit and a nice government job to Alex Greco in a pinch. And this despite the fact Alex was in a marriage to the man's daughter that was quickly dissolving. So yeah, I've wondered. Why did Schwartz go to bat for him?"

"I think there could be a thousand reasons," she said with a shrug. "I'm listening, Gerry. But I'm still not hearing anything to merit the level of concern you seem to have about him, I'm sorry." Gerry was a politician and opportunist to some extent, but Shelly also knew him to be smart and usually fair. Why he seemed hyper-focused on Alex as some sort of shady character—or worse—was perplexing and frustrating.

"Yes, there could be a thousand reasons," he said. "And one of them could be that Alex and Jonah Schwartz covered something up and then got him out of there. Or maybe not. The point is, he's not some amazing talent who fell from the sky. He's a guy who called in a favor and got to the Bronx. Maybe that's where he should have stayed. It's a lot less high-profile than where he is now."

FIFTEEN

"What's her name?" Nikki asked. She was mixing a drink in Alex's new apartment, the one in the Bronx he had just moved into with the decent raise he'd received when he took the job with the new citywide SCU. Most of his co-workers figured he'd relocate somewhere close to the new job in Manhattan, but the Bronx felt like home.

"Whose name?"

"There's a new case on your mind, I can tell. Does she have a name? Or he?"

"It's a 'she,'" he said. "Kim." He looked over at her and smiled, but otherwise didn't react as if she had caught him off guard, even though she had. Alex was used to that from his girlfriend, a doctorate level forensic psychologist who at times seemed to be able to read him like a magazine. Nikki had a way of deducing things from his moods, and she was usually right, or pretty close. "Kim Hadley."

"Ah," she said, dropping a cherry into the drink and walking it over to him. Nikki was tall for a woman and thin, pale with dark hair and almost goth-style bangs. She was sexier than she was pretty, alluring in a stealthy, quiet way. Her most interesting feature was a small, cherry-colored bow-like mouth, looking almost perpetually pursed. "What's the case?"

"That's the problem. I don't have one."

"So how is she on your radar?"

"It's more accurate to say she *was* on my radar, briefly. I think she's fallen off." With that, he explained what facts he knew, and how Kim had been identified, but still wasn't cooperating.

"Wow, that's odd. Any background on her?" Nikki settled in next to him on the new couch she had picked out for him.

"Yeah, I did a little research. She's an entrepreneur, apparently. Check this out." He opened his laptop and went to Kim's company's primary website, which was professional and sharply designed. Next to a description of her product line, called *Emily*, was her headshot. In it, she had a pleasant and bright but unsmiling look. Her hair was pulled back tightly, and she wore a simple gray blouse and small, diamond earrings.

"She's pretty," Nikki said. "But subtle. Classy. She looks smart, too."

"I would assume. She started a line of skincare products a few years ago, and she's got some traction. I found a couple of articles on her. She's been in New York two or three years, from what I can tell. I think she's pretty successful."

"Which I guess begs the question as to why she ran when the cops got to her. But it might be a part of the answer, also."

"Seems odd, though," he said. "People with this kind of

a profile are more likely to cooperate with us. It's the disenfranchised we lose. Outsiders, people with something to hide. She doesn't seem that way. She looks more like someone who's made it."

"Success is fragile sometimes," Nikki said with a shrug. "Who knows what she's been through, or what she's dealing with? Anyway, trauma creates different responses in different people, you know that. Is there a suspect?"

"Actually, yes. Arguably even more successful. Big in finance." He explained what he knew about Kevin Dunaway, and Angie and Danny's interview with him.

"Wow. And they think he's hiding something?"

"Angie more than Danny, but both of them got a weird vibe. At this point, though, it doesn't matter. Police in her neighborhood went by her apartment a couple of days ago. She didn't want to talk then, either. So even if there was a trauma response she was going through on the night of, it makes less of a difference now."

"True. But obviously it's still on your mind. It sounds like it wasn't your decision to let the case go."

"Of course not. It was Gerry."

"And you fought him on it."

"It was a brief disagreement," he said, winking at her. "I got shut down, as usual." He sipped his drink and looked out one of the big living room windows at the Hudson and Harlem Rivers, just down the hill from his building. Compared to the first nearly threadbare, one-bedroom walk-up apartment he had rented in Manhattan when he first arrived in New York, this one bordered on spectacular. It was considerably larger, and within his price range only because it was in the Bronx, albeit in a nice area across from Manhattan's thin northern tip. And thanks to

Nikki's taste, it was nicely decorated. In short, it actually felt like home, something Alex hadn't been able to achieve in his first few years in the city.

"This is where the psychologist would ask how that made you feel," she said. "If I was your psychologist, which I can't be."

"I don't mind that Gerry and I disagree. I would have chased things down more on this case, but Gerry's not unreasonable in thinking we need to let it go. I worry more about what he thinks of me in general."

"You've mentioned that. But he hasn't been overly critical, right?"

"No, not really. We're all new, it's hard to say. But I get a bad feeling." He narrowed his eyes, still looking out the window. "Like he's watching me. Waiting."

"Waiting for what?"

"I don't know. The other shoe to drop, or something. Some 'gotcha' moment. It's hard to put into words without sounding paranoid."

"I don't think you're paranoid," she said. "But maybe you over analyze, a little bit. You have reason to do so, though. I get that."

"I'm not proud of my past. But I have to live with it. And unfortunately, it tends to cling."

"You need to work on it clinging to you," she said. "Who knows what Gerry's problem is, but I'll bet it fades once he gets used to working with you and sees what you can do. In any event, Hon, the past is past."

"Yeah until it isn't." He looked at her and she frowned at him, but his face didn't soften. Finally, she turned toward the big window and sipped her drink. They were quiet for a long moment.

"Can you stay here tonight?" he asked finally.

"Sure. Do you have contact solution?"

"Yep. Brought it over in the move. You're covered."

"Then I'm all yours. That's a lovely view, by the way. I'm glad you moved here. What's this neighborhood called again? It's a Dutch name, right?"

"*Spuyten Duyvil*," he said, pronouncing it '*spooten doo-vil*' as he had heard it from the real estate broker who had shown him the place. But he had met a few new neighbors and a couple of cops who pronounced it differently. "Something about spiting the devil."

SIXTEEN

Sunday, September 24

The face in the glass next to Kim's was no longer Emily's. Emily had wandered a few doors down toward the corner. Kim was about to turn and call for her sister when she saw the reflection, smiling at her almost furtively.

"It's laid out so beautifully, I know," the voice attached to the face said. They were in front of a luxury cosmetics store called Lash, on Madison Avenue near Sixty-Fifth Street. "This store is the *bomb*." Kim turned toward the voice and smiled. The woman was, in a word, beautiful, and immaculately put together. That wasn't uncommon in the heart of the Madison Avenue, ultra-high-end shopping district. But it didn't happen as often as it used to, Kim had been told anyway, like back in the 50's and 60's when no women headed up that way without being dressed to the nines.

"It is, yeah," Kim said, her voice characteristically soft and light. She glanced around for Emily, her brow knitting when her sister wasn't immediately visible on the crowded street.

"She's over by that coffee cart," the woman said. "The

girl you're with." She pointed, gingerly and just with her finger, keeping her hand to her breast. "Right over there."

"Oh, ok. Thank you."

"I'm Megan," she said. She extended her hand a little further forward, and Kim shook it. Megan had soft hands, perfectly manicured, with a beautiful dark red shade of polish Kim figured was probably a gel. She was several inches taller than Kim with flowing light brown hair that went past her shoulders. Her eyes were brown with a corona of green near the pupils, bright and friendly. *Like a Texas beauty queen*, Kim thought. She was dressed for New York, though, in a tailored blouse and dark skirt.

"Hi, I'm Kim. And thanks for pointing out my sister. She tends to wander." Kim looked past Megan to Emily, who waved emphatically and then pointed at the cart.

"No worries," Megan said. "She looks like she wants something."

"Oh, I'm sure she does," Kim said, rolling her eyes a little. "She's a handful."

"She looks like she has a good heart," Megan said, glancing over at Emily. Kim smiled inwardly at the remark. It was unexpected, but nice to hear. Then Emily made a funny face and pointed again at the cart. Kim held a finger up, as if to say *wait one minute*, and then turned back to Megan, who was asking her a question. "Do you know this store? I love it. I come here all the time and just stare."

"I do," Kim said. "I'm in the business, actually. But not at this level."

"You look like it," Megan said, "if you don't mind me saying so. You're very well put together. I hope that doesn't sound weird."

"No, not at all," Kim said, smiling. "That's sweet of you

to say. I have to say, you are also. Do you work in fashion? Or beauty?"

"Nope, just a sales assistant. I work a few blocks away. There's something about this part of town, though. Kind of makes you want to up your game."

"Yes," Kim said, her shy smile widening. "I swear I was just thinking that, like there was a time when a woman wouldn't come near Madison Avenue without heels on."

"Gloves, even," Megan said. "I grew up in Jersey, but we came in on weekends sometimes. My mother wouldn't go into any part of Manhattan without dolling up when I was a kid." She paused for a moment, as if picturing it. "Anyway, go ahead and take care of your sister. I didn't mean to interrupt."

"No, not at all," Kim said. "It was nice to meet you. I hope we run into you again."

"I'll tell you what," Megan said, digging through her handbag and handing over a business card, "drop me a line sometime if you're up this way. I don't mean to seem pushy, but honestly, it's hard to make female friends in this town."

"Yes, I've noticed," Kim said. "Mostly it's just me and Emily. But yeah, that would be fun. Hang on, I think I have one also." Kim found one of her cards and offered it.

"Terrific, we'll meet for a coffee. Or better yet a glass of wine."

"I'd like that," Kim said. Then Emily was calling for her, drawing out her name over the sound of street traffic. "Ugh, sorry, gotta go. She's a handful, like I said."

"She looks like a pistol," Megan said, giving her a quick wink. "Have a great day, Kim. Nice to meet you."

Kim watched Megan walk north on Madison Avenue for a few seconds before turning back to Emily. She had a warm feeling about this woman, something she almost never experienced. It wasn't that she got bad vibes from most people, it was just that she rarely spoke to anyone outside of business dealings unless it was Emily. She had Evelyn, a wonderful confidant and sounding board, but Kim didn't see her very often, and their relationship was mostly one-sided, meaning it was mostly Kim venting or needing advice from Evelyn. Kim wished it were different, but Evelyn seemed even more intensely private than Kim, and in any event was very busy.

Whether she would even see Megan again was anyone's guess, of course. Kim had met many impressive and beautiful people in her industry who turned out to be flighty and made plans they never intended to see through. But still, the thought of maybe making a friend just to chat with now and then was kind of nice. And as an added bonus, Megan seemed like she would be kind to—and even comfortable around—Emily.

She would have said it had been a long time since she had seen an opportunity like that, but that would have been untrue. Kim Hadley had never had the opportunity for friendship. Not really. She smiled and reached into her purse for some cash for Emily.

SEVENTEEN

Monday, September 25

"So, Gerry pinched it, huh?" Angie asked, shaking her head. She and Alex were at a dark, cool bar called Tommy's not far from their respective offices. It was a little after 6:30 p.m. Outside the sun was descending, leaving a red and gold evening in its wake. Tommy, the bar's owner, had known Angie for years and gave her an inquisitive look as she finished her first glass of chardonnay. She nodded for another one and motioned toward Alex also, who was about to finish a pint of ale.

"Looks like it," Alex said, loosening his tie. "I'm sorry. I know you two put some time in."

"We get paid either way. But that sucks. The guy is wrong." New drinks arrived, and they smiled thanks at Tommy.

"Dunaway?"

"Yeah, Dunaway. He's smooth, but he's hiding something. And really? Gerry saying maybe *Dunaway* was the victim, like she assaulted *him*? That's ridiculous. We met Dunaway. He's a big fucking guy. Broad shoulders. Works out. And I talked to one of the sectors who checked in on Kim Hadley. She's a female at the one-three, Gina Milagros. She says Hadley looks and sounds like a china doll. That matches what Danny and I saw on the security cameras also. She's tiny."

"The tiny ones pack a punch sometimes," Alex said, and Angie scoffed at him.

"Yeah, right. Milagros also said there was no air of drama about her. She didn't deny anything. She just didn't want to talk. But she was polite. Not acting like she was on stage."

"Look, I'm with you, believe me. If you think he beat her up, he probably did."

"Might not be all he did. Remember, her skirt was torn. He might have raped her. Or tried. That's kind of what I think. I think she was able to get away from him. Maybe because she went at him with the champagne glass."

"Maybe. At this point we may never know. That's the thing, Ang, she ran. There's probably a reason, sure. But now patrol's been over there, and she's still not talking. I told Gerry we should do more. But really, at some point I start to look like a dog with a bone. He already thinks I'm on some kind of mission as it is."

"Mission to what?"

"Save the world, I don't know. He's got me pegged as some sort of drama queen."

"You'd make one ugly fucking queen."

"Yeah, no shit. Anyway, I didn't have much to argue with in terms of keeping things open. Gerry had made up his mind. I could tell."

"You could tell how?" she asked. He shrugged.

"I just knew."

"You think Dunaway knows someone who knows someone? Put in a call maybe?"

"A call to whom? The mayor?"

"Probably not that high. But maybe someone. You ever been to City Hall? Plenty of guys to ask favors of. Look, Dunaway plays at a high level. He's a major partner in a successful venture capital firm that works mostly in cosmetics. This town is central to that business. I did a little research. His firm makes serious money."

"That would have made his lawyers a joy to deal with, then," Alex said, grinning humorlessly. "The real marquis guys are a major pain in the ass to try a case against. I'm glad sector guys tracked her down, at least. We know she's okay now, more or less." He paused, took a sip of his beer, and then looked over at her, remembering something. "There was a rag or something they found, right? Bloody?"

"Yeah a handkerchief. I put a case number on it and sent it to the lab."

"Will they still process it? Gerry made it sound like your side was zipping it up also."

"Fuck Gerry, I don't work for him," she said with a grin. "Nah, unless someone flags it, it'll get tested in queue. I'll follow up, just for shits and giggles, make sure we at least get a report from OCME. It may never go anywhere, but what the hell? Maybe something weird will happen."

"Thanks. What do you think the timeline is?"

"For DNA? Month to forty-five days, probably."

"Here's to something weird, then," he said, raising his glass. She clinked hers against his and smiled.

EIGHTEEN

Across town from where Alex and Angie were killing a couple of hours and a few drinks after work, Kim was in front of her desktop computer screen in the little office area she had fashioned from a corner of the living room near the entrance to the kitchen. Her desk was littered with reports, invoices, catalogues and various papers and flyers related to product information; some hers, some her competitors.

She clicked on a Facebook message that had just come in and held her breath. It was from an acquaintance, but one she was friendly with and respected. Her name was Sylvia Chen and she worked for an Asian company that distributed beauty products. Sylvia was one of the first people to warn her about Kevin Dunaway after seeing them together at a trade show a few months before in Denver. Kim had chosen to reach out to Sylvia because she was secure in her position, not beholden to CIG or any other VC firm. Sure enough, she didn't seem to hold back in her message:

OMG, *Kevin? Tell me he didn't fuck with you*, the message read. Kim's fingers hovered over her keyboard for a few seconds.

Well. Yeah. But I'm okay, she wrote. *You were right, though. He's bad news.*

He's an asshole. I didn't hear anything else about Emily and CIG, and I figured it might have fallen through. Are you okay? Really?

Yeah, I am. It sucks. But. Oh fuck, Syl. I'm doing some digging, if you want to know the truth. Kim looked over the words for a moment, wondering if she really wanted to send them. Would she look vindictive? Bitter? Screw it, she hit the send button.

Digging for what? came the reply, quickly. *CIG? Kevin?*

Kevin. I don't care about CIG. I hated to lose them, but I'm doing okay. The truth is, Kevin hurt me. Physically. I don't want to dump this on you, but it was bad and I'm wondering if there are other women out there he's done this to. I know he has a reputation. But I'm wondering if there's some sort of a pattern. I'm wondering if I should say something. Report what he did. After sending the last message, Kim sat in front of the monitor, deeply uneasy with her features lit up in a ghostly glow. This was not like her, reaching out to, well, *anyone* and being so personal. From the living room, Emily snorted from her easy chair, asleep in front of the television.

Shit, Sylvia wrote back a few seconds later. *I'm so sorry, Kim. And yeah, there are women Kevin fucked with, and fucked over. I'm not talking about the rumors, either. I don't traffic in those and I don't think you do either.*

No, Kim wrote back, relieved to see Sylvia still engaging. *Not at all. I'm just trying to decide if I should come forward about my own experience. It's really not about me at this point, I hope you know that. I'm fine. The business is fine. But what he did was scary.*

I get that, came the reply. *Give me a minute, okay?*

Sure.

A few moments later, Sylvia typed out a name Kim wasn't familiar with.

Brenda Masterson.

Don't think I know her.

Well, I think the better word is 'knew,' Sylvia wrote. *She kind of disappeared after a run-in with Kevin and an opportunity with CIG maybe three years ago. It almost got him in trouble. Look, I don't want to start blabbing, but I don't mind telling you this. I knew Brenda. She was a start-up partner in a few projects with people I knew. She was—is, I hope—a good person. I talked to her once after she had gone through the ringer with Kevin. She never told me exactly what he tried to do with her, but I know it hurt her. And then he just blackballed her, all over the place. I saw it, too. Trade shows, conferences. He made her sound like some kind of psycho, and she's not. I'll include an email for her—it was a personal account, so hopefully it's still good. If anyone can tell you what he's capable of, it's her. She's not the only one, but she's one I know of.*

I really appreciate this, Kim wrote. *I won't misuse it, Syl. I'm not looking for gossip, I swear.*

It's mostly public knowledge, Sylvia wrote back. *Not the details about what he did to her. I never knew that anyway. But the backlash on Kevin for the mess he created for her was pretty public. He got away with it, but it soured him for some people. There were women who wouldn't meet with him for a while. CIG lost a few accounts. You know how it is, though—a few months later there was someone else with an idea needing funding and willing to work with them. Kevin took some time off, I remember that. And CIG bounced back of course. I guess Kevin did, too. I see him at industry events now, same as you. Anyway, I hope this helps. And don't worry, I don't care what Kevin knows I said or didn't say. He knows enough to stay away from me.* With that, Sylvia posted a little devil-face emoji, and then *Good luck, keep in touch. Emily is an amazing product line. You'll do great.*

A few seconds later, an email address for Brenda Masterson came through. Kim thanked Sylvia and switched off the computer. Emily was hungry, and there was other work to do. Whatever she would say to Brenda Masterson could wait another day or two.

NINETEEN

Thursday, September 28

You asked for this, she told herself, the phone trembling slightly in her hand, *so don't you run from it now*. Kim was in her living room, looking out the big window over the traffic below on Third Avenue. It was mid-afternoon, the middle of an otherwise typical hectic work day of calls, emails and paperwork. The voice on the other end was calm and measured. But there was a sound of defeat deep within it as well. Of resigned, eternal sadness.

"She was my sister," the woman, Ruth, said. "Her name was Brenda. I still watch her email account, and I saw yours come through. I hope it's okay to just call like this. I felt a little devious reading the message, but I feel strongly about the subject."

"No, it's fine," Kim said, glad she wasn't stammering. "I left my phone number on the off chance that she would call. I...I don't know what to say. Is she..."

"Dead, yes," Ruth said matter-of-factly. "It's okay. From the message I could tell you didn't really know Brenda. But did you ever meet, in professional circles, or anywhere?"

"No," Kim said. "I wish I had. I...well, I got her name from

91

another woman I used to work with in beauty. This other person had an email for her. Again, I'm just...so sorry."

"Thank you. Brenda died, about a year after Kevin Dunaway attacked her. I know this, which is why I decided to reach out to you directly. Brenda never told me the story, but she left some details in a letter that wasn't addressed to anyone. We hadn't been close for a few years, but we were once, so I like to think the letter was meant for me. Still, I don't know. I guess you could call it a suicide note, although it wasn't something she left behind. It was something I found later, when I was cleaning out her apartment in New York."

"Did she name him in that letter? Kevin, I mean."

"Oh yes," Ruth said, her voice taking on a momentarily conspiratorial tone. "It was all in there. What he tried to make her do. How she fought him. And then how he destroyed her. Piece by piece. Her career was over. She lost friends. That goddamn city is a pressure cooker on top of everything else. Suddenly she was ruined, alone and broke. Eventually it all became too much. She overdosed on some pills just before Christmas in 2016."

"I see," Kim said, a little above a whisper. "I hope it's okay to ask this. Did Brenda ever report Kevin to anyone? The police, I mean, or even to his company? Or seek help from a lawyer?"

"No, not that I know of. I knew my sister. She was proud. Self-made. Probably, well, the way you are. You look that way, anyway, in your ads. I pulled up a few things about you before I called."

"It's a very nice thing to say. Thank you."

"I don't think Brenda told anyone. Mostly, I know what she felt from the letter. Closed in. Beaten and alone."

"I don't know what to say. Again, I'm just so sorry. But I'm so grateful you called. I appreciate it more than you know."

"I guess I just felt like I had to," Ruth said. There was a brief sniffling sound, but otherwise her voice did not change. "I guess you felt like you had to also. Look for other victims, I mean."

"Yes," Kim said, holding back from choking on the word.

"I know I sound blunt. I've gotten that way, since Brenda died."

"No, it's good to hear honesty. I need that."

"He hurt you?" Ruth asked. "I assume that's why you reached out to me."

"He did. I was able to get away, but...some damage was done. A police investigation was started, but I wasn't the one who started it. It's kind of a long story, but I haven't cooperated with the police. Not yet anyway. I guess it's obvious, but I'm trying to decide what to do. If anything."

"You should do what makes you whole," Ruth said. Kim noticed her voice didn't seem to modulate. It wasn't monotone, but very steady. Like she was afraid of awakening something with it. "You should do the thing that helps you to survive. I wish my sister had found what that was."

"Me too, Ruth."

"I'm serious, Kim. Do what's right for you. If you don't want to tell the cops and take Dunaway on with some godawful courtroom circus, so be it. Whatever he did to you, all you had to do then was survive. That's all you have to do now. I would give my right arm to tell Brenda that." Kim was silent for a long moment.

"Thank you," she managed finally. "But I'm sensing I'll feel worse if I don't say something. Or do something."

"Maybe. I can't tell you what's best for you. I can tell you that another thing my sister felt was guilty. She felt guilty for not saying something. She worried about the next woman he'd push around. Or worse. But that's not on you."

"I guess not. But...well, we'll see. I've got some thinking to do. You've helped me."

"I wish I could help," Ruth said. "All I can say is, if anyone up there was interested in some dirt on Kevin Dunaway? I've got it. My sister left me those details, if not much else."

"Can I let you know?" Kim asked timidly.

"I hope you will. Good luck, Kim."

The phone went quiet in her hand, the call screen fading to black. Kim watched an ambulance weave expertly through the afternoon avenue traffic, lights and sirens blaring as it moved steadily up the East Side. The conversation with Ruth, the disembodied voice of the apparently middle-aged woman from Hollywood, Florida, would echo in her mind for some time. But the thing that stood out most and kept replaying in her mind was the way Ruth had phrased something. At least twice, Kim had heard it. What Kim was contemplating, at least the way Ruth seemed to see it, wasn't just an agreement to cooperate with law enforcement. It wasn't just the act of reporting a crime, enduring a few interviews, then standing back while justice took its course, so she could pat herself on the back and move on, vindicated.

It was more like taking on Kevin Dunaway. Personally. Like in a fighting arena. Perhaps that was the only way. She turned back toward the living area and caught a glimpse of herself in a mirror she had hung at the entrance to the kitchen. She forced her eyes back to the mirror, to the image of the woman, still bruised. Still swollen. After a long moment, she went to look for the card the female police officer had left her the week before.

TWENTY

Sunday, October 1

It was in the Washington Post that Kim first saw the house
she grew up in described as a "lab." She had been outside an
ice cream place with Emily, then just eight years-old, on a
sidewalk bench in idyllic little Dutchtown, Virginia. It was
less than seventy-two hours after the explosion that destroyed their house, now the subject of the newspaper story.

A walk from the shelter for women and families for ice
cream a few blocks away was their only respite from the
process that dominated that first week: Filling out forms,
talking to social workers, learning about Independent
Living. The newspaper had been left behind by another
reader and Emily had swiped it for the comics. Kim didn't
share the story with her, but instead folded it neatly and
placed it into her purse for later.

The Post reporter referred to the house—the charred re-
mains of it, anyway—as something that had been "according
to Tolland County sheriff's deputies, little more than a large
meth lab." This made sense to Kim of course, but still she
would have never referred to those filthy environs as anything so sophisticated. Her father made meth amphetamine

there, yes, although the real "cooks" were a string of older bikers, the last one a red-faced, pot-bellied guy named Lefty. Her father was little more than a mule, hauling materials and occasionally repairing equipment. His value otherwise was mostly ensuring quiet and unlimited access to the house, which had been in the family for generations. It was Lefty who did the real work as far as she could tell, manning the pans that blended lithium and ammonium nitrate in a miserable cloud of stink, breaking down the pseudoephedrine pills and blowing on crystals of meth as they lay cooling on sheets on the kitchen counters. He would move in a slow, methodical circle around the kitchen and in and out of an old pantry, his face beaded with sweat.

***

Kim smiled as she relived that afternoon with Emily at the ice cream store. Most of her memories were bad, but she enjoyed, at times, reliving her and her sister's first moments on their own, after the explosion and fire that changed everything for them. Those first few days alone had been a mix of fear and hope. She had never felt more isolated or afraid, between the uncertainty of what she was hurtling them both into and the gnawing realization that she was the only thing standing between Emily and God knew what. But at the same time, she had never felt freer. Those moments, the first ones where she finally felt like herself, she would remember until her last breath.

The memory faded as Kim heard the familiar email chime on her laptop, a reminder that she needed to be up early to catch up on work before leaving for the appointment she had made. On the easy chair a few feet away

Emily snored lightly, her mouth slightly agape and her hair in a wild tangle around her head. Kim pulled a throw blanket over her and walked to the bar to make a drink before getting ready for bed; she mixed a vodka soda, on the heavy side, but it had been a tough day. She felt the liquor move warmly down her middle.

She had made the call to the female police officer who had come to their door a week before. Officer Milagros had called her back within an hour. That had led to another phone call, and now she had an appointment the following day with an NYPD detective, a nice-sounding woman with a girlish voice named Angie. She was going to take that first step. Even though she had no idea where it might lead.

As always, she put Emily back in the forefront of her thoughts as she played out the possibilities. The idea of involving the law, a system that had never really helped her, was terrifying. Then again, the detective had assured her that nothing was set in stone and that their meeting would be informal. That she, Kim, would dictate whether it went past that. Kim could only speculate, but the detective had sounded genuine.

She figured she would have to tell Emily more about what was going on if a court case were to proceed. Emily could basically take care of herself during the day, so that wasn't an issue. But Kim wondered if the case would attract any kind of press attention, the kind Emily might be exposed to, and that might upset her. It seemed unlikely, but she couldn't be sure. Kevin Dunaway wasn't famous, but he was wealthy. There would be rumors flying around her industry of course. She had long since made peace with that. She only prayed this whole thing wouldn't affect her booming sales too terribly, and that it wouldn't alienate her from the chance to follow through with an-other venture capital firm when the time was right.

She also knew she couldn't remain silent. Pride was not a sin that haunted Kimberly Hadley. But there was a mea-sure of steely stubbornness in her, and even after a long trail of wrongs and suffering, there was a sense of justice that was not so easily quieted.

TWENTY-ONE

Monday, October 2

The place Detective Keegan suggested they meet was near Pier 40 on the Hudson Greenway, which in decent weather was an ever-active bike and walking path on Manhattan's West Side dotted with parks and public spaces. The day was gray and chilly, but mostly windless, even at the riverside. The detective was seated on a park bench talking on her phone when Kim approached after crossing West Street.

Kim had been told to look for a tall blonde woman in a navy-blue raincoat with a streak of purple in her hair, and sure enough, Kim noticed her standing beside a park bench. The coat was a nice one, Kim noticed. Sleek, with a waist belt. Recognition seemed to fill Angie's eyes as Kim approached and she ended her call, smiling as Kim bridged the distance and offered her hand.

"Detective Keegan?"

"I am. Ms. Hadley?" Kim had spoken with Keegan over the phone, and like most people, was surprised at the delicate high tone of her voice when actually in her presence. She was attractive, with a full but angular face, generous lips and beautiful light blue eyes. But she looked tougher than her voice; there was no other way to put it.

"Yes. Please, call me Kim. Thanks for meeting me, out here like this, I mean."

"It's fine. I'm Angie." She pulled out her notepad, then made eye contact with Kim. "I might take a few notes. But mostly, we'll just talk. Tell me what you can about that night. From there, it's up to you how far you want to take things. I'll be honest with you about what I can do with that choice."

"Thank you," Kim said. She took a deep breath. "Honestly, I'm surprised you even agreed to meet with me. I'm not sure I would believe me at this point."

"Why not?"

"Because I ran, for one thing."

"That happens sometimes."

"There was a side door I went out of. Through a trash room. I don't know if you all figured that out or not."

"Yeah, we put that together. That happens sometimes, too. People don't want to be seen or spotted. I'm sure you had a reason."

"I did, but it doesn't seem right. I was just...really scared."

"It's okay. Tell me what you can."

"I'm not sure where to start."

"Start anywhere." With that, Kim gave Angie the background of her interaction with Kevin and then the night she was attacked. She expected to feel more emotional when she related the worst details, Kevin grunting and cursing behind her, his hands pinching at her like hot, padded claws. But she was dry-eyed and calm, something she hoped wasn't off-putting to the detective.

"When you first turned away from him," Angie said, "and he grabbed you to pull you back. Tell me about that. Second by second. If you can." Kim looked over Angie's face. It was neutral, but there was belief in her eyes, not distrust or skepticism.

"I felt his hand, like his fingers, dig into my skirt. God, his fingers felt so big. I felt the skirt tear, at the zipper. He was pulling me back. Into his lap."

"Okay. And then?"

"That's when I found the champagne flute. I grabbed it by the stem. With my right hand. I swung it back, blindly. I felt it hit his hand. I can't remember if I heard it break or not. Probably. He yelled out."

"Okay. And then?"

Kim sighed at this. "Things happened really fast after that. We both jumped up, and then I was facing him. It was so fast. He punched me. I couldn't believe how fast and how hard. In the eye. Then in the mouth. I didn't even scream. I was in shock, I think. I turned around to run. He grabbed my ankle and I fell forward. I blocked the fall with my palms. That stung." She paused for a moment, looked around, and then back at Angie. "You wouldn't think I'd even feel that, the stinging, but I did."

"Sure," Angie said. "Then what?"

"I felt him grabbing at me, with both hands. His left hand is the one that got my left ankle first. Then his right, the bleeding hand. That got my right ankle. I could feel the blood on my heel. He was grunting. Saying things."

"Do you remember what he said?"

"He said...'fuck.' 'Whore.' Maybe both. I think both. Like calling me a name. He was kind of breathing it." She paused again, breathed deeply, and looked out over the blue-green stripe of the Hudson. A huge red and brown fuel barge was steaming steadily north.

"You're doing great. Take your time."

"He used his arms. He was opening my legs, like pulling them apart. With the bleeding hand, he tried to jerk me back, back toward him. His left hand was moving up my leg in grabbing motions. His hands felt so big."

"Was he able to touch your genital area? Or your butt?"

"Almost. He got as far as my underwear. I could feel his fingers, brushing the ... the crotch panel, you know?"

"Yeah."

"Then he said something. 'I've got you now.' It was... terrifying. I found some strength then. Reared back my right leg and kicked him. It connected somewhere on his chest I think. He howled. Roared. That was it, I was free. I got up, we exchanged some words. Then I left."

"And when you left," Angie said, at lower volume, like she knew it was a sensitive subject, "you left the building without going by the front desk."

"I did," Kim said, resigning herself to what she figured was the obvious, next thing to happen. Whatever justice she might have sought, for herself or anyone else, was out of reach. Her voice went to almost a whisper. "I went out a side door."

"Can you tell me why?" There was a long pause while Kim clutched her purse, and Angie sat patiently.

"I...have been in situations like that before. Violent ones, I mean. Not with men like Kevin. Really, it was family, to be honest. But I kind of learned that the response can be almost as bad as whatever happened. I'm not sure if that makes sense or not."

"It does."

"Well, given everything that happened, and what I did after, I wouldn't blame you for not believing me. I'm sure Kevin had an explanation."

"He did," Angie said slowly. "And I know it's bullshit." Kim paused, almost stunned, as this washed over her.

"But..."

"Kim, you don't have to convince me."

"Well, thank you. You don't, I mean, I'm not sure you know what that means to me."

"Well if it's good, I'm glad."

"It's more than good. It's almost shocking. Thank you."

"I listened to you," Angie said. "I listened to Dunaway. Carefully. I knew he was guilty of assaulting you. I wasn't sure how until now, but I knew it." Kim felt emotion rise up in her chest.

"From when you interviewed him?" she asked finally.

"Yeah," Angie said with an air of confidence. "About two minutes into the interview, I knew he was wrong. There was something else, though. Something I saw then, and I'm glad I remembered. But I didn't make sense of it until now."

"Okay."

"You said you were able to kick him," Angie said. "With your right heel."

"Yes."

"Connected on his right side somewhere."

"Yes. His chest, I think. I wish I had gotten him in the eye, to be honest."

"I'm pretty sure it was his chest also," Angie said. "You had to be there, but when we interviewed him, he kind of winced when he moved his body once, over the desk to shake hands when we were leaving. I'll bet there's a nice bruise where you got him."

"Well, I appreciate that. I suppose you're trained to spot liars also, but I would guess he's pretty smooth."

"People get away with lying to me," Angie said. "There are detectives who will tell you they can tell when anyone is lying, but that's bullshit, too. With some guys, you'll just never know, even if you do this job thirty years. But with him, I knew. He's polished, yeah. But I knew. Now, I don't have a doubt."

"He's charming when he wants to be, also," Kim said. "The whole bit. But I'm really glad you saw through him."

"Yeah, but that and five bucks gets you a nice cup of coffee. What do you want to do now? Try and go forward, talk to the DA?"

"Would a DA take the case?"

"Honestly I don't know," Angie said. "Like I said on the phone, officially it was kind of closed on that end. The prosecutor who was originally looking at it kind of felt like it got zipped up."

"Zipped up?"

Angie sighed, and said, "Look, there's only so much I can say. But I think his feeling was that his boss didn't want to deal with it. It's like I told you, there was some talk that Dunaway was really the victim."

"Oh yeah," Kim said quietly. "I could see that."

"Yeah, well I think it's nonsense. But I also think they could be made to see it differently. I wouldn't have encouraged you to come out here and repeat all this stuff if I didn't think I could do something with it. I'm still not sure, but it's worth a shot, if you want to go forward."

"Me?" Kim asked, and then realized how silly that sounded.

"Yeah, you. I have to write this up either way, but as

far as I'm concerned, this is a live case and you're a good witness. The next step is the DA. Their office 'papers' everything, which means they actually write up the charges. It's up to them whether they file them and bring the case to court. You might not even want that."

"I'm not sure either, but I think I should see this through. The truth is, I was contacted by someone. I heard rumors about Kevin from other women in my industry. Stories. So, after that night, I did some digging. Eventually I was contacted by someone. It wasn't someone Kevin attacked, actually. It was her sister. The woman Kevin attacked is dead, she committed suicide last year. So mostly I just can't stand the idea of him doing something like this to someone else. I'm willing to tell the truth, anyway. That's what I did with you."

"Okay."

"What's the prosecutor like?" Kim asked. "Would it be the same one you were talking about?"

"Yeah, I think so. His name is Alex."

"Good guy?"

"He is," Angie said, nodding, and something like a smile slipped across her face. "He gets it. The rest of the office is also pretty good. It's a new unit. They're supposed to take tough cases. So far, I think they're making good on that."

"So, I'm a tough case," Kim said. She sat up, forming her little mouth into a crooked grin, and glanced over at Angie.

"I have a feeling you're tough enough for it," Angie said. "Come with me for a few minutes. I'll explain what happens now."

TWENTY-TWO

Wednesday, October 4

"So, let's really commiserate," Megan said, flashing Kim a conspiratorial look. They were at a cozy, wood-paneled wine bar on Lexington Avenue on another gray, brisk October afternoon. "Have you dated much in this town?"

"Oh God no," Kim said, a little more forcefully than she intended, although Megan didn't seem to notice. "Not on my radar, I guess."

"Well you've been building a million-dollar business on your own," she said, tipping her glass toward Kim's. "Pretty understandable. Anyway, it's a nightmare. Men are the worst here."

"Aren't they pretty much the same everywhere?"

"I'm telling you New York is bad. This city is like a giant playground for them, there's always someone around the corner, younger and less wary."

"You can't have a problem finding dates," Kim said. She was nursing her second glass of pinot noir and felt a little lightheaded. It was a pleasant little buzz, something she hadn't felt in a while. She'd been surprised by a message from Megan a couple of days earlier—the same day she had met with Angie—suggesting a time and place to grab a drink. There was a place Megan suggested that was on Lexington not far from her office. Kim couldn't remember the last time she'd gone out like that, just meeting a girl-friend for a drink. Given the heaviness of the week, and the fact that she was scheduled to meet with the ADA the following day, it was a welcome diversion.

"Well, thank you," Megan said. "But dates are one thing. A decent guy not looking to run a game is another. Ugh, whatever. Listen, I *love* your product. The scrub?"

"Oh yeah, the signature one. We call that a hero product."

"Hero product?"

"Yeah. In the 'biz, it's the thing you kind of build your line around. That scrub was the first thing I came up with. I had Emily cutting up the ingredients next to me in our old kitchen, back in Virginia, if you can believe that."

"Oh my God, really? That is so sweet! How long did it take to come up with?"

"The scrub? Oh God, I can't remember how many things I tried. I have it all written down, though. I probably went through one hundred trials."

"And it's all organic?"

"Yep."

"That's genius," Megan said, as if making a bold but certain pronouncement.

"Not really. I just followed a trend. Maybe fifteen years ago, a bunch of stuff went around on the internet about some of the chemicals in beauty products." She glanced over at Megan, suddenly feeling conspiratorial herself. This was *fun*. "Want a tip? The better it smells, the worse it probably is for you."

"Get out."

"I swear. The really perfumed stuff? It's all chemicals. The big companies got away with that for decades. Then came the internet—God bless it—and a whole lot of information. Not all of it was accurate of course, but the basic stuff about organic ingredients really was. I riffed off of that. My ingredients are all things you could buy at a decent organic market. Fruit, sugar, salt. Things like that. There's a little more to it, and it takes forever to get the texture right, the color, all of that. But really, it's about purity and just going with what's natural. After I had a basic formula, the other products kind of flowed from it. That first scrub is what I had patented, though."

"And it's still made the same way?"

"Basically," Kim said with a shrug. "I have a manufacturer now, so there's a process. I fight cutting corners, even if it costs me more in production costs. It's a struggle to really stay true to the ingredients, but it's doable. And there's quality control and all sorts of regulations and such. Ugh, stop me, I'm boring you!"

"You're not," Megan said. "Seriously, I love talking to someone who actually did something like this. I googled and found a couple of articles on you. I hope you don't mind. You're like a big deal."

"I don't mind, and thank you," Kim said, feeling a warm glow inside. She felt a little silly admitting it to herself, but the fact was, she needed an ego boost like this after what she'd just been through. "I'm really just a little fish, it's a relatively small business. I've started something good, I'm just hoping to get it past the finish line, that's all."

"Meaning?"

"Meaning sell the business, if I can. For me, that's

the goal. Some women want to run the whole thing and build an empire. Me? I'll sell for the right price, get out and then, well... I don't know really. Hang out with Emily. Travel, maybe."

"That sounds nice," Megan said. For a split-second Kim saw a faraway look in her eyes. Not sad, really. But almost wistful. It was a little like the one she saw when Megan was talking about her mother, coming into the city all dressed up. "How do you do it all? I mean running the company and taking care of your sister. It's got to be exhausting."

"Oh, it is. But I've got a small staff now. My manufacturer is in New Jersey, so he's not far. It's tough, but it's manageable. I spend most of the day on the computer, keeping up with it all. The thing is, to really get to the next level, you have to have a different infrastructure. Like a lab, not just a kitchen counter. I'm in over my head already. If I can get out while the getting is good, I won't hesitate."

"That's awesome," Megan said. "I'd like to think I'd do the same thing, if I ever had an original idea."

"The ideas are in there," Kim said, smiling at her and pointing playfully. "What are you passionate about?" Megan seemed to ponder this. Her lips were pursed, and Kim noticed they were particularly full, probably collagen infused. If so, they were very well done.

"The perfect margarita," she said finally. "I doubt there's a fortune in it, though. Look, I'm not complaining. I have a good job. A decent apartment. My family isn't far. I just love meeting people who take charge, you know?"

"Of course," Kim said. "And I really appreciate that. And getting me out for a drink, too. It's been a long time." She wasn't going to add the next thing, but the wine had loosened her up a little bit, and out it came. "I'm in the middle of something, actually, and it's kind of scary. So, this is nice diversion."

"Uh-oh," Megan said. "Something with Emily? Is she okay?"

"No, she's fine. It's a court case. Or it could be one. I don't want to dump all this on you, though."

"You don't have to tell me anything, but I'm a decent listener. And if someone is suing you, I know some pretty cutthroat lawyers."

"That would be so much easier." Kim said. She sighed and weighed her options. Megan was brand new to her life, such as it was. But she seemed sincere. And really, other than Evelyn, Kim had no one to talk to. "The truth is, it's a criminal case. A couple of months ago, a guy attacked me. So, I'm a...crime victim, I guess."

"Oh God, I'm so sorry. You mean someone was arrested and there's a case going on?"

"No one's arrested yet. I met with a detective in Manhattan. I meet with a DA tomorrow. I think his office decides if it's officially charged, or whatever."

"Oh Kim, I'm sorry. Was it some wacko, like on the train? I've had a few run-ins. It used to be a lot worse around here."

"I swear, I think that would be easier also. No, it was a guy I was working with. A partner at a venture capital firm. It happened after a dinner meeting, if you can believe that."

"I can believe anything," Megan said, throwing her a dark look. She motioned to the bartender for another round. "Tell me whatever you want to tell me. Or nothing at all. But I promise, nothing will surprise me." With that, Kim explained the basic details, minus most of the gory stuff, and how she had come to report the crime after all. Megan seemed to listen with patience, nodding from time to time and appearing unfazed by what she was hearing.

"I'm probably a handful as a new friend," Kim said when she had finished. The explanation was exhausting, yet she also felt an odd sense of lightness, like something had been lifted from her shoulders. "I hope it doesn't freak you out."

"Please, of course not. Are you okay now? Physically I mean?"

"Yeah, I'm fine. I had a nasty shiner for a while. Fat lip. A few other bruises. But I'm okay. He didn't get to my goodies. How's that for plain talk?" At this, Megan stared blankly at her for a moment, and then let out a chortle.

"Oh God that's priceless! And if we're really talking plain, did you get a good shot at him? Like maybe his balls?"

"No, but I got him with a broken champagne flute," she said. "He needed stitches in his hand. The detective told me that. Good God." She shook her head and reached for her wine glass.

"Well, good for you," Megan said. "Not that it matters, but physically you're a small woman and I'm sure he's a lot bigger. I'm just glad you got away before it got even worse."

"Thanks," Kim said. She was looking down at the space between them, to the floor under the barstools. But also smiling inwardly. This had been a good idea. She could feel that inside. "Me too."

TWENTY-THREE

Thursday, October 5

"Please, call me Kim," she said, as she smoothed her skirt and took a seat in front of Alex's desk. "I very much appreciate your time."

"I appreciate yours," Alex said. "You made a good impression on Detective Keegan as well. We were both hoping we'd meet you eventually." Kim smiled shyly at this. Alex's first impression of Kim Hadley—similar to Angie's—was that she actually looked doll-like, with small, neat features, bright green eyes and dark brown hair pulled tightly in a bun. She was dressed in a conservative, dark business suit with low heels. She looked incredibly well put-together. He still wondered why she had run from responders the night she'd been attacked. That, more than anything, was what he needed to discuss with her at this first meeting. "Also, did Ms. Levin explain that she could be present while I talk to you?"

"Oh, Judy Levin? Yes, she was great, thank you. But she figured I'd be okay talking with you alone, and I am. She asked me to stop by her office afterward. I'll do that."

"Well, I'll take that as a compliment," he said. "Do you

have any preliminary questions for me? If not, we can start with the facts, when you feel ready."

"You mean between Kevin and me," she said. She maintained eye contact, intensely. Her speech was clear and metered.

"Yes. But in addition to that, I need to know everything you remember. What I mean is, how you got out of his apartment, and what was behind the decisions you made from there."

"Of course," she said, glancing down. "I'm not proud of how I reacted." Now she lifted her chin a touch. "I'll understand if the case can't be prosecuted. Everyone here has been very good to me. I don't want to waste their time. Or yours."

"There's nothing for you to be ashamed of, first of all," he said. As he often did with crime victims, he lowered his voice and leaned forward a little in his chair, hands clasped in front of him. "There are all sorts of reasons people react the way they do in traumatic situations. I can't say for sure whether my office will agree to press charges in your case. It's not solely my decision." There was no need to tell Kim, but it had taken some convincing on both Alex and Shelly's part to get Gerry to reconsider pursuing the case, at least to the extent of bringing the victim in for an interview. The new unit was all about taking tough cases, after all. Even Gerry had to admit that with a willing complaining witness, this one fit the bill. "But I can tell you this. Just because you fled the scene doesn't mean I can't prosecute your case."

"Really?" She seemed genuinely surprised at this. "Honestly, I thought you were going to thank me for coming in, but then tell me how it just wasn't possible to press charges. The detective wasn't sure."

"A few years ago, that might have been the case. We've come a long way. I've won cases with challenging facts. And that's all they are. Challenging. If I understand them, and we're truthful with each other, I can put them into context."

"You mean in front of a jury."

"Eventually, if there's a case and it goes to trial, yes."

She nodded, sighed, and said, "Where should I start?"

"Wherever you'd like. This is a safe place. If you need a break while we talk, let me know. Okay?"

"Okay." With that, she relayed pretty much everything that she had told Angie. Alex nodded occasionally but didn't interrupt her. Her recitation was smooth, seemed natural, and also matched the write-up Angie had done after meeting her the day before. He had no problem with her credibility so far. He had a feeling a jury might not either. She paused after explaining how she finally smashed the champagne bottle, challenged Kevin with it and then made it out of his apartment.

"And then?"

"Then I found the stairway," she said. "I...didn't want to take the elevator."

"Did that have to do with the elevator itself?"

"No. It was because I knew I'd have to walk past the doorman to leave the building," she said, her voice lowering to almost a whisper. "I didn't want to do that."

"Okay. Can you tell me what was going on in your mind?" As usual, he avoided "why" questions. They usually came off as sounding judgmental.

"I was panicking. But not about what Kevin had done to me." Her eyes, which had been cast downward, now snapped up into his. "I've experienced physical violence before. Sexual violence, too, as a child. I was shocked by what Kevin had done, but not entirely surprised. Does that make sense?"

"It does, yes."

"Well, you'd think that would mean I'd be calmer. Collected, I guess. Ready to face the police. Or ask someone to call them. But I didn't want that." She paused, and Alex waited patiently. "I wanted to find another way out of the building. I didn't want to be seen, or report anything. I know that's wrong. I can only imagine how it looks."

"It's not wrong. And let me worry about how it looks. Just tell me what was going on in your head, and how you reacted. Take your time."

"I was bleeding, I know that. I found a handkerchief in my bag. I held it to my mouth at first. That's where the bleeding was, mostly, although my eye felt like it had exploded. Anyway, I got to the bottom of the stairs, and wandered around until I found what looked like another way out. It was the door to the trash room, I guess. I was terrified someone would see me. I went through it past the dumpsters and found the side door to the building. When I got out to the alley, I'm not sure what happened. The air hit me. I was woozy all of a sudden. I fell. I remember lying there for a few seconds, or...well, I don't know how long. But I could hear foot traffic on the street behind me, on the busier street."

"West Broadway," Alex said.

"Yes, exactly. I tried to get up, but I just couldn't. I crawled toward the street his building is on. Wooster, I guess."

"Do you remember dropping the handkerchief? It was found right outside the side door."

"No. I didn't realize I had dropped it until I was in a cab, on the way home. I was looking for something to put over my mouth. That's when I noticed it was gone."

"It was one you used often?" he asked, scratching out a few notes.

"Mostly for Emily. My sister. If she makes a mess on her face with an ice cream cone or something, it comes in handy. It was in my purse all the time unless I was washing it. For years, I guess. I was actually sad when I realized it was gone."

"Ah, okay." He paused and looked up at her. "Emily. Is she an adult?"

"She's twenty-three, yes, although disabled. She's pretty functional, but I take care of her. And she can be messy."

"Gotcha," he said, and smiled. "We'll get to know each other during this process." After a moment, she smiled back. "Anyway, the handkerchief. Were you and Emily the only ones to handle it, or was it also handled by a third party? A boyfriend maybe or a housekeeper?"

"No, just us. All we have is each other, Emily and me."

"Understood. Okay, so let's go back to after you dropped the handkerchief. You were telling me you were making your way out of the alley?"

"Yes," she said, her eyes seeming to darken at the memory of it. "I was on my hands and knees, almost to the street. I was thinking I had to get up again when the doorman came running out. And then a guy from across the street showed up. The doorman was nice. The older guy was kind of bossy."

"We have their statements," Alex said.

"They wanted me to stay where I was. But again, I just... couldn't. I wanted to get out of there. Far away from where I was."

"Okay."

"I was ashamed. I was terrified. I just wanted to get into a cab. I hate that I did it. But that's the truth."

"The truth, about what you were feeling and how you reacted, is all I need right now. You're doing great. Take a moment if you need to."

"Thank you," she said, and cleared her throat. Her eyes had welled up with tears, but only slightly. Alex slid the ever-present box of tissues on his desk toward her. "I snapped when I heard sirens and saw the blue lights. All I could think of was to get away. So, I got to my feet. By that time there were a few other people nearby, people who had stopped to look, I guess. Between them and the thought of the cops showing up, I just turned and ran. I got to West Broadway and found a cab almost immediately. There were a ton of them and it was a nice night, so people were walking. The cab driver didn't ask me anything. He didn't even look at me. I got home maybe fifteen minutes later."

TWENTY-FOUR

"The police," Alex said after pausing to take in what Kim had told him. "Were they your biggest fear? Or was it just everything, like the people around you, the response in general?"

"Both, I think."

"Do you understand why I'm asking?"

"You mean am I wanted by the law?" she asked, a tiny grin creeping onto her face. Alex returned it.

"Some people have had bad experiences with the police. Some people are just intensely private, and they avoid contact with authority, strangers, whatever. And yes, some people are wanted. But I don't assume that about you."

"Well, I'd assume you'd know if I was," she said. "It's got to be a part of your job."

"You assume correctly," he said. "But you have no criminal record that I'm aware of. And even if you did, I wouldn't shy away from your case because of it. Judy, who you met earlier? She'd have my head if I did."

"Well, good on Judy," she said. She grinned again, a tight, narrow grin. Alex noticed she rarely smiled wide enough to show her teeth, even though they were bright and even. He wondered if that hadn't always been the case.

They talked at length about Kim's career path and how she had intersected with Kevin and Callisto Investing. Alex didn't know anything about the beauty business except for the few things Angie had mentioned, but Kim's description of it, and her foray into it since college, sounded reasonable to him. After that, he explained how the process would go. He'd talk to his bosses about the case. If they agreed it could go forward, he'd write up a charging document. She would sign it, and a case would be presented to a grand jury in Manhattan, probably within a couple of weeks, depending on how fast the paperwork flowed.

"Will he have to appear in court, then?" she asked. "Kevin, I mean?"

"Yes, and he's got counsel already," Alex said. "Because of that, as a courtesy, I'll tell his lawyer when charges will be written up. Dunaway will have to surrender himself at a precinct and appear in court for an arraignment. After that a grand jury will meet to decide if the case can go on to trial. You should know, Kevin has a right to testify in front of the same grand jury you would. But usually, defendants don't do that. Then, if the grand jury returns a true bill, the case will get held over for trial. That's a months-long process, but we'll talk more about it later on. The defendant can always plea out, of course. I'll talk to you about that too, before any decisions are made."

"I doubt Kevin would plea to anything," she said, shaking her head. "So, the charge would be...?"

"Like I said, all of this is contingent on what my boss decides. I'll have to discuss it with him or the deputy, maybe both. But most likely, it would be attempted rape. I'll also add an assault charge." Kim winced at the reality of those words. The reality of what was done to her. Attempted rape.

Assault.

Alex picked up her expression and responded in kind. "They're ugly words, I know."

"Attempted rape?" she asked. Her eyes widened a little. "Really?"

"Yes. From what you described, I think the facts fit the statute."

"Oh, okay. I mean, that's fine. I just figured, maybe an assault charge was all there would be."

"Do you believe Kevin was trying to have sex with you against your will?"

"I do," she said after a pause. "Yes."

"So do I," he said, "based on what you've told me. Again, I'll discuss it with my superiors here. I'll let you know more as soon as I do."

"Okay," she said, as if resigning herself to something long and arduous, which of course Alex knew was correct. "Thank you."

"No, thank you. You came forward, however long it took. That's good for everyone."

"Except you, maybe," she said.

"This is what I signed up for. I'll be fine. Oh, Detective Keegan mentioned that Dunaway claimed you were texting someone, just before you left his apartment. But you weren't, right? That's what Angie wrote up."

"No," Kim said, her brow furrowed. "I checked on Emily once during dinner. Other than that, I didn't use my phone until the next day."

"That's fine. We'll pull your phone records so we can verify that. Speaking of your phone, do you mind if I contact you on your cell?

"Not at all," she said.

"Thank you. I'm going to give you mine also. I don't do that with everyone, but you seem pretty decent."

"I guess I should take that as a compliment."

"Yes, you should. Anyway, this case is going to be tough, assuming it goes forward. For now, I'll stay in contact every step of the way, as will Judy. Detective Keegan can also assist you, if you can't reach us. Any other questions for now? I'm sure a ton of them will come up."

"There is one," she said, slowing her speech a little. "If I go forward with this, would I have to submit to any examinations? Mental, or physical?" He pondered this for a moment.

"I don't see how you would. Based on the facts, and the delay in reporting, I can't imagine how a physical examination would be relevant to the charges I'm considering. In terms of a psychological examination, again, I can't see how that would be relevant. You seem functional and competent to me. But you have to know, I can't promise anything." She raised her eyebrows.

"Really? So, a physical or a mental evaluation is actually a possibility?"

"Kim," he said, taking a moment to meet her eyes, "anything is a possibility. Any lawyer who makes you a promise about litigation is one you shouldn't trust. I can't see how any examinations would be allowed in a case like this. But I would never state that as an absolute. Kevin Dunaway is a man of means. The more robust the defense, the more likely they are to throw anything at the wall and hope it sticks, or that it just makes you not want to do this anymore. I don't want to dissuade you based on those concerns. But I can't promise anything. You have to understand that."

"I do," she said, like a bride. "Thank you. I do."

TWENTY-FIVE

Friday, October 6

Kim felt herself finally starting to relax after a long and tough week, almost melting into the examination table in Evelyn's little Brooklyn office. Evelyn, with her penlight in hand, examined her face and gently palpated the area around her eye.

"Does this still hurt?" she asked, lifting her fingers. Kim smiled and shook her head. Evelyn's scent was different this time. She had a lotion on, something with eucalyptus maybe.

"No. I think it's okay now. It's still tender, but it's healing okay."

"I think you're right," Evelyn said, and took a seat on the rolling stool next to the table. She looked at Kim with tired eyes. "You're lucky. I'm happy for you."

"And I'm healthy otherwise?"

"As far as I'm qualified to say," Evelyn said with a shrug. "How do you feel?"

"Other than the healing injuries, one hundred percent."

Kim hadn't seen her since that first Monday after the "incident." That's what she was calling it—the "incident." Alex Greco had referred to it as the "assault," which Kim assumed was per his legal training. Detective Keegan tended to go with the more impactful "attack." Kim felt both of those words were true, but it still felt weird using them in her own mind. For the time being she was sticking with the "incident."

"There's something else I wanted to see you about today," Kim said, sitting up and letting her legs hang over the side of the table. She clasped her hands together in her lap. "Not just the follow-up."

"You don't say," Evelyn said, lifting an eyebrow and smiling. She had a tired smile, Kim noticed, and not for the first time. It wasn't that it seemed disingenuous, like the smiles of so many people she'd met in her industry, the kind that ended far below the eyes. It was more like the smile was naturally hesitant, almost fearful. Like whatever reason existed for it could be swept away quickly.

"I spoke to the police. And a prosecutor, in Manhattan."

"Okay."

"There might be a court case," Kim said. "I wanted you to know." With that, she gave Evelyn the complete rendition of who Kevin was and what had happened that night. Evelyn nodded occasionally but didn't interrupt. She seemed concerned, but unsurprised.

"Well, I'm proud of you," Evelyn said when she had finished. Kim hadn't known what to expect in response, but that was an appreciated one.

"I figured you'd want me to think about Emily," Kim said. "I want you to know I have. I think she can handle it. But I *am* worried."

"Of course, you are. But I agree with you there, she can handle it."

"I'm scared, Ev."

"I wish I could tell you there was nothing to be afraid of."

"This is why I come to you," Kim said, holding her gaze and smiling. She felt a wave of emotion rise through her. It felt great just to be back in Evelyn's company. "No bullshit. Ever."

"No time for it. There's love, though. Got plenty of that."

Kim looked down and said, "Evelyn, I know I've asked you to watch over me, the way a doctor would. And I know I should a find a real doctor. It's just that you're the only one I really trust."

"I understand. It's okay."

"Well, it's just...with this case, I'm putting myself out there. The DA doesn't think there would be any physical or mental examinations, or questions about my health. But he was pretty straightforward in telling me he couldn't guarantee anything. This guy Kevin is loaded. He can send lawyers or investigators in to poke around."

"There's a doctor-patient privilege that applies to us under my license. Don't worry about that."

"Yeah, but what if there was a subpoena or something?"

"Chances are no one will ask me anything," Evelyn said, putting both of her hands on Kim's knees and looking intently at her. "If they do, we have a privilege and neither of us has done one thing to break it. And no matter what, I'm not breaking it. Not for anyone. Not even for an army of lawyers. Don't worry about me. You have enough to worry about."

TWENTY-SIX

She didn't see Emily get hit. She had seen the bat, though, the one Phil, a meth user who frequented her father's home, used to nearly bash her sister's skull in. It wasn't intentional. Phil didn't seem to give a fuck about Emily or the twins, but he never purposefully looked to harm them either. For most of the men who drifted in and out, the kids were just a part of the background, essentially invisible. That was preferable, of course, to the occasional customer who lingered and took an interest in one of them.

It was a scarred, wooden baseball bat and Phil toted it everywhere. He swung it around and around in his right hand. When he was tweaking, it was like some sort of security blanket. Phil got paranoid. A lot of guys did, but he was worse. Even when he was seemingly relaxed, the bat was in hand, doing its meaningless loops through his thumb and fingers. But when he was high, pacing back and forth or perched rigidly on the couch in what passed for the living room, everything, every thump, every screech of the door on its hinges, sent Phil to his feet, his bat at the ready.

Why Emily chose to cross his path that night, a little shadow between the couch and the flicker of the television set, was anyone's guess. She probably needed to pee and was making her way to the little half-bathroom on the kitchen side of the house. She shouldn't have been downstairs in the first place, but maybe she had come down to the kitchen hoping to find something to snack on. Meth-heads left all sorts of junk food lying around, donuts, cookies, bags of chips. Most mornings there were open boxes, packages and paper bags all over the place.

Emily tiptoed into the living room where Phil was sitting, fidgeting on the couch with a cigarette in one hand and the bat in the other. The figure in his peripheral vision must have startled him. He swung in the dark and connected.

She didn't hear the sound of the bat connecting with Emily's head. Instead she heard Phil's audible "whaaaa" sound as the light from the TV revealed the thing he had actually struck. By the time she arrived, darting through the kitchen from her bedroom, Phil was standing over Emily, his chest heaving, the bat dropped to the floor next to the child it had just flattened. He turned toward her and made the same sound, a kind of wail. His eyes were wide, searching and terrified in the glow of the TV. Emily was on the ground, eyes closed, blood leaking from the right side of her head, over her ear.

"I didn't..." he started. "I mean. Fuck. Oh fuck. I didn't mean to."

"Oh Jesus," she breathed. She fell to her knees in front of Emily, wanting to do something between cradling her and shaking her awake, and then remembered something about not moving wounded people. So instead of touching her, her hands floated helplessly around her head while she choked back sobs.

"What the fuck?" She heard him some moments later, maybe seconds, maybe a minute. It was her father. He had run in from the meth cooking area, probably at the sound of Phil's wailing.

"I didn't mean..." Phil started again.

"You worthless fuckin' scumbag," her father started, but by that time Phil was bolting out through the kitchen toward the back door. Then their father looked down at Emily, and then over to her.

"Stop the bleeding," he said. "Put something over the wound and press on it."

"I'm not sure we should touch her."

"She's fucking bleeding to death, goddammit!" He retreated through to the kitchen and was back in a few seconds with what looked like an oven mitt. He knelt down and pressed the mitt to the site of the bleeding. For a few seconds Emily didn't respond at all. Then she grunted and spewed some white foam out of her mouth. She made a gurgling sound, then vomited, a thin, yellow gruel cascading over her chin.

"She needs an ambulance, dad. Where's your phone?"

"She'll be okay. Just hold that, over the wound 'til it stops bleeding." Gingerly she took her father's place holding the now-bloody oven mitt over Emily's head. A few seconds later, the head jerked to the side. Her arms and legs shot straight out in their sockets, like she'd been electrocuted. She vomited again, a pathetic sputtering sound.

"Dad, she's turning purple. Please!"

"Carry her upstairs," he said. "Now."

"But–"

"To her bed. Now. Clean her up and watch her." She scooped her sister up, the now nearly blood-soaked mitt still resting against the wound. Emily's head seemed to loll about, her tongue protruding from her mouth, the vomit all over her chin, neck and nightclothes. From time to time her body jerked, like she'd been struck again by some unseen hand.

"We need a fucking ambulance!" she screamed. "She ain't right!"

"We can't."

"Then give me the car, I'll take her somewhere."

"Just get her upstairs," he said, his eyes moving nervously over Emily's jerking frame. "Now."

"But–"

"Now, goddammit! I'll call someone."

"Someone? Who?"

"A fuckin' doctor, goddammit, now go!"

The next thirty minutes were a blur. She replaced the oven mitt over Emily's head with a washcloth she had torn into strips but didn't press on it as her father had. That had seemed to make it worse. After a few minutes the bleeding slowed. Emily's breathing was erratic at first, but then it settled into a quick, shallow rhythm.

She was watching her breathing when the "doc" arrived. He was, as far as she could tell, just another biker. Like many of them, he was heavy-set and bearded, and wore a Pagan's leather vest with a dirty T-shirt underneath. But unlike many of them, his eyes were quick and alert, not sleepy or glazed. He had a military-style camouflage pack with him.

"Are you the doctor?"

"I'm a doc, yeah. Gimme some room." She did as he said and stood a few feet away, her arms crossed. He didn't look like a doctor, but he moved like one, his hands oddly gentle but firm over Emily's body. He reached into his pack for a penlight, and stabilized her as she shook in bed again, jerking in place.

"She keeps doing that," she said through tears. He seemed

not to hear her. Instead he pulled a packet of gauze from his pack, tore it open and gently removed the washcloth strips. He shined the penlight onto the wound.

"Ah, shit," Doc said.

"God, what?" she asked, tears welling up.

"Someone put pressure on the head wound, to stop the bleeding."

"My father. He said we had to."

"Yeah well he was wrong. I think she's got a fracture. The pressure could have killed her. Still might."

"We've got to call an ambulance, then. I mean, right?"

"Ain't gonna be no ambulance," he said, mumbled really, as if he was resigned to the fact. Where this guy goes to treat people, she thought, real doctors don't follow. She felt panic rising up in her chest.

"Please. What can we do?"

"I need time with her," he said, looking carefully at Emily and the bandage he had just applied. He glanced back toward his pack, and then up at her. "Leave us be for a few minutes. I'll come find you."

"I can't. Please, I can't—"

"Believe me, kid, I've seen worse pull through." He looked over Emily's little frame and her purple, swollen face, and she could have sworn she saw pain in his eyes, or at least empathy. It was as if the rough exterior was cracking, letting something else show through. "Go on now," he said softly. "Leave me with her. I'll come get you when I know more."

About an hour later, one torturous, endless hour, the doc appeared in her bedroom door. He remained expressionless, but without the same vigilant look he had worn before, when he was looking Emily over for the first time. For a moment panic seized her, but then she relaxed. It was very *strange, but she was beginning to feel like she almost knew this man. The look in his eyes was relaxed, but not resigned. Emily wasn't dying.*

"She'll live," he said, as if on cue. "She's stable again. Breathing is okay. Pulse is steady. Eyes are reacting to a penlight, more or less. She's deeply concussed, though. I have no idea what kind of damage she might have going on up there."

"I need to get her out of here," she said, her hands on her chest. "That's what I thought."

"You can't tonight, so just relax, okay?" His reddened eyes fixed on hers. "Look, I can't be sure, but I think she's turned a corner. What happened tonight won't kill her. But I don't know about long-term."

"Oh God," she said, nausea blooming through her body. "Like she might have a brain injury?"

"Hard to say. The brain is one fucked up organ. But yeah, I wouldn't be surprised."

"What the hell am I supposed to do?"

"Take it easy, like I said. I gotta go. I want you to watch her. Sit by her. That stuff you saw her do before. Remember?"

"Like she was flipping out."

"Yes, the shaking or scrunching up, making fists, maybe. That's a seizure. Watch for those. She might throw up. Make sure she doesn't choke on it. If you don't see any seizures in the next few hours, I'd say she's good to go for the short term. I cleaned her up and bandaged her good. But you'll have to change the bandages. Twice a day. I left you plenty of stuff. Figure out how to use it."

"I can't do this," she said, barely a whisper.

"Yeah you fuckin' can," Doc said, raising his voice a little. He seemed to check it then, dialing it back. "You can. My

guess is you've gone through a thing or two in this fuckin'
dump. You can do this."

"Okay," she said, looking bewildered. "Okay." There was
long moment of silence.

"I know you probably think your old man's a piece of shit
for callin' me instead of an ambulance," he said finally. She
just shrugged. "He is a piece of shit. But the truth is, when it
comes to this type of injury, I'm about as good as you were
going to get anyway tonight. This is what I see all the time.
Head wounds, mostly from bike wrecks. But sometimes
from baseball bats, just like this. Or tire tools or whatever.
I've seen this kind of injury a million times. Kids, too."

"Okay," she said again. She didn't know what else to say.

"But you gotta get her outta here."

"You just said I can't."

"I don't mean tonight. Tonight, she was fucked. If she was
gonna die, she was gonna die here. But she didn't. When you
can, make a move."

"A move?"

"Don't act stupid. You know what I mean. Get her the
fuck out of here. I don't pretend to be a fuckin' neurologist.
She needs follow up. And I don't have a good feeling about
what she'll be like long-term. Get her out. Get her help."

"I don't know if I can," she said, her voice cracking.

"If you care about her, you will. And listen." He waited
until she got control of her emotions and looked up at him
again. The doc's eyes, in a pink nest of dirty wrinkles, narrowed on her little, angular face. "Don't let anyone get in
your way when you do. You hear me?"

"Yeah," she said. "Um, thank you." He seemed ready to
scoff at this, but then wrinkled his upper lip and nodded.
Then he turned and was gone.

***

Kim hadn't been dreaming about the night Emily almost died. Instead she'd been replaying it in her mind, laying sleepless in bed for hours after seeing Evelyn. Emily was asleep in her chair in the living room, snoring loudly. Kim's bedroom door was open, as Emily preferred, and she listened to the rhythm of her sister's breathing down the hall. The reality of it, at once annoying and life affirming, chased away the terrible "what ifs" that almost sixteen years later still fluttered through her brain.

She wondered if he was still alive, the "doc" who saw to Emily's head wound and Kim's near hysteria with such odd dexterity and near-tenderness. She doubted it. His type didn't live long in her experience. She had always wanted to thank him, though, to tell him what a difference he had made. She'd been alone that night, with Emily, and she would likely have died in her arms had Doc, whoever he was, not handled things the way he had.

Nevertheless, it was long ago and far away. She and Emily had finally made their escape from that wretched place to this one, and they weren't going back. Kim took fierce pride in that fact. But she had taught herself never to take any good thing for granted. More importantly, she never allowed herself too much credit for the tumbling, shifting circumstances that had landed them where they were now. There were almost angelic creatures, like Doc, whose presence in their lives arrived with such perfect timing it seemed impossible to deny the providence behind it. But there were also demons, like her father and Kevin Dunaway, who seemed ever-present, sniffing her out with forked tongues like snakes in tall grass.

TWENTY-SEVEN

Monday, October 9

Alex expected to hear from a defense attorney on Kevin Dunaway's case even though he hadn't taken any action yet, other than a preliminary meeting with Kim Hadley. The well-heeled defendants usually brought their lawyers in early, especially if they knew they were being investigated and there was a chance at getting the case resolved without charges being brought.

What he didn't expect was Jack Hooper as the person requesting a meeting on behalf of Dunaway. Hooper was younger than Alex, maybe thirty-five or thirty-six, and looked even younger than that. He had been an ADA himself in Brooklyn, but just long enough to fulfill his post-law school, three-year commitment to the office. Since then he had come out swinging, starting his own firm with an older defense attorney named Bram Kluger. Kluger was famous for raging against the system and going after the NYPD in particular. Jack was similarly aggressive, although he had found a niche defending police officers as well, which made their pairing an odd one indeed. Mostly, Jack was known as a ball-buster, an expensive if somewhat flashy dresser, and a dogged self-promoter. He had pulled out some decent wins in his years in private practice, although his tactics were edgy and had been called into question once or twice.

That any defendant would want a bare-knuckle fighter in his corner made sense, but Alex expected a guy like Kevin Dunaway to go a little more high-end, maybe a lawyer with less of a billboard-style reputation. But who knew? Hooper also framed himself as a hard-charging man of the people and a voice for the little guy. Maybe there was something strategic in the choice of Hooper for a rich venture capitalist charged with a crime.

"I've heard a few things about you," Jack said as he followed Alex back to his office from the unit's main lobby. He was tall and thin, with an athletic build. Since he had begun to lose his hair early, he kept it baby-fine and shaven, little more than a shadow over a well-shaped head.

"I'll bet I've heard more about you," Alex said. He invited Jack to sit, and then settled in behind his desk.

"I don't know, man. You're like, on the rise around here. This new gig has got people talking, too. SCU." He made air quotes around "SCU" and smiled a broad, toothy grin. Jack had a great smile, framed by a stylish three-day growth of beard and brilliant blue eyes. He was dressed in a fine, navy-blue pinstripe suit. Alex could see how he could be a jury charmer, especially in Manhattan where he now spent most of his time.

"Thanks, the gig's been interesting so far. So, what can I do for you?" Jack's smile disappeared.

"Talk some sense into this woman, Kim Hadley. Get her to back off on pressing charges, if that's what she's doing."

"She's not the one who papers the case."

"I know. But if she's pushing, and I think she might be, you don't want to give in to her. I'd say 'trust me,' but I won't bother. It'll be obvious if it isn't already."

"What will be?"

"That she's a hustler with a very sketchy past, and now has a desperate need to clean up a situation she royally botched. She's taking that out on my client." A *sketchy past*. Alex wondered if Jack knew something he didn't, or if he was just making assumptions. Kim and Alex hadn't discussed much about her past, but she had seemed forthcoming about the basics, which were more or less that it was awful, and that she had escaped it.

"That's quite a pitch," Alex said. "But she sounds truthful to me, so far. And whatever her past is, I doubt it's relevant. Or admissible."

"Okay, let's talk about the present. Dude, she fled the scene!"

"That happens sometimes."

"Yeah, when the person has something to hide. Look, we know what happened, okay? She left my client's apartment looking to get high. She got beat up, probably by her dealer, and probably for acting like a strung-out nutcase. That's exactly what was happening in my client's living room, and it ended with her assaulting him with a champagne flute. The only reason she surfaced was in hopes that Dunaway would pay her off to go away. And I can tell you, that's not happening."

"She didn't surface, Jack. We found her."

"And at first, she didn't want anything to do with the cops, right?"

"Correct. But she changed her mind. That happens, too."

"Right. She agreed to come in and talk to a detective, like she's making some sacrifice for justice. Look, I feel for her, okay? You've probably learned about her company, and the successes she's had. She's smart, she came up with a skincare product. It made her a few bucks, so she came up here to the big city. Things were looking good. But she couldn't keep it together. Whatever else she's done with her money, it looks like she also got involved with drugs, and that's a big part of what killed her relationship with CIG. My client got the brunt of that. He found out, and almost too late, that she wasn't a good investment. When that was starting to look obvious and the night went south, she took it all out on him. Then, someone else roughed her up. We know that, because she took off when the cops got there. She might have had drugs on her–hell, that's probably why she ran. So now she's sniffing around a criminal prosecution? Really Alex, it's embarrassing."

"All I can tell you is I've interviewed her, and so has a very good detective I work with. Neither of us get this 'hustler' vibe you're describing."

"Well, I hope it becomes clear before you get too far into it," Jack said, shaking his head. "Usually in cases like this, we come to you, feel you out, see what you have, and see if there's any wiggle room for anything. But a case like this? Honestly, the only thing I can say is do some digging before you step into this mess. This is almost a courtesy."

"To me."

"Yes, to you." Jack looked around the office and spread his hands out. "To this new, bold project the city took on about going after the tough cases. It's a nice idea. But something like this will hurt more than help. You'll look like you over-reached. It'll be humiliating, Dominque Strauss-Kahn, take two. You don't need that."

"All I can tell you right now is that I'm still investigating, and I'll present a case if and when I think I have one. There was physical evidence recovered also, you should know that. A handkerchief, with a decent amount of blood on it."

"Okay," Jack said. His tone indicated he knew this already. Alex wasn't sure how, but he wasn't entirely surprised, either. "I'll trust you to save me some extract. I doubt my client's blood is on it, but if it is, we know why. She cut his hand open. He bled all over the place."

"You'll have extract for your own test, sure," Alex said. 'Extract' referred to an amount of raw DNA material pulled from the original item, in this case the handkerchief, that the defense had a right to have preserved for testing with an independent laboratory. "I haven't talked to anyone at the lab yet, but I know it's in queue."

"Tell them not to hurry. I doubt this is going anywhere. You look like a smart guy."

"I'll take that as a compliment," Alex said. "Everything else, I'll take under advisement. Can I get you something before you go? Coffee?"

"I've never been in a DA's office or a precinct where the coffee didn't suck," Jack said with a grin. "Thanks, but I'll get my six-dollar latte downstairs." Despite the cocky attitude and rant against Kim, Alex found something oddly endearing about him. He made a mental note to be wary of it.

"Yeah I don't blame you," he said, and sighed. "Listen, you did your job, you made your argument. No decisions have been made. If we decide to paper, I'll let you know before it goes into the system. That's my courtesy."

"Focus on where she came from," Jack said, gathering

his overcoat.

"It's actually not far from where I'm from. She's from outside of D.C., way outside."

"Oh, I know where she crawled out of," he said. "I've got an investigator. He's beyond thorough."

"I'd be shocked if you didn't have more than one."

"I might," Jack said with a shrug. "But honestly, this guy's a bloodhound, and he's just getting started. She's got a sketchy past. That's all I'll say."

"From what I know so far, it's a tragic past. That doesn't disqualify her."

"All right, all right," he said, offering his hand. Jack seemed to sense he'd pushed things far enough. "Enough of the bullshit for now. But really, you seem like a decent guy, and you've been at this longer than I have, so I'm not trying to school you. But this one stinks. I'll show myself out, thanks."

***

Alex sat thinking for a few minutes after Jack left. The stuff about Kim's past was something he knew he'd need to look into, although Angie had already determined she had no criminal record. He had found nothing else that seemed like it might hurt her credibility, other than the fact that she ran from the scene of her attack and her initial reluctance to cooperate once police found her.

He made a mental note to talk to her about the possibility of Dunaway's defense team reaching out to her in a variety of ways. Some defendants, depending on resources, would offer a payout for silence in various forms, some that could be legally formalized and some that couldn't.

Whatever the motive, his lawyers had a right to contact the "alleged victim" as well, and any other potential witnesses. Ethically, he couldn't tell Kim not to speak with them. He could only tell her it was up to her.

Beyond that, Alex had a feeling Jack's reference to the "bloodhound" on his team was a warning. The really well-heeled defense teams sometimes sent investigators after the detectives, the prosecutors and even the judge as a part of their strategy. This is what Alex had referred to at the bar with Angie a few days before. Working against the big players, and on cases where the stakes were high, was no joke.

For the present though, he didn't find anything about Kim to be concerning. Her record was clean, and her past was her past. As far as he could tell, she was an enterprising and hard-working woman who had escaped a terrible upbringing with a disabled sibling in tow and had made something of herself in a very tough environment. He also knew another thing very well: If Kim Hadley had indeed made her way to New York City after fleeing something in the rearview and perhaps making some tough choices along the way, she was hardly alone. The city was made up of people like that. Few people knew it more than Alex himself.

TWENTY-EIGHT

Friday October 13

"His name is Jack Hooper," Alex said. Kim was back in his office, the morning he planned to file the official criminal complaint against Kevin Dunaway. He had explained how Dunaway would be formally charged. "He's aggressive, which isn't surprising. And of course, his client is wealthy, so he's been able to dispatch an investigator. Jack's probably blowing smoke, but he's suggesting there's something about your past that's somehow an issue. Or could be."

"I don't know what to say," Kim said. "You can ask me anything. I'm sure his lawyer told you I'm some crazy person or redneck hustler, though."

"I'm immune to his opinion, don't worry," Alex said. "Look, there's nothing about your past that bothers me. I also don't see how it's relevant, but when it comes to attacking the credibility of a witness, judges let all sorts of things in. I'm not sure where Jack could go with this, but I've learned enough to know that it's better to be prepared for anything." With that, he slid a short stack of documents over the desk towards Kim. She leafed through them and looked up at him.

"The fire department report from the explosion, in 2002. I saw this years ago, when Emily and I first got to Dutchtown."

"Right. The reports say you and Emily went missing the night of the accident. They assumed you were dead, at least at first."

"I know they did," Kim said, nodding. "If I thought there was anyone left behind who would care, I wouldn't have run."

"You were sure there wasn't?"

"As sure as I could be, yes. We grew up in a meth lab, Alex. And before it was that, it was just a violent and dirty place. About two years before the explosion, my mother left. If my father knew where she was going or where she ended up, he never told us. We never had much of a relationship with her to begin with, so it didn't really affect us. We raised ourselves, almost completely. We went to school on our own, but my father told the county we were home-schooled the last few months, early in 2002. He was afraid of what attention Emily might attract because of her injury.

"My brother left when he turned eighteen. He was looking for a way to get all three of us out, but we didn't know how that would work with Emily. She was injured while he was gone and he came back after it happened. He was there when the house blew up. So was my father, Tom, and a guy he worked with named Lefty."

"I saw that in the reports," Alex said quietly. "There were no bodies found. Most of the ground floor was blown to bits, from what they put together."

"I helped them put it together, once they located us. We didn't hide in Dutchtown. Once we got to the shelter, they did a full intake on both of us. They called the

Tolland County sheriff's office. Detectives interviewed us that day."

"I saw that, too," Alex said. He gestured towards the documents. "Their concern was that you took off with Emily that night."

"I did, and I'd do it again," she said, with steel resolve in her eyes. She paused, looked away and breathed deeply, then turned back at Alex. "I was outside in the yard when the house went up. There was a part of me that always half expected something like that. We had plenty of near-misses. There was a leak once that sent us all running out of the house, throwing up in the middle of the night, eyes burning. Anyway, the explosion lit up the whole sky, like all of a sudden it was daylight. I knew no one survived it. There was no way anyone could have."

"I saw the pictures. I believe you."

"The only other thought I had was of Emily. We had a neighbor down the road, an old woman who lived alone. She took us in sometimes. The night this happened, Emily was with her."

"Dolly Griggs," Alex said. "I saw her name in the detective's statement. They questioned her, from what I could tell, wanting to know where you and Emily had gone."

"Yes, Dolly," A slow, sad smile crept across her face. "She was, well, I can't really put it into words. She was just always there. I went to get Emily, and I figured we'd end up calling someone from Dolly's, but I had no idea who to call."

"No aunts or uncles?"

"None that would take a call from us," she said, looking almost apologetic for saying it. "It's not easy to imagine how I grew up, I know that. We had extended family, somewhere. At least my father did. But we never knew them. My parents isolated themselves. They knew bikers and drug dealers. That was about it."

"But your mother..." he started.

"I had no idea where she was. I still don't. We never saw her again."

"Did she ever try to contact you?"

"Sort of," Kim said. "A detective from Tolland called me once, maybe five or six months after we got to Dutchtown. He was one of the men who investigated the explosion. He said my mother had asked about us. Not that she was looking for us, just that she was in town, and had asked. He felt wrong about giving her my contact information, so he gave me hers and left it up to me. By that time Emily and I were getting settled on our own. I never reached out."

"Okay."

"Look, I knew the right thing to do was to cooperate. I should have called the police from Dolly's. I should have waited for my mother to show up, or at least reached out to her later, when I had the chance. But I just couldn't."

"And Dolly didn't suggest it," he said. "That's what I'm guessing."

"No. Dolly had another idea. She had a sister who ran a shelter for women and families in Dutchtown. She offered to help us get there. You know the rest. It was my choice to go, and to take Emily with me."

"It sounds like it worked out. Did you ever see Dolly again?"

"No, never," she said, and Alex could tell she was regretful about it. "Her sister Rebecca ran the shelter, but they weren't close. I don't think Rebecca even mentioned her when we got there. Everything just kept moving forward after that. There was no time to think about the past. The women at the shelter were great. They cared for us and helped get both of us on track. We saw a social worker. Emily saw a doctor. We both saw a dentist for the first time in I don't know how long. When I applied for guardianship of Emily, I saw those same reports you have. After that, nothing. Dolly died a few years later. Rebecca's alive, but I haven't talked to her in years. I think she's retired." She paused and seemed to search Alex's face. "Can I be honest?"

"I hope you always will."

"It seems like a dream, sometimes, that whole time in my life. Everything I've worked for, for Emily, for both of us. The business, my life here. That came from hard work, and a little luck. But those first few weeks after the explosion? I still don't know how to feel about it."

"I'd say relieved or at least grateful to be alive and have a chance to start fresh," Alex said. "It's miraculous you two weren't blown up with the rest of them."

"Lives were lost that night. I don't care about my father. I'm sorry for how that sounds, but he was a terrible man and I spent most of my life hiding from him. Lefty never hurt us, he was just a cog in a wheel, but he knew the risks. And my brother, well…" She trailed off and let out a heavy sigh. "I lost him." She seemed to crumple almost, becoming even smaller in her chair, but she didn't cry. She just looked suddenly exhausted, an effect of relaying old trauma Alex had seen many times before. "But otherwise, yes. It does seem miraculous."

"Take a minute," he said. "You've told me enough. More than you needed to, probably. But it's good context, in case Jack tries to make an issue out of any of it."

"Do you think he will?"

Alex paused, wanting to think through his answer rather than just spitting out something mollifying.

"You made a decision to run the night Kevin attacked you. You made a decision to run the night your family was killed. You had perfectly understandable reasons both times. Juries have a way of relating to those things, even unconsciously. I don't think Jack will get very far bringing any of this up anyway, but I think he's a fool if he does."

TWENTY-NINE

Wednesday, October 18

On a dreary, gray morning at the First Precinct, Kevin Dunaway arrived in the back of a black Lincoln SUV flanked by Jack Hooper and a younger attorney from Jack's office. Angie and Danny were there to greet them. Per procedure, the arrest warrant authorized by Alex after charges had been filed had to be served on Dunaway at the precinct. From there, Angie and Danny were required to transport him, in custody, to the criminal court at 111 Centre Street less than a half of a mile away. No pictures were taken, but Angie told Alex later that she had seen a couple of guys who looked like they could have been reporters.

The scene in the arraignment "part," or courtroom, was similarly low-key, for which Alex was grateful. Dunaway was dressed conservatively in a dark suit and tie, and answered quietly when the judge addressed him, pleading not guilty and otherwise letting Jack do the talking. The bail argument also went pretty much as Alex expected. He made the usual points, that the charges were severe, and Dunaway was a person of means who posed a flight risk. Hooper argued reasonably that Dunaway owned an apartment in the city, had deep ties to the community, and no criminal record. Jack also made a few well-rehearsed statements on the record about how the charges against Dunaway were "extremely weak" and would almost certainly be dismissed, either by the grand jury or at a later stage. The judge–a squat, bearded, older man who looked more like a rabbi–seemed unimpressed with both of their positions. Bond was set at $100,000, which Dunaway was prepared to post immediately. Angie was given custody of his passport. It was pretty much exactly what all of them had expected.

The bail hearing took less than twenty minutes. Alex hoped it would be emblematic of how the case would play out, if not completely below the radar, then at least below the level of a circus. But as he put on his raincoat outside the courtroom, the first of the texts started coming in. A few people, including his namesake and old colleague from the Bronx DA's office, Alexa, had sent a message to tell him they'd heard about the arrest. It was slow, but news was getting out—a wealthy financial figure was being charged with the attempted rape of a young female entrepreneur. Neither Dunaway nor Kim were well-known people, but their roles in city life, and the fact that they were young, attractive and white, would for better or worse, move them quickly into a public spotlight. But neither they nor anyone around them could have prepared for just how much.

THIRTY

8:20 p.m.

"Try this when you get home tonight," Kim said. She set a small, black jar in front of Megan. "It's not in my line, but it's wonderful. I know the woman who makes it."

"Thanks! Is it a scrub?" Kim nodded. Megan inspected it for a moment and ran her fingers along the top of Kim's beautiful vanity and makeup mirror. She was seated cross-legged on the plush chair in front of it while Kim lounged on the bed, surrounded by beauty magazines the two had been going through. "This is beautiful, by the way."

"Oh, the vanity? Thanks. It's a little school-girlish for this room, but I love it." Kim reached over and handed her the pint of gelato they were sharing. The vanity was white, hand-painted with pink and purple flowers, and was an anachronism in Kim's otherwise modern, minimally decorated bedroom.

"Is it from childhood?" Megan asked. "It looks like you refinished it."

"Oh no," Kim said, with more feeling than she intended. "I never had one. I swore to myself I would, though. Someday. Of course, I found the frilliest one possible. This one was refinished, actually. It's pretty old. I found it in a little town in the Shenandoah Valley."

"I love it," Megan said. "And you keep it so neat. If I had one it would be a mess."

"Thanks. Yeah, I don't touch it with my phone, my laptop, nothing. No work in that space. It's a treasure chest. If it helps me look and feel good, it's in there."

"Kim, come watch!" Emily called out from the living room. "This shit's funny!" She was reclined in her easy chair with her sizable feet in the air, hooting at a sitcom on TV.

"In a minute, Em," Kim said. And then to Megan, "Thank you again for bringing dinner. I can't believe how much of it she ate!"

"So glad she liked it. I love that place. Come on, let's go sit with her."

Megan had brought Thai food with her and the three women were spending the third chilly, rainy Wednesday of the month at Kim and Emily's apartment. Emily, who wasn't big on trying new foods, had nevertheless eaten some chicken and jasmine rice when Megan made a plate for her, promising her she would like the taste. She may have, but Kim was just impressed with how comfortable Emily seemed around Megan after just meeting her and only seeing her a handful of times. Since their first outing, Kim and Megan had been getting together almost once a week, and Megan had been to the apartment two or three times, either to pick Kim up or drop something off. Emily didn't pay much attention to Megan as she didn't like most people other than Kim, but she never seemed threatened or intimidated by her presence either. This was a godsend for Kim in terms of measuring Megan's potential as a friend.

Kim and Megan took their places on the sofa around the coffee table. When the sitcom was over, Emily announced she was going to the bathroom and plodded off toward her bedroom. It had a bathroom attached which also opened into the hallway.

"She'll probably be a few minutes," Kim said, concealing a grin. "She usually is when she announces it like that. I'm just glad she wasn't more forward about it."

"Let her be blunt," Megan said with a shrug. "The world could use more honesty."

"Oh, that she is. To a fault."

"Well good for her," Megan said. She gestured toward the easy chair. "Is she the only person who sits in that chair? My father had a chair like that. Literally, it was his. No one else sat in it."

"Pretty much," Kim said, "and it's just as well." She looked at the chair a little disdainfully. It was food-stained in a couple of places and the cushions concealed a never-ending cache of crumbs underneath. It was also sunken-in like a mold of Emily's considerable frame. "I bought it for her when we moved in. She saw it in a furniture store down south and had to have it. It's a little bit of a mess, but whatever. She relaxes in it."

"She's a hoot," Megan said. "I hope she's okay with me being here. I know it's been mostly just the two of you together."

"I really think she is," Kim said, smiling. "And I'm very attuned to her moods, trust me. I think she likes you."

"Well, I'll take that as a compliment," Megan said, raising her wine glass. "But you don't think she's jealous or anything, do you? I would never want to get between you two like that."

"I worried about that at first," Kim said, "but now I really don't think it's an issue. Emily is...a mystery. I don't know how else to put it. There are things most people, even smart, perceptive people, would assume about her that are just miles off."

"She has a brain injury, right? From a long time ago? I remember you telling me, the last time we were out, but I was probably a few glasses in."

"Yes. In terms of her condition, she has what's referred to as a traumatic brain injury, or TBI."

"Right, I remember now. I hope it's okay to ask these things."

"Of course, it's fine. Emily is my life, mostly. Anyone in my life has be okay with her, and vice versa. I think it's also better when they understand her. You can ask me anything, really."

"Well, she seems...a little slow I guess," Megan said, her brow knitted. "But not like, well, you know, full-on..."

"Mentally retarded is what it used to be called," Kim said. "Don't worry, it's not a bad thing to say. Except the terms have changed, and it's called 'intellectually disabled' now. But no, that's not her issue. Her intelligence level seems to vary depending on what she's doing, but in general, she's slow. For a while I sort of believed she was just mentally stuck where she was when she was injured, as an eight-year-old kid."

"That's kind of what I would assume."

"Many people would, it's an easy answer. But it's a lazy one, and I'm still kicking myself for believing it as long as I did. I mean, she might be somewhat trapped in the place she was when she was hurt, but it's nowhere near the whole picture. I've learned that the hard way, but it's a blessing in the long run."

"Ah. She surprises you."

"Definitely. Emily can be clever sometimes. You'll see it eventually. She can also be…well, very adult. We can put it that way."

"Oh," Megan said. "So she knows about sex and stuff."

"Oh yeah," Kim said, her eyes widening a little. "Emily has some experience, for better or worse."

"No way, really? Boyfriends?"

"No, hook-ups. Never really a boyfriend. The first guys were ones she met in some of the programs she was in. That happens a lot."

"Like guys who had the same condition?"

"Well, they were usually disabled guys, but almost always in another disability category. There aren't a lot of TBI cases out there being treated. Sometimes the boys had autism. Sometimes they were emotionally disturbed. Sometimes a combination of things. A lot of people think kids with disabilities are automatically asexual or something. Believe me, they're not."

"Well, it doesn't seem fair to stop her. I mean she's an adult, right?"

"Exactly," Kim said, nodding and tipping her wine glass. "Every now and then I get a lecture from one of her doctors, asking why she was out doing this or that. I get a little freaked out by some of the things she tells me, too. But really, she's an adult. She can't get an apartment or buy a house on her own, but she's still her own person. Of course, I watch out for her. But she's got a subway pass and a few bucks to walk around with. I don't keep her on a leash."

"Can she work?"

"She works for me. She and I packed thousands of orders before I hired a fulfillment center, but I still send samples personally, so she packs those. Or she helps me experiment in the kitchen, or whatever odd job I need help with. I would like to get her a gig of her own, though. I'm working on that." She paused for a moment. Yet again, there was a hesitation in Kim's mind for fear of sharing too much. But this felt okay. "The other side of the coin with Emily is anxiety. PTSD to be exact."

"Oh yeah from childhood," Megan said, at lower volume. "I know we haven't talked about that much. We don't have to, but I'm sorry for whatever you both went through. I hope you know that."

"Thanks," Kim said, looking away for a moment. "It's okay. I guess right now the big focus has to be on the case I'm now officially in the middle of."

"Yeah for sure," Megan said, with feeling. "He was arrested on that, right?"

"Sort of. He surrendered himself, and there was an arraignment today. Do you know what that is? I didn't."

"I've heard the word, but I get all those legal terms confused. Isn't that where you enter a plea?"

"Yeah. He pleaded not guilty, of course, and bonded out for a lot of money. Alex said it goes to a grand jury now, probably in a few days. We'll meet tomorrow so he can help me get ready for that."

"Oh wow, you have to testify?"

"I do. It's supposed to be pretty easy compared to the trial, but there will be a whole room full of people. My stomach turns at the thought of it, believe me."

"Does he have to? Testify I mean."

"No. Alex says he has a right to, but they almost never do. It should just be me."

"His name is Kevin, right?" Megan asked.

"Yep. Dunaway. Real piece of work."

"Have any newspapers picked it up?"

"I haven't looked yet," Kim said, and an icy sliver of dread cut through her. She'd been worried about that since her first meeting with the detective. A mix of facts and rumors were circulating in her professional circles, that much she knew from a few closer acquaintances who were willing to tell her directly. That didn't faze her very much, but the idea of attracting attention from the press was scarier. "A few people told me they saw his name on Twitter, that he was accused of sexual assault. It's mostly accounts that people in my business follow, though. He's not a celebrity. Just a rich guy. Word could spread, though."

"I guess it's rippling around your industry," Megan said, softly, as if she'd read Kim's mind. "I hope that's not too bothersome."

"I expected it," Kim said with a shrug. "People talk. I'd say more so in beauty, but really, I'm sure it's no different from any other industry. Anyway, sales are still good, and people are still answering the phone when I call. At this point, that's all that matters. Believe it or not, I've been through worse."

"I'm sorry for that. I hope you'll tell me about it."

"Oh, I won't lay it all on you now," Kim said. "But after enough late nights and bottles of this stuff, you might hear a story or two."

"In for a penny, in for a pound," Megan said. She raised her glass again and clinked it against Kim's. "It's all good. I'm glad we met."

"I am also," Kim said, and meant it. She had noticed her own heart beating faster with fear at the idea of scaring Megan away with the reality of her past, even the sad but mundane details. Yet deep down, and for the first time since meeting Evelyn, she felt she might be able to share some of that stuff with Megan after all.

It would happen over time, of course. And maybe not all of it would come out. Only Evelyn really knew how deep it went, but Evelyn was effectively a therapist. That informal part of what she did was an adjunct to her occasional treatment of Kim for whatever was going on in her life. Kim loved Evelyn, but it wasn't quite a friendship. Megan, so far at least, was becoming something Kim had never had. A pal, a girlfriend. A confidant. And that was very good indeed, because Kim sensed she was heading into a firestorm with the case of the *People of the State of New York v. Kevin Dunaway.*

THIRTY-ONE

Sunday, October 22

By Sunday evening, Kim was starting to feel the pressure of media attention. It was still low-key, but it was present and getting harder to tune out. As she had told Megan the night of the arraignment, the first rumblings she had seen were on Twitter. That night and the following day there were only a few vague posts with no names, just reports that a principal at Callisto Investment Group in New York had been charged with a felony sex offense. But by Friday morning, Kevin's name was popping up.

Kim only used Twitter for business, but she knew how it worked. A search of Kevin's name brought forth more results steadily through Friday and Saturday, including a few details she had not heard otherwise. CIG was "separating" from Dunaway, several tweets claimed, but it was believed he was walking away with plenty of money. Still, Kim assumed, that had to hurt. She didn't know investing the way she knew her own industry, but in many ways the two were intertwined. Kevin had done well and would probably stay rich, but his ability to make more money was now truncated.

Worse still for Dunaway were the other accusations that started to appear as the weekend passed, not only on social media but eventually in different news sources as well. The first separate accusations were mentioned in a couple of online industry publications that Kim read regularly. One article interviewed three women who described Dunaway acting toward them in a similar way, leaning on them, becoming physical, threatening to stall careers—or worse—if sexual demands weren't met. None alleged rape or attempted rape, but one woman stated plainly that she felt obligated to give in to sex with Dunaway or she would have been forced.

All three women were public about who they were, and their photos appeared in the article. One was African-American, the other two white, and appeared to be around Kim's age. All were similar to her in that they had either created beauty products or discovered them and had gone to CIG and found their way to Dunaway. Kim had not met any of them, but one, named Gayle, looked familiar. Kim wondered if she had run into her at a show or a conference. Then a day later, one of the other two, a woman named Rhonda Viecho, reached out to Kim through email via her website. The message was brief and to the point:

Hi, Kim.
I don't want to intrude on your privacy, but I wanted you to know Kevin Dunaway did something very similar to me a few years back when I was VP at Tarrant's. I guess the details don't matter but it was horrible, and I never told anyone. Then I saw a story about the charges and heard through the grapevine that it was you who was pressing

them. I will leave you alone—I just wanted you to know how much I admire what you did. Kevin is scum. I hope he pays for what he did to you. I'm so sorry.

Rhonda

Kim read the email over and over again as a crisp, fall Sunday afternoon darkened to evening. Tarrant was a small but successful beauty company that had been acquired by one of the giants—Revlon, or L'Oréal, Kim couldn't remember which—a few years before. Rhonda's email wasn't the first she had received since the arraignment. Quite a few women and even some men she had worked or networked with over the years had reached out to her, all supportive, and most offering something to the effect of 'good for you' or just 'good luck and I'm sorry it happened.' Sylvia Chen, the woman she had reached out to a month back when deciding whether or not to report Kevin at all, wrote her a lovely message thanking her for her courage. But this woman, Rhonda, was the first person who had reached out to her as a fellow victim. She thought about writing back, just to say thank you, but figured she should ask Alex first. They had the Grand Jury presentation scheduled for the morning, but Kim wondered if he would mind if she called him that evening. Then as if he was reading her thoughts, the phone rang about five minutes later.

"How are you?" he asked.

"So far so good," she said. "We're still on for tomorrow?"

"We are. Be at my office at eight-thirty if you can. Angie and Danny will drive us over to court around ten. You feel ready?"

"Yeah," she said, although her stomach was in knots. She had gone to lunch with Emily but could barely finish a small salad. Eating for the rest of the night was likely out of the question. "I'm a little nervous, of course. I guess you've seen some of the social media coverage?"

"I have," he said. "The traditional media has picked it up also, although it's still slightly buried. Something could be building though, especially if Dunaway is sued or charged in other cases."

"Are you surprised?" she asked. "About the others? I'm not sure if I should be or not."

"That he probably has other victims? No, that's common. Guys like him rarely do something like this once. Most people don't report it, though. Men like him depend on that. But the world's changing."

"Oh God," she said, mostly to herself. "Now I'm part of a trend."

"Don't worry about it. For tomorrow at least, I don't think we'll encounter any media. Has anyone reached out to you personally?"

"Acquaintances have, people I know in the business. Everyone has been supportive. But I did hear from one woman who says she was victimized by Kevin a few years ago. She was in an article I saw a couple of days ago. It was in a trade magazine I read online."

"Can you give me her name?"

"I'll send you the link. There were three women interviewed. Do you think it's okay to write this one back, just to say thank you? She wrote that she never told anyone what Kevin did to her. She seemed grateful that I came forward. I don't know to how to feel about this."

"It's up to you, Kim. I can tell you it's probably best to keep things short if you do, no details or facts about the case. That seems like how you'd handle it anyway."

"Yes," she said. "It is."

"Then sure. I think a short thank you to her is okay. Look, I know it's scary. But this media attention is bad for him, not us. At least for now."

"For now?"

"Media attention is tricky. To be honest, I hate it, even when it's directed against the person I'm going after. But for now, it seems like he made the bed he's gonna be laying in for a while. Better him than us."

THIRTY-TWO

Monday, October 23

The presentation of the case to the Manhattan Grand Jury, not unlike the arraignment, had gone about as well as Alex could have hoped. Kim had testified calmly and concisely before about twenty-five assembled jurors in one of the big, wood-paneled grand jury rooms, projecting her voice when he asked her to make sure everyone could hear her. Alex kept the background between her and Kevin to a minimum. The panel got the basic facts of their business relationship, and then the second-by-second details he had developed from their meetings. He tracked the statutory requirements on his yellow legal pad as Kim gave her testimony.

Alex wasn't sure if he was imagining it, but there were a few grand jurors who seemed aware of the case and raised eyebrows when Kevin's name was mentioned. No one had any questions for his witness though, and they returned a true bill within a few minutes of him reading the charges. Now with the legal decision he needed to move forward, he sat down in an alcove nearby to make some notes after Angie and Danny escorted Kim back to her apartment. He had forgotten to ask Angie to take a known DNA sample from Kim in the form of a swabbing of the inside of her cheek and was about to make a note to himself about it when the phone rang. It was Jack Hooper.

"You found out already?" Alex said. "I was getting ready to call you."

"No, but I assumed it was probably over. True bill?"

"Yes. Bond's continued, I'm sure. We'll get a motions date in a few days."

"I have another question," Jack asked, his tone less casual. "What's this social media attack, man?"

"On whom?"

"My client. Don't tell me you haven't seen it. Accusers, coming out of the woodwork."

"You think that's coming from me?"

"Actually, I don't think it's coming from you," Jack said. "I've done my research on you, too. You don't seem like the type. But your complainant could be working angles you don't even see. God knows she is on other stuff."

"I don't think she's a leaker. It's not coming from us. My guess is it's a combination of the news cycle and social media. I think your client has to answer for this one."

"My client's a womanizer. Not a rapist. This is becoming a witch hunt."

"The world's changing, I don't know what to tell you."

"Whatever. Okay, I'll see you in motions. Hey Alex? Don't say I didn't warn you, man."

"So long, Jack."

THIRTY-THREE

Friday, November 17

Waiting on an oil change in the mechanic's garage a little before noon, Alex sat in a cracked plastic folding chair in his suit and tie, working on his laptop. It had been three weeks since grand jury on the *Dunaway* case, and he was answering Jack's first pretrial motions, this one about discovery.

Above him hung a calendar featuring topless models from a tool maker somewhere in Mexico. The garage was on Cromwell Avenue, a couple of blocks from the 44th Precinct in the Bronx, a neighborhood that resembled the developing world about as plainly as any other in New York City. It was no longer a dangerous area, during the day at least, but it was dirty, noisy and hopelessly congested.

"*Listo!*" Raphael called out, smiling as he wiped his hands clean with a towel. *Ready!* A Special Victims detective had introduced Alex to Raphael Ramirez, the mechanic who was keeping his old Jeep Cherokee alive. He paid Raphael in cash and tipped Raphael's assistants individually. The way things were done in the Bronx seemed very natural to Alex; there was no other way to put it.

"*Perfecto, gracias,*" Alex called back as one of Raphael's

young workers backed the SUV onto the crowded street. Alex handed over a couple of twenties for the oil change, and another one to the kid who had done the work. He waved goodbye and got in the car to head back to the city. He was about to check a traffic app when his phone rang from a 703 exchange. It took a second, but he recognized it as one his brother sometimes used at work. His older brother Pete was an EMT and firefighter in Alexandria, Virginia, the place Alex had called home up until a few years ago.

"Alex, it's Pete," he heard. And something sounded wrong.

"Petey, what's up? Everything okay?"

"Not exactly. I'm at 4320. Jonah Schwartz was admitted this morning. I just heard about it."

"What the hell happened?" Alex pulled over so a dented panel van, honking at him from behind, could pass. "4320" was cop and EMT slang in his hometown for Inova Alexandria Hospital, because it reflected part of its address. "Was he at home?"

"No, we got a call from his secretary, at the office in Old Town. He collapsed at his desk. Severe abdominal pain."

"Shit, were you on the call?"

"No, I'm working an evening shift. I just heard about it, and I ran over here to see what the deal is. Everyone at the station was talking about it. Hoping it's not what we think it is." Alex nodded to himself. That a bunch of EMTs were waiting to see why a wealthy real estate developer had collapsed at his desk was actually not a surprise. Alex's former father-in-law was not only rich—he was also highly philanthropic, particularly to the emergency services in Alexandria. A few years before, he had outfitted all of them with new firefighting and life-saving equipment. He was brash and controversial in other ways, a bare-knuckled brawler in business and currently dating a woman a little younger than his own daughter. But for better or worse, he was more of a father to Alex than his own. Theirs was a friendship forged largely in horror and secrecy, but it was hard and fast.

"So, no diagnosis yet? What now?"

"No, they're doing a special MRI later today. There'll be blood work and a few other things. It might take some time to pinpoint what it is, but the guys on the truck had a bad feeling. He's got jaundice, so probably a blocked bile duct. And the abdominal distress? It could be cancer, dude. And if it is, it could be bad."

"There's cancer that isn't bad?"

"If it's pancreatic, it's bad. Believe me."

"Okay," Alex said, sighing. "Any idea if Dara knows?" Dara was Alex's ex-wife and Jonah's daughter.

"Yeah, I think she's here someplace. I'm surprised she hasn't reached out to you."

Alex hesitated and then said, "You never know with her."

"Yeah man, I know," Pete said, and Alex could sense the quiet understanding in his voice. Alex and his older brother weren't very close, but when it came to Dara and the pain they had all endured around the death of Alex's son Jordan, Pete knew more than most.

"Do you think I should come down there?"

"I don't know, man. Look, I wasn't there and I'm not an oncologist. The symptoms could be caused by a bunch of things, but it's not adding up well. I heard he was having type-two diabetes symptoms lately too, out of nowhere. I've seen this before, and I just don't have a good feeling about it. Dara may know more by now. I mean, not sure if you want to reach out to her, but…"

"My guess is I'll hear from her at some point regardless," Alex said. "I'll drive down today, I don't have court. I can be there around six."

"Need a place to stay? Sam and the kids would love to see you. She'll get the guest room ready."

"If it's no trouble, yeah. Thanks Pete. I'll touch base when I'm in range."

THIRTY-FOUR

6:30 p.m.

"Jonah, my God," Alex said, kneeling beside the hospital bed. Alex was surprised at his own emotions. It wasn't a kind thought, but seeing Jonah, tubed and wired up with a life-threatening condition was worse than seeing his own father in the same place.

"Feh," Jonah managed, with a weak wave of his hand, and then he smiled. "I'll live. For now, anyway." But there was a hollowness in his eyes that suggested something else, and his color was all wrong, pale and yellow, as wan as Pete had suggested it might be.

"What do they know?"

"They won't tell me until they know for sure, but I have feeling the news won't be good. Pancreatic cancer, most likely."

"But, there's no history in your family, right?"

"From what they're telling me there usually isn't. Someone spun the wheel. I lost. It happens."

"Please don't jump to conclusions."

"It's okay. I've had suspicions for a while it might be this. My regular guy didn't want to mention it, but I think the idea of no longer being able to bill me was breaking his heart. Same with my dentist. Jesus, will he be sorry to see me go."

"No jokes, please."

"In the end, it's all we have," he said, the last word coming out as barely a breath. "Did you hear from Dara?"

"She texted when I was on the road, said the two of you got into a fight last night. And of course, she's blaming herself, like somehow she brought this on."

"Of course she is. She's downstairs, I think. If you want to avoid her, go out the back."

"I'll look for her," Alex said, dropping his eyes. Dara was a wealth of bad memories and interminable anxiety. Still, there was no way he wouldn't seek her out, especially under these circumstances. "I couldn't come down here for something like this and not reach out to her."

"You know I love her," Jonah said. "More than life."

"Yes."

"But you know what?"

"What?"

"She's a goddamn lunatic!" He put a deep stress on the last word and then coughed. Alarmed, Alex looked up at his vitals monitor, as if anything there would make much sense to him other than a flatline.

"We're all crazy," Alex said with a shrug, once Jonah had settled back onto his pillows. "She doesn't hide it well, that's all."

"I can take crazy," he said. "It's fools I can't tolerate. Oh, and she's gone Christian. Did you know that?"

"She's what?"

"Christian, so she says anyway. She's got some spiritual advisor. That's what she calls him. Although she writes checks to a life coach. *Life coach*. Like that's a thing?"

"I've heard of them. Okay, so she found a life coach?"

"Advisor. Jesus whisperer, I don't know. Christian! Can you believe that?"

"She was married to a Catholic," Alex said, and smiled weakly.

"Haha, *Shaygetz*," Jonah said, using a disparaging but usually joking word for a non-Jewish boy. He patted Alex's arm. "You're no more Catholic than I am."

"Yeah, true. What do you know about this guy, then?" Alex assumed that Jonah had already done some digging on this "life coach," whoever he was. Jonah wasn't paranoid or particularly nosy with regard to his daughter's life, but he was protective, and Dara often needed protecting.

"Nothing. I didn't know he existed until a few days ago."

"Is that what the fight was about? The one last night?"

"It was a few things," Jonah said, and sighed. "If you ask, I'm sure she'll tell you."

"She's downstairs? The main lobby?"

"Yeah I think so. Her mother was here, but she left. Dara's with her coach or whatever. They were in here before. Praying over me."

"I'll go down and say 'hi,'" Alex said. "What about Louisa? Is she here?" Louisa Ricci was Jonah's on-again, off-again girlfriend, a former Italian model. She lived in New York most of the time where Jonah had a lavish apartment but spent time with him in Alexandria and when they traveled abroad.

"She's in Rome," Jonah said. "She comes in tomorrow. She knows I'm alive."

"I'll be here tomorrow, too. Get some rest, okay?"

"Alex, I'm worried," Jonah said, looking over at him. At once he looked haunted and resigned, his eyes searching.

"You're in good hands," Alex said, his tone low and

soothing, the way he might talk to a child victim. "You'll beat this."

"No," he said, taking breaths between each word. "Not about me. Dara. I'm worried."

"About what?"

"This guy. Life coach. This fucking guy. She trusts him. I can see it."

"Well, maybe that's a good thing, Jonah. I don't know."

"No!" he said, more forcefully and with an almost frightening effort. "No. I mean she *trusts* him."

"With what? Money?"

Jonah rolled his eyes and shook his head.

"I don't give a shit about money. Not mine. Not hers. That's not the point. She trusts him. You know what I mean?"

"I'm not sure I do."

"She'll..." he paused, lifted his head, and coughed. Then he winced with the pain of it.

"Please, just lie still. Dara will be fine. She's a survivor."

"She'll *talk* to him!" he managed, and fixed his eyes, red-rimmed and pain-lined, on Alex's. "She'll fucking *tell* him things. I know she will."

For a moment Alex searched for some mollifying words to say but found none. Finally, he shook his head. "It's okay. Really. Dara won't. She's a little nutty, I know that as much as anyone. But...she won't. And anyway, you can't worry about that. Okay? You've worried enough. You've worried for all of us. Right now, just rest."

THIRTY-FIVE

In the main lobby, busy with traffic as visiting hours came to a close, Dara was seated with her head down and her hands between her knees. Alex found her quickly in the crowd in a black sweater and jeans, the jeans tucked into her boots. Beside her was a young man, white, thin, perhaps early thirties. He wore a plain black shirt underneath a tan sport jacket. He also had his hands folded between his knees. He was speaking to her in what seemed like a low voice, and Dara nodded occasionally. Finally, she looked up and over the room until her eyes found Alex's. The same spark, the one that had been there since they were children growing up as friends until their teen years plunged them into love, fired through Alex as she smiled in recognition and her eyes lit up. The man with her seemed to recognize Alex as he walked over, but Alex didn't get a jealous vibe from him.

Dara Schwartz was, as Alex reflected from time to time, simply pretty, and in the most subtle and un-coaxed way he had ever known. There was nothing vampish or striking about her. She was of average height and build, a little pear-shaped, with generous lips, dark, heavy eyebrows and a cute, pug-like nose with a sprinkling of faded freckles around it. Her hair was perhaps the most alluring thing about her; it formed a corona of rich, brown, naturally curly lushness that went past her shoulders.

Alex was no longer in love with her. An ocean of horror and grief had mostly washed that away. He loved Nikki, and was comfortable in his relationship with her, with New York, and with a new life that was finally taking wing. But there was no denying that he shared something with his ex-wife, deeper than memory, deeper than shame, that he would share with no one else. It was just that natural, and timeless.

"Hey there," he said as he reached the two of them, seated on a lobby sofa. Dara stood to hug him, and fresh tears welled up in her eyes.

"Oh Alex, thank you. I knew you'd be here."

"I'm sorry, Dara."

"It's not good news," she said when there was space between them again. Her mouth quivered. "They won't say for sure, but they think it's cancer. Did you talk to anyone upstairs?"

"They can't tell me anything," Alex said with a shrug. "I saw him, though. I know it doesn't look good. But he's as tough as leather. We'll see."

"I'm scared for him," she said. "Probably more than he is for himself." Then she seemed to snap to attention, like she had forgotten her manners. "Alex, I'm sorry. This is Walter, my...coach I guess." Her pout gave way to a little smile.

"Hi, Alex," Walter said. His face was smooth, somewhat long and V-shaped. His eyes were dark and intense beneath a full head of brown hair. "I've heard quite a bit about you. I'm sorry for the circumstances, but really happy to finally meet you. Call me Walt."

"Thank you," Alex said, unsure of how to take any of that. Neither Walt's words nor his tone was off-putting, but Alex was still uneasy. He guessed the idea of anyone "hearing" much about him and Dara was going to make him feel that way. "And thanks for being here. For Dara and her father."

"Of course," he said, smiling. "Dara and I work together. I'm glad I could be here."

"Yeah, Jonah mentioned something. You're a life coach, I guess?"

"I'm working on certification. It's a new career path for me. Dara agreed to take me on, which I'm grateful for."

"He's a natural," Dara said. She smiled and hooked her arm inside of Walt's. It was an affectionate gesture, not a flirtatious one, but Alex could tell she felt very close to him. "He's made a huge difference. With everything." Dara set her eyes on Alex's in an almost conspiratorial way.

"Well that's terrific," Alex said. He looked over at Walt, who looked self-satisfied. "Thank you."

"She's doing all the work," he said. At this, Dara announced that she was going to say goodnight to her father. She gave Alex one last hug, told him she would keep him informed and told Walt she'd be back in five. After she left, Alex stood for a moment feeling awkward, then put out his hand one more time to the other man.

"I'd better get going," he said. Walt shook his hand and smiled. He didn't seem to feel the awkwardness at all.

"She still loves you," he said. Alex looked back at him, nonplussed. "It's okay. There's no need to say anything. It's just a fact."

"We've known each other most of our lives," Alex said, unsure of what else to add. He was about to say something like *and we have a history which I'm sure you know about,* but stopped himself.

"That really shows. I expected to see a connection between you two. But it's more intense than I realized."

"Well, I care about her. And her father."

"Ah, her father," Walt said, with a knowing nod. "Seems like a great man. Unfortunately, he doesn't like me. Certainly doesn't trust me."

"He's a skeptic by nature. Protective."

"Money magnifies that, I think," he said. "The protective thing. I think he thinks I'm after her money. For what it's worth, I'm absolutely not."

"You'd really have to ask him," Alex said. Now he was feeling slightly turned off by Walt. Or something. There was something vague in the air now, hardly there but definitely negative. The murky thing about whatever 'connection' this guy sensed between him and Dara. Now a dig, possibly, about Jonah. "Nice to meet you."

"Dara's working through something, Alex," he said as Alex turned to leave. Alex stopped and turned around slowly. Walter looked relaxed but guarded. "Something profound. I don't mean to sound cryptic."

"Well, you kind of do. I mean, we just met, and..."

"Yes. I understand. And I apologize. The thing I'm talking about, the thing Dara is near a break-through on? I sense it involves you. I also have a feeling her father might be dying. I'm sorry for saying that so bluntly, but I have feelings about things, and usually they're right. When he is gone, she may be leaning on you again, emotionally, from time to time. I just feel like you should know that."

"Okay."

"I sense you're a private person."

"I am, yeah."

"Understood. Thank you for listening to me. I hope we

meet again." With that, Walt's mouth seemed to slide into a neutral position, neither a frown nor a grin. His stoic eyes never left Alex's. He seemed collected and confident. Alex didn't know what to make of any of it. He was uneasy.

"Perhaps. Good night."

THIRTY-SIX

Tuesday, November 21

"The media attention has increased on this case," the judge was saying to both Jack and Alex. It was two days before Thanksgiving, and they were once again in front of the judge overseeing the pretrial process in the *Dunaway* case–a mild-mannered, unassuming man about Alex's age named Craig Kullinan. Judge Kullinan briefly examined and then handed a copy of the *New York Daily News* to his court attorney, a meek-looking woman with coke-bottle glasses who sat just below him. The headline, which Alex had seen that morning, was prominent in the local section of the paper: '*Finance Mogul's Rape Case Heats Up in Manhattan*.' Below the headline was a photo of Kim from her website next to one of Dunaway at an earlier court appearance.

"We're aware, Your Honor," Alex said. "I've referred all media inquiries to our press office. That won't change."

"We're trying to stay above it, Your Honor," Jack said. Beside him, his client sighed and shook his head. Kevin Dunaway, Alex noticed, didn't look good. He was still a strapping figure in a well-fitting suit, but his face looked puffy, with a five o'clock shadow even though it was barely ten in the morning. Alex had been in the business of putting people on trial, sometimes for their lives, for fifteen years at that point. Regardless of who was in the chair and for what, he didn't wish the experience on anyone. And Kevin, it appeared, had made his situation worse by leaving a trail of victims behind. Now that trail had caught up to him, fueled by the unblinking eye and ceaseless appetite of the internet and social media.

"It's going to make picking a jury a lot harder," Kullinan said. "That'll be the trial judge's problem, but I don't want to leave that judge with a poorly prepared case."

"We're considering a motion for a change of venue," Jack said. Both the judge and Alex knitted their brows at that. A change of venue meant holding the trial outside of Manhattan, maybe in a suburban county like Westchester, or Nassau out in Long Island. "We agree it will be very difficult to get an unbiased jury here, I'm afraid."

"That's a heavy assumption, Mr. Hooper," the judge said, frowning. "Let's not jump to conclusions. But let's also make sure that both parties here are handling the media attention responsibly. Mr. Greco and the government have a higher burden of course, but Mr. Hooper, you're also obligated to be careful with what's communicated about this case, and any witnesses. Do we understand each other?"

"Of course, Your Honor. We're asking for a trial date after the holidays. We'll see where we are then."

THIRTY-SEVEN

Wednesday, November 22

"This is the kind of thing that worries me," Megan said, thumbing over something on her phone. They were standing in Kim's small kitchen, while Kim made a list of things she would shop for the next day.

"What is?"

"Articles like this," Megan said. "Have you seen this?"

Kim had to squint, but she could see what Megan had brought up. It was an online article of some sort with a colorful top banner by a woman who called herself "Cosmetic Junkie." The title was YES, I CAN SAY 'WHAT IF.' *What if Kimberly Hadley is a wannabe beauty titan who's going after a venture capitalist because she was jilted?*

"Oh yeah, she's a blogger, I've seen her stuff. She's made a career out of claiming to say what no one else will in beauty. I'm not surprised."

"It bothers me. I see the positive comments and I'm glad most people are supportive. But what if it turns? What if Kevin's team is out there planting things about you?"

"They probably are," Kim said with a shrug. "Alex said they might."

"I just wonder if this is worth it," Megan said. They moved over to the little kitchen island where Kim refilled their wine glasses. As usual, Emily was in her chair in the living room, watching TV. "I don't trust the system, Kim, I'm sorry. Men run it. In the end, they protect each other."

"I get that. But I'm in it now."

"You know I work at a brokerage agency," Megan said. "One of our brokers negotiated the lease for the building CIG is in. We still have connections there." Kim knitted her brow. Megan had never said much about her job, other than it was boring and most people there were assholes.

"Really?"

"Yes, really. Listen, it's a long shot, but I wonder if I could get a message to Dunaway, through someone at CIG. I know he's not working there now, but still."

"A message about what?"

"About money," Megan said, lowering her voice. "A lot of it, for you. For what he did to you."

"But, how..."

"Think about what he's probably paying his lawyers," she said. "And there's no guarantee he'll win. Imagine if he could pay you instead. It doesn't make it right, I know that. But what if he was willing to? Then you've got something, guaranteed, and this process is over."

"You mean...hush money?"

"It's all hush money," she said. "That's how I see it. And I think he'd be willing to pay something real. Maybe through his lawyer. Maybe through someone else. We could try to find out."

"Yeah, but then what? If some guy brought me a bag of cash, what then? I'd have to go to court and say it didn't happen?"

"You've told me a bunch of times they're not forcing you to go forward. You have a right to say, 'I don't want to do this anymore.' Or hell, I don't know. You could say you don't remember. I'm pretty sure you wouldn't be the first."

"I couldn't. I just couldn't, Megan."

"Just think about it. Didn't your doctor mention Emily also? She's been through a lot, too. It's gonna get worse after the holidays when the trial starts."

"Emily's fine," Kim said, glancing over the kitchen counter toward her sister. "Believe me, I've got my eye on her."

"I know you do. I'm not worried about how you care for her. I worry about what guys like that can do with the connections they have. What if someone sends a lawyer after you, trying to take her away?"

"What?"

"She's not competent on her own, right?"

"Well no, but she's–"

"So maybe the city comes in, says she needs a guardian. Wants to put her in a group home or something. They can do all sorts of terrible things. I wish it wasn't true, but I've seen it."

"You're scaring me, Megan," Kim said. "Please don't."

"I'm sorry," she said, placing her hand on Kim's. "Really, I am. Listen, you're like a hero to me, okay? I have a sales assistant job in a shitty brokerage firm and a shitty studio on the East Side. But you? I see what you've accomplished, and it's amazing. I also see what this guy did to you. Call me cynical, I can take that. But I don't trust the system, and I don't want to see you get hurt."

"I can see that," Kim said. Her eyes finding Megan's. "And thank you. Emily and I will be okay. She's not all there, but she's still an adult. I don't think anyone will take her away from me. As for the money, I just couldn't do it. I couldn't try extorting him, even if I thought it would work. If he pays for this, he'll pay the right way."

"I understand. Just remember, you've got him against the ropes now. The other women coming out? The rumors? He's vulnerable *now*. You never know when that might change."

"Like you said once," Kim said, with a shrug. "In for a penny, in for a pound. It's almost Thanksgiving. Let's open another bottle."

THIRTY-EIGHT

Thursday, November 23

Alex and Nikki went up to her sister Pam's in Westchester for Thanksgiving dinner. It had been a decent day, weather-wise, and traffic was only moderate getting up there. Alex got along well with Nikki's family, and he knew how much Nikki loved to see her niece Wendy who was now almost seven. On the way back, Nikki rubbed his neck with one hand and monitored the Waze app on her phone with the other. The relative darkness of the Taconic State Parkway had them both squinting; they were not used to being outside of the constant sodium glow of the city.

"Did you hear from anyone back home?" she asked.

"My brother texted earlier. They send their best. My father spent the day with them. Hopefully that wasn't a disaster."

"Anything from Dara or Jonah's girlfriend?"

"No. But every time I ask, the news gets worse. Every test result comes back with something else blocked, or another spot, or growth."

"Palliative care at this point?" she asked. "That's the general term for keeping you comfortable when there's nothing else that can be done."

"I think so, yeah."

"Call her," Nikki said after a few seconds. He looked over at her in the glow of the Jeep's dash lights.

"We text, it's okay."

"Alex, call her. It's Thanksgiving. You know I'm okay with it." He sighed and searched for her number.

"How is he?" he asked when Dara picked up.

"A little worse than yesterday," she said. She sounded exhausted. "We just got back from the hospital."

"Lousy place to spend a holiday. I'm sorry."

"It's okay. It was that or a big table at my mother's with a bunch of very nice people I'm not in the mood for." She was silent for a few seconds, and then said, "I talked to him about hospice today."

"How did he take it?"

"Well, you know him. His attitude at this point is, 'might as well get it over with.' He's actually in good spirits. I think I'm in a state of grace or something, but it's kind of okay."

"Good. How is Louisa?" Alex half expected to hear that she had disappeared. She and Jonah had been together on and off for the last few years. He had no idea if Jonah was planning on providing for her, although he wouldn't put it past him.

"She's been great, actually," Dara said, almost as if she was surprised by it. "She's like this smiling Italian presence, swishing in wearing ungodly expensive leather boots and making us all laugh. She's going back to Europe for a few days, but she's been staying at his house down here otherwise. I'm pretty sure she'll be here until the end." *The end.* The phrase sank through him like lead.

"Okay," he said. "I'll come down soon. Take care of yourself Dara."

"I'm fine. Walter helps. He has me meditating."

"Does it work?"

"It steadies me. You know I can use that."

"Okay," he said with a sigh. "Keep me updated."

The call disconnected, and Alex put his phone in the cup holder.

"Thank you," Alex breathed looking at Nikki. She smiled and took his hand.

"It's in the mail for all of us, Hon."

"Nice thought, Doc."

"Is she thinking about hospice?" she asked. He nodded and swallowed a lump in his throat. He had shed tears in front of Nikki before, but rarely. And he didn't want to now. "Yeah. Soon."

"Is he still lucid?"

"For now."

"Go see him while he still is," she said. "Say whatever's left."

"I think he knows how I feel."

"Don't think, Alex. Know. Okay? If you think you owe the man, you owe him that."

THIRTY-NINE

Saturday, December 9

The room seemed small, too small for the giant of a man who lay dying in it, but that was an illusion. It was actually sizable and private, decked out with sleek blinds, a mounted widescreen TV and cool, beige walls. The facility around it was also well-appointed, quiet and orderly. Kind-faced nurses with clipboards and little cups of pills nodded politely at the living, whether gathered in the rooms or outside in waiting areas. Dara had chosen his hospice carefully, Alex figured. Jonah enjoyed comfort and had lived well, but he wasn't the type to dwell on the process of his own death. He'd drop dead wherever the universe willed it, like windfall fruit or seagull shit.

"Come in," Dara said when she saw him in the doorway. She was perched on the chair beside the bed, holding his hand. "He's been waiting for you. I think he's waking up." Alex smiled weakly at her and then willed his eyes over to Jonah, wishing he could mask the shock he knew was clear on his face. He'd been warned about what to expect, but it was ghastly seeing him this way, emaciated and sallow. Jonah seemed to sink into the bed, propped up at an angle.

His eyes were still animated, although probably with pain. He was taking less medication than the hospice staff was offering. Then the eyes locked in on Alex's and brightened.

"I've been awake," he said. His voice was gravely and low, but clear. "Jesus, don't talk like I'm not here. Plenty of time for that soon enough." He turned to her and said, "DeeDee," an old nickname Alex hadn't heard in decades, "give us a minute." Then to Alex, "Sit down, *boychik*."

"I didn't come to say goodbye," Alex said, his voice cracking as he settled heavily into the chair Dara had just left. It sounded pointless and petulant, and instantly he regretted it. He closed his eyes.

"So, I'll say it. I call you *boychik*. You know why, right?"

"You've been doing it for so long I forgot," Alex said, smiling. He hesitated for a moment, but then took the man's hand in his. It was cool and dry. Jonah squeezed back. If there was any awkwardness in the gesture, it was gone almost instantly. Alex felt so much like crying he feared his face might burst.

"The son," Jonah said, his eyes moving in slow circles over Alex's face. "The son I never had. Should have been you."

"I think we're closer than that." He held Jonah's gaze once it finally settled.

"I love my daughter, but I didn't wish her on you. Still, I wanted you as a son. But I knew, Alex. I knew she was bad for you. I knew like your father knew."

"Fuck him," Alex said, the second thing in five minutes he now regretted uttering. But Jonah just grinned, along with a tiny snort.

"He's a tough customer, your old man. I should have told him that when I had the chance." Alex, who had very little affection for his father, smiled in spite of himself. For Jonah, the term "tough customer" was about the highest compliment a person could be paid. "Anyway, Dara. I love her. Like life. But Jesus, she scares me." The last two words, *scares me* were almost a gasp. Alex felt a coldness slide through him, as if Jonah had transmitted it through his hand.

"She's a good soul, Jonah. A tortured soul, sometimes. But good."

"I've wanted to believe that," he said, then coughed and winced. "Maybe I do. She's reckless, though. Something destructive there. Something terrible. Always has been." Alex stared back him, the cold feeling deepening.

"It was a moment," he said, barely above a whisper. "A moment of madness, Jonah. That's all it was."

"It was inevitable," Jonah said, and his eyes drifted to the ceiling. "It'll always be inevitable with Dara." They shifted back, dark and cutting. "Don't forget that, Alex."

"I'll always take care of her," Alex said. He had a sudden and fleeting urge to get up and run, as if an unseen threat had just breathed hot and foul air onto his neck from behind. He shook it off. "Whatever happens. Whoever she is. I never stopped, and I never will."

"A thing about that," Jonah said then, as if an idea had occurred to him. "There's a guy. In New York. I want you to talk to him."

"I have a girlfriend, but thanks."

"Shut up," he said, grinning and then wincing. Alex winced also, a reflex. "He'll be in touch. Next day or two."

"Okay. Whatever you want, you know that."

"I want you to take care of yourself," he breathed. "I know you'll be there for Dara. I'm talking about you. Your life. Tend to that, Alex. It's the one you fought for."

"It's the one you gave me," Alex said, his eyes brimming with tears. "I tend to it pretty well. Let me worry, now, old man. It's my time to."

FORTY

The original thousand-watt smile is what Alex thought of when he first greeted Dale Friedlander, standing at the bar of a steak place called Porterhouse on Columbus Circle. It wasn't just that the guy had a nice set of teeth and a welcoming display of them. It was like the smile really did light up his entire face like a movie set lamp. The face was otherwise pleasant and tanned, with a prominent nose, strong eyebrows and a wide forehead.

"Thank you for meeting me," Dale said. He was much shorter than Alex, maybe five-six or five-seven, and handsomely but casually dressed in a tailored shirt and slacks. His feet were shoulder-width apart, and his stance was serenely poised, that of an athlete utterly comfortable in his own skin.

"You're welcome," Alex said, not knowing what else to offer. He knew almost nothing about what this meeting would entail, other than Jonah had arranged it. An assistant of Dale's had called him earlier in the day, seeing if he could meet for dinner.

"I hope you're hungry. And feel free to take your tie off. Mine's gone by eleven most days."

"Uh, sure. I don't know anything about why I'm here, though."

"I think Jonah wanted it that way. Don't worry, I'll fill you in. C'mon, let's sit. Great view up here."

"So, you're a friend of Jonah's?" Alex asked. Dale glanced backward as they fell in line toward their table.

"No. A lawyer."

***

The view, looking east along Central Park South, was splendid. It was a cold but clear night, and the treetops and light posts in the park had crisp outlines, their shadows sharp along the paths. Above it all, the great city twinkled. Alex mouthed a 'thank you' as a gray-haired waiter poured more cabernet into his glass. He had no idea what it was, but it was delicious, and the waiter seemed impressed with Dale's choice.

"I hope I didn't come off as suspicious before," Alex said. "I just didn't know what I was getting into."

"I'd be worried about you if you didn't," Dale said, frowning at the menu. He looked up. "Do you have a preference for steak?"

"Anything, really."

"Sides?"

"Whatever you like. I'll eat anything."

"I think we'll get along just fine," Dale said, nodding. He motioned to the waiter, ordered, and then leaned toward Alex. "Listen, I know you've never heard of me. Jonah wanted it that way. That went for a lot of people, not just you. I know a great deal about you, though. More than most people in Jonah's life, to be frank." Alex didn't know what to do with this.

"Okay."

"I've done a lot of work for him. I'm doing more now that he's dying. He told me you visited this weekend. That's good, I don't think there's much time left."

"Probably not," Alex said. "I don't expect to see him alive again." He swallowed hard and took a moment to compose himself. "I'm sorry, it's hard to think about."

"Don't be sorry. I'll be settling some of his affairs when the time comes. And I'm taking care of a few things now."

"Is there something you need from me?"

"Other way around," Dale said. "Some money will come your way. And maybe some information, and some responsibilities. It's kind of up to you. Jonah wouldn't force anything on you. But he's hoping you'll accept."

"I don't want his money. Any of it. It's not like that."

"If you did, you wouldn't be getting it. Truth is, he probably would have given you his apartment up here, but the taxes would have just forced you into a sale anyway."

"Yeah, I've been to that apartment, I think you're right."

A few minutes later the steaks arrived, sizzling and aromatic. After some small talk about the city and a little about Jonah, Alex returned to the one subject he wanted to make clear. "Listen, I don't know what to say, except Jonah is like a father to me, more than my own. The last thing I want to do is somehow profit from that. I love the guy. Really."

"And I don't," Dale said, meeting Alex's gaze as he twisted a pepper shaker over his steak. "That's why I'm his lawyer. I'm the help. You're the son-in-law."

"Former."

"Not the way he sees it."

"I'll do whatever he wants," Alex said. "Whatever it is you need, when the time comes. Obviously, you know how to find me."

Dale nodded and asked, "How's your steak?"

"Fantastic."

"Good. So, there's this guy. Walter Lynch." Alex stopped mid-chew.

"The life coach."

"Yeah." There was no longer a grin. Or a trace of one. "He could be trouble."

"For Dara, I know."

"For both of you, possibly." Dale set his fork down and looked neutrally over at Alex. There was nothing in his de-meanor that seemed the least bit threatening, but now Alex's guard was up.

"I'm not sure I understand."

"I'm not sure I do either, but I don't need to. What I'm telling you is just what Jonah wants you to be told."

"Well, I can tell you he's already expressed his con-cerns to me about Lynch."

"I understand that," Dale said, taking a sip of the wine and then pouring the rest of the bottle between them. "I'm just here to let you know you're supported, and you will be after Jonah is gone. You'll have resources, depending on how you think you need to protect Dara. That's what Jonah really wants, Alex. He wants you to protect her. And yourself."

For a long moment Alex sat quietly. Dale seemed not to notice and helped himself to more scalloped potatoes. Alex had been trained to be wary, hammered into that mindset both professionally and personally. But nothing about Dale seemed amiss. It was more just the shock of it, the idea that, maybe, Jonah had revealed something to someone outside of their dreadful, three-person circle. But even that wasn't clear. Maybe Dale was being circumspect, or ostentatiously discreet, or maybe not. Maybe he didn't know any details and was just doing exactly what his job was, communicating Jonah's wishes. Alex wasn't inclined to trust anyone, but for now, at least, Dale seemed decent, and wasn't asking for information. He told himself he would try to confirm things with Jonah, and then realized with a bitter stab of pain that he might not have that chance. That was the whole point of the meeting now.

"I'll always protect her," he said finally. Dale nodded.

"He knew you'd say that, too. I'm glad. So, do you know anything about this guy? Lynch?"

"No, not a thing. But I assume Jonah had him checked up on."

"Somewhat, yeah. There's no smoking gun there. No criminal record, no evidence he's pauperized a string of old ladies, nothing like that. He's never been married from what I can tell. Dara knows all of this, by the way. I don't mean to imply she's in the dark and we're not."

"All I got from Dara was that he was working on accreditation in life coaching. There's some federation that gives out certificates. They met at a networking event. She says he agreed to work with her for free, but she's paying him something. Nothing that would raise eyebrows I guess."

"Yeah a couple hundred bucks a month or something," Dale said. "The money didn't bother Jonah at all. It was more that he just seemed to come out of nowhere."

"I was wondering about that. Where did he come from?"

"He was in Atlantic City before he got to Northern

Virginia. Ohio before that, it's where he grew up. He has a mostly insignificant past. He went to a small college in Pennsylvania but didn't stay long. Did some odd jobs. Then he ended up in A.C., where he worked on the production staff for a few shows and did different things at a few hotels."

"Does he have any money?" He wasn't sure how Dale would know that, but he knew that Dale did.

"Not real money, but enough to get by on for a while. His father has been gone for years. His mother died a couple of years ago and left him maybe twenty thousand. He's got some in a checking account, but not much in the way of investments. No debt, either. He moved to Arlington a couple of months ago."

"Dara told me that," Alex said. "She says it's a tiny place in a not-so-great neighborhood. He's living small until he can get his business going. She says he doesn't mind, though. He's not materialistic. That's how she put it."

"Seems that way," Dale said, nodding. He paused for a second. "It doesn't appear romantic between them, either. For whatever that's worth."

"I know her pretty well," Alex said. "I didn't get that vibe either. If it was, though, that would be fine as long as he was good to her. I've got a girlfriend up here now."

"Yeah, Jonah told me. He likes that you do."

"Good to know." He flashed a weak smile and Dale returned it. "So, there's no obvious threat, right? Jonah's just being overly cautious?"

"I'm not sure what Jonah's worried about," Dale said, his face going blank again. "I'm just letting you know what I know. The rest is between you and Dara, once Jonah isn't here anymore. If you need more information, or maybe someone to help you do some digging, I hope you'll come to me. That's all."

"Thanks," Alex said. He held Dale's gaze, not wanting to appear cagey or anxious, even though Dale wasn't telegraphing a hint of judgment or even curiosity. Alex suspected it was a developed skill, and a good one for the kind of lawyer Dale seemed to be. Below the surface, though, Alex felt fingers of disquiet wrapping around his insides. Jonah was worried about what Dara was telling this guy. It's exactly what he had said when Alex first saw him in the hospital. Alex knew now that he needed to be worried about it, too.

FORTY-ONE

Wednesday, December 13

Alex knew when his phone rang, a low, toneless rattle a little after five that morning. Beside him, Nikki breathed deeply and steadily in slumber. She was a heavy sleeper, and not much outside of a fire alarm could wake her. The window next to his bed was frosted in the corner. Normally he had a good view of the railroad bridge over Spuyten Duyvil, a smaller version of the view from the living room. But now it was opaque and clouded, like the porthole of a cold, black chamber.

"He's gone, Alex," Dara said when he picked up. He rubbed his eyes with his free hand and sat up in bed. His heart sank at the words, even though he expected them.

"I'm sorry. Did it just happen?"

"Maybe ten minutes ago. You're the first person I called."

"He loved you more than anything," Alex said. There were a few other things he wanted to say, things that felt appropriate, but that was all he could get out. Emotion climbing up the back of his throat threatened to render him choking with sobs.

"It was horrible, Alex. He just kept...breathing. We'd think it was over, and then...another one. It went on for hours, I swear." The vision of that, of Jonah clinging to life despite life's every effort to cast him out, actually pushed aside his urge to cry, replacing it almost with a dark grin. He had no idea why, but it did, and he was grateful for it. He sighed instead.

"It's hard, I know."

"Of course," she said. "I know your mother went through it."

"Is Louisa with you?"

"No, she went back to Dad's to sleep. I'll call her next. Walter is with me."

"I'm glad for that. Do you need help with anything right now? I can get down there, maybe tonight."

"No, Daddy made sure everything was covered. The hospital will release him later this morning, and he wanted to be cremated, so that's all set up. Just come down tomorrow if you can. We'll do a small memorial service at eleven, and then sit shiva at my mother's."

"She's okay with that?" he asked. The break-up between Jonah and Dara's mother Lois had been many years before, but it had not been pleasant.

"Not really, but she'll do it for me. There'll be a larger memorial service in a few weeks. Hey, you can bring your girlfriend, you know. It's really okay." Alex looked over at Nikki, turned away from him and wrapped in a white sheet, her shoulders exposed, and smiled.

"She'll come for the later memorial service, I'm sure," he said. "Tomorrow, it'll just be me. I'll let you know when I get into town." There was a long pause, and Alex was almost certain Dara was about to say 'I love you.'

"Thanks, Alex," she said instead. "It means everything. I'll see you tomorrow. Remember the rule."

"The rule?"

"No living things to a *shiva* call, so no flowers. We're Jews, we like food."

"You got it, Dara." And he had to stop himself from saying 'I love you' himself. It was habit, he figured, a pattern revisited when fresh tragedy sparked the old dynamics back into motion. Still, even without Nikki sleeping beside him, it would have been grossly inappropriate.

He set the phone down and spooned his girlfriend, drawing her warm body toward him under the comforter. She stirred, mumbled something unintelligible, clasped his hand where he had cupped her breast and fell quiet again. A deep sadness was sinking in, the permanence of death replacing the anxiety of waiting for it.

But more than that he felt abandoned and rootless, as if the sturdy ground he'd been able to plant himself on and stride across had now given way to something rocky, steep and dark. He figured that's how it probably felt for many men who lost their fathers. He heard Nikki mumble.

"Baby, you okay?" He wasn't sure if she was entirely awake, and in any event wanted to deal with it all later, so he stayed silent. A second later she snuggled her butt tighter against him and seemed to fall back into sleep. He closed his eyes and took in the scent of her hair. For the moment she was all he needed, a fragrant, feminine bulwark against the approaching morning. Against the reality that the only father figure he had ever known, who had saved his life, was gone for good.

FORTY-TWO

Thursday, December 14
12:45 p.m.

In her cubicle on the eleventh floor of the Office of the Chief Medical Examiner on First Avenue in Manhattan, Cassie Fitzsimmons looked over the results, still preliminary, regarding the DNA evidence extracted from the handkerchief Kim Hadley had dropped in the alley. Technically known as a "criminalist," Cassie was in her ninth year with the city and loved her work. But unlike many of the people she worked with, she took almost no interest in the outcome of any case in which evidence became hers to examine.

It wasn't that she felt it was wrong to do so, it just wasn't who she was. Most of her colleagues had more context for the items they examined, be it bloody underwear, stained bedsheets or cigarette butts. They enjoyed being a part of getting the right guy, or, in the alternative, ensuring the wrong guy was let go. For Cassie, though, just doing the job right was the priority, and in fact she kept a measured distance from the humanization of the stains, spatters and spots she spent her days with. What she loved about being a DNA examiner was the series of puzzles the work presented to her, and the challenge of doing it cleanly and correctly.

For that reason, she was a little annoyed with herself for feeling concerned over the results she had gleaned from the sole piece of physical evidence in the case involving a defendant named Kevin Dunaway. *People v. Dunaway* had become a "press case," meaning one that attracted major media attention. For that reason alone, whether she wanted to know the details or not, she was absorbing a few of them in the local news and office scuttlebutt. Among those details were a couple of photos of the complainant in the case, Kim Hadley, in news stories online. To Cassie, Hadley looked decent and earnest, not someone looking for a payday or drama. The defendant, Kevin Dunaway, on the other hand, looked like an arrogant prick in the photos she'd seen. Dunaway was also facing a media crisis related to the case. Several more women had come out accusing him of the kind of behavior Hadley had eventually reported.

These kinds of impressions, Cassie knew well, were the kind that could get a scientific examiner in trouble. Bias, in favor of the guilt of the defendant whose case she was evaluating, was a creeping, sometimes unconscious thing. She had training on it, she was aware of it, and thankfully she worked in a fully accredited lab where there were blind cross-checks and confirmation. But even above that, she knew she needed to keep herself in check.

Still, in cases where she was working with a prosecutor she felt comfortable with, there were occasional situations where a red flag could be made known, if such a thing in testing became apparent. Cassie knew, as all criminalists did, that there were ADA's you could reach out to if you wanted to, beyond the strict perimeters of the job, simply because you had grown to trust them. That didn't mean the results differed. Every case, whether for an ADA she liked or loathed, got her full analytical commitment. But for a trustworthy ADA, she was willing to make a call when it looked like a bombshell was about to explode in the middle of his or her case. This was one of those cases.

Five days earlier, at her workstation with goggles, lab coat and hairnet in place, she had unpacked the handkerchief from the sealed evidence bag, initialed by the sergeant who had supervised its collection from the alley, per evidence collection protocol. She had visually examined the handkerchief, finding three areas, or stains, where biological material was. She had circled each stain with a sharpie marker. From there, she had cut out pieces of the fabric, conducted a test for blood on two of the stains and amylase, a chemical present in saliva, on the other. Not surprisingly, the tests had confirmed her visual impressions. Two of the stains were blood, the other more likely saliva. Each swatch had then been placed into a chemical-filled tube that became the first part—extraction—of the elaborate process of developing a human DNA profile from the material itself. From there, Cassie sent three tubes via a dumb-waiter system to another part of her lab. Now she was trying to make sense of the results.

The first area, Area One, was a singular spot of blood less than a centimeter wide. Area Two was the larger, yellowish saliva stain. The final area of interest on the cloth was the bigger blood stain, the one that covered the largest section of the handkerchief as Area Three. Dunaway, the defendant, had provided his DNA in the form of a "buccal swab," or a swiping of the inside of the cheek, when he was arrested. Cassie had already developed Kevin's DNA profile, and it matched perfectly with the DNA of the small blood spot on the handkerchief, or Area One. With regard to that spot at least, Cassie could document and testify that Kevin Dunaway had "donated," or left his biological material in the form of blood, on the handkerchief. That left Areas Two and Three for comparison, but in order to do that, Cassie needed a buccal swab from Kim herself. She looked through the file again to be sure. It hadn't come in yet. There was a request to have it provided, still open.

Cassie had, however, developed still anonymous DNA profiles from both Areas Two and Three. Area Two, the saliva stain, contained a mixture of human DNA, which was not surprising given that Hadley reported using the handkerchief to clean her sister from time to time. But what was really troubling was Area Three. Cassie didn't know all the facts of the case, but she knew it was reported that Hadley had used the handkerchief to stop her own bleeding after being struck by the defendant. If that was case, then the large blood stain would almost certainly match Kim's DNA.

But that didn't seem possible, unless something had gone wrong during the testing process. She looked over the results again, going through everything painstakingly. Yes, she decided, this was odd. Then she went back to the file and confirmed who the ADA was. Alex Greco, from the newly formed Special Crimes Unit. Alex was a good guy, and Cassie had known him since he had worked homicide cases in the Bronx a couple of years back. He was the type she was comfortable making a call to.

FORTY-THREE

1:00 p.m.

"Alex, can we talk?" the voice came from behind him. It was familiar. Alex had just stepped away from the crowd at the *shiva* call onto the huge back porch that overlooked the swimming pool. The house Dara grew up in, and that Alex had been in hundreds of times, was lovely and well-appointed, although not lavish. It was on a quiet street in an area of Alexandria known as Beverly Hills, and was set back from the road, shaded by several old trees. The outside air was cold and crisp. Weak afternoon light coated the sky like old paint.

"What is it, Walter?"

"First, I'm sorry for your loss. I know this is hard for you, harder than most people think."

"Thank you," he said, not sure what else to say. He had come outside for a breath of fresh air, and maybe a cigarette if he could find something to use as an ashtray. He felt his phone vibrate and excused himself for a moment. The call was from a 212 number he couldn't immediately place, but he had a feeling it was the medical examiner's office. If so, it was probably Cassie Fitzsimmons, the criminalist on the case. In his experience, Cassie wouldn't reach out to him by phone unless there was a reason to. Cassie also had a relationship with Angie and would talk to her, so he sent the call to voicemail and shot off a quick text to Angie: I *think Cassie at OCME might be trying to reach me. Can you call her and see what's up? I can't get away for a couple of hours, but text if it's urgent.*

"You probably want a cigarette," Walter said when Alex looked up. Alex's brow knitted. He wasn't sure how Walter knew he smoked. Maybe Dara had mentioned it, or maybe Walter had seen his hand fidget.

"Mostly I just wanted a minute to myself."

"I completely understand, and I'll try to be quick, but this is important. Do you remember, when we talked, that night I met you at the hospital? There was something about Dara I was concerned about. Something I felt you needed to know about." Behind Walter, through the big french doors, Alex could see Dara walking back and forth across the living room, opening the door and greeting the new callers. There had been dozens already and they had only been at the house for an hour. Catering staff in crisp white aprons moved between the kitchen and the living and dining rooms with trays of hors d'oeuvres.

"Okay."

"Well, I think it's closer than ever. Things are happening pretty quickly. It's not the death of her father, though. That's actually incidental to this. I hope that doesn't sound cold."

"Walter, I don't mean to be rude. If you've been good for Dara, I'm glad. That's all that matters. But you and I don't have a relationship."

"I think we need to forge one, though," he said. He

looked thinner than Alex remembered, in a simple but well-cut black suit with a gray T-shirt underneath. His manner was earnest, but there was something behind it, almost as if he was reluctant. "It doesn't have to be permanent, but I'm sensing it's important right now. Very important. Please bear with me, I can explain."

"It's really not a good time," Alex said, and rubbed his forehead with two fingers. He was straining to stay polite, but it was getting difficult. The air outside was exactly what he had craved—cold, clear and silent. Walter's presence was a blunt intrusion on all of that. "This has been hard, like you said. I don't have much time here, and I'd like to spend it mourning my friend before I have to leave." With that, he walked past Walter toward the doors. "Please excuse me."

"I can't excuse it," Walter said, now behind him as Alex opened one of the doors. "It's not for me to excuse."

"It's not...what?" He pulled the door shut and turned around.

"I'm sorry," Walter said, almost sputtering. "That's not how I meant that to come out."

"Meant what? What are you getting at?" Alex took a few steps toward him, and Walter backed up. Shadows widened in the yard as a heavy gray cloud passed overhead. A stiff breeze picked up.

"Wait," Walter said. "Wait, I see it now." His voice lowered. "There was blood. Dara said there wasn't, but I see it. It was on your face, wasn't it?" His eyes darted away, as if his attention had been summoned to the left. Alex felt a deep chill, utterly independent of the air making their breath visible.

"My face? What?"

"Cheek," Walter said, barely above a whisper. Their eyes met. "Cheek or chin. Pink." For a moment Alex was stunned. His breath caught in his throat. He could feel it again, the razor sliding with a neat, thin sting across his cheek, just below his lip on the right side as Dara's first wretched scream reached him, upstairs in their bathroom. He saw his younger face for a terrible second, back in the old mirror, a trickle of blood mixing with the shaving lotion. Mixing pink.

At first there was a rush of dread, like vomit crawling up his throat. Then he banished it, replacing it with anger. He was sure now what this was. When he spoke, his voice was a controlled growl.

"Who told you that?"

"No one told me. I saw it. Just now."

"Yeah right. Dara told you something. Some detail about that day."

"She didn't," he said. "Don't blame her, please." He raised his hands as if to ward off a blow, and a second later Alex became aware of his hands, balled up into fists. He concentrated on releasing them and trying not to shake. Anger would eclipse all other thought, any second now, if he didn't maintain control. For a few reasons, he couldn't let that happen.

"You know what? You're going to disappear. Whatever arrangement you had with Dara, friendship, mentorship, whatever? It's over after today."

"That's not your decision to make, Alex."

"I'm making it anyway. You will leave her life. I will see to it."

"It's too late anyway. I could never talk to her again, it won't change what I know. And believe me, I didn't want to know it. But I do." For a moment the anger was blinding. Alex felt a deep, dizzying sensation move through him.

"You know nothing," he said through clenched teeth. "You're some kind of fortune teller, and you got to her. But now you're dealing with me, and I will hurt you, so help me God."

"Why would you do that?" he asked, a look of honest bewilderment on his face. He took a step back, now almost against the porch railing, but otherwise didn't appear frightened. It was like he had prepared for the confrontation. "What about that day is so hidden for you, Alex? For both of you?"

"Back off and disappear," was all he could manage. "Seriously, you don't know what I'm capable of."

"Oh, I think I might, actually. Look, if you're prepared to kill me, I won't be able to stop you. If you're not, then maybe think about letting me help you. And Dara."

"Yeah, that's funny."

"No, it's not. This isn't a joke, Alex."

"Oh yeah? What, then, a game?"

"No, not that either. I know things that are tearing you both to pieces. They already tore you apart from each other. Now they're coming for you separately. I know how to stop them."

"I'll tear *you* apart if you don't get away from me this very fucking second. Try me."

"There's only one way out," Walter said, as if he hadn't heard the threat. "I'm not being disingenuous and I'm not being cruel. This is the truth. There's a shadow, over your son's grave. You can remove it. It can really be over."

"This conversation is over," Alex said. He could feel his heart thump, the adrenaline wild in his blood. He had already let things get too far. He had to call it back, all of it, for now. He needed to talk to Dara, but that would have to wait until later, not while she was dealing with guests, prayers and the caterers. He took a few deep breaths, willed a cold calmness back into himself and then locked his eyes on Walter. What he would say next was something he needed to be ready to follow up on, and that was best delivered without emotion. "You've been warned, Walter Lynch. It's the only warning you'll ever get."

FORTY-FOUR

3:00 p.m.

Angie lit a cigarette as she and Danny walked past the truck-bomb barriers outside the doors. They had just left the clean-lined, beige, brick and glass building that was the Office of the Chief Medical Examiner. Behind them the flags of the United States and the City of New York whipped in the cold December wind atop the flagpoles before the entrance. Angie and Danny had been across town from the OCME earlier and came in to talk to Cassie in person when Angie heard from her.

"We gotta call him," Danny said. "This is bad."

"I know, but he's at a funeral. And there's nothing he can do about it right now."

"Ang, for Christ's sake, wouldn't you want to know? Like immediately?"

"Let's see if we can talk to her first. She works from home most of the time, and she lives like ten blocks away. Maybe we can figure out what's going on. At least then we've got more to tell him." She looked at her phone for a few seconds, dreading making the call for some reason she couldn't quite fathom. She had dealt with liars before, even very good ones. Untangling their garbage was a part of the job. There was something unreal about it, though, the idea that Kim Hadley had made this up. She had known something was off. But not this. Finally, her thumb hit the button.

"This is Kim Hadley," Angie heard on the other end.

"Kim, it's Detective Keegan. Listen, we need to talk. Are you at home or on the East Side by any chance?"

"Yeah, I'm working from home," Kim said. Angie gave Danny a thumbs up.

"Is Emily with you?"

"No, she's up in Bryant Park. Some kid's exhibit or something she wanted to see. Is everything okay?"

"Yeah. Is it okay if we come by?"

FORTY-FIVE

Kim made coffee for Angie and Danny and invited them to take the couch while she perched on an ottoman. Angie had been watching her as she answered their small talk and walked in and out of the kitchen. She seemed no more guarded than usual. The whole thing was surreal.

"Kim, we were at the Office of the Chief Medical Examiner today," Angie said. Kim nodded and sipped her coffee.

"Oh, sure. About the DNA?"

"Yes."

"You probably need a sample from me, right?" Kim asked. "And Emily also? I'm really sorry—Alex asked me a few weeks ago about it, and I just keep forgetting. I can call Emily though, have her come back."

"No need for Emily's right now," Angie said. "We will get yours today. There's an issue with the DNA we need to talk to you about." Kim's brow furrowed and she set her mug down.

"Okay."

"How much do you know about DNA?"

"Not much."

"Well, the bloody handkerchief you dropped at the crime scene had a few spots on it. DNA was found on three of them, and one was a mixture of individuals."

"Mixture meaning DNA from more than one person?"

"Yes," Angie said. "The mixture was found in a saliva stain. Once we get exemplars from you and Emily, parts of both of you will probably match that mixture. I don't know all the science, but that's how I understand it." Kim nodded at this. She seemed curious, but not the least bit anxious. "There were blood spots, too."

"Sure," Kim said. "Alex Greco figured most of it was mine but was hoping they'd find Kevin's blood there also."

"Well they did find Kevin's blood," Angie said. She glanced over at Danny whose face was a practiced mask of neutrality. "Of the two blood stains, one was pretty small, and one was much bigger. The smaller stain has Kevin's blood on it. The DNA is an absolute match."

"I guess that makes sense," Kim said. To Angie, she still seemed relaxed and unconcerned.

"Well, that left the other blood stain, the larger one. The DNA analyst assumed the larger stain would have your DNA in it, you know, especially because you pressed it against your mouth, to stop the bleeding."

"That's right," Kim said, nodding. "That's exactly what I did, so sure."

"Yeah, but Kim, that other blood stain doesn't *have* your DNA in it, that's the thing. The DNA profile from that stain is from a male. Do you understand?" Angie saw it then, the change in Kim's face. A draining of color there. "You need to tell us if any other male used that handkerchief that night, or if another man was involved with you. I don't like doing this, Kim, but I have to." *This is it*, Angie thought. *Now she tells me some other asshole really did it.* The thought was more than disturbing. It was strangely sad.

"When you say 'male' and 'female,'" Kim said, slowly and with odd deliberateness, "I guess I don't know what you mean. DNA tells you that?"

"Yeah," Angie said. "The numbers don't tell us anything about characteristics. But there's a sex marker, it tells us whether the donor of the evidence is male or female."

"I think I understand," Kim said, barely above a whisper. She placed her hands together in her lap.

"We know you were beaten," Angie said. "No matter what, you didn't deserve that. But if it was someone other than Kevin, it changes everything. And we need to know." "We just need the truth," Danny said. "Nothing will shock either of us, Kim. But we've gotta know." Kim sat silently for several seconds, then looked up at them, meeting their gazes one at a time.

"You need to know who the male profile is on that larger stain, because it's not Kevin Dunaway," she said. Angie could hear that Kim's breathing had deepened. She looked close to tears, but also as if she was exerting herself to control her emotions. The small, angled face seemed set, the jaw clenched when she was silent. Angie steeled herself. *Here we go. At least she seems like the type who will just spill it, and not dig deeper.*

"We need the truth," Angie said. "Whatever it is. We're not looking to jam you up for it, but we need to know." When Kim spoke, it was even and measured. Whatever emotions she had been fighting seemed to have been tamed. Her eyes went from Angie to Danny, and then back again to Angie.

"The truth is that the male profile belongs to me. I was born male."

FORTY-SIX

For a long moment, no one said anything. Angie and Danny looked at each other, then back at Kim. She seemed princess-like in that moment, a statue of a woman perfectly poised, but frozen as if in a tedious pose for a portrait while wearing a Lululemon outfit.

"Kim, what?" Angie asked finally. She almost stuttered on the 'K.'

"I was born Andrew Ray Hadley," Kim said. The voice continued in that calm, perfectly paced way. It was as if modulating it might somehow wake something inside. "I told Alex I lost my brother the night my house blew up. But really, I lost a sister. I've lived as her ever since." Angie searched Kim's eyes for something maybe she missed before, something like complete and utter dissociation from reality. But nothing like that was there. Kim looked as sane, present and oriented as ever. Angie looked over at Danny, who just looked back and shrugged, his eyes a little wide.

"But you don't..." Angie started, then paused, "...you don't seem *male* to me. I mean at all. And I've been doing this a long time." She glanced at Danny, who shook his head with a look of wonder on his face.

"I never have seemed male," Kim said. She still maintained that steel-like posture, as if relaxing a tiny bit might cause her to crack into a million little pieces.

"Yeah, but..." Angie started, then trailed off. "Have you...had any surgery?"

"No. Hormone therapy, though. I do that. Umm. I tape a little, too, body parts, I mean. There are things you can do. Undergarments."

"Does Emily know?" Danny asked.

"She knows me as Kim. The nature of her disability has probably impacted her memory, and maybe her ability to perceive what's happened and when. But I never gave her a full explanation, no." She paused, and then a look of horror crossed her face, the pose shattered. "Listen, whatever I've done, or laws I've broken, please don't let this reflect on Emily. None of this is her fault."

"I don't think you broke any laws," said Danny, who seemed genuinely perplexed. He looked over at Angie, whose mind was racing a mile a minute, taking it all in. "Right?"

"I don't think so, no," Angie said, still thinking it through. She could feel her face, contorted into an unbelieving stare, and tried to soften it. "You're not...you're not in trouble, Kim. That's not what this is. We needed the truth. We've got it now."

"But how? How could I not be in trouble? I wasted your time. Everyone's. I'm sorry. To both of you. To all of you. I'm just worried for my sister. I can explain this to her. I should have a long time ago. I feel awful. And exposed. And now I'm so scared..." Finally, tears did come, as mightily as it seemed she had tried to hold them back. They only leaked out, though. Kim swept one tear away with a quick hand and cast her eyes down.

"Did Kevin Dunaway attack you that night, Kim?" Angie asked after a few seconds. Kim looked back at her.

"Yes."

"Did it happen exactly the way you told me?"

"Yes."

"Did anyone else hurt you that night?"

"No."

"Did I ever ask you what your gender was?"

"Well...no."

"Did Alex Greco, or anyone at his office?"

"No. No one did. But..."

"You haven't lied," Angie said with a shrug. "About anything."

"This case, though," Kim said, looking from one to the other, cheeks stained with tear tracks. "It's over, right?"

"We don't make that decision," Angie said. "That could be, but I wouldn't assume it yet. What I can tell you right now is you're not in any trouble, at least not with us. Neither is Emily. I don't know what will happen with your case, but don't worry about the other stuff."

"You know, there's a call I gotta make on another case," Danny said, standing up. He cleared his throat. "Kim, do you mind talkin' to just Angie?"

Kim looked as if the question was surprising. "No, not at all."

"Alright, we'll be in touch again soon. Take care, okay?" He shifted his eyes to Angie. "I'll be downstairs. Take your time." Angie looked after him as he walked out. For a second or two she kept her head pointed away from Kim, trying to hide a sliver of a grin.

"Do you think he's okay?" Kim asked softly when the

door shut behind him.

"He's fine," Angie said, still looking at the door. "He's a good guy. This is *how* he's being a good guy."

"I'm not sure I understand."

"He wants to let us talk," Angie said, looking back at her. Now the grin fought its way out over her freckled face, constrained just enough. "Woman to woman."

FORTY-SEVEN

6:00 p.m.

As usual, the meeting place was Jordan's grave, the neat, rectangular stone with "Beloved Son" and the carving of a reposed lamb below it. He figured there were other places, by now, where he could get Dara to meet him. But given what they had to discuss, this place, after dark with the visitors and attendants gone and nothing but the dead for company, made the most sense.

He arrived early and spent a few empty minutes in the cold, staring at the grave and feeling the familiar weight of grief settle over him like a heavy blanket. Here, a stone's throw from the house he grew up in, there was no big city to shield him from the past with its exhausting stimuli and eternal pulse. He could see Dara was still tending to the grave site regularly but noted with some relief that it had tapered off. So maybe she was coming by once a week now instead of daily. That was progress for her, he figured, and the thought was tinged with some new melancholy. Still, he was glad for it.

He tried to focus on that feeling as a way to keep the anger at bay, the anger he was feeling and the pressure of what he had to discuss with her. The conversation had to be calm. He had to be firm, but not unkind. Whatever she'd done, whatever she'd said to Walter, it wasn't something he had the right to shove back in her face.

"Alex," she said as she approached. He hadn't heard her walk up the path, and she emerged out of the shadow of one of the street lamps like an apparition. She joined him at the headstone and followed his eyes down to it; the dates, the notation, the lifeless outline of the lamb. They stood in silence for a moment.

"It had to be here," he said. "You know I don't like meeting here. But tonight, it had to be here."

"It's okay," she said with a shrug. "I feel at home here. I know you don't like that, but I still do." And then, as if she'd read his mind, "But I don't come as often, now. I don't freak out when a blade of grass pops over his stone. It's getting better."

"I can tell. That's good."

"You're mad about something else, though. I could tell when you left the house."

"Yes. I'm trying not to be. But I am."

"Tell me."

"You're putting us both at risk," Alex said, turning to her, his voice cracking. "Terrible risk. Jesus, after all we've been through, that's the one thing I thought we'd never to do each other."

"It's nothing I've told him," she said, and her face was placid and sad. There was no 'gotcha' look as if he had caught her somehow, and this amplified his disquiet. Her eyes stayed on his. "I saw you two on the porch. What did he tell you?"

"Something he couldn't have known. A *detail* he couldn't

have known, about that morning. So, tell me, Dara. Tell me what you told him, so I can deal with it, somehow."

"I've told him nothing that isn't publicly known. I've admitted nothing to him. It's scary, I know."

"It's bullshit is what it is!"

"Alex, I didn't. He just knows."

"That's not possible. Do you understand me? He doesn't just *know*. He knows because you told him. There are three people—now two—who know the details of what happened that morning, and even your father didn't know every…"

"Please listen," she said, raising a petite hand. Her breath had sped up and she was gulping air in shallow bursts, something he had seen many times before. "I don't know how it works. But I know it's real."

"It's not real. He tricked you into giving him details. He's extrapolated some story from them."

"He *sees* it! It's not words exactly. I mean, yes, of course, he tells it to me in words. But what he sees…"—she sputtered between bursts of breath— "…are like pictures or something."

"What?"

"I *don't know*! All I know is what he tells me when it happens, when it comes over him. There's no regularity to it. We'll be talking about something, anything. Then his eyes will shift, like he's looking at something to his left or right. His left, I think. His head jerks a little, too, like he's being pulled that way. And then he says things."

"Oh, I'm sure he does."

"No, listen to me. He just blurts things out, okay? Things he's seeing." She paused for a moment to control her own pulsated intakes of air, like a foot pump filling a mattress. "The milk from the cereal bowl that morning. It dripped off the table when Jordan flipped his bowl over. It was green. Do you remember? That cereal was so gross, and it was nothing but sugar. I was just so desperate for something he liked and that he would eat."

"Lucky Charms," he said, a familiar and terrible pain cutting up through his middle, into his throat. But underneath that was something else. A flutter of unease.

"Yes. It was Lucky Charms. Well, guess what? Walter *saw* that milk. Pale green, dripping down from a table he can describe, and that we threw out years ago."

"No."

"He sees more every time. It scares me, too, believe me, but there's nothing I can do to stop it-"

"Dara, for God's sake," he said, interrupting her, but without the arrogant self-assurance coupled with disgust he'd purposely projected before. He couldn't summon that now.

"Just stop," she said, shaking her head. She was suddenly calm. Typical of her in their closest moments together, she seemed to seize on what was spreading through him, truncating his pig-headed swagger. "Stop trying to trivialize this." Her breathing was slowing, becoming normal.

"That's not what I'm doing."

"Yes, you are. Because it terrifies you, I can see it. And I'm glad you're scared, Honey. Not because I think it's funny, but because you need to understand it, too." Her breathing was fully in control now. He was shocked by it, how quickly she was regulating her emotions. He knew Dara very well, and this was new. "First things first, okay? I know I'm crazy."

"We're all crazy."

"You know what I mean. But you also know *how* I'm

crazy. I don't make things up. And I don't see things that aren't there. You know this, Alex. You, more than anyone else in the world." He was poised with another stern and rational reply but then paused, his mouth hanging open. What she was saying was true.

"Okay," was all that came out.

"Some of what he sees," she said, still chillingly calm, "are things I saw. The kitchen that morning. His toys on the floor. Just listen to me, it's been almost four years. I can talk about it without cracking up. And you need to hear it."

"I'm listening."

"When this happens, it's like Walter is behind my eyes." She turned away from him, staring into the darkness beyond the lamplight. Her breath announced itself in little clouds. "It's like...like he can see everything. How Jordan reacted. How he screamed, his red little face all scrunched up. How he spit at me. How I just...erupted." For a long moment she said nothing, as if reliving the moment, but now in some resigned, zen-like manner that was utterly unlike her. Alex's heartbeat was a slow, steady thud, like a hammer on soft wood.

"Dara, have you told him what actually happened?"

"That I pushed him? No."

"Okay," he breathed. Her assurance, at least, that she hadn't made some kind of a confession, provided comfort.

"But I don't know if he's seen it anyway. I think he might have. He sees so much. It's terrifying."

"Can I say something?"

"Of course."

"You're describing trauma. Just listen for a second. I'm not minimizing what you're saying. And you're right, it's scary. But really, Dara, this is something another person could imagine, and then put together, if they had enough information."

"I never gave him that information."

"I think it's possible you did, and you don't realize it."

"I didn't," she said, and then fixed him with a wicked look, a gleam appearing in her eyes even through the red-ness and the tears. "You and my father. The two of you always thought you had me figured out, like some puppy whose reactions you could predict. Well, you're wrong."

"That's not fair."

"Sure it is. But I'm not your wife anymore, and whether I still love you or not, I don't care anymore about what you think. And my father is dead. I know what I did that day. It was murder. And I know who I told, it was you. I never even told my father. He never asked. So don't—not for one second—tell me who I said what to, or who I shared information with."

"Yeah, well let me tell you something," he said, anger rising again in his chest. He checked it and lowered his voice. This was information that, up until now, even Dara didn't have. Only Jonah had known, because Jonah had as-sisted him. "I reviewed every single report that was gen-erated about Jordan's death. Every report, Dara. I received envelopes I had no business receiving. I broke into city offices and filing cabinets in the middle of the goddam night, all those shitty months right after. I copied things. I took things with me once or twice." He paused to let this sink in, however it might. Dara simply stared back at him, her eyes neutral. "There is nothing in those reports about the color of the milk, or how it dripped from the table. There's nothing about our son's face. If he's claiming to see things like that and you think they're accurate, it means you gave him the information. Somehow.

"And please, no more assumptions about me, okay? We've both done a lot of growing up the last few years. You're right, I've been patronizing at times. I'm sorry for that. But Dara, I'm telling you. Without realizing it, you've said things to him, things you don't remember. Things no one would remember. He's clever. Probably a professional. Maybe he's even guessed right about some details. But at the end of the day, he's recreated something already given to him, and your mind is accepting it."

"Whatever you say," she said, a faint grin lengthening those full, dark lips. After his weighty speech, his model of rational discourse—where he even threw her a bone!—this was what he was getting in return: a maddening little grin and mocking, mean-girl acquiescence.

Yeah, and you deserve it.

This, too, after all, was Dara, now up close and personal again, after pain and time had, for Alex, dispelled her into some gauzy ether. This was her sly side. Her slippery, tongue-over-the-teeth side. He felt a stirring in his crotch, foolish and monstrously out of place. He sighed and rubbed his forehead with his fingertips.

"Fine, let's say you're right. What the hell do I do with this? Do I go up to Walter and say, 'hey, so I understand you have some sixth sense, and that I need to acknowledge it, with regard to my dead son, because you've got some fucking opinion about it?' Is that what I'm supposed to do?"

"I really don't know."

"Well then what if, Dara? What if he does claim he saw you push our child? Then what? You admit it to him?"

"You know, what if I did? What if somehow that's what I *have* to do? Why is that so terrible?"

"Because you'd be giving him license to blackmail you. How do you know he's not recording you?"

"What? How? Of course, he's not!"

"I work in a business where people are recorded without their knowledge all the time. There are a thousand ways to do it and you'd never know."

"It's not like that. That's not who he is."

"You don't know who he is," Alex said. He took his voice down a notch. Around them the cemetery was cold, still and silent. "Listen, you're a wealthy woman now. I mean for real. You can't allow yourself to fall for–"

"I haven't fallen for anything," she said, lifting her chin. "And I would never—*ever*—implicate you in anything I told him. If it's yourself you're worried about, don't. You were there for me when I needed you. I would never betray that."

"I don't think you would," he said. "But we're intertwined. Our *stories* from that day are. Jonah is out of danger now. But we're not, Dara. Neither of us."

"I get that," she said. "Listen, I have no desire to spill my guts, to him or anyone else. But you can't imagine how much better I've felt in the time I've known him. He's just a good presence for me. And if he's unlocking some terrible stuff, I don't think he wants to hurt me with it."

"There's no privilege in your relationship with him. You know that, right? He's not a therapist or a rabbi. He's…I don't know what the hell he is."

"Yes. I do know that. I know I'm not as savvy as you are. I never pretended to be. But I'm not stupid either. Walter and I met before anyone knew my father was ill. He barely accepts what little I pay him. There's no reason to believe he's setting me up. Honestly, I'm not sure what he gets out of helping me, but I think it's genuine. I think he wants to make a life out of doing this kind of thing. I think he's good at it, too."

"He wants something," Alex said. His head, his heart, even his cock were all a miserable cauldron of conflicting sensations. Anger, lust, heartache, shame, nostalgia, fear. "Find out what he wants, because everything else is just conversation."

"Let yourself be scared," she said, barely above a whisper. "Just once, darling Alex. Let yourself be scared of something you can't control. It's liberating."

"Oh, I'm scared, don't worry. But it's not about whatever mumbo-jumbo this con artist has filled you up with. I'm scared of what he *wants*, Dara. You should be also."

FORTY-EIGHT

The last moments of his life as Andy Hadley began a little before 10:00 p.m., a little past full dark on the first Tuesday of August 2002. The air in his bedroom was hot and thick. He'd been sitting cross-legged on his bed, shirtless in a pair of running shorts, reading a fashion magazine swiped from the laundromat earlier that week. He heard a bump against the door and then his sister Kim burst in.

"Put these on," she said, tossing a pair of her jeans and a girl's yellow V-neck T-shirt at him. They landed in his lap. They were clothes he'd worn before, in secret except from Kim herself. He and Kim were fraternal twins, but as feminine and slight as Andy had always been, and as tomboyish as Kim was, they were basically the same size. They had also always looked alike, almost startlingly so when Andy, if his hair was long enough, fashioned it like Kim's or put a little make-up on.

"These are yours," he said, looking down at them.

"Duh. Put them on. There isn't much time."

"Time for what?"

"Andy please," Kim said. For the moment, she avoided his gaze. "Just do as I say. I'll be right back."

"But Dad's here," Andy hissed. He held the yellow shirt up. "I can't be wearing this!"

"You're leaving," Kim said, with dead evenness. "Tonight, and for good. Emily is going with you. She's at Dolly's. You'll pick her up there."

"Dolly's? But it's past ten! You didn't go get her before? You should have told me, I would have gone and–"

"Goddammit, just do what I say!" She was gone. A minute later he was in front of the mirror, in Kim's jeans and T-shirt. His hair was a little longer than normal, and he tucked it hesitantly behind his ears. If it were another inch or two longer he could easily pass as a flatter-chested version of his sister. He let his gaze linger in the mirror, snapping out of it only when he heard her coming down the hall again.

"I grabbed a few things," she said, handing him an old gym bag. "But it's not much. You can't be seen with much, or they'll ask questions."

"They? Who are 'they'?"

"There's a change of clothes in here for both of you," Kim went on, as if she hadn't heard the question, "and a few toys she won't want to part with. All that stuff, you can say was at Dolly's anyway. Everything else, you'll get on the road."

"The road? What road? Kim, what..."

"Andy listen to me," Kim said, her eyes boring into his. "You're leaving. You and Emily. Tonight."

"Kim, what the hell?"

"You are leaving," she said, punctuating each word. "Take this, too." With that, she handed over something Andy hadn't seen before. It was a fat, smudged, manila envelope, sealed with tape. Andy stared at it for a second, and then took it. It was satisfyingly weighty, and the heaviness sent a shockwave through him.

"What's in here?"

"Money and a few documents, that's all. The less you're carrying the better, but it's stuff you'll need."

"Need to do what?"

"To live as me," Kim said, her gaze unwavering. For a few seconds he could only stare back at her. "Please, just do what I say. You need to go. You need to take Emily with you."

"W-what about you?"

"I'll go soon enough. Somewhere far away. But first, you're going. Do you understand?" She drew in a sharp breath. "You're going as me."

"But I'm not you!" This was wailed as much as it was said, with a familiar and bitter, despairing resignation.

"You are now. You're Kim Hadley. And listen to me. I'm you. I'm Andy. From this moment on. Say it."

"Say what?"

"Say your name. Mine's Andy. Tell me yours."

"Kim, please."

"Not 'Kim Please.' Just Kim. Say it."

"I can't."

"Jesus Christ, of course you can." She lowered her voice to drive the point home, leaning into his space. "No one will know as long as you stay away from here, and you will."

"But...what do I do? How do I even tell Emily, let alone–?"

"Tell Emily whatever you think you need to tell her when the time is right." Kim said this patiently, as if there were some guilt in it. It was as if, despite having engineered this elaborate escape, she knew this was the one part she couldn't spell out for him.

"This is just ... wrong."

"It ain't wrong," Kim said. Andy saw tears forming in her eyes, something Kim almost never let show. She gestured around his room. "This is wrong, all of it. You're gettin out."

"But I can't just..." he trailed off, realizing his own heart was now pounding in his chest, and it wasn't all dread and foreboding. Although it would take some time to admit it to himself, there was something else going on. It was an absolute, deep-seated thrill. But then another thought occurred to him, one that sent a look of horror across his face and that Kim seemed to recognize immediately.

"I told you, I'm leaving also," she said. "Soon."

"But I don't understand. How can I be you, and...?"

"You'll be me just fine. You're more me than I ever was."

"But then what will you do? What?" Andy felt as if he might hyperventilate. His words were staccato and breathy. "You...you want me to live your life? Your life?"

"Better one of us lives it than neither of us. I'll figure out something else. Maybe as Andy, or maybe as someone else."

"Can't you just come with us?"

"Not yet. Go to Dolly's. She's got some more info for you. She'll explain when you pick up Emily."

"Explain? Explain what? Dolly never says anything!"

"Trust me. Just go."

"Kim, please," he said, now a full wail. "If we're going, come with us!"

"Uh-uh," she said, reaching for him. He clutched her and sobbed. "I can't right now. But everything will be clear to you soon, okay? Dolly knows someone. Just trust me." She breathed into his ear. "Be strong for me, sister. For Emily, too. I love you. You're going to be fine."

FORTY-NINE

The two crept downstairs, cringing with each creak of the floorboards, but no one else in the house was within earshot. Their father and his crew for the night were in between the kitchen and what was once a dining room, moving materials and product in and out. The sounds of mumbling and occasional curses floated over with the stink of the process.

They slipped out the big front door, ran across the porch and then down to the front walk. Kim led him to the gnarled oak tree in front of the house and packed the envelope into the gym bag. She nodded toward the end of the driveway, about one hundred yards from the old front porch steps.

"When you get to Dolly's she'll tell you what to do next, but you'll be on your own for a while after that. You've got some money but be very careful with it. Keep it on you or hidden." She paused and said, "When you can, email me and tell me where you are. We'll go from there."

"Kim, where will you be? Don't lie to me."

"It's Andy, goddammit, don't confuse things. I'll be here, for a little while. After that, I don't know." He was about to answer her, but she put a finger to her lips. "Go on, now. Dolly's waiting."

***

The night was sultry and moonlit. Andy felt giddy, almost like he was outside of himself as he walked down the drive toward the two-lane road that ran past their house. He couldn't imagine what Dolly was supposed to tell him or clue him in on, after a life of saying almost nothing to any of them other than things like "go to sleep" or "are you hungry?"

She was an old woman Andy and Kim had known for most of their lives simply as "the neighbor lady." She had been married once, at least they assumed, but no one had ever seen or known of a man in her life. She lived alone in a small brick house that looked diminutive and lonely on a broad, flat piece of land about a quarter of a mile from the Hadley house. The land had been farmed at one point, but now all Dolly maintained was a garden.

She wasn't motherly or even particularly friendly, but she was kind. Since Andy and Kim had been little children, Dolly's two-bedroom ranch style house had been a haven; it was a tidy, quiet place they could go and hide from one or both of their parents, or whatever madness was going on in their own home. Dolly never asked questions, even when the kids showed up hungry, bruised or worse. She never suggested, let alone threatened, to call the authorities. She just took the kids in from time to time and directed them to the TV or a board game. She provided hot, fresh food and sometimes a place to sleep. Usually that was the living room couch, or sometimes Dolly's "guest room" although neither child ever saw a guest in her home other than themselves.

By the time they were twelve and Emily was three, Kim and Andy had begun to take Emily to Dolly's, sometimes staying with her and sometimes just leaving her in the old woman's care. If Dolly felt uncomfortable about not calling authorities, or if she ever questioned her own wisdom in taking in a toddler or one or two pre-teens for hours or a night on end, she never expressed them.

His thoughts moved to Emily, and where they would sleep tonight, if not at Dolly's. And for how many nights after? And until when? Until Kim rejoined them, he supposed, but...

Panic gripped him. His guess, a correct one, about Kim's entire plan became clear in the blink of an eye. He drew a breath, turning back to call out for her, but then clamped down the urge and kept walking.

Jesus, Jesus, Jesus, what is she going to do?

He looked ahead at the road, damp and warm from the day, placid in the moonlight. He looked back toward the house. Distantly, he could hear voices. For a moment he stood frozen, then dropped the bag in a gully by the road and ran back toward the house.

He pulled the screen door open, happy it wasn't creaking, and tiptoed into the living room. Kim was standing with her back to him, talking to Lefty.

"What the fuck you wanna talk to him about?" he heard Lefty ask.

"Just get him in here," Kim said.

Andy opened his mouth to call out to her, but then shut it again. It didn't look like Lefty had seen him. In fact, Lefty seemed oddly focused on Kim, almost like he was afraid of her. A few seconds later, Andy heard his father's voice in the kitchen.

"What the fuck do you want?" he demanded as he came into view. He stood beside Lefty, both of them just behind the stained propane tank, large and squat in the center of *the kitchen. Both men were still focused only on Kim, and neither looked as if they'd seen Andy yet.*

"What's in there, anyway?" *Kim asked, pointing at the tank.*

"What?" *her father, Tom, asked, squinting at her.* "Why?"

"It's ammonium nitrate," *Lefty said. The speed of his breathing seemed to increase. Andy couldn't tell if his father was frightened or not. But Lefty was. Andy could feel it.*

"What the fuck is this?" *Tom demanded. Then his eyes flicked toward Andy. Startled, Andy took a step back.* "And why the fuck are you dressed like that again?" *Now Kim whipped her head around.*

"God fuckin' dammit, Andy! Get the fuck out of here!"

"No, you stay where you are," *Tom said, a low growl.* "What the fuck is goin' on? What kind of sick fuckin' Halloween prank are you two..." *Tom Hadley's voice trailed off as he saw the revolver in Kim's hands. A second before, Andy had seen her reach for it from the back waistband of her jeans. Now Lefty seemed to have stopped breathing altogether. His face was bulging and flushed.*

"Andy, get out!" *she yelled, but this time she didn't look behind her.* "You two fuckers stay where you are!"

"Or what?" *Tom said with an exaggerated shrug.* "No, I've had it with this shit ..." *He took a step forward, and Kim cocked the hammer back.*

"Tom, fuckin' calm down," *Lefty said. He was back to breathing again, but it was rapid and shallow.* "She's got it pointed at the tank." *He put his arm out to stop the other man from moving forward.*

"Put that goddam gun down," *Tom said, his teeth clenched. Lefty's beefy arm stayed right out in front on him like a tollbooth barrier.* "Put it down, Kimberly."

Andy stood paralyzed, less than four feet behind his twin sister, a poised, coiled thing with a pistol in her grip. Her breathing became audible, the air moving in and out of her nose as if driven by a piston. She turned and shrieked at Andy.

"RUN!"

Like he'd been shocked, he turned and bolted. The conversation, fading behind him, degraded to screaming.

"PUT IT DOWN, KIM! PUT THE FUCKING—"

Andy heard the screen door slam behind him. He jumped the porch stairs as he had thousands of times before and ran as fast as he could toward where he had left the bag. A second or two later, the outline of the trees in front of him and the field across the road lit up in garish yellow and orange. The boom was deafening. Most of the house he'd grown up in was blown to bits, along with everyone inside of it.

FIFTY

Neither Kim nor Andy really believed in God, but both believed that something beyond the borders of their world had given them Dolly. When Andy knocked softly at her door, about ten minutes after running from the mass of fire that had been his home, she answered the door in her bathrobe and horn-rimmed glasses and looked him up and down. She was short and thin, and her head seemed to sink between her shoulder blades. When she spoke, her voice was soft with a touch of a southwestern Virginia accent that turned her "r's" into "ah's."

"Andy. Are you hurt?"

"There...there was an explosion," he said. He felt numb, stupid and utterly ridiculous standing at Dolly's door in his sister's clothes. Dolly seemed to notice nothing out of the ordinary.

"I said are you hurt? Physically?"

"Ma'am? No. I'm okay." His voice sounded alien coming from his throat.

"Good," she said, nodding and glancing for a split second toward the columns of smoke that were rising from the woods where the Hadley's home had been. "Come in. Emily's asleep, but I'm about to wake her. I'll get some food in you, and then you need to get on your way."

"I don't understand what's happening," he said, a whisper. A layer of shock was still numbing the grief, but it was prying its way in with cold fingers. The idea of his house and his father gone meant nothing, but the thought of what had just happened to his sister would eventually cut through everything else—the fear, the uncertainty and the forbidden excitement beneath all of it. It was going to hurt like hell when it finally did.

"Don't try to understand it right now," Dolly said. "Focus on Emily and getting her through tonight." She sat him down at the kitchen table with a cup of hot chocolate and went to wake his sister.

***

"The name of the woman you're going to see is Rebecca Connor," Dolly said when she came back with Emily in tow a few minutes later. Emily clutched her favorite toy for the moment, a raccoon Beanie Baby with oversized eyes. She brightened when she saw Andy, but she didn't smile. Instead, she hopped into a chair at the table beside him while Dolly fixed her a snack. "She runs a shelter for women and families in Dutchtown."

"Dutchtown?"

"It's down I-81, not far from the big college. Virginia Tech."

"Okay."

"She's my sister," Dolly said, still turned away from him, spreading peanut butter on toast for Emily and cutting up apple slices. "We don't talk much anymore. But she'll help you get started down there."

"But it's a shelter? For..."

"Women and families," Dolly said, bringing Emily her plate and then a glass of milk. She said it with no change in tone, as if there was nothing to dwell on. "You'll want to leave tonight. There's a late bus that will take you to Dutchtown from Warrenton. You'll get there in the morning. Rebecca knows to look for you. I'll give you the address, though, just in case."

"Does she know...?" Andy trailed off. He had no idea what to think, let alone say, next.

"She knows what's important," Dolly said again, as if it was a mundane detail. Beside them, Emily munched happily on her toast and apple slices. Dolly turned and looked Andy squarely in the eye as she wiped her hands on a dishrag. "We don't need to talk much. You just need to get ready to go. Now are you hungry?"

"No, ma'am. Thank you."

The goodbyes were brief. Emily left Dolly with a hug as if she would see her the following day. Andy, as Dolly had suggested, said very little. Dolly shook his hand in an awkward moment, but there was something in her eyes that was searching and sad, and also looked like respect. He gave her a weak smile, then turned with Emily behind him and the bag over his arm. They never saw her again.

***

"Home's that way," Emily said as they reached the road and began walking toward the larger Route 50. "Where are we going?"

"Well, we're kind of on an adventure," Andy said. "The truth is, something happened to our house. It...well, it caught on fire, and we're probably going to live somewhere else for a while."

"Our house?" she asked, craning her neck toward that direction. "Oh! Smoke!"

"Yes, Hon. Lots of smoke."

"It caught on fire!" The word came out "fahr". "Is it okay?"

"Probably not, Honey. But we're okay. We've got everything we need, and everyone is safe."

Emily nodded, seeming to accept this with a blessed evenness. Then she asked, "Where's Kim?"

Andy opened his mouth to answer and realized he might sob. He had never felt the need to cry so much, and yet at the same time an inner command to be strong. He swallowed his emotions and waited until he had them under control before he spoke again. "Kim will come for us when she can, okay? But we may not see her for a while."

"How long?"

"I'm not sure, Em."

"Does she know where we're going?" She was still craning her neck to look back at the house, but they were about to round a bend in the road, and the column of smoke was disappearing.

"She does, Honey. She planned this for us. So we need to be brave, okay? She sent us on adventure. Remember when we saw An American Tail on TV?"

"Yeah," Emily said.

"Well, that's kind of like us. Kim is okay. We'll see her soon."

"What about Dad?"

"I'm not sure about Dad," Andy said. "But he knows we're on an adventure, too. We just have to be brave. It'll be fun, too, though. I promise." All of this seemed to swirl around Emily's over-sized head. Andy tried to watch how it was happening, but Emily's thoughts were a mystery. Finally, it seemed to settle through her.

"Okay," she said.

They reached the larger and busier Route 50 and turned east. Andy was careful to keep Emily on the side away from the cars and stayed off the highway a few feet so they were less exposed to the headlights. Andy had no idea what the response would be to the explosion at his family's house, but he knew there would be one. In a way, that was good. Pretty much every cop and firefighter within miles would likely be dispatched to it. Still, the last thing he wanted was to attract attention, a teenager and a child, homeless for all intents and purposes, walking down the road alone in the moonlight. It's an adventure indeed, Andy thought ruefully, a tiny, humorless smile crossing his lips. Kim hadn't lied about that.

And then the next thought—deep, clear, and as terrifying as it was hopeful.

I am Kim now.

The familiar lights of the Shell gas station and the 7-11 next to it came into view. The person who had been Andy Hadley tightened her grip on her little sister's hand and smiled down on her.

"How's the adventure so far?" she asked. Emily looked up and shrugged, sucking on the ear of the Beanie Baby.

"What are we gonna do now?" she asked, muffled by the toy.

"We're gonna call a taxi cab. And a nice man is gonna take us to a bus station a few miles away." Emily, who had never been in a cab or on a bus other than for school, just nodded. "Then, we're gonna take a bus ride, but you'll probably fall asleep. In the morning we'll be in a new town, and there's a nice lady there who's gonna help us."

"Like Dolly?" Emily asked, perking up.

"Yes," the new Kim Hadley said, almost choking on the word. Once again, she swallowed the emotion rising through her. "Yes, Honey. Like Dolly."

FIFTY-ONE

7:30 p.m.

The text had been from Angie.

Call me later. It's important, but it can wait. About the DNA. Writing up a supplement now.

Alex had seen it earlier, around six, just before meeting Dara at Jordan's grave. Now walking through Union Station in Washington on the way to catch his train back to New York, he pulled up the text again. The last sentence jumped out at him.

Writing up a supplement now.

A detective's supplement. That meant there was something she needed to document, and in a full and formal way. That was a little odd, and he wished he had read it closer earlier. He hit the button for Angie's number, and she answered almost immediately.

"Alex, what's up?"

"You tell me. Something about the DNA?"

"Yeah, there's something we learned. Listen, are you sitting down?" He paused and pulled the phone away from his ear, giving it an odd look as if she could see him doing it.

"No. But whatever it is, I don't think it'll shock me."

"No offense, Hon, but you're the second man that's said that today and ended up being wrong about it."

FIFTY-TWO

10:12 p.m.

Around the time he was passing Trenton on Amtrak, Alex received an email from Angie with a draft of her supplemental DD-5 on the Dunaway case. His mind was already aching from the drama of the day. He had been greeted by dozens of former acquaintances at the memorial service and Dara's house. They were men and women who had been at his and Dara's wedding as well as Jordan's *bris*, and still looked at him with pained smiles, as if they were greeting a terminally ill person and trying to remain cheerful. The cryptic talk with Walter had utterly freaked him out, as had Dara's explanation of it. His last words to her, that they needed to be scared of whatever Walter Lynch wanted, at first felt deeply satisfying to say, as if he was regaining control.

Well that's your role with her, always the grown-up, because someone has to be.

Oh bullshit, another side of him argued. *What you've really always enjoyed was having the last word, and guess what? She saw right through it.*

Now on top of everything happening with Dara and the surreal sting of losing Jonah, was this bombshell in his professional life—the consequences and "now what?" of Kim's revelation, staring down on him like a jury in judgment. If nothing else, there could be a question about why Kim's DNA hadn't been pulled prior to the regular testing. He had asked Kim once about getting a DNA exemplar from both her and Emily but hadn't yet followed up. He had thought about it the day of grand jury, but then the defense attorney, Jack Hooper, had called, and it had gone out of his head again. It was as simple as Angie taking buccal swabs from the two of them and dropping them in bags, but it hadn't happened. He doubted anyone would assume he had avoided gathering them on purpose. There was still plenty of time, and it was common for known exemplars to follow evidence for weeks or more. But Jack might suggest something sinister.

Aside from that, he had a great deal more work to do. Angie's supplement mentioned the same reports Alex already had in his files and had considered. They concerned the 2002 police and fire investigation around the deaths of Tom and Andy Hadley, and the biker "cook," Lefty, who had worked with Tom. Those old facts weren't ones Alex wanted to deal with, and they weren't supposed to have much relevance to his case. But without a doubt, he would have to deal with the efforts—certainly illegal—the former Andrew Hadley had used to live as his late sister, even back then. From what Angie knew, Andrew had used Kim's birth certificate at least, possibly her social security card, and had applied for a new driver's license once the real Kim's original one expired, sometime in 2009 or 2010. All of this, from the stunning fact of who Kim actually was to the most banal detail of a document she might have passed at some point in her life for a benefit for herself or Emily, was "exculpatory evidence," meaning facts that would have to be turned over to the defense.

Jack Hooper was going to have a field day, of course. But the anticipation of Jack's glee, for Alex, was nothing compared to the apoplectic reaction he knew he was going to get from Gerry Ramos. And what about the people above Ramos, in the mayor's office? God knew. It had been a long day, but the following day, Friday, was going to make it look like a cakewalk.

He had purposely put off calling Nikki, not because he didn't want to talk to her, but because, however oddly, he wanted to be prepared to do so. It shouldn't have been that way. They were in a romantic relationship, not a therapeutic one. But sometimes he felt better thinking about talking to her before he did so. He had long since become comfortable with that. Finally, as the last of the dark and desolate Trenton streets slipped from view, he called her.

"Hey you," she said. "Where are you?"

"Trenton. It's lovely."

"Always is. How's the train?"

"Wobbly. I'll be home in an hour and a half."

"How was today?"

"Not good."

"Wanna talk about it?"

"Later. I've got something else going on." With that, he told her what he had learned, and Nikki listened in silence.

"How do you feel about it?" she asked as Alex's train lumbered away from the stop after Trenton, a sterile, suburban office area called Metro Park. The train was emptying out, the last tired-looking passengers mostly bound for Penn Station New York. Outside there was an inky blackness slowly giving way to the orange glow which would mark the approach to the city. Alex sighed.

"I'm not sure how to feel."

"Nothing would be inappropriate."

"I'm not angry. Not at her, anyway."

"I think that's a good thing."

"I actually feel...almost like it makes sense. It's not like I had a clue. I didn't. But it feels, I don't know. *Complete*, somehow."

"Like a puzzle with a piece that was missing," she said.

"Yes. Like that." He loved her for many things, not the least of which was how she could distill his thoughts so concisely.

"Angie seems to have handled it well, at least."

"She did. She didn't make any promises or predictions about what would happen next, either. But she was supportive. She reassured her. That's key. If she had flipped out, Kim probably would have shut down."

"Ah, so you think there's still a case," Nikki said. The train rushed through the momentary glow of the Secaucus rail station, then back into the blackness of the Meadowlands. The skyline rose in the distance, getting closer. He would lose her soon, in the tunnel.

"It won't be up to just me. But I think I could salvage it. Maybe."

"Do you believe in it?" she asked.

"I do, yes."

"Do you believe in her?"

"Yes."

"When can you talk to her? My guess is she's feeling pretty awful about keeping this from you."

"I'll text her now," Alex said. His watch read 10:00 p.m.

"I'll see if she can come in tomorrow. I can't talk to her by phone, though, not until everything is clear between us. I'll have enough to write up and turn over to this guy's attorney as it is."

"Well, I doubt she's asleep," Nikki said. "And my guess is she'll want to talk to you as soon as possible. Call me later, or just come over. I'll be up for a while."

FIFTY-THREE

Friday, December 15

"Oh, dear God," was all Alex's boss Gerry Ramos could seem to say. He muttered it three or four times while Alex stood before his desk. As usual, Shelly was seated on the couch a few feet away. "Dear God, Alex. What have you done? What have we done?" It was seven forty-five the next morning. He was scheduled to meet with Kim that day, but first he had to deal with Gerry, whom Alex had texted the night before, saying he had an important topic to discuss first thing. Gerry was an early riser.

"We indicted a case," Alex said. "If I'm allowed to, I'll see it through."

"You indicted an attempted rape case," Gerry said, almost barking the word *rape*. "This is New York State, and rape here still involves *both* a penis and a vagina. And Hadley...Hadley is a fucking *man*? It's..." Gerry sputtered, looking for the word, "impossibility!"

"It's factual impossibility," Alex said, slowly and at low volume. "Not legal impossibility."

"Not legal impossibility?"

"No. Her actual gender doesn't invalidate–"

"Her," Gerry said, lifting his hands. Alex continued as if he hadn't been interrupted.

"-Dunaway's intent. Dunaway believed Hadley was physically female. He believed that about Hadley when he attempted the rape." He flicked his eyes toward Shelly and then back. In his periphery a few seconds later, he saw Shelly nod.

"He's right, Gerry," she said. Her voice also seemed controlled as if she, too, was afraid of setting off whatever powder keg was inside of their boss. "There's no legal defense to the indictment." Gerry opened his mouth as if to fire off a reply, then shut it again. He reached for the blue New York Penal Law Guide ever-present on his desk, flipped through a few pages, and turned his chair away from them. When he turned back around, he looked calmer, but no less distressed.

"You're right," he said, looking first to Shelly and then, reluctantly, to Alex. "There's no legal defense." Now he focused his bright, lamp-like eyes on Alex. "But there's nothing left. Nothing. There's nothing Dunaway will plead to and there's nothing we can prove."

"I don't believe that," Alex said. He remained arrow-straight, his back once again aching with stress and damp with sweat. He checked his breathing. *Calm.* He was ready for this. He had been up the entire night thinking about every angle.

"Hooper warned you about this," Gerry said. "He knew something was wrong, maybe not this, but he knew something was up. And he was right. This will humiliate the office. All of us. You, too. But it's a crusade, isn't it? Your crusade. That's why you're still all in. I've got half a mind to think you suspected something like this all along."

"That's not fair," Alex said with continued evenness. "There's nothing about Hadley that would indicate she wasn't female. No one suspected anything. Not Angie, not Danny, not Judy, not me."

"No one who met the victim suspected anything like that, Gerry," Shelly said. "Apparently, she does hormone therapy, but she was passing as female long before that. From what Alex has uncovered, she's always been, well, in the wrong body. It happens."

Gerry frowned and shook his head.

"Has there been a sex change? Like an operation?"

"No," Alex said. "Hormonal treatment is all she does, like Shelly said."

"Legally?" he asked, as if seizing on something.

"As far as I know, yes. But I'm looking into it."

"Nightmare," Gerry said, almost a whisper. "That's what this is."

"It's a case, Gerry, that's all. It's one I think I can win. There wasn't much press coverage about the case at first, but it's been building. Several other women have come forward on social media and in a few other places, pointing fingers at the same guy for similar conduct. He's facing more legal trouble, possibly even criminal charges depending on when it happened and who the women talk to. Time isn't on his side in terms of influencing a potential jury pool, or whether he'll want to testify. He's vulnerable. He might even be willing to plea to something."

"What's Hadley want?" Gerry asked. "Did you talk her to about a possible plea? Before this, I mean. Right now, I'm not sure he'd plea to spitting on the sidewalk."

"She's not concerned with a specific outcome. She

wants justice, that's all. More than anything she wants to be the last person he does this to. Ultimately, she had the guts to come forward. She deserves her day in court for that."

"Justice for what? A lie? One she's been telling for sixteen some-odd years?

"The only lie she's ever told was in response to a desperate situation where she felt she had no choice. That's a lie I can explain. I was up all night thinking this through. Believe me, I know it's a problem. But it's not insurmountable."

"Even if you can, she allowed us to proceed with a completely different understanding about a key characteristic of who she was. Christ, Alex, she's not even a *she*."

"So? She didn't lie about her gender. She wasn't asked."

"She withheld information."

"But it's not relevant information. She's not obligated to tell me or anyone else every private thing about how she lives her life or presents herself. Think about it."

"We're talking about gender!" Gerry thundered, slapping his desk with his fist. "We're talking about the core of who this person is!"

"The core of who she is as an individual? I don't think so. Gender isn't what it used to be, Gerry."

"Ah there it is," he said, turning to Shelly and flashing a sarcastic, over-sized smile. "Alex Greco, the crusader, here to reinvent the law and drag us all into some tolerant new age." Alex considered replying to this but thought better of it. At this point, whatever Gerry's opinion of him was, it was set in stone. He was either going to allow the case to go forward or not, and now even that decision was complicated by the fact that there was a live indictment out there. The office could still move to have it dismissed, but that was rare, and a public admission of failure, even incompetence. Gerry shook his head a few more times, then gave Alex a resigned look. "You know what? Fine. Run with this thing. I won't dump the indictment. I'd like to say you'll own the verdict, but that's not how it works. We'll all own it."

"I know it seems hopeless," Alex said. "But this has touched a nerve with a lot of people. Dunaway is making the news, like I said. More and more people believe he's a predator."

"Yeah the news," Gerry said, lightly pointing a finger in Alex's direction. "That's where you see yourself going, isn't it? A few more cases like this and you'll be yucking it up on the tube with Chris Cuomo or Anderson Cooper. Never mind what you leave behind here."

"If you knew anything about me, you'd know that's the very last thing I'd ever want. My concern right now is this case, and her welfare."

"You see?" Gerry said. "There it is again. *Her.*" Then he glanced over at Shelly, as if he had been, or was about to be, caught saying something decidedly un-PC. Shelly's eyebrows were raised, but she said nothing.

"She identifies as–" Alex started.

"Yeah I get that," Gerry said. "And you know what? That's fine with me. I'm not anti-transgender, and I won't be labeled that way. But you're going into a court of law. *Law.* So now that you've got your way, let me give you some advice, Alex. You need to start thinking about these pronouns. You can use them all you want with Hadley, but you need to get her ready for reality. I guarantee the defense team will be all over this, demanding *she* be referred to as *he*, in court, in front of your jury." He paused and rubbed the stubble on his chin. "What's her real name anyway?"

"She was born Andrew Ray Hadley," Alex said. "But Kim is her name. And I'll fight for that, too."

FIFTY-FOUR

3:00 p.m.

As Kim Hadley sat clutching her small black purse in Alex's office, her eyes cast downward, an expression of Nikki's came back to him, something she had said long ago in a conversation about a client she was working with who had been sexually assaulted. *We're embarrassed for what we do, but we're ashamed for what we are.* Shame was the emotion coming off of Kim in waves. It was palpable in Alex's office, and he hated it, but knew no way of ameliorating it.

"I can't say I understand what you're going through," he said. "But please understand I support you. Okay? I support your case. My office supports it. I found out for sure this morning."

"My sister Emily," Kim said. She looked up at him, her eyes red and swollen. "Could she be taken away from me?"

"What?"

"She's all I have. She's all I care about. And...*fuck*...I should have thought more about her before doing this." Alex was taken aback, only because he had never heard Kim curse.

"I'm not a family law expert, but I don't know why someone would."

"I'm about to be a publicly exposed freak," she said, looking away. A single tear escaped her right eye. "I've been hearing things, like someone could go to court, try to have a guardian appointed on her behalf."

"Was a guardian ever appointed for her as a disabled adult? Here, in New York?" Kim shook her head and squeezed her eyes shut.

"No. I got guardianship when we were in Virginia, but she was a child then."

"And it's worked out, hasn't it? She's happy and safe with you. Listen, like I said, this isn't my area. But I know someone." He pictured Dale Friedlander and smiled to himself. "Someone who can put your mind at ease, I think."

"I don't deserve that," she breathed. He handed her the tissue box and she wiped her eyes. "I don't deserve another second of your time. I didn't come here hoping you'd still prosecute this case. I came because I knew I owed you an apology in person. I'm sorry, Alex. I'm so...very sorry."

"Let's talk about that." He shifted in his chair and leaned forward. He kept his voice measured, but now raised it, just enough to where it was apparent. "What are you sorry for?" She seemed surprised by the new tone of voice, which was what he wanted.

"What?"

"What are you sorry for, Kim? Escaping an abusive environment? Working your ass off to make something out of nothing? Building a comfortable, secure life for you and your sister and raising her on your own?"

"Well...no, not that stuff."

"Then what? Are you sorry you were targeted by a rich psychopath who beat you? Who tried to rape you?"

"Of course not," she said, meeting his eyes fully for the

first time that morning. "But I'm sorry I didn't tell you the full truth about what I was. I'm sorry for that." He could see it now, a steely edge creeping into her expression, freezing her mouth in place. She was tough, probably a hell of a lot tougher than he could appreciate. He needed that toughness now.

"You're not a 'what.' You're a 'who.' Why did you owe me that anyway?"

"For God's sake, it wasn't fair, not telling you everything. You know it wasn't fair."

"Ah, fair." He lowered his voice again. "Let's talk about that, too. What's fair? The body you were born into? What happened to Emily? Was any of that fair?"

"No," she said. "It wasn't."

"Exactly. Neither is this city, or how you made it here. Forget fair, Kim. The fact is, there were questions maybe I didn't think to ask. That's not unfair to me."

"I don't see how you could have anticipated..." she made a gesture down her body with her hands "...this."

"Yeah, well, that's a compliment to you, isn't it?"

"I still wish I had told you."

"So now I know. And this case isn't over, unless you want it to be." She seemed to ponder this.

"Okay. So, what now?"

"We tell each other the truth," he said. "I think you've done that so far. Except about one thing."

"You mean my past," she said quietly. "And who really died in my house that night, other than my father and Lefty."

"Personally, I don't give a damn. I've tried to make that clear. What matters to me is what happened to you back in September. Not what happened some terrible night when you were a kid. But I need to be able to account for anything you lied about, whether it was then or more recently." She sighed.

"I don't know what it's worth, but I'm being honest when I say I've never felt like I was lying about who I was, and who she was—my sister Kim I mean—even before that night. I think Kim wanted to get it into my head, the idea that I would live as her eventually. She wanted me to believe it. I know that sounds crazy, but it's true. We felt like each other. All of our lives. Toward the end, we tried to make it official, at least between ourselves."

"I think I can make sense of that to a jury," he said. He paused for a moment. "So, Kim never made it out of the house that night. You went on from there as her."

"That's right," she said, and now Alex saw her lower lip tremble. "She didn't. I'm not sure how much else you want to know."

"Nothing more," he said, and meant it. "What you've told me matches up with the investigation. Your statements to me, today, account for the identity issue. We don't need to push it any further."

"I know you have obligations," Kim said. "Ethical ones. You seem like you take them seriously, and I respect that."

"I do," he said. "And I'm meeting them. I have no further reason to press you about a fifteen-year-old event. We can agree on that, okay?"

"Okay."

"So, let's get back to the present, and what this case is about. Are you ready to tell me everything? Now that I'm finally informed enough to ask?"

"Yes. Of course."

"Are you ready for some really tough questions? About your body, I mean? Your sex life even?"

"I haven't had a sex life," she said with a shrug. "Not a consensual one, anyway. My genitalia were never fully developed. I know more about it now than I used to, but it was always obvious. I don't have much of a libido, either. It's just not a part of me. But of course, you can ask me anything."

"Anything I don't ask, you better bet the other side will find a way to. Are you ready for that?"

"I am."

"The media attention this case has already received. You know that might jump, right?"

"I assume so, yeah."

"I can almost guarantee it. Chances are, Dunaway has a media expert on his team. They'll leak stuff. They make sure things get around." At this, Kim just shrugged.

"I think there was a part of me that always knew this might happen," she said. "Maybe a little part that almost wanted it to."

"What about your business? Your brand, whatever? Can you deal with that fallout? I don't know anything about what you do, but I want to be sure you've thought things through."

"Other than my sister, my business is all I think about. Will it be hurt by this? I really don't know, but I've got money put away for Emily already and I'm willing to chance it. Anyway, we both know it's too late. You could drop everything today, there's going to be news about what the DNA revealed. That's on me for not knowing how it worked."

"Probably true, but the buzz will go way up if the trial is still going forward." At this, Kim just shrugged.

"I'm in if you are. The only thing I care about more is my sister."

"I never promise anything, but I think your sister will be just fine. And like I said, I've got a lawyer for you if anyone threatens you with trying to take Emily. But I don't think that will happen. You've talked to her about the case, right? About what to expect?"

"Yes. She's..." Kim trailed off, her little face breaking into a grin for the first time in days. "She's actually really okay with it all."

"Good. That helps. What's your schedule like today? Can you stick around for a while? Is she okay?"

"Yeah, she's fine, I'll call her to tell her where I am. She's got everything she needs."

"Do you want coffee? We're going to be here a while."

"Your coffee kind of sucks," she said, grinning for the second time. "Can we go the Starbucks on the corner?"

"We can," he said, standing to grab his suit jacket. He waited until they made eye contact again. "Thanks for being willing to continue this with me." She waved him off.

"You're welcome. But you know I caused a shitstorm, Alex."

"No. Kevin Dunaway caused a shitstorm. Now you and I are going to give it right back to him."

FIFTY-FIVE

9:30 p.m.

"Hey, Kiddo," Kim whispered. She had just walked in the door after spending the afternoon and some of the evening with Alex Greco, and it felt like she had been gutted out like a melon. Emily was asleep on her chair, an empty bowl of soup and an open package of crackers beside her. There was a stray noodle on Emily's plaid shirt, and Kim picked it off. Emily opened her eyes and frowned.

"Where you been?"

"With the lawyer, Honey. I told you, remember? That's why you had your soup without me." Emily raised her eyebrows, then looked over at the empty bowl. Recognition seemed to fill her eyes.

"Oh, yeah. Are things okay?"

"Yeah. Can I talk to you for a minute?"

"Is it bad?"

"No. I'm gonna make a drink first. You want something?"

"That sounds bad," Emily said. Then she brightened. "Orange soda."

"I think we're out. How about orange juice?"

"Sure."

"So, you know the case I'm involved in, right?" Kim asked, settling in on the couch next to her. "The court case?" Emily blinked and nodded.

"That guy. Who hit you."

"Yep. He tried to hurt me, too, Em. Sexually. You know what I mean?"

"He wanted to fuck? And you said 'no'?"

"That's right. So, he got really mean. Men do that sometimes. It's terrible."

"Fuckers," she said, looking away.

"Well, it's okay now. But the thing is, since I told the police, you know we're going to court about it."

"Yeah."

"So, some stuff is going to come out about me. Some private stuff. And some stuff about when we were younger. Does that make sense?"

"Why?"

"The newspapers pay attention to court cases sometimes," Kim said. "And people online do too. So, my name might come out in a newspaper."

"Your name's already out," she said. "Lots of people know who you are."

"I know, but that's my business, Honey. This would be different. Some people might say mean things."

"They better not."

"Doesn't matter," Kim said. "But listen. Here's what I have to tell you. And I should have told you a long, long time ago." Emily scooted up in her chair, her face suddenly anxious.

"Are you leaving?"

"Emily, no! Of course, I'm not leaving. I'll always be with you. Just listen. Do you remember our brother? Our brother Andy?" Emily went quiet for a long moment. Her eyes seemed far away.

"You mean when there were two of you?"

"Yes, when there were two of us. One of us was Andy. One of us was Kim."

"I don't really remember both of you together," she said. She had calmed, but Kim could tell she was still distressed. "Did something happen?"

"One of us died, Emily. I told you that, remember? It was a long time ago. When our house blew up."

"The fire," Emily said, almost as if she was dreaming it.

"Yes. The fire."

"Well, there's just us now."

"That's right, there's just us. But the thing is, I...well, I used to be called Andy." At this, Emily's face scrunched up in confusion.

"You were called Andy?"

"I was," Kim said. "The truth is, I was born a boy. In some ways, I still am a boy. But I've been Kim to you, pretty much as long as we've been on our own. I live like a woman does. People do that sometimes. Does that make sense at all?"

"Fuck, I don't know," she said, squinting as if she was fighting off a headache. Kim suppressed a grin.

"It's okay, Em. I know it's confusing."

"Do you want to be Andy again?"

"No, Hon. I'm Kim now. It's who I was supposed to be. But there was another Kim once. She really, really loved you, too."

"You're the only Kim I know."

"I know. And I'm sorry for that, just because the other Kim was pretty great. But you've got me. Forever."

"Well, do you like being Kim?"

"I do. I love being Kim." She reached out and patted Emily's arm. Emily looked at her arm, then up at Kim.

"So, who cares who you were before?"

FIFTY-SIX

Monday, December 18

There was a small, free newspaper called NYC-GO that guys handed out at the entrance to subway stations. At the Brooklyn Bridge/City Hall Station just south of the court buildings, Alex grabbed one and winced at the headline:

FINANCIER SEX CASE IS DAVID VS. GOLIATH (AND YES, WE MEAN DAVID!)

Below it was the same photo of Kim he had seen before online, apparently taken unawares as she walked down the street on her phone. The shot of Kevin was one taken at a court appearance, but he couldn't remember which. In it, Kevin looked calm and defiant.

He stuffed the newspaper into his computer bag and pulled out the heavy manila envelope he had prepared for Jack Hooper, who was there to meet him a little after 8:30 that morning. Jack was on a park bench, on his phone and turned away from the cold as a bitter wind swept south down Centre Street. Jack clicked off as Alex approached, his eyes going to the envelope.

"What's that, your novel?"

"It's discovery. A lot of it. You're entitled to it."

"What the hell? Why isn't that a motion to dismiss?" A flap of Jack's overcoat whipped against his face, as if the coat, too, felt agitated.

"We're not dismissing the indictment. I spent the weekend writing up everything I found out about last week. You know everything I know, and we still have a case to try."

"You're kidding."

"I don't kid much, Jack. You might say it's not in my DNA."

"Oh, that's rich. Dude, this is crazy."

"Take it." Around them, commuters and delivery guys scurried across the station grounds and through City Hall Park, looking for shelter. The wind had a knife's edge.

"What you were doing before was foolish," Jack said, stuffing the envelope into a supple leather briefcase. "This? This is reckless. I'm not sure it's ethical."

"Don't go there. I just wrote up forty-five pages for you to chew on. We'll be in court again after New Year's. Be ready."

"Have you seen that little rag they give out at the train? The headline?"

"Yeah, just now."

"Well, that's just the beginning."

"So, you're telling me your media team is spreading this stuff around?"

"It's organic," Jack said, stressing the word as if it had some independent majesty. "I haven't had to do anything. It's all over the place."

"It was the independent accusations against your

client that made this a press case. Remember that."

"Yeah, and Hadley being transgender is going to kill it. You want to push this? Fine. It's my job to go after people like Hadley in court. I don't always enjoy it. But you know what? This time, I will."

FIFTY-SEVEN

5:07 p.m.

"He tried to be a mentalist," Dale said. He and Alex were at the bar in another steakhouse in midtown, downstairs from Dale's law office. *The Christmas Waltz*, by Doris Day, accompanied by tinkling bells, crooned from hidden speakers around the room. The bar had an old-school feel to it. Just after five, Alex and Dale had the place mostly to themselves. "He washed out, but that's what he was doing for a while in Atlantic City."

"What the hell is a mentalist?"

"You've never seen one? They do mind-reading tricks. They guess which hand the coin is in, stuff like that." Dale paused and sipped his old fashioned. "I saw one in Vegas once. He was damn good."

"So, it's a trick?" Alex asked. He gulped down the rest of the bourbon in his glass, and Dale motioned for another. The bartender seemed to know him. "It didn't feel that way. I don't want to sound crazy, but he freaked me out."

"There are tricks," Dale said. "What Lynch does? I just don't know. All I can tell you is that's what he was trying to do for a while. He worked on a show. There's a guy he was associated with, Kenny Luxe. Probably not his real name. He still does a show at a smaller hotel, but he moves around."

"So, Walter was on stage with this guy?"

"Yeah, but not regularly. Like an apprentice or something. He never got his own show, I know that."

"Wizard's apprentice," Alex said, shaking his head. "Jesus, I swear, I don't believe in any of this shit."

"I don't either, but what you're telling me would freak me out, too."

"But he didn't make it, right? As a mentalist, I mean?"

"No, but the guy I talked to says that's not unusual. Even when they have talent, or whatever. The competition is tough."

"So maybe he thinks he has some gift. Or maybe he does." Alex ran his fingers through his hair. "I can't believe I'm telling you this."

"I've heard worse."

"Dara believes it. And you know what? That scares me. After all the years I patronized her, for all the times I treated her like a child? She's smarter than I am. I think half the time that's *why* I treated her the way I did. The point is, her problems are complex, but she's not gullible. She doesn't fall for this kind of thing."

"But you don't think there's any other way Lynch would know the things he knows?"

"Not the details. No. I just don't see how."

"I don't know," Dale said. He put his glass down on the bar and clasped his hands together. "But I think there's a way you can understand this without buying into magic. Like you said, maybe it's lucky guesses based on a few nicely picked facts. And remember, it builds on itself. I don't know much about fortune-telling, but I know they watch your reactions. It's a 'getting warmer, getting colder' thing. A lot of smart and sane people get fooled by it."

"So maybe that's it," Alex replied, even though it didn't feel that way at all. "Thanks for getting me the info."

"That's exactly what I'm here for." He paused for a second. "Dara hasn't revealed anything damaging to him, right?"

"No," Alex said. "But I'm afraid she will. He's got this angle, I can see it. Something about freeing her. Freeing *us.*"

"With some kind of acknowledgement of what happened that day." Dale said. It wasn't a question. "This is a privileged conversation, by the way."

"I know," Alex said, emptying his glass. "Thank you. And yes, it's something he thinks we did, or didn't do. At least that's the feeling I'm getting. I won't burden you with all of it. But if he is seeking to get Dara to make some penance, then why? Just for her sake? I mean, maybe that *is* what it's about. Maybe I am too goddamn cynical."

"Not for my taste," Dale said, frowning.

"I hate the idea of giving him some kind of power over her. Over us."

"I don't blame you. Look, we'll talk again. As long as Dara is being cautious, I think you're okay for now. What are you doing for Christmas?"

"My girlfriend and I are going to Aruba on the twenty-sixth," Alex said. "Thank God. What about you? It's still Hanukkah, right?"

"Yeah, but my wife and daughters love a Christmas tree," he said, grinning. "I'm glad you're getting out of town for a few days, Alex. I can tell you need it. Merry Christmas."

FIFTY-EIGHT

6:15 p.m.

"But that's hopeful, isn't it?" Dara asked. Alex had called her after leaving Dale at the steakhouse and was now walking up Fifth Avenue. Above him it was adorned with banners, huge wreaths and Christmas lights.

"I'm not sure what it is," Alex said. Around him were families with small children out and about. The kids were laughing and pointing excitedly at the decorations and various items in the storefronts. His heart ached watching them. There was a reason he avoided places like this where families tended to congregate, like Central Park or midtown at Christmastime.

"Well, it sounds like he's got some kind of a gift. You've got to admit it would explain some things. How did you find out?"

"There's a lawyer I talked to. A guy who worked for your father." He had no intention of lying to Dara, and Dale had not encouraged him to.

"Of course, there is," she said, sighing. "I'd ask who, but I probably don't know him. There's so many of them. Anyway, I know my father had Walter checked up on. If there was something bad, I would have heard about it a while back."

"I'm not hiding anything from you, either. But I'm involved here, too. That's why I looked into it."

"I know, I'm not blaming you. So, what do you think?"

"I don't believe in magic."

"You don't believe in anything," she said. "I'm not sure either, but I'm hopeful, okay? For the first time in a while. Please don't take that away from me."

"Hopeful for what, though?"

"I don't know yet. Clarity, maybe. Some sense of peace. I think he can give me that."

"And I'd love for you to have that," he said. "But you know what my concerns are."

"Of course, I do. And I told you, I'm being careful. No full-on confessions, so don't worry. We're taking a break for the holidays anyway. He thinks I need some time after Dad's death."

"Whatever Walt says," Alex said.

"Ugh, whatever." He could tell she was about to change the subject. "What are you doing for Christmas?"

"Nikki and I are going to Aruba, through New Year's."

"That's great, Alex. I'm glad." She sounded like she meant it. "I might go away, after I get things settled. Speaking of that, you'll probably have some money coming your way. You know that, right?"

"I don't want his money, Dara."

"Life's just so unfair, isn't it? Merry Christmas, Darling."

FIFTY-NINE

Sunday, December 24

The Christmas tree Emily had picked out around the corner from their apartment was now alive with lights and ornaments, a few of which Emily had made herself over the years, and some that were crafted from small sample bottles in Kim's product line. The TV was on, and she and Kim were wrapping each other's presents, a tradition they had started years before. It seemed silly to wrap things Kim had bought for both of them and that they were just going to tear open the following morning, but it had become a ritual, and Emily loved rituals.

Kim hadn't looked at her computer since the previous evening, but her biggest fear, that her sales would take a hit, had been utterly unfounded. If anything, it seemed like she had gotten a bump since the eighteenth, even more so than the final Christmas shopping rush. She recalled a mentor years before who had said there was no such thing as bad publicity in the beauty industry, as long as your product wasn't tested on animals, found to cause cancer or have spider eggs in it. Most of the business contacts she had spoken with in the last few days acted like nothing was different. "Hi, Kim, it's so-and-so," the voice-mails would start, like always. The emails were all the same. The language was vague, things like "really proud of you" or "you go, girl," but it was nonetheless comforting.

There was another side to it though, and she was learning to train herself to take the rush of publicity in small doses. Judy Levin, the victim-witness person from the DA's office, had given her some good suggestions. *'You might be the focus of some arguments online,'* she had said. *'Try to tune them out, because they have nothing to do with you even though it seems that way. Even people who claim to be on your side will distort things. It'll drive you crazy if you try to internalize it.'*

That was an understatement. Overnight, it seemed, she had been at once adopted and rejected by the online transgender community, or at least a segment of it. The disparagers were people who thought she was being disingenuous and even harmful to the trans community by simply passing as female in order to get ahead in business. In a way, Kim understood those reactions. She had never really identified as transgender and hadn't planned to until the moment it was forced on her. The other side praised her, evoking her name as a revolutionary or some boundary-breaking hero. Then there were the trolls who just said horrible things to say horrible things.

She deserved what she got, leading a man on.

She's a monster, why are we talking about this circus side show?

Hey, "Kim," let's see how much face cream you sell now that we know you have a dick!

You are going to HELL. REPENT!

The worst comments, usually responses to an online

piece or a social media post, were no surprise. Kim had known cruelty, up close and personal, for much of her childhood. But now there was a threatening dynamic associated with seeing that kind of thing on the internet, especially from strangers. She would reel with shock at some venomous comment next to the photo of someone who looked normal. Then she'd be buoyed by someone responding to it in her defense. On balance, she was more supported than not, but the whole thing was a little dizzying. She tried to remember Judy's advice, and stopped herself when she started to read a lengthy thread on Twitter.

"Phone," Emily called out, breaking the word into two syllables. She pointed to it on the coffee table. Kim was about to ignore it but glanced over anyway and froze when saw the name on the screen.

"Megan?" she asked, scurrying up to take the call. Emily seemed un-phased by it and continued her messy wrapping job.

"Hi, Kim," Megan said. "I'm sorry I haven't reached out in a while."

"No, I understand," Kim said, nearly stammering. Her heart was pounding. "I really don't know what to say." Of all the people in her world, even Emily, Megan seemed the hardest to approach after the news came out. Kim hadn't called her. They didn't talk much on the phone anyway. She had just sent out a text on the nineteenth telling Megan she hoped they could talk. There had been no answer until now.

"I brought something for Emily," Megan said. "Is it okay if I come up for a moment?"

SIXTY

The soft bundle Megan brought for Emily was neatly wrapped and tied with a big bow. Emily tore through the wrapping and grinned wide when she saw what was inside. It was a plush, pink bathrobe, large enough to swallow Emily in.

"Shit, this is awesome," Emily said. The bathrobe had a hood also, and Emily slipped it over her head. "Kim, look!"

"It's lovely," Kim said. "Em, say thank you."

"Thanks, Megan."

"Merry Christmas, Emily," Megan said. "I'm glad you like it."

"It's cool yeah," she said, reaching backward for the cloth belt. "I'm gonna look in a mirror." With that she walked off toward her bedroom.

"That robe was not cheap," Kim said, giving Megan an admonishing look. Megan just smiled.

"It's okay. I was hoping she would like it. I've seen her point them out on TV."

"It's a beautiful gift, and yes, she'll love it." Kim paused for a second. "How did you find it in her size?"

"I looked around. Listen, can we talk, just for a minute? I've got a train to catch."

"Of course," Kim said, interrupting her lightly. "There's a Christmas movie she wants to watch. I'll start it for her in her bedroom."

"Just need to pee," Megan said, pressing her knees together. "It was a long walk here."

"Oh, no worries. Go in my room, Emily's bathroom is a mess. I'll meet you in the living room."

***

"I don't know what to say," Kim said, emotion rising through her. They sat close together in the living room, two glasses of wine in front of them. The hurt of not hearing from Megan for six days had been more than she was prepared for. But in addition to that, she felt guilty. She felt like she had betrayed a friend. "I should have told you."

"I'm not mad you didn't tell me. I'm hurt because you didn't think you could, I guess. I just feel like I don't know you. Like I never did."

"You do know me. You just didn't know one big thing, although I guess it's so big it kind of changes everything."

"It's just...I became friends with a woman," Megan said. "There's a difference, or at least I thought there was. But if you feel like a woman, then it doesn't matter. I'm sorry, Kim. It just freaked me out. I should have reached out before now."

"It's okay. I'm the one who should be sorry. Look, I've lived this way a long time, and almost always on my own. My body is, well, it's hard to explain. The parts of me still there that don't fit are like an old injury or something I don't think about anymore. So, I don't tell people about them. They don't notice, so I just go on the way I am."

"I get that," Megan said. "I just hope you feel like you could have told me, eventually."

"A part of me really wanted to. It's just...I was just loving having a friend, Megan. That's all. I never had a real friend before you."

"It's been nice for me, too," Megan said. "Really nice."

"I know it sounds empty now, but you can ask me anything. Really."

"It's just such a mystery to me," Megan said. She seemed genuinely perplexed. "It seems like it would be a lot of work. But you're so...natural. I mean it, Kim."

"Thank you. I've always been feminine looking. I'm not entirely natural, though. I've never had surgery, but I do hormone therapy."

"Is that with the doctor?" Megan asked. "The one you told me about?"

"Yes," Kim said. "She's not a physician though. She can't prescribe, but she knows how to help me get the drugs I need."

"Are they legal? It sounds a little scary, I hope you're careful."

"They're mostly legal, yeah. There's a lot of DIY hormone therapy going on out there. Evelyn knows her stuff, but ultimately, the responsibility is on me. I should find an endocrinologist, but it's tough to do that with any privacy. I guess it doesn't matter now."

"I'm glad you have Evelyn," Megan said. "I'm a little jealous. I guess she knows you better than me." She put her hand on Kim's, and Kim squeezed it.

"Evelyn knows more than anyone else," she said. "But you know about the most important things. You know about my dreams, and the things that scare me. You've gotten to know Emily. This physical part of me? I know it's important. It's everything, I guess, to most people. But I'm just me."

"I'm glad you feel that way," Megan said. She turned away and then looked back. Her face looked pained, but something there seemed different to Kim. She seemed conflicted, but not miserable, the way Kim was. Kim supposed she deserved that. "I'm glad we talked. But listen, I know you've heard me say it, but I'm worried. Protect yourself, please."

"What?"

"I *do* know you pretty well, and you're great. But the world doesn't know you, Kim. Instead it's making up things about you, and you could get hurt over them. It doesn't matter if people think good things or bad."

"That was always a possibility, though. I didn't want to be exposed this way, but I have been. And I'm dealing with it."

"So deal with it privately." She put a deep stress on "privately." "Focus on your business, that's what matters. You need to retreat. Don't you see that?"

"Retreat how?"

"Drop this stupid court case and go back to your life, for starters. You've got a good life, you know that? You don't need a public trial stomping on it."

"I'll be all right. Business is still good. Things haven't changed that much."

"It's only been a week." The brown and green eyes, so pretty, bore into hers. "The holidays are making everything seem less serious. But wait until January, when your case starts up again. That's when they'll crush you. It's a system, I've told you before. They'll protect each other. They'll use you in the process. That DA you like so much? He's as much a part of it as any of them."

"I don't think he is."

Megan seemed poised to say something else, but then her eyes softened. "Look, I'm sorry. I shouldn't be saying these things to you on Christmas Eve. Go be with Emily. I've got to get going anyway."

"Will I see you after the holidays?"

"Of course," Megan said. "I'm taking a couple of weeks off after New Year's, but I'll be back mid-January."

"Will you see your family tonight I hope?"

"I'm headed down there now," she said. "On a smelly train packed with whiny kids I'm sure. Merry Christmas, Kim."

SIXTY-ONE

Wednesday, January 10, 2018
3:30 p.m.

Bill Petrazzo, Jack Hooper's senior investigator, had thought about approaching Emily for weeks. Initially, Jack had been against it. It didn't seem like Emily had much to offer, and she would just complain to Kim who would in turn piss in Alex Greco's ear over it. But the fact was, she was in her twenties and clearly got out on her own. They had a right to reach out to her, and now, with the case pretty much in tatters for the government anyway, they had less to worry about regardless.

It was also easy. Emily regularly walked from Kim's apartment over to Bryant Park, a rectangular space in midtown that also contained the main branch of the New York Public Library. Jack's law office was on Broadway, which ran diagonally just west of the park, and only a few blocks down. Bill knew she took the route from her home to the park three or four times a week unless it was raining or snowing. Cold weather didn't seem to bother Emily, but then again she was dressed for it. There were no stylish, sleek overcoats for her like the kind her sister Kim Hadley favored. She wore a wool New York Jets hat, clamped down over her hair, gloves, and a bulky, down ski jacket. She looked a little like the Michelin Man in it, stomping up the avenue with a stupid, determined look on her face.

At 3:30 p.m. on that Wednesday, Jack spotted her exactly where he expected her to be. She was behind the library near the northwest corner of the park, along a concrete walkway where tables and chairs were set up in better weather. Today she was just perched on a bench, munching on a pretzel.

"Hi...Emily?" he said as he approached her. Bill wasn't an avuncular looking guy and he didn't try to be. Rather than smiling or trying to appear overly friendly, he took an approach of honest concern instead.

"Yeah?" she asked him, looking up and squinting into the weak sunlight. Bill was thin and of average height, although his slimness made him appear taller. He was dressed lightly for the cold in slacks and a waist-length black jacket.

"Do you remember me?"

"Uh-uh."

"Oh, well that's okay. I know your sister, Kim. I'm here about her, actually." She stopped nibbling on her pretzel while it was still in her mouth.

"About Kim?"

"Yes," Bill said. "I have some questions about her. Truth is, I'm trying to help her out with something."

"Help her out with what?"

"There's a court case coming up. You know that, right?"

"Yeah, so?"

"Well, my boss and I are working on that case, too. We're trying to make sure everyone has all the information they need, for Kim's sake. It's up to you, but...do you mind talking to us?" Bill waited, holding his breath. It was quite likely the big woman in front of him was going to give him the finger or start yelling, or just walk away. But instead, Emily looked both ways, and then back at Bill.

"Where? Here?"

"Actually, it's pretty cold out here. My boss and I work just down that way. Do you mind walking with me? It's a nice office. We can talk there. It won't take long at all."

"Can I get another pretzel?"

"Sure," Bill said. This was happening more easily than he anticipated. "C'mon, we'll grab one on the way."

SIXTY-TWO

Kim expected Emily back by 3:30 or 4:00 p.m. It wasn't exactly freezing outside, but it was still January, and it would be dark early. At 4:00 p.m., she sent Emily a text. At 4:15 p.m., she called. The call went to voicemail, which for Emily was just the automated recording with her phone number. Kim wasn't worried, yet. Emily could be flaky with her phone. Kim made sure it was charged every night, but sometimes Emily would stuff it into a coat pocket, especially in wintertime, and just forget it was there.

At 4:30 p.m., Kim called again with the same result. She had a tracker on Emily's phone, so she pulled it up to get her location. She figured Emily was probably on her way home from the park by now, hopefully somewhere on Lexington Avenue or Third. But the tracker was showing her phone on Broadway, around Thirty-Seventh Street. Kim squinted at the little blue indicator. That location wasn't the other side of town, but it wasn't on the way home, either. And Emily was a creature of habit. She almost always went up Third, with the traffic as if that was something a pedestrian should do, and down Lexington, also with the traffic. Kim went to Google and pulled up a photo of the location. It looked like an office building.

Why the hell would her sister be at an office building in midtown Manhattan without her? She called one more time, followed with a text that just said, *Em where are you?* Then she looked for her keys and overcoat.

SIXTY-THREE

Jack's receptionist treated Emily with kindness, taking her coat and hat, and offering her something to drink. Emily chose a coke. The can was now sitting in front of her, at the head of a large conference table. Jack, in a blue suit and red tie, was seated a few feet away, with Bill Petrazzo just one chair down. Jack studied Emily closely, trying not to be obvious about it. He really had no idea what to expect from her, but Bill had told him she'd been cooperative so far.

"Emily, this is my boss, Jack Hooper," Bill said. "He's the one who has the questions. Do you feel okay talking to us for a few minutes?"

"I guess."

"Hi, Emily," Jack said brightly. Unlike Bill, he did try to seem friendly. It was unclear if Emily cared.

"Hi."

"Well, we'll get started," Jack said. "Emily, this device records what we're saying. You can listen to it later if you want to. We just have it on so we don't miss anything. Is that okay?"

"I guess so. This is about Kim, right?"

"Well, it's really about you," Jack said. "I very much appreciate you coming to speak with us, Emily."

"He said it was about Kim," Emily said, her eyes narrowing on Jack. They flicked over to Petrazzo. "Does Kim know I'm here?"

"She doesn't have to know," Jack said. "Emily, you're a grown woman. You're here to tell us what you know about Kim, if you're willing to do that. It's important, or I wouldn't ask."

"Important to who?"

"To the court, Emily. You know there's a trial coming up, right?"

"Yeah."

"Well, both sides in this trial—I mean both of the lawyers—have a right to know what the witnesses might say in court. You're here because you know things about a witness. That person is the one you live with." He paused and slowed his speech, making sure he had eye contact. "The person who calls herself Kim."

"She is Kim."

"Actually, she's not, Emily. We know that for sure now. Look, I don't know how Kim explained things to you. Or even if she did." He looked down and paused, as if his task was now to relate some terrible sadness. Then his blue eyes shot back to hers. "But we know that Kim is not who she's been saying she is. Kim is a man, Emily. She has male body parts. She's been posing, living as a woman. For years, she's lied to you about it. Almost all of your life." At this, Emily stared back impassively, still as a statue. He waited for a few seconds. Then a few more. "Do you understand, Emily, what it is I'm telling you?"

"Yeah," Emily said in an almost dreamy fashion. Then she shook her head. "But Kim isn't a man." She drew out the word "man," so it was almost two syllables. There was a slightly bemused look on her scarred, round face.

"She is," Jack said, a bit more forcefully, as if the dimwit in front of him needed to have the fact drilled into her head before it dawned on her. "The person you live with is not Kim, and you deserve to know that. It's really your bother, Andy."

"I ain't got a brother. I've got a sister. That's Kim."

"I wish I could tell you that was true," Jack said. "But it's all been a lie. You could be angry about that, too. It would be okay." With this, Jack sat back and smoothed his tie, once more taking on the air of a man who has just performed a solemn, if heart-breaking, duty.

"So, you're sayin' she's got a dick," Emily said, matter-of-factly. Jack opened his mouth to speak, then shut it again.

"She...has a penis, yes," he said finally. Emily grinned widely.

"Penis, sure! Cock! Prick! Pecker! Tube-steak!" The words, fired out of Emily's mouth in rising volume, silenced Jack, who now stared wide-eyed back at her.

"Emily, this is serious," he said. A part of his mind was wondering if this was how you were supposed to talk to crazy people. It seemed like he had seen it on TV, somewhere: stay calm. Don't change your tone. Continue to stress the idea of how it all Must Be Taken Seriously. "Yes, you're correct. Kim has male body parts, and a penis is one of them. But really, the bigger point is that–"

"It's a tiny, one, though, right? Her penis, I mean. Probably a nub is all. There was a black guy I met up here once. In the park. Now he had one big..."

"Emily, please," Jack said, wishing he had some water nearby. "We don't have to talk that way." His throat was now bone dry. He glanced over at Petrazzo, as if questioning how this woman could even be competent enough to testify. Bill just shrugged.

"Okay," Emily said, nodding and pursing her lips, like a farmer acknowledging a bad outlook for winter weather. "So, Kim doesn't have a hole down there. That's what you're sayin'."

"You mean a vagina," Jack said, just above a whisper. He had never, ever so desperately wished to be elsewhere in his entire legal career. Whatever the fuck this was going to accomplish, it wasn't worth it.

"Yeah. A pussy. Kim ain't got one."

"No," he said, with a sigh. It was getting harder and harder to stay composed in front of this fat freak. Plus, it was all being recorded, and God forbid a jury ever heard it. He was going to end this, and soon. "She doesn't have female body parts. This is what I mean, Emily. Kim lied to you."

"Kim ain't never once lied to me," she said, spat really; her eyes narrowed to a glare. She was looking at Jack as if he was a roach she was taking aim at with a shoe.

"She did, Emily. She lied about being a woman." He sat up straight in his chair. As far as he was concerned, the interview was over. He just hoped she wasn't about to leap over the table at him. But the anger in Emily's eyes had disappeared, as quickly as it had emerged. Far from threatening, she suddenly looked oddly composed and wise, like an old woman relating an aphorism.

"Havin' a hole down there ain't what makes Kim a woman," she said. "It's bein' pretty. And strong. And takin' care of me. That's what makes Kim a woman." For a moment, both Jack and Bill just stared at her. Shame, an emotion that hadn't plagued Jack Hooper in some time, was now burning within him in a way he was positive was visible.

"You can go now, Ms. Hadley," he said. "Thank you for coming in to speak with us. Someone will get your coat for you."

"There's one more thing, though," she said, rising to leave, her voice quiet.

"What is it?" he asked, an exasperated tone just below the tenor of his voice. Emily, he would swear later, actually looked at the recording device, as if she knew she was speaking into posterity, before she shifted her eyes to him and answered.

"My sister Kim's more a woman than you are a man, you cocksucker."

SIXTY-FOUR

Kim's heart was pounding as she reached the address where Emily's phone indicated she was. The blue dot hadn't moved at all. It still showed her at that location, somewhere. She scanned the ground floor, but the only retail shops were a florist and a Dry Bar salon, and it wasn't likely that her sister would be in either place. There was a McDonalds on the next corner, and she darted over there to search the crowd. Still no Emily.

It was as she was crossing the street again at Thirty-Seventh, going south on Broadway, that Kim finally saw her, zipping her coat up with her gloves in her mouth. She was right in front of the main entrance to the building where Kim had been just moments before, a massive steel and glass structure with a cavernous main lobby. Kim had no idea why Emily was where she was, but she was obviously fine and there was no need to make a scene. She thought briefly of playing it off, acting like she had been out walking around and—oh wow, there's Emily! But Emily wasn't always so easily fooled. Emily, Kim noticed, still hadn't seen her. Instead she was turned toward someone else, a gaunt looking older man with gray hair who looked like a cop. He was standing a few feet away from her on the sidewalk.

"Tell your boss I took a shit in his bathroom," Emily called out as she pulled the gloves on. The cop-looking guy seemed surprised to see her there but did not reply. Then, he saw Kim approaching and froze.

Kim also froze, but not because of the cop-looking guy. What stopped her was the sight of a young woman standing next to the guy, a woman who looked like she wanted to disappear behind him. The two were maybe ten feet beyond Emily on the sidewalk, maybe twenty feet from Kim. The woman was tall and beautiful, immaculately dressed and made up, with long, flowing light-brown hair. She shivered in the cold, without a coat on.

It was Megan.

"You told me she was gone, Bill," Megan said as Kim drew closer. She said it to the cop-looking guy, but her eyes were on Kim.

"She was supposed to be gone," Bill said. "I guess she made a pitstop first." For a few seconds there was silence, which Emily finally broke when she saw Kim approach.

"Kim, what're you doing here?"

"I was looking for you," Kim said, forcing calm into her voice and smiling. Then the smile disappeared as she addressed the man, the one Megan called Bill.

"What was my sister doing here?"

"You'd have to ask her."

"Megan," Kim said, looking at her. Her voice rose on the second syllable, as if she was pleading. "What the hell is this?" Megan stared back at her, eyes wide. Her mouth opened and closed a few times, but nothing came out.

"You should go, Ms. Hadley," Bill said finally. The tone he infused it with was authoritarian, pure police. "We're done here."

"Who is 'we?'" Kim said, snapping back to him. "Who do you work for?"

"Ms. Hadley is your sister a functioning adult or not?" he asked.

"What?"

"You heard me. Can she make decisions for herself or not? If she can, then you need to ask her why she volunteered to come here. If she can't, then maybe someone needs to check on what kind of care she's getting."

"Bill, please," Megan said to him. She turned to Kim, who felt like she'd been punched. "Kim, please go. Get Emily out of here."

"Why are you here?" Kim asked. Her eyes were brimming with tears. "Tell me that, at least."

"I tried to warn you. It's their system."

"But Megan, why?"

"Kim?" Emily asked. Kim heard the uncertainty in her voice.

"Coming, Em," she said, still staring at Megan. Megan stared back, dry-eyed but now stone-faced and defeated looking.

"She has nothing to say to you," Bill said. "I told you, you need to leave."

"She was a guest in my home," Kim said, keeping her voice tightly controlled. "She acted like a friend. If she's not, I have a right to know."

"That's right," Bill Petrazzo said. He walked a couple of feet toward Kim and lowered his voice. His eyes, cold as stones, bore into hers. "She was an invited guest. So think about the things she saw, the way you live your life. The illegal drugs you take. Think about it, and walk away. Walk away from all of it, Kim Hadley. Don't be stupid."

"You won't get away with this," Kim said. She could feel Emily's presence next to her, brimming with anxiety. She had to stay calm and strong for her, if nothing else. "Neither will Kevin Dunaway."

SIXTY-FIVE

5:43 p.m.

"I'm so sorry, Kim," Judy said, lightly rubbing her back. They were sitting in the chairs in front of Alex's desk. Kim had, Alex noted, kept it together very well through most of the description of the afternoon. But the betrayal she was feeling about Megan seemed to have pushed her over the edge emotionally. Now she couldn't stop crying.

"I'm sorry," Kim said. "God, I've got to stop this."

"Not right now you don't," Judy said. "I've been doing this a long time. I can tell when someone really needs to get it out. It's okay, you're safe here."

"Thank you. I'm not usually so dramatic and here I am sobbing like an idiot."

"You've been holding all of this in for a while," Judy said, her voice soothing and steady. "All of it, I can tell. Just relax and let go, okay? We're not going anywhere." Kim nodded, broke into another round of light sobs, and grabbed a handful of tissues. Judy glanced up at Alex, who mouthed 'thank you.' He was grateful to her for staying late. Kim had called a little before five explaining what happened at

Hooper's law office. Alex could have scheduled a morning meeting but didn't want to wait.

More than that, he was grateful to Judy for knowing how to respond to the level of emotion Kim was finally letting go of. Alex was good with victims, women and children especially, but he wouldn't have understood Kim's reaction the way Judy did. And of course, she was right. It wasn't just the loss of this "friend," Megan, or the sick feeling of being duped that Kim was reacting to. It was, in general, having to hold herself together throughout this entire nightmare. She'd been groped and beaten and then she'd been thrown into public scrutiny, exposed as something she'd hidden for half of her life. Now she had to accept that the only real friend she'd ever known was probably a plant from Kevin Dunaway's defense team. Through all of this, she had a company to run and a disabled sister to stay strong and cheerful for. At last, she had reached a breaking point.

Slowly, though, she steadied. Her face went back to its usual poised, pleasant affect. But she looked exhausted, and it was more than the tear tracks and dark circles under her eyes.

"Can I get you something?" Alex asked.

"No, thank you. I feel a lot better." She looked over at Judy. "Thank you very much."

"Of course," Judy said. Then to Alex, "Can they get away with this?"

"Probably," Alex said with a tired shrug. "It's low, but I don't think it's illegal."

"The drugs he mentioned," Kim said. "The hormones. They're all legal, I'm pretty sure. But some require a prescription. I never got one."

"Did he mention any of the drugs by name?" Alex asked.

"No. Just that he knew about them."

"Did you keep them in a medicine cabinet? I'm sure she had access to your bathroom, right?"

"She did, but that's not where I kept them. I think Megan knew where to look. I told her where I keep things. I have a vanity in my bedroom. She would have known they were in there."

"Did you notice any missing?"

"No, never. I guess she could have taken photos, though. I don't know."

"Okay," Alex said, as if reassuring himself. "Okay. The healthcare person you mentioned. Evelyn Robinson. I know she's not a M.D. Did she procure anything for you?"

"No," Kim said. "She advised me, that's all. Most of what I use, I found online."

"Give me a list of the things you take," Alex said. "I'll look into it. I think we're fine, Kim, really. But I'll look into it."

"I don't want to get Evelyn in trouble. Whatever else I've ruined, that can't happen."

"If she wasn't prescribing, she's done nothing wrong," Alex said. "Nothing else is ruined. Let me deal with it. I'm sorry. I really am."

"I'm the one who should be sorry."

"You couldn't have known," Judy said.

"Maybe, but I can see it now. I really should have sensed something. I don't think she's completely heartless, either. I think she saw me as a job, but I think a part of her really did believe I was better off letting this case go. I imagine that's what she told herself, anyway."

"How's Emily?" Judy asked.

"She's fine. She doesn't really understand it. Everyone other than us, people in our lives, they've always kind of come and gone. Megan's just the next one I guess."

"Did Emily tell you what she told them?" Alex asked. "This guy and Jack Hooper?"

"Not really. She told me she just fucked with them. Sorry to be blunt, that's exactly what she said."

"Maybe she did," Judy said. "Good for her."

"I'll probably never know for sure," Kim said. "Emily describes things vaguely sometimes. She can be a little lazy that way. It's like she remembers what happened, but just doesn't feel like it's important enough to tell it to me in detail. Anyway, there's nothing she could tell them that would be damaging. I'm not sure what they thought they'd get out of her."

"I can ask one of our investigators to look into Megan Heatherton," Alex said. "I can't really go after her for trying to take advantage of you, although I wish I could."

"I didn't expect that," Kim said. "I'd rather just move on anyway. But thank you both."

"Well, if you hear from her again, let me know. Especially if she threatens you or demands anything."

"I wish I knew more about her. She said she was from New Jersey. She talked about growing up there."

"Did she say where?" he asked, scribbling it down.

"Hammonton. She said there isn't much there, but it's on the way to Atlantic City." He wrote down the name of the town, and then Atlantic City. Then he paused and stared down at the words on the paper. He stared at them long enough that eventually Judy called his name.

"Alex? Everything ok?"

"Yeah," he said, snapping back to the present. "Sorry, I got distracted for a second."

SIXTY-SIX

8:30 p.m.

Dara's phone went straight to voicemail again, and Alex cursed it. It was hard enough getting through the last moments of his meeting with Kim and Judy without looking like he was panicking, and now she wasn't picking up. He was typing out another text to her when she finally called back.

"What is it?"

"Where are you?"

"At the house, why?"

"Is Walter there?" Alex knew 'the house' meant the guest house, a tiny but comfortable cottage on the grounds of the home Dara grew up in. Dara had lived there since she and Alex split up after Jordan's death.

"Walter? No, he had class tonight."

"Is that where he is? Class?"

"It's, well, what? Almost nine? Probably not. He's probably at home. What's this about?"

"Dara, we need to talk. I need you to tell me when you first met Walter, and how."

"What? I told you how we met. It was a networking event in Old Town."

"Right. When? Do you remember?"

"Exactly? I don't know, a few months ago."

"It is in your phone? The event, I mean." He knew Dara kept a meticulous calendar.

"Um, maybe. Hang on, I have to look at the phone." There was a short pause, and Alex counted the seconds. "October fourth. It was a Wednesday." His heart sank.

"Okay. Listen to me. Did he approach you? Or the other way around?"

"Did he what? It's not like that. We're not dating."

"I know, that's not the issue. Please, do you remember? Did he talk to you first?"

"You know me, I'm pretty shy at those things. So yeah, he probably was the one who spoke to me first. But I don't remember exactly. What is this?"

"Dara, I have to tell you this. I can't be sure, but I have a bad feeling."

"About what?" Her voice seemed to go flat, like whatever energy was projecting it had fizzled out.

"I think Walter was sent by someone. To get to know you. I think he has an agenda."

"What? That's crazy!" Her voice was animated again, as if the scary thing quieting it before was obviously a figment of Alex's imagination.

"It's crazy, but I think it's true. Please listen." With that, he explained it to her as best he could, the basics of the case and Kevin Dunaway, what had happened to Kim and the timing of it all. He hated the way it was coming out of him, like some kind of conspiracy theory, not to mention one focused entirely on him. But when he finished, Dara said nothing. She didn't launch into an immediate denial. She didn't accuse him of being jealous, or crazy, or just plain mean. Instead she was silent for so long Alex was afraid she might have set the phone down and walked away.

"Did my father suspect this?" she asked finally. "D-Did you both know?"

"No. Your father didn't trust him, but he didn't know this. I didn't either. I still don't know for sure."

"Oh God, Alex. I can't. Really, I can't." The last word, 'can't,' was a gasp, swallowed in tears.

"Can't what?" There was more silence on the other end, then weeping. It sounded miserable and hopeless, and it was dreadfully familiar to him. "Dara, can't what? Can't believe it? Listen, I don't know for sure either, but…"

"No!" she said, shocking him into pulling the phone from his ear. She was wailing. "No, I *can* believe it, it's… *fuck*! Alex, why are you doing this to me!?"

"Believe me, I don't want this to be true."

"He's all I had," she said, between sobs. "Walter, what he sees, however it works. It was all the hope I had. Don't you understand that?"

"I don't…I don't know what you mean."

"He told me I could *reach* him, Alex. Jordan. He told me I could apologize. For real. He could *see* it, how it would be."

"Dara, no." A dark, deep chill cut through him. "He can't do that."

"He does something, though. You felt it, too, don't lie."

"I'm not lying. He scared me, yes. It could be he can sense some things, I don't know."

"So then why wouldn't he be able to help me reach our son?"

"I don't think he has that ability. I think he's telling you that so you'll say things to him."

"But why would he…" She trailed off, racked with sobs.

"Ultimately I think he wants to blackmail me. I think that's what he was sent to do, through you. I'm sorry Dara. I wish I was wrong." More silence.

"You're not wrong," she said finally, a whimper. "Things have happened."

"What things?"

"Guys. Calling him. Wanting money he owed them. He pretended it was something else, like a bill collection agency. But I could tell they weren't those kind of debts."

"Did you ever know who was calling?"

"No. But I answered his phone once when he was in the shower. There was a guy on the other end. Some guy with an accent. He asked me where Walter was, but it was aggressive, like in a threatening way. I panicked and said he wasn't there. He asked if I had fifty-thousand dollars. I said 'no,' and he said I couldn't help him, and that he'd call back. That was it, he hung up."

"Did you ever talk to Walter about it?"

"No," she said. "I guess I didn't want to believe it, or I didn't think it mattered. I mean, no one has a perfect life."

"Yeah, but if he owes people that kind of money, I think it's an indication."

"Of what? He's some kind of scam artist?" She sounded utterly defeated.

"Something like that, yes. I'm sorry."

"I didn't tell him anything about us, I told you that."

"And I'm grateful for–"

"But I wanted to. Not about you, just about me. I was trying to figure out how I could do it, but I didn't think it would work if I lied."

"What did he want you to say, Dara?"

"He told me he saw a shadow," she said, barely a

whisper. "He said he saw a shadow over Jordan's grave. He said he could take it away, and Jordan would know. He told me I could free myself if I apologized to him. He told me Jordan would hear it."

"Did he want you to tell him about that morning?" She made a 'tsk' sound at this.

"Of course, he did. Ultimately, he said that's what I had to do. He said it would cleanse me. No more guilt. No more torturing myself. And he told me Jordan would know. That he would feel it."

"Okay," Alex said. He sighed and rubbed his forehead with his free hand. "Okay."

"I didn't do it, because I couldn't figure out how to do it without talking about both of us and putting you at risk. I couldn't do that to you. You're doing good things. You still have a life that matters."

"So do you."

"No. I don't. You should know by now I don't care about my life. Walter could record me saying whatever horrible things he wanted and go straight to the police and I could be in jail forever. I wouldn't care if he could do what he promised." She blew her nose. "But I couldn't do that to you."

"Thank you."

"Just once, Alex, I wanted to know I could reach him. And now I don't know what to do."

"Let me help you," he said. "I'll be there in three days." Jonah's larger memorial service was Sunday afternoon, and he and Nikki were leaving on Saturday to stay with Pete's family overnight. "In the meantime, there's no reason to confront him."

"We talk every day, though. I could hear from him tonight."

"Ignore it, or act like nothing's wrong. You've got an excuse to be busy with the service coming up."

"It'll be weird if I don't ask him to go."

"Well, if you think it's best to ask him, ask him. But either way, I'll be there, okay? We'll talk this out."

"Will you bring Nikki this time?"

"Yes, she'll come with me."

"That's good, I'm glad you won't be alone."

"I'll be there for you, too. Nikki understands that. Listen, I'm coming to help you with this. It's happening because of me, and I'm coming to help you."

"No, Alex, it's not. Everything that's happening, everything that's happened. It's not because of you. It's because of me." She hung up and he stared at the phone. Part of him was relieved Dara wasn't completely rejecting his theory. It hurt, but he could tell she was taking it seriously. He hated how she sounded though, particularly the last thing she had said. It was the enervated voice again, the exhausted, almost dead-sounding one.

SIXTY-SEVEN

9:30 p.m.

His next call was to Dale, who thankfully picked up on the second ring.

"Alex? Everything okay?" Alex could hear a television in the background and a young girl's laughter fading into the distance.

"I'm sorry it's late, I hope I'm not interrupting."

"You're not. My wife just left to put my younger one down. After that we watch *The Bachelorette*, but it's recorded anyway."

The kind of life I might have had, Alex thought with a bitter stab of regret. "Thanks, I'll be quick. The information you got on Walter Lynch. Do you have someone who can dig deeper?"

"Of course. But it might take a few days."

"Can you ask him to get started?"

"It's a 'she,' actually."

"Really?"

"Yep. Retired state trooper. She's a stand-up lady with ethics like the Pope, but she knows how to poke around. Did you hear something?"

"I think I figured out what Walter Lynch wants. There's this case I'm working on. I'm prosecuting a man for an attempted rape."

"The venture capital guy, I know," Dale said. "Looks like a schmuck."

"Yeah, him. He's got big bucks, and I think Walter's on his payroll."

"Jesus, you think his defense team put this guy on you? On Dara?"

"I'm not positive, but the timing makes sense. That and a few other things."

"Okay. What do you need?"

"Just information. I have a feeling Lynch got into some trouble in Atlantic City, with whatever skills he has, or convinces people he has. From what Dara says, he owes people money, and I don't mean a bank loan. If he's running from something or hoping to make money to pay off other debts, it would help to have the intel."

"I'm on it," Dale said. "You're going down there for the memorial service, right?"

"Yeah, I'll head down Saturday."

"Weather is supposed to get ugly, so be careful. I'll let you know as soon as I hear something."

SIXTY-EIGHT

Saturday, January 13

The snowstorm predicted for the Washington D.C. area on Sunday rolled in early. It bore down on the I-95 corridor Saturday afternoon, turning Alex and Nikki's trip from the typical four-hour drive to something closer to seven. Thankfully she was easy to travel with and had an over-abundance of patience with traffic. She read over some reports and fiddled with the radio while they inched toward his hometown. There was plenty of time to talk, so she was also up to speed on what was going on.

Even with Nikki present and supportive, his nerves were frayed. It had been a busy week at work, with two other sentencing hearings and a new child homicide case to review. He had reached out to Dara once more on Thursday and twice the previous day but hadn't heard back from her. It was odd, especially under the circumstances.

"She might be withdrawing a little bit," Nikki said as he set the phone back in the Jeep's cup-holder after getting her voicemail again. "If she's trying to stay out of reach from Walter, she probably just finds it easier to shut out everyone."

"I guess. It's just not like her."

"I know you've been through a lot together. But this would be new territory for almost anyone." He nodded and eased the car onto the expressway that would take them past the Jefferson Memorial and over the bridge to Virginia. It was already dark at six, and sleet slashed the windshield in icy spatters.

***

"This is all Jonah," Pete said. They had just finished dinner and he and Alex were now out on the front porch, Pete with a cigar and Alex with a cigarette. The sleet had turned to snow, and the normally active neighborhood was still and silent as the yards and houses were gently coated white.

"What is?"

"The storm. It's Jonah's way of saying 'enough already, give it a rest, I'm gone.'" Alex smiled. Through the living room window, he could see Nikki with Pete's wife Samantha, polishing off another bottle of wine and talking like old friends. Sam and Pete had a ten-year-old boy, Hunter, and an eight-year-old girl, Devyn. They were sweet and loving kids, and from time to time one of them would come up from their playroom and interrupt the conversation. Alex felt another strange twinge of regret, imagining the life he might have had in a house like his brother's. The feeling was cut short, by the sight of Nikki still in the picture; that was his real life. He was lucky, and he needed to remember that.

"You're probably right. He'll still get a hell of a crowd tomorrow."

"Yeah, this'll taper off by then," Pete said, taking a pull

from a healthy glass of Jameson. He and Alex didn't look much alike as Alex inherited their mother's refined looks and Pete had their father's more rough, rounded ones. He had a beard and mustache, a barrel chest and a generous beer gut. "Where the hell is Dara, anyway? Anybody know?"

"Dara?" Alex had just begun to unwind, and now tensed up again. "At her mother's I guess. You know, the guest house."

"No, she's been staying at her old man's place, down by the water. The police department is sending an honor guard to the service, and a buddy of mine is on it. You remember Rich Swain?" Alex nodded. "Anyway, he's been trying to get ahold of Dara since yesterday about some detail. He tried her mother, but she hasn't heard from her either."

"Not yesterday or today?" Alex asked. "Really?"

"Not since Thursday from what I understand. I told Rich I'd see you tonight and ask if you spoke to her."

"We talked Wednesday night, but not since then."

"I'm sure there's someone else Rich can ask," Pete said. "But it's kind of Dara's thing, you know? The details and all."

"I'll try her again tomorrow morning. Nikki thinks she might be withdrawing or something. Let's get inside. It's cold out here."

SIXTY-NINE

Sunday, January 14
10:00 a.m.

"How are you, Alex?" Lois greeted when she picked up the phone. On the other end, Alex was a little surprised that his phone number was still recognizable to Dara's mother. He supposed it was probably programmed into her home phone at this point. The kind that announced who was calling when it rang. He and Lois had never been close but got along well enough.

"I'm okay, Lois, thanks. I'm looking for Dara, actually."

"You and everyone else. Are you in town?"

"I am. I got here last night."

"Oooh, in that storm?"

"It's okay, I made it." Lois, like Dara, had a tendency to focus on the mundane just when he was trying to get to the bottom of something. "Have you heard from Dara at all today?"

"No, not since Friday morning. The woman at the synagogue had some questions about the service, and she called here looking for her. We texted about it, and Dara said she'd call her back. You know I don't want to be involved, Alex."

"Of course. I understand."

"He was my husband, but still. It's no place for me."

"I completely understand."

"He loved you, though."

"Well, he wasn't married to me," Alex said. "Or vice-ver-sa." With this, Lois let out a clipped but hearty laugh.

"You're a pisser. I guess he was, too."

"So ... Dara's not at the guest house?"

"She's been staying at her father's, off and on. She's got things to go through there. His closets. You know."

"Yeah sure. Listen, does she seem okay to you? She's been a little absent the last few days. I mean, we've been talking more recently, since Jonah died."

"Eh, you know how she is. She's been sleeping a lot, kind of sluggish. But it's that time of year." Lois said this as if it was a particularly salient point. "You know how she hates the winter."

"I remember. Okay, I'll see if I can find her."

***

By the time the service began at 3:00 p.m., Alex still hadn't heard anything from Dara. The synagogue was one of the largest ones in the city, along a wide street that also ran past the hospital. He and Nikki had waited in a long line of cars to get into the parking lot. Inside, Alex found a staff member to ask if Dara had responded regarding the final details. To his relief, she had, and everything was set. But they hadn't seen her either.

Alex guided Nikki to the standing area in the back, hoping to interact as little as possible with anyone in the crowd, many of whom he'd known all of his life. There had been a few quick handshakes and awkward smiles, but so far they had been able to keep mostly to themselves. He noticed his brother, sister-in-law and the kids seated with a big group of police, firefighters and their families. Most local politicians were present. There were more lawyers, including two or three from his old office, than he could count.

Dara texted just as things were about to begin.

Alexx are u there? at th servic I mean? He looked twice at the text before showing it to Nikki. Good God, was she drunk?

Yeah we are here. Where are you? Everyone is asking for you. Music began, and Alex tried to appear inconspicuous.

I can't

You can't what? Are you okay?

Yeah but I can't. I can't do it. but ur there for me thank you so much

That was it. Nikki asked to see the texts once more, then they both turned to the front of the sanctuary as the rabbi opened with a prayer. About forty-five minutes later, as things began to wind down, she leaned over and whispered to him.

"Can we step out?"

"Now? It's almost over."

"Please."

He shrugged and followed her outside. The snow had stopped, and it was still and cold in the diminishing afternoon light. A few other people were slipping out early as well, no doubt to beat the rush out of the parking lot. That was Nikki's plan too.

"You got a hot date to get to?" he asked, grinning sideways as they wheeled easily out onto the main drag. The larger crowd was just emerging from the building. Nikki wasn't smiling.

"When did you hear from Dara last?" she asked. "Before that text in there?"

"I told you, Wednesday night. Where are we going anyway? Back to Pete's?"

"How did you two leave things?"

"Like I told you. I told her to avoid Walter if she could, and that we'd talk it out when I got here. God knows it's been a lousy week for her. Plus, she had this whole service to plan."

"And she barely got that done," Nikki said, more to herself.

"Dara's an odd duck, what can I tell you? Not much surprises me."

"What did her mother say?"

"About what?"

"When you talked to her. Did you ask how Dara was? Did she say anything about her recent behavior?" She seemed impatient, and Alex frowned, trying to catch up with wherever her brain was. He turned left toward Pete's house.

"She said Dara was spending time at her father's place. Going through his things. You know, how people do when someone dies."

"What else?"

"She said she's been sluggish," he said. "That's the word she used." Now he looked over at her, and pulled the car over. "Why?"

"Did she say she was sleeping a lot?"

"Yes."

"You told me Dara hung up on you the other night. What was the last thing she said?"

"You mean word for word? I'm not positive."

"Think, Alex. What?"

He sighed and said, "She said it was her fault. This fucking thing with Walter, I tried to tell her it was because of me, but she said no, it wasn't. She said everything that was happening was because of her." He was starting to get it now. The unease in his eyes reflected in hers. But as usual, she was one step ahead of him.

"Where is Jonah's townhouse?"

"South Old Town, down by the water."

"Can you get in if she won't answer?"

"I have a key, yeah."

"Go. Now."

SEVENTY

4:05 p.m.

Jonah's townhouse was one of the newer, classic-style colonials on the Potomac River in Old Town Alexandria, on a lovely little street called Gull's Quay which ended at a dock and a tiny, private marina. The quay and the houses were only a few years old, but they melted perfectly into the atmosphere of the old riverfront street that ran past them.

Alex knocked, and knocked again. He tried the door, found it locked, and flipped through his key ring. Then his phone went off. He was about to ignore it, but then saw it was Pete.

"Petey?" He sandwiched the phone between his cheek and shoulder, still fumbling through the keys. Beside him, Nikki glanced impatiently around the multi-million-dollar homes and boats. She didn't seem to feel the cold.

"Hey man, are you two coming back to the house? Sam's gonna thaw some steaks."

"Uh, yeah," he said, producing the key at last. "Actually, stay on the line with me a minute, okay?"

"Yeah sure. Where are you?"

"Jonah's townhouse, down off of Union Street. Can you stay on a second?"

"I'm right here, man."

Alex opened the door into a neat vestibule with a marble floor and a table for the mail. It was dimly lit and chilly inside, as if the heat had been turned off. A scent much like pipe smoke drifted out. Nikki seemed to judge what direction to move in based on the scent and entered the living room. Alex followed her past a large marble fireplace and some bookshelves. The walls were a deep cranberry color. Alex hadn't been in this house for a long time, but it always reminded him of a scene out of that old board game "Clue."

"Shit!" Nikki yelled out as she walked into the next room. "Alex!" The room was Jonah's dark, wood-paneled study. In addition to a large desk and chair, there was an ornate cream-colored chaise lounge and a coffee table. Sprawled out on the chaise lounge, her feet trailing off the edge, was Dara. She was dressed in pajama bottoms and a sweatshirt.

"Hey, what's going on?" Pete spoke into his ear. "Something wrong?"

"We just found Dara. I think she's unconscious."

"What?"

"In Jonah's study. She might have taken something."

Nikki knelt beside Dara and took her hand. Alex had an absurd, fleeting sense of what an odd first meeting this made between them.

Yeah, assuming she's still alive.

"Does she have a pulse?" Alex asked. Nikki was feeling for one on Dara's neck. She nodded.

"Dara, wake up!" She patted Dara's cheeks, then shouted it. "Wake up!"

"A pulse?" Pete said into Alex's ear. "Yo, what the hell's going on?" Nikki motioned for him to give her the phone.

"We think she took something," she said. "She's alive but her breathing is really shallow and it's slow. I can't wake her up."

"Call an ambulance," Pete said. His voice, like Alex's, carried, and Alex heard it even up against Nikki's ear. "But one of you stay on with me. Give Alex the phone. Call from yours." Nikki handed the phone back and dug in her purse.

"Number thirty Gull's Quay," Alex said to her. "Pete, what can we do?"

"Look around. You see pills? Bottles? Anything? I'm coming with a jump bag, but stay with me." Alex heard him call out something to Samantha.

"I'm looking." The coffee table in front of the chaise lounge was cluttered with books, newspapers and mail. There was also an empty wine bottle and a smudged glass. Then he saw them, two amber prescription pill bottles. "I see two pill bottles and an empty bottle of wine. Red, I think."

"Are there labels on the pill bottles?" Pete asked. Alex heard what sounded like the door to his pickup slamming shut, then the engine turn over.

"Yeah. The first one is ... ami ... amitrip ..."

"Amitriptyline?"

"Yes."

"Okay, that's a benzo. What's the other one?"

"Uh, it's a sleeping pill I think. This label's hard to read though, it's gotten wet. But I can see where it says don't take with alcohol."

"Try to read it."

"It's a something 'pam.' Starts with a 'C' maybe. Or an 'O.'"

"Shit," Pete breathed into the phone. "She fuckin' looked this shit up."

"What can we do?"

"Dara!" Nikki yelled. The ambulance on its way, she had returned to trying to rouse her. Dara's eyes opened, fluttered, then fell closed again. "Dara! DARA!"

"Whaa?"

"Dara talk to me!" Nikki shouted. Dara's eyes opened again, unfocused and blank. Then to Alex, Nikki said "Talk to her!"

"Dara, it's Alex! Talk to me!" Her eyes shifted toward Alex, and then widened.

"Al..." she started. She lifted her right arm as if to reach for him. "Al..."

"Pete, she's awake," he said into the phone. "Sort of."

"Can you stand her up? Put me on speaker, set the phone down." Alex did as instructed and then reached for her. Nikki draped Dara's arms around his neck, and slowly he pulled her to her feet, her legs wobbly and uncertain. When they were face to face, her eyes opened more fully, and rolled. "Dara? Can you hear me?" She opened her mouth as if to say something, and then threw up all over him.

"Whoa, she puked?" he heard Pete ask. He sounded relieved.

"Yep. All over my suit." A sour smell of red wine, mixed with whatever else she had taken, wafted up from his midsection.

"That's probably good. I'm five minutes out. Medics should be there any second."

"I'll look for the ambulance," Nikki said. "Keep her on her feet."

SEVENTY-ONE

8:00 p.m.

The hospital room was dark except for the green glow from a light on a monitor, and a sliver of honey-yellow light from the hallway. It was deathly quiet other than the occasional cough or sniffle from down the hall. Nikki was alone with Dara in the chair closest to the bed. Alex had stepped out of the room for few minutes, and Dara's mother was talking to the attending physician and Dara's psychiatrist. Nikki hadn't realized how tired she was, but in the cool silence of the room, she was beginning to nod off. Dara's voice snapped her awake.

"Hi." It was a girlish, sweet sound. Nikki looked up and smiled. "Dara?"

"Nikki?"

"Yes."

"It's nice to meet you, Nikki." She offered a hand. Nikki took it to shake, but Dara seemed to want to hold it, so Nikki obliged.

"How do you feel?"

"Like someone shit in my mouth."

"That's probably the activated charcoal. You were awake for a little while before. Do you remember?"

She paused and let out a deep sign. "Yeah, sort of."

"Your mother is talking to the doctors right now. Alex just stepped out for a few minutes. Can I get you anything?"

"You saved my life," Dara said, smiling and still holding her hand. "I'd say you've done enough for me today." Nikki wasn't surprised, but she was almost shocked at how unassumingly pretty she was. Her face, even puffy with sleep and sickness, was bright and open, almost childlike. When she blinked, even in the dark, it was like little lights flashing.

"I'm just glad you feel better."

"I'm really sorry. To both of you."

"Please don't be."

"No, I should be. I've caused Alex nothing but grief. This is just the latest thing." Her eyelids fell, the look almost dreamy. "The truth is, there's a sin between us, him and me. It's terrible. And it's been after us, ever since the day I committed it."

"Dara, you should rest."

"It's okay, I know you know. I'm glad you know. I don't want Alex to be alone with it, especially now that my father is gone."

"Okay," Nikki said, unsure of what else to say.

"This sin. I'll never be able to outrun it. I don't deserve to. But Alex can. With you, he can. Please help him."

"I'll try. But Alex wants you to be well, too, Dara. He wants that very much."

"I guess it's all that's left," she said with a shrug. "I mean, killing myself didn't work." Nikki almost smiled at this. After the last few cryptic thoughts, this was uttered like a description of a stop at the post office. Dara looked over at her. "I think we could be friends, maybe."

"I'd like that," Nikki said.

"I know it's weird."

"Not really."

"You're a psychologist, right?"

"I am."

"Hmm." Dara's eyes wandered around the darkened room, then back to Nikki. "You love him, right?"

"I do, yes."

"I'm really glad. But is it okay if...I mean I'd never try...I couldn't anyway. But is it okay if I still do too, just a little?"

"Yes," Nikki said. She brought her other hand forward, so she was holding Dara's with both. "It's okay."

SEVENTY-TWO

8:30 p.m.

"Walter, it's Alex," he said. He was calling from Dara's cell phone which he had swiped before the EMT's arrived. He took a chance on the passcode still being 0407, Jordan's birthday. Sure enough, it hadn't changed.

"Alex? Is Dara okay?"

"She's at Alexandria Hospital. She collapsed at her father's place." That wasn't entirely false. "She's asking for you." That was false.

"Oh my god," Walter said. "Collapsed? What happened?"

"We're not sure yet, but she's doing better. She'll be here overnight, though."

"Wow. I'm so sorry. Who, I mean, who found her?"

"My girlfriend and I did, after the service. She didn't show up for it, so we went by her father's townhouse to check on her."

"Well thank God you were there. Jeez. I wasn't at the service either. Truth is I haven't talked to Dara for the last couple of days. I should have known something was up."

"I think she's okay. It might be an issue with her medication. They're looking her over. She's alert though, and wants to see you. Can you come by?"

"Of course," he said. "But isn't it too late? Aren't visiting hours over?"

"Technically, but I can get you in. I spent a lot of time at this place when I worked down here."

"Okay, sure. Should I call you on her phone when I get there?"

"Yeah do that," Alex said. "There's a side door I'll direct you to, we can get you in that way. When you get into the lot, go left and park anywhere. The door is about half-way down on that side of the building."

***

Alex was unaware of the cold as he stood in the open vestibule of the glass side door he had described to Walter. He had used it before, and it wasn't usually locked until much later in the evening. It opened to an almost always empty hall that ran the length of the building, away from the lobby. Dara's phone rang as he was putting out a cigarette.

"Walter?"

"Hi, just getting here." Sure enough, Alex saw a dark compact car turn the corner from the front lot.

"See me?" Alex asked.

"Yes. I'll be right there."

Alex watched as Walter parked his car, climbed out and slammed the door behind him. As he was walking, he put his hands in his pockets. He had a black overcoat on, topped with a maroon scarf. When he reached the doorway, Alex stepped out and offered his hand. Walter took it to shake, but Alex grabbed a hold of it, spun him around and wrenched Walter's right arm behind his back. Then with all of his weight, Alex slammed him face-first into the cold brick of the vestibule.

"What the–"

"Shut up or I'll break your arm."

"What? Alex what is this?"

"What, you didn't see this coming?" Alex surprised himself at the force he had used. He hadn't acted violently toward anyone in years, not really ever, other than one or two awkward playground fights as a kid.

"See what coming?"

"You didn't get a picture of it in your head?" Alex whispered, his head next to Walter's. He tugged upward on Walter's arm, and he yelped. Alex glanced over to the door. The hallway was empty. "Don't scream."

"Okay, but please! What are you doing?"

"For now, pinning you up against a wall. So tell me, why couldn't you see this? Not just this. I mean Dara, today. Or yesterday for that matter. Why couldn't you see it? That's what you do, isn't it?"

"No, it's not what I do. That's not how it works."

"How does it work? Tell me."

"I don't know how it works, okay? I wish I did. Let me go, for God's sake."

"When I'm ready."

"Are you crazy? There are cameras here, it's a hospital!"

"I was a prosecutor here for ten years. You don't think I know where every single camera is? Every blind spot? No one can see us here, Walter. It's just you and me."

"Well, what do you want?"

"Not sure yet," Alex said, his breathing heavy. He pulled up on the helpless left arm. "Maybe I just want to hurt you."

"God, please!"

"My name is Alex."

"Alex, please. Don't break my arm. I don't know what you think, but–"

"Use your right arm," Alex said. "Take out the recording device. Throw it on the ground."

"What recording device?"

"The one you use to record Dara. I know it's on you. Take it out. Throw it on the ground."

"I didn't bring anything like that." At this, Alex gave a substantial tug to his left arm, and Walter made a welp-like sound, almost a squeal.

"I'll snap your arm right here, right now. If you scream, I'll cover your mouth."

"Okay," Walter breathed. "Okay." With that, he fished for something in his coat pocket, and produced a small black rectangular device with only one button and a micro USB port on one end, not much larger than a cigarette lighter. He tossed it on the ground.

"Now your phone," Alex said.

"What?"

"Your phone. Give it to me."

"But why?" Alex didn't answer, but tugged again at the arm, prompting something between a scream and a squeal. Alex was about to speak when Walter reached into a pants pocket. With his now shaking, free hand, he pulled out his phone.

"Drop it." Walter did. It hit the pavement with a plop into the snow.

"Why are you doing this?" Alex noticed then that his voice was different. The light confident tone was gone, replaced by something flat and even.

"I'm going to take your phone to people I know who

can pull every piece of data from it," Alex said into his ear. "I'm going to extract information about guys you've talked to. The ones you owe money to." For a few seconds, Walter didn't say anything.

"I didn't expect this from you," he said finally.

"Oh yeah?" Alex kicked both the cell phone and the little recording device a few feet away into a shadow. "I guess you aren't that talented after all."

"I know enough. You're monsters, the two of you."

"Who sent you?" Alex asked as if he hadn't heard the insult. His hand still gripped Walter's arm.

"I never met the guy. The guy you're prosecuting, I mean. I dealt with some ex-cop."

"What's his name?"

"Petrazzo," Walter said with a sigh. "William, I think. Or Bill."

"And what did he want?"

"What do you think he wanted? Something he could hold over you."

"Have they paid you yet?"

"Just expenses."

"Good, so you're not out of pocket. I'm glad."

"Screw you," Walter said, his teeth clenched. He had turned his head so his ear was pressed against the wall rather than his nose. "Just break my arm, you fucking hypocrite. Go ahead." Instead, Alex released him. Slowly, like an animal unsure of whether he had escaped a trap, Walter turned around until they were face to face.

"Drive far away from here," Alex said. "Don't stop at your shitty apartment. Don't stop to piss. Put as much distance between you and me as humanly possible, and hope that somehow I'm satisfied with that." Walter stared back at him.

"You prosecute people. Not just rich rapists, you go after people who kill children."

"What's your point?" Walter looked poised to answer, then just shook his head. "The information I'll get from your phone? Hope I don't use that against you. But know that if I ever hear of you coming within one hundred miles of this city, or my ex-wife, I'll have that information ready to turn over to people who I'm fairly certain will put you in a place like this. Or worse."

"You win," Walter said, spreading his hands out in a gesture of surrender. "But she'll crack eventually. I was paid to get the truth from her, about both of you. I almost got it. But believe me, it'll come out on its own eventually." With that, he turned and walked back to his car. Alex watched him until he was out of the parking lot.

SEVENTY-THREE

"Darling Alex," Dara said. Still in his overcoat, he took the seat Nikki had occupied. Upon his return, she had left for a cup of coffee.

"Please don't do this again," he said. He wasn't sure what to expect as an answer, but Dara just smiled back at him.

"I don't think I will."

"I wish I knew how to take the pain away."

"You do, sometimes," she said. "And you saved me. Both of you. That makes things different. It's hard to explain."

"I hope so," he said, his breath becoming ragged as he fought back tears. "God, I hope so."

"There's a road ahead of me," she said. "I'm not out of the woods. But things are clearer now. It's weird. I mean, I meant to do it. I wanted to do it. But then when it didn't work, it was like, 'well, this isn't the way out.' Does that sound crazy?"

"No, of course not. What does the psychiatrist say? How long will they keep you?"

"He'll call my regular one tomorrow, they'll make up a plan, blah, blah. I'll be okay."

"I borrowed your phone," he said, producing it and setting it on the bed. She looked at it and then up at him.

"I thought my mother had it."

"I took it."

"You took...wait, did you call Walter?"

"Yes." She sighed and shook her head.

"Please tell me you didn't hurt him."

"Of course not, he's fine. But I sent him away."

"What did you do? Tell me?"

"He was coming in here with a recording device. I took it from him. I took his phone, too. I can get data from it. He knows that."

"Alex, leave him be."

"He tried to-"

"Leave him be. Promise me you will. Take his phone and just throw it in a pond."

"Dara, he-"

"He failed," she said, and took his hand. "He didn't get anything from either of us, except for a very weird vibe, I guess."

"And what else? Visions?"

"Maybe," she said with a shrug. "We'll never know. But it doesn't matter."

"It matters to me."

"Promise me," she said again, squeezing his hand. Finally, he nodded.

"Okay. I promise."

"I got to know him a little. I'm sure he doesn't think I did. I'm sure he thought he played me, right down the line. Mostly that was true. But it wasn't that clean. I saw things he tried to hide from me." She looked up at him. "It's terrible for him, Alex. He's so sad."

"He deserves to be."

"Whatever. He has a talent, I'm sure of it. But he can't

control it. He can't focus it. He tried to do something with it and he got nowhere. So now what? He rips off gamblers and goes after sad women so he can maybe blackmail someone else? That's hell, Alex. We've been through hell. Walter puts himself there."

"Some people aren't tortured by that. Some people just get a kick out of it, I hate to tell you."

"You *have* told me, a bunch of times. It's depressing. I hope you don't lay that all on Nikki."

"What are you, kidding? Nikki makes me look naive. It's darker in her head than it is in mine, believe me."

"Ugh, fine. Then you're perfect for each other. But she's good for you. I can see it."

"Thank you. I think so, too." He stood to leave. "Get some rest, okay? I'll call tomorrow."

"Go win your big case," she said. "I've got plenty of support here. Call me sometimes but go be with Nikki."

Their eyes locked, and there was a long, weighted pause where Alex almost said 'I love you.' It wouldn't have carried the same kind of weight and it would be true in a different, complex way. But it was wrong to say it, especially out loud, and he knew it.

"Alex?"

"Yeah?" His breath caught in his chest. If she were to say it, he wasn't sure he could resist not saying it back. The moment seemed to still the clock on the wall. Then her mouth broke into a little grin.

"I'm sorry I threw up on you."

SEVENTY-FOUR

Monday, January 15

Hey sis-

Not sure how to start this. I thought of a thousand differ-ent ways and what to say, but I'm not so good at all that. So here's some stuff to know, as you go on as a woman.

There's lots to say about blood. Carry a regular size tam-pon in your purse. Always. Believe me, you'll get women asking for them all the time. Make it a regular one, but if there's room, carry a light or super also.

Read up on ovulation—like how it feels. For me, it's just cramps, like indigestion. Some women get a tingle or a little extra pain on the side where they're ovulating. I think for most it's one side each month.

Have a story about your first period. You'll get asked at some point. You can use mine—I went to pee in sixth grade—from Mrs. Arnold's class. I saw it when my underpants were down. It was Mrs. Arnold who gave me a pad.

You can probably guess what a period is like. Mostly it's just inconvenient, but sometimes it really sucks. Cramps usually come beforehand for me, although everyone's dif-ferent. You feel bloated. Your boobs hurt, and usually they *get a little bigger. You won't have much to work with there, but it doesn't matter. Girls with small tits bleed, too. God's an a-hole.*

You can put make-up on better than anyone I know, so you've got that down. You know to put lip stuff on every night. We all do that, too. And carry a little bottle of perfume with you.

Be aware of your surroundings more than you would as a man. There's a difference, and other women will notice it.

You've got the other stuff down.

I know you're crying while you're reading this. Stop, ok? Yeah, I know crying is a woman thing, but stop it for now and just read what I'm telling you with an open heart. You're gonna be fine, sis. You're more of a woman than I ever was. Take care of Emily and you'll have earned every bit of this back, whatever it's worth.

I love you very much.

***

Kim handed the letter, which she had carefully folded and placed in her purse that morning, to Evelyn as the two sat in their usual places in Evelyn's office, with Kim on the exam table and Evelyn on her rolling stool. The letter was written on yellowing, lined school paper. It had been among the money and documents the real Kim had given her that night. Evelyn took it in her fingertips like she was handling old parchment, as if it were even more delicate than it was. She read it, read it again and then looked up and smiled.

"This is beautiful. Thank you for sharing it with me."

"It's all for nothing if this hurts you," Kim said. "I can protect Emily. But I'm worried about you."

"Kim, I'll be fine. The hormones you use are all legal."

"Not all without a prescription."

"You haven't committed prescription fraud," Evelyn said. "You have some online sources. Maybe some of them call themselves pharmacies, whatever. Believe me, people do far worse and the government does not care."

"Yeah, but they're not under a microscope like I am. What if they come after you, try to ask you questions, or put you under subpoena?"

"I have nothing to hide," Evelyn said. "And anyway, I'd never hurt you. Never. What does the ADA say?"

"To let him worry about it."

"So, let him."

"I don't deserve this," Kim whispered.

"Believe me, I wish I could give it to someone who did."

"No, not the bad stuff. I mean the good things, Evelyn. What you do for me. What Alex is doing. I don't deserve it."

"Yes, you do. Just like you deserved that letter from your sister."

"I feel like I need to earn it every day," she said, choking up. She felt like she'd been on the verge of tears for days.

"But that's just it, Honey, you didn't. You never had to earn it."

"She's why I did all this, why I went to the police. I wasn't going to. Even after talking to that poor woman in Florida, I was set against it. But it was right after that, right after talking to her. I saw myself in the mirror, a little square one we have in the living room. It was suddenly different, you know? I wasn't looking at myself the way I do when I go to brush my teeth or wash my face. It was like...like I got caught. Like I was looking at someone else just then.

"I saw Kim in that moment. Not me. The *real* Kim. My sister. And my sister wouldn't lie down for what Kevin did." Now the tears did come. Kim was not a crier and she was tired of how much emotion was pouring out of her lately, but it was like the ocean's tide, steady and unstoppable. Evelyn stayed silent, letting her cry. "I miss her so much, Evelyn! God, even now."

"You'll always miss her, honey," Evelyn said, standing to hug her. They embraced for a long moment, and then Evelyn pulled back to look in her eyes. "The thing is, you've never given yourself the proper time to miss her. There was no time. You need to make time. Then, it'll get better, I promise."

"I don't understand."

"You've been running. Marching. Moving in one direction, however you want to put it, since you were eighteen. I could say you've put Emily and your business ahead of yourself, but it's actually worse than that. You've been hiding. Hiding inside yourself. I can't imagine how much energy that's taken from you."

"It's all I've known."

"It doesn't have to be," Evelyn said, searching her eyes. "Not anymore. There's only one good thing about what came out in your DNA. In a way it set you free."

"I swear, I don't know what that would feel like."

"You will, because you've already started. Your sister let you live the way you were meant to live. That was her gift to you. But now you can be *all* of who you are."

"I don't have a choice. Alex says there will be questions at the trial. He says it'll feel like I've been through a washing machine."

"Okay. So maybe get used to it. Who are you?"

"Kim Hadley."

"And who is Kim Hadley? Who is she, really?" Kim thought about the answer, then looked suspiciously at Evelyn.

"A transgender woman," she said, slowly, punctuating each syllable. She had never said it out loud.

"Yes. A transgender woman. That doesn't make you good or bad, but it's the whole of who you are."

"A transgender woman with underdeveloped and majorly useless sex organs," Kim said with a sardonic grin. "Wow, this is freeing!"

"We're just getting started, girl," Evelyn said. She reached for her tablet. "Let's talk about your hormones."

SEVENTY-FIVE

Friday, March 9
4:50 p.m.

"I always loved that bag," Kim heard from behind her. She was on Lexington Avenue, a block from the post office she visited with samples to mail out almost every Friday. She could ship from home, but she liked the little ritual of going to the post office at the end of the week, like she had back when she had nothing.

"What do you want?" she asked without turning around. Megan sidled up on her left.

"A minute of your time, Kim. Nothing else." Slowly, Kim raised her eyes up Megan's body. She was decked out in black boots, leggings, and a supple looking gray leather coat.

"I can't imagine why I'd do that," Kim said. But she made no move to stomp off. She held her sample bag, a Kate Spade leather tote, in her right hand. Around them, pedestrians made their way into after-work bars and bistros in the darkening late afternoon. The air was crisp and cold.

"These are for you," Megan said. She held a manila envelope out to Kim, who stared at it and then up at her. She looked as lovely as ever. "Take it, please."

"What is it?"

"Photos. The ones I took of the pill bottles in your vanity. I'm giving them back to you."

"Why?"

"Because I don't want them. And I don't want Jack Hooper or anyone else using them against you."

"Oh God, please," Kim said. She felt suddenly exhausted, drained far beyond the product of a typical hard winter week. "What do I do now? Take your word that they're gone from your phone, and these are the only copies?"

"They *are* gone, and these *are* the only copies. I printed them out for Bill Petrazzo, that grave-digger you saw with me that day at Hooper's office."

"Your word means nothing, I'm sorry."

"It wouldn't matter if there were other copies. Your name isn't on any of the bottles, and even if it was, they're not worth anything without me there to identify them in the photographs. And I won't be."

"So why are you giving them to me?"

"It's a gesture," Megan said. "I don't expect it to mean much. But I felt like I had to do it." She was still holding the envelope out. Kim took it and leafed quickly through the photos. Sure enough, they reflected what was nestled in the lower left vanity drawer. The dull looking little bottles with the generic names, the estrogen, the anti-androgens. The bottles were sterile, white and marked in Arial font, so unlike the beauty product vessels she had studied, and then designed, her whole life. She looked up at Megan after stuffing the photos back in the envelope.

"I think it's mostly an empty gesture. I'm not a complete idiot, Megan. The ADA doesn't think evidence about the meds would be admissible anyway."

"Well, at least this way you know there won't be a question. My shadow won't be over this case, whatever happens with it."

"Your shadow will stay over me for a long time," Kim said. She was willing herself not to cry, to blubber in front of this person, but she was shaking and sad. So sad. The fact was, she missed her friend, even if she existed only in her imagination.

"I'm an out-of-work actress," Megan said. "Past my prime and alone. I don't work at a brokerage firm. This is the work I have to do, sometimes. I took an opportunity and I regret it. I can't go backward. This is all I can do."

"Is your name even Megan Heatherton?"

"Yes. You wouldn't have to go deep to find me. I'm surprised your ADA hasn't tried already. He probably has."

"He would have told me who you were by now if he knew."

"Maybe," Megan said with a shrug. "But maybe not, if he thought it would upset you more."

"What's that supposed to mean?"

"He needs you ready. He wants you to be an effective witness, and that's all he wants. Go ahead, smirk. But I told you many times, and I was telling the truth, at least about that. It's a system. It's their system. You won't win."

"There's no winning," Kim said, almost sympathetically. The urge to cry had faded, vanished as quickly as it had appeared at the sound of Megan's voice. The burning loss was still there. The longing for the friend who never was, was still there. But the sadness inside her had morphed. Now she was sadder for this beautiful, terrible creature than anything else. "There's only survival. I survived Kevin Dunaway. I'll survive you, too."

SEVENTY-SIX

Monday, April 2

"I've read your motions," the judge said as both lawyers and the defendant looked up at him in anticipation. He was a broad-shouldered, dark-skinned man named Harris Lowe. "Is there anything else, briefly, from either of you?"

Alex and Jack looked sideways at each other. The word "briefly" almost certainly meant that Judge Lowe had made his decision on the defense's motion. Jack had filed it immediately after Lowe had been assigned the case as trial judge. The motion asked for a ruling that the complaining witness, Kimberly Hadley, be referred to by "his" given name Andrew, or at least by "mister" when addressed in court. It was exactly what Gerry predicted months before, and Alex had spent weeks researching the issue with a couple of other lawyers from his unit. Now, Alex tapped a finger silently on the prosecution table, waiting to see what last arguments Jack would toss out. Beside the judge was his court attorney, a likable guy named Evan who both Jack and Alex had dealt with as *People v. Dunaway* moved slowly toward trial. Alex looked for some sign on Evan's face as to which way things were going, but Evan was sphinxlike.

"We think the motion speaks to justice, Your Honor," Jack said, standing up. "More importantly it simply speaks to truth and common sense." Jack turned toward the gallery, where Kim sat expressionless between Angie and Judy Levin. Almost everyone else in the full courtroom was a reporter. Jack looked at Kim for a few seconds, as if inviting others to do so, then turned back to the judge. "Kim Hadley is not female. I should not be compelled to address or refer to Hadley as a female in defense of my client." Jack paused for effect. His speech was slow and measured, something Alex noticed with grudging admiration. "This is especially true when literally everything turns on Hadley's credibility. That credibility was destroyed years ago. The prosecution should not be able to mask it now by pretending their complainant is something that he is not." Jack placed faint stress on the word *he*.

"The jury will be fully aware that Kim Hadley is biologically male," the judge said. His voice was deep, and he stressed the word "biologically." Alex perked up. This was a great sign. "I'm not sure I see what's gained by hammering that fact home every time Hadley is referred to by you."

"I'd say an appreciation for the truth is gained, Your Honor," Jack said. "A full appreciation for it. At last."

Alex waited for the judge to look over at him for a rebuttal. Instead, he kept his eyes on Jack. Another good sign. Both Jack and Alex had been apprehensive about Lowe as the trial judge. On one hand, he was known as very defendant-friendly. He had been a successful and admired defense attorney, making his way to the bench through a very liberal Democratic political machine. Alex's colleagues had groaned when they heard he had drawn Lowe. But on the other hand, it was hard to say what a judge's progressive tendencies might lead to in a case like this.

There was very little guidance from case law, a fact both lawyers learned when researching the issue in the weeks previous. It was more or less a case of first impression in New York State, and Judge Lowe was destined to be carefully scrutinized, however he decided. For the prosecutor, that usually meant defeat. When in doubt, rule against the government. It was appeal-proof in the event of an acquittal, and probably easy for a jurist like Harris Lowe. But this didn't seem to be going Jack's way.

"The jury will know the truth about the complaining witness," Lowe said in his sonorous baritone. "I'm confident both parties will address it from *voir dire* onward. Mr. Hooper, you're asking me to allow you to effectively humiliate the complaining witness at every turn regardless of that. I don't see how justice is advanced just because the complaining witness's assigned gender-"

"Not assigned," Jack said. "I'm so sorry to interrupt Your Honor, but for the record, his gender is male, it's not just *assigned...*"

"Says whom?" Lowe thundered. Alex suppressed a grin. "Mr. Hooper, who do you think you are?" Jack stared back, shocked into silence. Lowe turned to Alex. "Mr. Greco, could Kimberly Hadley testify to choosing her gender at birth?"

"Sir? No, of course not. Hadley was an infant, I mean..."

"Correct," Lowe said. He turned back to Jack. "Mr. Hooper, your motion is all but eaten up with references to how many years the complaining witness lived as a male. You refer again and again to how Hadley grew up—*grew up*—as a boy."

"Yes, Your Honor," Jack said. He lowered his eyes. It

was all but over. Beside him was Dunaway, who looked tired, but otherwise stoic and unreadable. Also at Jack's table was a young, attractive female attorney named Crystal Haidt. A few of the ADA's in Alex's office had suggested she was a plant, there to feminize the defense. She was often seen whispering to Kevin, sometimes with her hand on his back or shoulder. There was nothing untoward about it, but the intended message seemed clear: if this woman attorney was comfortable with Dunaway, the jury should be too.

"So then, Mr. Hooper, you would agree that this court could take judicial notice—let's call it common sense as you so artfully evoked a moment ago—that Kimberly Hadley, once Andrew Hadley, was *assigned* a gender at birth?"

"Well, yes," Jack said. "I suppose we all are."

"Yes, we are. I doubt you or anyone else can say with complete satisfaction to this court what gender is, outside of how it's defined for us and assigned to us."

"I'm not sure I understand," Jack said.

"No, Mr. Hooper, you don't. And I'm not sure I do either. But I have researched far beyond your motion and the people's response in considering this issue. I need not burden the record with the conflicting research, theory and speculation that I encountered. Suffice to say, gender is a loaded and uncertain term. Now I have certain powers in this courtroom. One of them is the ability to prevent undue harassment or embarrassment to witnesses. I agree fully that your client has the right to present evidence of the complaining witness's apparent change with regard to how she views her gender, and how she lived previously. I agree it goes to her credibility to an extent. But that's as far as it goes. I'm requiring you to refer to the complaining witness as "Ms." when you question her, and to refer to her with the pronouns she has used for herself for almost half of her life. The motion is denied, case is set for trial."

SEVENTY-SEVEN

Tuesday, June 5
2:12 p.m.

"The man who did these things to you," Alex said, carefully phrasing his very last direct examination question to Kim Hadley. Alex's voice filled the large, wood-paneled room beautifully. He was never more comfortable than on his feet in a space like this. "Do you see him in this courtroom?"

"I do."

"Can you point him out for the jury, please?"

"He's at that table," Kim said. Her voice didn't resonate like Alex's, but it was clear and steady. "Wearing a gray suit and a dark blue tie." Kevin Dunaway looked back at her, his handsome face blank.

"Thank you, Ms. Hadley." He turned to the judge. "Nothing further, Your Honor."

After two weeks of jury selection and last-minute legal wrangling, the trial was finally underway before a jammed courtroom, one of the largest in the New York County Criminal Court Building on Centre Street. The jury, evenly split between men and women, was older than Alex would have wanted. But retired jurors in particular were the most likely picks for a trial that had attracted a decent amount of media attention and could last longer than a week. There were two younger women on it, one African-American and one white, both within a few years of Kim's age. Like the rest they seemed attentive and neutral, but beyond that Alex couldn't tell how they were leaning, if at all.

Kim was testifying beautifully so far, dressed in a tailored blue suit, her hair, nails, shoes and jewelry all perfect. Alex was immensely proud of her as she relayed the background and the events of the previous September. He had agonized about the questions about her childhood. In the end, he asked only a few, and got them out of the way early. By doing so he hoped to take the wind out of Jack's sails when he began his cross-examination. If there was something negative out there the other side was likely to address, it was better to get out in front of it.

Kim was Alex's last witness, and the two before her had been very quick. Gina Milagros, the patrol officer, testified about how Kim still appeared bruised on September twentieth when she visited Kim and Emily's apartment, five days after the incident. Angie testified next and answered a few questions about the investigation, also identifying photos of Kim she had taken on the day they met. There was no need for testimony on the DNA as Jack had previously stipulated to the presence of his client's blood on the handkerchief.

Both Gina and Angie's testimony had gone smoothly, but neither was particularly effectual. Jack didn't go after them much on cross because he didn't need to. His client had reasons for everything the prosecution had brought out so far. It was Kim who was the crux of the case. In preparation with her, Alex had tried to downplay that. The responsibility for the case, he said again and again, was his, not hers. That was what he told all victims who would testify in his cases, whether they were six or sixty. But at the end of the day, how the jury would view things was riding almost exclusively on how they perceived her.

SEVENTY-EIGHT

"Your witness," the judge said to Jack as Alex completed his direct of Kim. True to what Alex suspected, Jack was maintaining his confident "I *got this*" mien and was comfortable and folksy with the jury. Alex braced himself as Jack stood and buttoned his suit jacket.

Enduring the cross-examination of one's own witness was nerve-racking. *She's been great so far*, he told himself, *sympathetic, unassuming, humble. The jurors seem to like her. Going after her aggressively won't be smart, so he's not likely to do that.* But when Jack looked up from his notes, his eyes seemed to sharpen on Kim.

"You were Andrew Hadley prior to August 10, 2002, correct?" No preamble. No 'good afternoon, Ms. Hadley,' or 'you can ask that a question be repeated.' Just the question. And a cutting stare.

"I was."

"A male."

"Yes."

"And biologically, you are still male, correct?" An accent on the word *still*. Alex tensed up. The question was a little vague, potentially misleading. Kim could have tried to be creative with her answer, something Alex had asked her not to do for any answer, no matter how tempting.

"I am," she said. Alex smiled to himself. *Good answer. Clean and simple, like she doesn't have a care in the world, or an axe to grind.*

"You have male genitalia?"

"Underdeveloped," Kim said. "But yes."

"And you lived as male until you were eighteen, correct?"

"I did."

"Until that fateful night in August of 2002."

"Correct."

"That night," Jack said, glancing down at some notes and then back up her, "your father was killed, along with another man he made meth amphetamine with, correct?"

"Yes."

"Your sister was also killed, right?"

"She was."

"And that was in an explosion that at least one of you planned, and that you *knew* would happen wasn't it?"

"Objection!" Alex called out. "Nothing like that has ever been insinuated."

"It's a reasonable conclusion from the investigation that's been done on that case, Your Honor. It goes to her credibility."

"It's not relevant," Alex said. "We're not trying a case about an explosion in Virginia in 2002."

"Don't argue in front of the jury," the judge said. "Come forward." At a sidebar, he leaned down as Jack and Alex gathered at the bench. "Mr. Hooper, what is this?"

"Your Honor, the night Andrew Hadley decided to assume his sister's identity speaks volumes about his credibility. It's not just the act of deciding to become his sister.

I believe there was more to it."

"And if Mr. Hooper had been a fire department investigator in rural Virginia in 2002, that might be interesting," Alex said. "As it is, this is an attempt to try a case within a case."

"Her credibility is everything," the judge said, shifting his eyes to Alex. "And you did ask her for some of this background on your direct."

"The basic background of how she became who she is and what prompted it, yes. But that doesn't mean Mr. Hooper gets to re-hash every detail of that night."

"I'll allow this line of questing," the judge said, scratching at his chin. "But only to a point. You have the right to explore dishonest acts the complaining witness may have undertaken to the extent that it goes to her credibility. But don't overdo it. Mr. Greco is right, we're not here to rehash an old accident."

"I don't believe it was an accident," Jack said, looking at Alex. "That's the point, Your Honor. It's just accepted that the complainant assumed his sister's identity. For all we know, he stole it."

"You're saying Kim Hadley is guilty of something related to the explosion?" Alex said, trying to keep his voice to a whisper. "Really?"

"Step back," Judge Lowe said. "We don't need to argue this here. Mr. Hooper, you have your perimeters. Continue."

***

"Both your sister and you," Jack said when they had taken their places again. "You both knew that house would be blown up that night, didn't you?"

"Objection. She can't speak for her sister."

"Sustained."

"So, you knew, correct?"

"I didn't," Kim said. She looked bewildered in general, but not uncertain about the answer.

"You're telling this jury," Jack said, turning toward them, "under oath, that you weren't aware of a plan to blow your house sky-high, taking out your abusive father and one of his cronies?"

"Correct. I had no idea that was going to happen."

"It would have been convenient, though, right? The house blowing up, I mean."

"I don't understand," she said before Alex could object.

"I mean, if everyone was out of the way," Jack said, "your abusive father, the actual Kim Hadley, then you could live as her, right?" Now Kim's eyes darkened. She shook her head.

"That was never my intention."

"You left the house immediately after it exploded, didn't you?"

"Yes. I was in the front yard when it happened."

"That's convenient also, isn't it?"

"Our house was an unpleasant place, Mr. Hooper," she said. "I was often outside, especially when it was warm." *Beautiful*, Alex thought. *Hold steady, Kim.*

"So, you walked away from this terrible explosion," Jack said, taking a few steps away from the defense table and toward the witness box.

"Yes. I went for my younger sister, Emily."

"Yes, Emily," Jack said, looking down at his notes. "She was at a neighbor's house."

"That's right."

"The same neighbor who helped you leave town without a trace."

"We left later that night from her house, yes."

"And without talking to a single fireman or investigator?'"

"That's right."

"Were you not even curious," Jack said, stressing each word of *not even curious* and glancing at the jury, "as to the fate of your family members?"

"The explosion was terrible," Kim said. She was still poised, but Alex could see her face was rigid and flushed. "I didn't think anyone survived it."

"But you didn't stay to find out, either."

"No."

"Your sister is disabled, correct?"

"Yes. She has a traumatic brain injury. And PTSD."

"Right. And when you got to the shelter where you stayed," Jack looked again at his notes, "in Dutchtown, Virginia. They helped you get an apartment of your own with Emily, correct?"

"Yes."

Jack paused for effect before the next question.

"They didn't ask a lot of questions at that shelter, did they?"

"No, not really. They asked us health-related questions. Some background things."

"But for the most part, they took your word for how your situation came about, correct?"

"I suppose, yes."

"So, you and Emily were allowed to just start a new life, right?"

"Yes."

"And you had some funds to start out with, didn't you?"

"I had some money, yes."

"Right," Jack said. "Money you took from the house that night."

"My sister," Kim said, looking away. "She gave me..." she trailed off, her mouth trembling. The jurors were enraptured, all of them leaning forward. Kim seemed to go rigid again. She lifted her chin and looked back at Jack. "She gave me some money."

"That night?"

"Yes," Kim said. "She wanted to send me away. With Emily. But I didn't know...I didn't know what would happen."

"So you say," he said, and took another step toward her. His focus was laser-like, his posture perfect. *Whether or not this strategy is going to work,* Alex thought, *he's playing the part well.*

"When you established yourself in Dutchtown, you enrolled Emily in school, didn't you?"

"Yes."

"You obtained benefits for her, correct?"

"Of course, yes."

"And among the documents you passed in order to do this," Jack said, walking back to the defense table as his co-counsel, Crystal, leaned forward to hand him a document, "was her birth certificate, wasn't it?" He took the document and turned back to Kim.

"I believe so," Kim said. "Probably." Jack walked over to Alex and handed it to him. Alex recognized it instantly as a typical Commonwealth of Virginia birth certificate with blue, ornate corners, lavender shading and a watermark of the state seal in the middle. *Sic Semper Tyrannis.* Thus Always to Tyrants. Alex handed it back and stood up.

"Counsel has presented to me what appears to be the birth certificate of Emily Hadley," he said. "We'll stipulate that it's a copy. I don't see the relevance of any of this as to whether Kevin Dunaway attempted to rape Kim Hadley on September 15, 2017."

"Overruled."

"You used Emily's birth certificate to obtain benefits and services, didn't you, Ms. Hadley?"

"Yes. I'm sure I did."

"So, you had it on your person the night you left that house," Jack said, now only a few feet from her. His voice was controlled, but the contempt in it was clear. "Right after it blew up with everyone in it, didn't you?"

"We had planned to leave," Kim said, so low the court reporter looked ready to ask her to repeat it. "My sister and me. For some time. We kept a few documents and some money with us sometimes."

"You just walked around with vital records," Jack said, shaking his head. "Just waiting for something to happen."

"I was ready to leave," Kim said. She looked utterly drained, even more exhausted than she was miserable. Her shoulders now sagged. "We were desperate to leave. We planned to do so as soon as we could."

"And you just got really lucky that night," Jack said. "That's what you want us to believe?"

"All I can tell you is an opportunity presented itself, counsel. I was faced with a choice and I made it."

"That was some opportunity," Jack said. "But I'll bet you don't miss opportunities when they present themselves, do you, Ms. Hadley?"

"Objection," Alex called.

"Sustained. Mr. Hooper, enough about old business.

You've made your point. Turn your attention to the night in question, please."

SEVENTY-NINE

Jack made what points he could after that, highlighting the most questionable points of Kim's behavior both when the police arrived and in the days after. But Alex had taken Kim through all of that on direct examination, so the effect was blunted, and Jack was smart enough not to belabor what was already known. Alex could tell he was looking for a high note to end on.

"You would agree with me, Ms. Hadley," he said, "that our world is changing rapidly with regard to its response to sexual assault and harassment, wouldn't you?" The question didn't seem relevant, but Alex hesitated to object.

"I suppose so," Kim said.

"You're familiar with the phrase and Twitter hashtag *metoo*, are you not?"

"A little bit, yes."

"Well, people have expressed support for you under that hashtag, haven't they?"

"I've seen that," Kim said with a shrug. "It's not something I've ever posted on or written about myself."

"And your company," Jack said. "Your brand, Emily. It's fair to say it hasn't been hurt at all in the wake of these allegations, has it?"

"No, it hasn't."

"And that's true even in the wake of revelations about your biological status, isn't it?"

"I'm not sure what you're asking," she said. "Are my company's sales doing well? Yes, they are. I'm not sure what that's attributable to. I'd like to think we make a good product."

"Your company's value is also up, correct?"

"Yes," Kim said.

"In fact, you've attracted the attention of other investors in the wake of these allegations and revelations, haven't you?"

"There might be new opportunities, yes," she said. "I haven't had much time to consider any of them." Alex knew this to be true as Kim had told him as much. A few of the beauty blogs and magazines were reporting it as well. Emily, the brand, was far from suffering, either because of Kim's case or her revealed gender.

"I see," Jack said, his eyes lingering in hers. He looked poised, maybe purposefully, to ask another question. Alex was praying he would, because it would almost surely be the one question too many that would allow Kim to reject Jack's insinuation, that the allegation against Kevin was part of some major publicity stunt. But Jack, not for the first time, acted impressively. "Nothing further, Ms. Hadley. Thank you."

EIGHTY

4:23 p.m.

"You did great," Angie said to Kim. They were in the hallway outside the courtroom where it was cooler. Alex had
just rested his case after the remainder of Kim's testimony, and they were on a twenty-minute recess. "I know it
never seems like it from up there, but you did."

"It felt awful," Kim said. "He wants them to think I'm
a murderer." Dressed for court, Angie was in a black
Theory suit that Kim found impressive. Angie smiled and
squeezed her hand.

"I've spent years in that chair," she said. "I know what
it's like. He came after you hard, but you never took the
bait. That means a lot, Kim. If you go after a witness and
try to make her look like an asshole and she doesn't bite?
Then *you're* the asshole. I didn't go to law school, but I
know that. He was doing well with that jury, but I think he
crossed a line with you."

"He spent more time on that night years ago then on
the one where I was attacked. Alex warned me about that.
But it was still a shock."

"I know it was. But sometimes that's what they do. He

didn't have much to break you down about where the charges are concerned. That's why Alex took you through all of it on direct, why you ran when patrol got there and why you didn't come forward for a few days. It all made perfect sense. Hooper could hit you with more questions about that stuff, but then he'd just be making the same points Alex was making. As far as he was concerned, the biggest thing he had to slam you with was this ancient thing where your family was killed."

"It could look fishy from the outside," Kim said. "I can see that a lot more clearly now."

"It's still old business, and you handled it perfectly. Believe me, if you had started getting cagey or defensive with all that stuff? He would have scored points. But you never let him. Let Alex worry about this part. I learned that a long time ago."

"Thanks. I'll try. Do you know what happens now?"

"Well, Alex rested. There'll be some motions from the defense to dismiss before it goes to the jury. They'll get denied, and then the defense case will start, if they have one. Probably tomorrow." Angie went to check her phone, and Kim was about to do the same when they saw Judy Levin walking toward them with an anxious look on her face.

"Kim, is Emily here?" Judy asked.

"No, she's at home. Why?"

"There's a defense witness you need to know about," Judy said. "I just found out."

"Oh, God," Kim said. "Is it Megan? I told Alex, she said she wasn't getting involved."

"No, it's ..." Suddenly Judy's voice faded in Kim's ears, replaced by an intense, high ringing. There was a pale, thin woman in her line of sight, standing next to Crystal

Haidt and the investigator, Petrazzo. She was maybe fifty but looked older, with dark, gray-streaked hair pulled back to a bun. She stood in the hallway with her arms folded, wearing a plain blue dress and flat, black shoes. She had cold eyes and a grim line for a mouth.

Kim was trying to breathe but felt a terrible heaviness in her chest, and her knees felt weak. She felt Angie and Judy grasp one arm each, steering her away from the sight in front of her and toward the women's bathroom down the hall.

"I'm not sure if I should go in there," she said, still breathing in short, shallow bursts. She could feel the granola bar she had eaten for breakfast about to come back up. "I just spent an hour admitting I'm not really a w-woman."

"Fuck all that," Angie said. She and Judy got her into the bathroom and then gave her some privacy in a stall as Kim threw up.

"Oh God, I'm sorry," she said from inside, her voice echoing into the bowl.

"It's okay," Judy said. "I'm surprised you even recognized her." Kim was quiet for a long moment. She got to her feet, opened the stall and walked over to the sink.

"Twenty years," she said finally, staring into the mirror and turning the water on. Behind her, Judy and Angie watched Kim with something like awe. "But yeah, I recognize her."

EIGHTY-ONE

Wednesday, June 6
9:30 a.m.

"Her mother?" Alex said, hoping incredulity was dripping from his lips. He was in Judge Lowe's chambers with Jack, Crystal, Kevin and the court reporter. Dunaway had appeared indifferent throughout the entire trial, not betraying emotion whether the jury was present or not. Mostly he seemed worn out, which made sense given the psychological burden of being on trial for what amounted to one's life. But now he seemed nearly buoyant, almost smiling as his eyes went from his lawyers to Alex.

"She's here to testify to the complaining witness' reputation for truthfulness, Your Honor," Crystal said. Apparently, this was her witness. She was, as Alex had noticed before, beautiful with long, blonde hair and great features, maybe early thirties. She spoke confidently, her words crisp and non-accented. Alex could see the fire of ambition in her eyes as well, plenty of it. "It's an accepted concept and as old as evidence itself."

"It's an antiquated concept," Alex said.

"Still applicable, though," the judge said, frowning. "What's her name again?"

"Holly Jones, Your Honor," Crystal said. "She was Holly Hadley from the time of her marriage to the complaining witness's father Tom Hadley in 1985 until sometime in 2003. She dropped her married name after the mysterious death of her husband and son." Crystal glanced over at Alex for effect. "Or the child she believed was her son at the time."

"Haven't we re-hashed that night enough?" Alex asked.

"It's not the night in 2002 we're interested in," Crystal said. "Mr. Greco's direct examination of the complainant touched on the fact that her mother disappeared about two years prior to that, so he should know. Ms. Jones is here to testify about the years before that, in regard to what reputation her son Andrew had for truthfulness in her community."

"When she was what, a teenager?" Alex said.

"*She* at that time was Andrew Hadley," Crystal said. She kept her eyes on the judge, but Alex could see them, glowing with alacrity. "There wasn't yet a ruse in place that Andrew was female."

***

"Is there anything else you can tell me about her?" Alex asked Kim. They were in a windowless witness room across from the courtroom, seated in thick, hardwood chairs.

"Not much," Kim said. "You know the basics. She was born in '67. She had us in '83, when she was sixteen. She dropped out of high school. Eventually my parents got married, I think we were two or three then. They never talked about it. It's not like there was a wedding album lying around. I think it was just a quick Justice of the Peace thing."

"You said she was mostly inattentive," Alex said. "Was she ever cruel, to any of you?"

"Before my father got into making meth, not really. There were a few times she even tried to protect us from him when he was drunk. But when the business started, everything changed. The house was a wreck. She had more money, but only spent it on liquor."

"Did she use meth?"

"Not that I knew of," Kim said. She seemed lost in thought for a moment. "She actually kind of rebelled against it, in her own way. Never tried to stop my father from what he was doing. She took the money though, and never cared what the house looked like anyway. Usually she was drunk and on the floor by noon most days. For some reason, she got really religious the last two or three years that she was home. I remember that."

"Your mother went to church?"

"No, she almost never left the house. Just watched TV preachers. She sent money in, that kind of thing. My father probably beat her for it once or twice. She sent cash, which you're not supposed to do, but it's all she had."

"About her being cruel," Alex said. "You said that changed when your father started in with making meth at your house?"

"Yes," she said, and looked away. "There were some bad years, before she left. I was afraid of both of them for different reasons. I think for her, some of it was actually related to finding religion. I know that sounds crazy."

"It doesn't, not at all. Kim, what I'm asking about is... who you were, before you became who you are now."

"When I was Andy," she said, looking back at him.

"Yes, when you were Andy, but feeling more like a girl," Alex said. He was trying to phrase things sensitively even though he and Kim were mostly beyond the point of having to do so. "Did your mother notice that?"

"They both noticed it, of course. It was terrifying."

"Tell me about that."

EIGHTY-TWO

11:30 a.m.

"Ms. Jones," Crystal asked, standing in front of the defense table. Holly Jones had been sworn in a few minutes before, and her direct examination was underway. "Just to be clear, did anyone force or coerce you to testify today?"

"No. I was contacted by an investigator working on your case. I came of my own free will."

"Where do you live now?"

"In Colorado Springs, Colorado."

"Do you have family there?"

"No. I have no one left. I live near my church."

"Are you being paid for your testimony?"

"My expenses are being paid. That's all."

"Ms. Jones, how old were your children when you left your home?"

"The twins, Andy and Kim, were sixteen," she said. "Emily was six."

"Without going into too much detail, because the purpose of your testimony is limited, did you leave because you wanted to?"

"No," Holly said. "I left because I had to. I was in a situation that was out of control. I couldn't care for my children. I was in a spiral of addiction and despair. I'm not proud of it, but I left to find myself. To find God, if I could. I wanted to return. But I never got the chance."

"Did you eventually find out that two of your children had survived the explosion that destroyed your home?"

"My daughters, that's what I was told. Kim and Emily. A detective where we lived took my information to give to Kim, but I never heard from her. I was still drinking then. I should have followed up. But eventually it all slipped away."

"When did you become aware that the actual surviving twin was the boy you once knew as Andy?"

"When your investigator, Mr. Petrazzo, informed me. It was a terrible shock at first. But then it started to make sense."

"Well, that's what we're here to talk about," Crystal said. "Ms. Jones, this may sound like an obvious question, but before you left, did you spend time with your children, including Andy?"

"Of course."

"Were you aware of how Andy was perceived, at home, in school and at the places you frequented?"

"Of course, I was. Andy was my son. I was not a very good mother to him or the others. I've never denied that. But yes, I knew how he was viewed, and how he interacted with others."

"And did you develop an opinion about Andy's reputation for truthfulness in the community you shared? To be clear, Ms. Jones, I'm talking about the person who lives as Kimberly Hadley today." Holly's thin lips curled at the mention of Kim's name. She had appeared round-shouldered and slumped in the witness chair, but now sat up straight.

"Yes, I have." The jurors didn't seem to warm to Holly as a witness, which wasn't a surprise to Alex. He knew his own bias was probably playing into it, but even with a tragic backstory, the woman looked mean and unfeeling. Nevertheless, they were paying close attention to her.

"And what is that opinion, Ms. Jones?"

"Andy was a liar. I guess there were reasons. But it's all he did, and everyone around him knew it."

"Nothing further," Crystal said, as if it was obvious there wasn't anything left to say in the entire trial.

Alex's mind raced as he stood for his cross-examination. The smartest course of action, and the one his instinct tended toward, was to keep it very short. Crystal had done her job in laying the foundation for why Holly would have known about her then-son's reputation for truthfulness in the "community," although that was a bit of a stretch since Andy would have been a child. Regardless, she had tracked the evidence rule closely and remained within its limits. As Alex had alluded to in judges' chambers, "a witness's reputation for truthfulness in the community" was an ancient impeachment technique, far more practical when, for example, a blacksmith or a chandler had a reputation as a businessman among other similarly stationed men in a town or village. The evidence rule and the testimony that underpinned it were purposefully narrow.

That could change depending on Alex's cross-examination, though. His questions, if they went too far afield, could lead to a re-direct which would allow Crystal to let Holly spew all sorts of things. He would be wise to avoid any chances for that.

Ask three or four questions, tops, he thought. *Stress that the "community" she's talking about was really just a family. Argue later that family dynamics are a poor barometer for any "reputation for truthfulness." Don't be stupid. Stay in control.*

"Ms. Jones," he started, deciding in that moment to ignore the advice he had just given himself, "you lived with the person you knew as Andy Hadley for about sixteen years, correct?"

"He *was* Andy Hadley," she said, lifting her chin a little. "He still is."

"But," Alex started, stepping around the prosecution table, "he never really felt like Andy, did he?" Holly wrinkled her brow at this. Crystal seemed poised to object but didn't.

"What?"

"Andy didn't want to be a boy, did he, Ms. Jones?"

"Objection," Crystal called out. "This calls for speculation on what the witness wanted..."

"Rephrase," the judge said, interrupting her.

"Andy didn't act like a typical boy, did he?" He took another step toward the witness stand. Holly stared back at him.

"I guess not, no."

"I wouldn't think you'd have to guess, Ms. Jones. You were a part of the community he shared, right?"

"Yes. Of course."

"Indeed, you were his mother."

"I was."

"So, you saw how he acted, didn't you?"

"I guess."

"You saw for instance, that instead of G.I. Joes, he played with dolls, right?"

"Sometimes."

"He wore dresses, didn't he?"

"He...yes, sometimes."

"He wore his sister's clothing, didn't he?"

"Sometimes."

"He wore make-up that he and his sister Kim had purchased or otherwise gotten a hold of, didn't he?"

"Yes."

"And it infuriated both you and Andy's father Tom, didn't it, Ms. Jones?" Alex turned toward the jury and waited for her answer.

"It...well, I wasn't always there."

"Objection!" Crystal called out. "This witness can't speak for what Tom Hadley was thinking."

"Sustained."

"Withdrawn. But you—you, Ms. Jones. As Andy's mother. You were infuriated that Andy dressed like a girl, weren't you?"

"Wouldn't you be?"

"I ask the questions here, Ms. Jones. Should I repeat that one?" Holly's eyes darkened, two black spots of contempt.

"I heard your question. Yes. It angered me."

"Andy was punished for those actions, wasn't he?"

"Yes."

"He was punished by both you and Tom Hadley, wasn't he?"

"We did what we felt we had to do at the time."

"Which meant beating Andy, didn't it?"

"I...I didn't always beat him."

"But you did, didn't you?"

"Yes."

"And Tom also beat him, didn't he?

"Yes."

"You were aware that Tom was sexually abusing Andy as well, weren't you?" This question seemed to hit Holly like a slap in the face. Her eyes grew wide. Her mouth almost disappeared her lips were so tight.

"No, I never saw that."

"I asked if you were aware of it."

"I couldn't control what Tom did."

"That's not what I asked you. You knew, didn't you?"

"I may have suspected it. You have no idea what it was like living with a man like Tom."

"Very well, but Andy's beatings, at least. We can agree that you witnessed those, right?"

"There were a few times, yes."

"And you approved of those beatings, didn't you?"

"I thought they were necessary at the time."

"Right, because the way Andy wanted to live offended you, didn't it, Ms. Jones?"

"It offended God's law," she said. "It doesn't matter how I viewed it. I didn't want to hurt Andy, but I had to. Do you have children?"

"Again, Ms. Jones, you can't ask the questions here. So, you felt you had to hurt Andy, to punish him, yes?"

"I was trying to correct him," she said. "I don't know what his father was doing. You could ask him if he wasn't murdered." Holly looked poised to say something else but seemed to clamp down on it. Out of the corner of his eye, Alex saw Crystal and Jack tense up.

"But Andy didn't correct himself in the way you wanted, did he Ms. Jones?"

"Not that I ever saw, no."

"Right. So, until you left, Andy was still desperately

trying to be something he wasn't allowed to be, wasn't he?"

"I was losing control over him," Holly said. For the first time, emotion, and not just anger or contempt, seemed to be rising up within her. "I was losing control over the situation."

"I understand, Ms. Jones," Alex said. "But before you left, it's safe to say that Andy was forbidden to live the way he wanted to, isn't that right?"

"We couldn't allow that. No one would!"

"He was forbidden to talk about it as well, correct?"

"I...I don't remember what we told him about that."

"Are you telling this jury he was free to discuss his feelings in public, or with neighbors?"

"No."

"In school?"

"Well, no."

"So, there was nowhere," Alex said, taking another step toward the witness stand, "that Andy was allowed to talk about who he was, isn't that correct?" Holly shifted in the chair. She looked like she wanted to spit at him.

"No."

"There was nowhere he could be truthful," Alex said, drawing out *truthful*. He took a final step toward Holly and planted his feet. He could feel all the jurors' eyes on him now. "Nowhere within his *community*. Isn't that right, Ms. Jones?"

EIGHTY-THREE

Thursday, June 7
11:17 a.m.

"Did you see Kim Hadley after that night, Mr. Dunaway?" Jack asked. He was almost finished with Kevin's direct examination, which had taken a little more than an hour. Kevin looked and sounded calm and confident. He was dressed professionally, but not ostentatiously, in a dark business suit.

"No," he said, shaking his head just slightly. "I never saw her in person again until this trial started."

"Did you speak to any detectives about that night?"

"Yes. I believe it was a few days later. On the nineteenth, I think."

"Were you cooperative with those detectives?"

"I was. I didn't even know Kim had been hurt before they came to my office. I told them what I knew. I showed them my hand."

"Did you tell them the same thing you've told this jury?"

"Absolutely. Almost word for word, as far as I remember."

"Mr. Dunaway," Jack said, planting his feet before the witness stand, "I'm going to ask you to address the jury with this question. Sir, did you harm Kim Hadley on the night of September 15, 2017?"

"No," Kevin said, turned to them. All twelve simply stared back.

"Did you attempt to rape Kim Hadley on the night of September 15, 2017 or any other night?"

"Absolutely not," he said. "I felt horrible when I was told Kim might have been hurt. I wouldn't want that for anyone. I can't tell you how much of a shock it was to be accused of something like this."

Almost, Alex thought. But that statement wasn't nearly enough to open the door to a line of questioning about other accusations. Jack had been careful.

"Nothing further."

EIGHTY-FOUR

Defendants like Dunaway, Alex knew, were usually eager to testify, to look the jury in the eyes and state under oath they didn't do it. They were used to a position of respect in the community, and indeed, they wanted more than just to say it wasn't so. They wanted to appear hurt and surprised that they had been pegged for something as damning and life-altering as a serious criminal act. They wanted to trumpet who they were, and who the world saw them as.

The world, though, had seen a different side of Kevin Dunaway since the charges had been filed. Alex was keeping track of the accusations against him, which now numbered more than eight complaints made either in civil suits or to the police in various places. The jury knew none of this. They had been chosen precisely because they didn't know about any of the press or rumors, positive or negative, about Kevin or Kim. As it was, Alex was forbidden to cross-examine Kevin on the other accusations. They were unproven and would probably be inadmissible even if he had been convicted of them.

Alex hoped Kevin might go too far in his testimony and "open the door," as it was said in legal circles, to questions about those accusations. If Kevin had said, for instance, that he had never been accused of anything like this, Alex would have had a potential open door to walk through. Jack was coarse and edgy, though, not foolish, and he had kept Kevin well within the perimeters. In the end, Alex saw only two areas he could explore, and he planned on doing so quickly.

"Your testimony was that Kim Hadley had been texting before she left your apartment, correct?"

"Yes," Kevin said. "I believe I told that to the detectives also."

"So according to you, she began texting someone, you went to use the bathroom, and she was still texting when you returned, correct?"

"That's correct. It's what I remember, anyway."

"She told you that person was some kind of a connection, someone she was going to meet?"

"Yes. She didn't say exactly what about, but I assumed it was a drug dealer of some kind. She said she was going to meet whoever it was around the corner."

"You're aware, though," Alex said, "that Kim Hadley's cell phone wasn't used at all during the time of this incident, correct?" The jurors seemed to perk up at this. Alex took Kim's phone records from the table and handed them to Jack, who had seen them already in discovery. Neither Jack nor Kevin seemed concerned at the question, which wasn't a surprise. Jack knew this was coming and he had prepped for it. But Kevin's answer was a killer.

"I don't use illegal drugs, counsel," Kevin said. "But in my experience, it's not at all uncommon for people who do, to have a separate phone they use to communicate with people who sell them."

Alex masked the *fuck* reflex he was feeling by keeping his eyes on Kevin, as if the answer had been almost humorous.

There was nothing he could do with it, nothing that wouldn't invite further damage. Jack knew that and had almost certainly prepped Kevin for it. It was time to leave it behind.

Alex had one more area to visit, and it was one he hadn't discovered until late the previous evening. It had been there all along, a small observation in Angie's typically meticulous report. But he hadn't picked up on it right away, and he hadn't asked Angie about it when she testified. That had been a mistake, but there was one last chance to make the most of her work.

"When you met with Detective Keegan and Detective Lopez on the nineteenth," Alex said, "Detective Keegan asked you about some pain you seemed to be having, didn't she?"

"My hand, yeah," Kevin said. "There are days it still hurts."

"I'm not talking about your hand," Alex said, slowing his speech. He tapped his index finger on the right side of his chest. "I'm talking about your chest."

"My chest?" Kevin asked. Now, for the first time, he seemed uncomfortable. Then a light seemed to go on.

"Yes, your chest," Alex said. "On the right side, not far below your collar bone. Detective Keegan asked if you had injured it, didn't she?"

"Objection," Jack called. "He can't speculate as to what Detective Keegan might have suspected was an injury."

"That wasn't the question," the judge said. "The question was whether Keegan *asked* if he had been injured. Overruled."

"You can answer, Mr. Dunaway," the judge said to him, and Alex continued. "Detective Keegan asked you if you had injured your chest, on the right side, in about the very same place Kim Hadley testified that she kicked you with a high-heeled shoe…"

"Objection, argumentative!"

"Sustained. Mr. Greco refrain from commentary."

"She asked, yes," Kevin said. His face took on a guarded look.

"And you answered that it was an old injury, correct?"

"It was—it is—an old injury."

"So, you didn't deny to Detective Keegan that you experienced pain in that area, correct?"

"I didn't deny it."

"On that part of your body, correct?"

"Yes."

"When you went to shake hands with the two of them, correct?"

"You know, I don't remember exactly," Kevin said. He forced a smile, but it wasn't nearly as comfortable as the ones he'd flashed previously. "It was a long time ago and it really wasn't a big deal."

"Thank you," Alex said, avoiding the temptation to push further. As it was, Jack was probably going to do a brief re-direct on the source of the "old injury." But the damage was done. The jurors were looking differently at Kevin. Not with cold suspicion, but with something different than they had before. "Nothing further."

EIGHTY-FIVE

Friday, June 9
9:45 a.m.

"The anatomy of a lie," Jack said, standing to begin his closing argument. He looked over at Alex as if disappointed in him. Alex had just completed his first closing, which he had kept relatively short. Rebutting what Jack was about to say, here and now, was where he was going to earn this conviction if that was at all possible. Jack pivoted and looked back to the jury. "That, ladies and gentlemen, is what this travesty of a case is about." He moved around the defense table and stood before them. "Kim Hadley is a liar. It's all she's ever done. Her entire life is a lie. Everything she has, everything she knows, everything she's built. It's all...built...upon...a lie.

"Now, is this her fault? Most likely, it's not. She was raised in an abusive environment. We know that, and no one is denying it. She was beaten and mistreated for having gender dysphoria and wanting to live as a girl instead of a boy, and no one is denying that.

"Folks, we didn't bring Holly Jones into this courtroom to present to you the mother of the year. Ms. Jones is a sad person. A bitter person. We don't expect any of you to admire the way she raised Andy Hadley, the boy she came here to testify about. But Holly is also human, however tragic her story. Her bitterness and her anger, however they were formed, weren't formed by accident. And they were cemented on the night most of her family was killed." He turned back to the jury, letting that hang in the air.

Son of a bitch, Alex thought. He hadn't used the word "murdered." But he had come close.

"Well, you might say, she left, right? She had been gone for some time when her husband and her real daughter were both blown to bits. That's true. She did leave, and she told us why. She was in a situation she could no longer control, and that she felt the need to escape from. She ran in order to re-group and return when she felt stronger. Unfortunately, that day never came.

"Regardless of this, this isn't Holly's story. I'm sure many of you have wondered why we took such pains to bring her here in front of you. It wasn't for you to embrace her, or even to feel sympathy for her. No, we brought her here—and she came on her own volition—to tell you the truth about the person who calls herself Kimberly Hadley. Holly Jones had one job to do here, and that was to tell you how Andy Hadley—the actual person the complainant was and still really is today—was perceived in his community. She told you the truth without passion. Without rancor." With this, Jack turned and looked at Alex. "Sure, Mr. Greco dug into her as well as he could. He tried to minimize the truth of Holly's testimony, mostly with an appeal to sympathy for the complaining witness. But none of that distracted from the sad, simple truth of Holly Jones's testimony. The complainant, the person who calls herself

Kim Hadley, *lies*. That's what this person was known for in the community. That's what Andy Hadley did. That's what Andy's present persona, Kim Hadley, does.

"And by the way, ladies and gentlemen, if you also have sympathy for Kimberly Hadley, then you're not alone. You *should* have sympathy for her." Jack paused, turned and looked at Kim, seated behind the prosecution table, flanked by Judy, Angie and Danny. He held Kim's gaze for a few seconds, then turned back. "I have sympathy for her. Kevin Dunaway had, and even still has, sympathy for her. But my sympathy ends when yet another of Kim Hadley's lies threatens to destroy the life of an innocent man. Hadley should be pitied. She should be treated professionally, not for her choice to live as a woman, but for the abuse she suffered because of that desire.

"Let me be clear that this case isn't a statement about who Hadley is, thinks she is, or wants to be. Those are not issues for us to decide. What's to be decided is simply this: whether any of you can possibly find beyond a reasonable doubt that Kim Hadley has told you the truth about anything. The answer is clear that you cannot. We have no burden to prove anything here. We had no burden to present a case to you at all. As you can see, we didn't present a very big one. Trust me, that's not because I'm shirking responsibility for this case. Just ask my wife and daughter, they'll tell you about the other duties I've been shirking." A few of the jurors smiled, and Alex kept his eyes glued to his notes to keep from rolling them. "It's because we didn't need to. The government's case rests entirely, one hundred percent, on the testimony of the person who calls herself Kim Hadley. It requires that you believe Kim Hadley against every other reasonable inference. That simply isn't possible. I'll remind you of the high points now but remember this point above all others. It may not be Kim's fault that she knows, practices and lives only lies. However, it's not Kevin Dunaway's either."

EIGHTY-SIX

"She's spent a lifetime lying. She has no concept of truth. That's Mr. Hooper's argument to you." Alex stood before the jury box, his hands clasped.

"Truth." He unclasped his hands and spread them out. "Lie. These are important words." He moved his eyes from one juror to the next. "They're not just language we play games with. They're not just rhetorical fodder. They backstop the concepts that make this process possible." He paused and gestured around the courtroom. "The law isn't the only place where the truth is crucial, and that lies must be banished. It's the same in art, science, engineering, cooking. Truth is light. Truth is guidance. Truth allows us to move confidently, and safely, with each decision we make.

"So, Mr. Hooper is right to stress the importance, not only of these words, but of these concepts. But when it comes to evaluating them, ladies and gentlemen, he has it exactly backwards.

"Mr. Hooper wants you to believe that Kim Hadley is incapable of truth for the most inaccurate reason possible—because she refused to accept a lifetime of lies that were forced upon her. He wants you to believe Kim is incapable of speaking the truth when in fact she's been fighting for the truth her entire life. And she's won.

"Think about what you've heard. Kim told you about her past, indeed, we've heard as much about it as we have the events that brought us here. And the defense wanted it that way. They bore deep into her past hoping to find something you might distrust her for. Instead, what did they really accomplish? You know about Kim. You know about Emily, her younger sister with disabilities who Kim has cared for her entire life, most of it singlehandedly. You know about the love between them, the love that has sustained them through horrors most of us are happily unfamiliar with as to make them impossible even as nightmares. Is any of that a lie?

"Look at Kim's company, the one she built from nothing and that millions of customers and every beauty magazine raves about, that every business analyst praises. Mr. Hooper pointed your attention to it also, so let's look closely at it. Is any of it a lie?

"Look at the chains Kim broke, the ones placed on her as a child through ignorance and cruelty. They are chains she threw off to live as she has always known she was supposed to live. Look at the truth she grasped when she accepted the gift of a new identity from the woman who probably loved her more than herself—her twin sister. Look now at what she's accomplished with it. Look at every truth Kimberly Hadley has built, and that you've heard about during the course of this trial.

"Her path to truth is what some call a lie because it serves other ends, whether it's narrow-mindedness, doctrine, oppression, or just plain human meanness. But Kim has overcome that. She lives more truthfully than most of us could ever hope to do. Kim has found truth. Kim has lived truth. Kim has told you the truth." Alex walked across the courtroom in Kim's direction. He gestured with one hand toward her and spoke to the jury, his voice resonating with power.

"This. Is. Kimberly. Hadley. That is the truth." Then he extended his arm and pointed at Kevin Dunaway. He took a few steps toward him, looking not at the jury but at Kevin.

"He tried to rape her. That is the truth."

EIGHTY-SEVEN

5:15 p.m.

The jury had been out for almost five hours when Alex ducked out for his sixth cigarette of the day, the fifth since 2:00 p.m. As he had done his entire career, he brought paperwork with him to sift through as he waited on the jury. There was no shortage of new cases coming in, and the unit was in for a busy summer and fall. And, as he had also done his entire career, he gave up on trying to concentrate on it. It was the one part of the job that never got easier, the painstaking wait for deliberations to bear fruit.

Outside, it was a gray and cool early summer day, owed mostly to an approaching line of storms. A damp wind swept through downtown; thick, dark clouds pressed down on the skyscrapers and distant rumbles of thunder could be heard on the Jersey side. Alex squinted against street dust as he left the courthouse from a rear exit and crossed Baxter Street to Columbus Park. There was plenty of tree cover, and he found a quiet bench out of sight. He lit up and breathed deep. For a minute or two, he just watched the cigarette burn and let his thoughts drift.

"I hope there's someone in your life who's trying to

get you to drop that habit," he heard. The voice was clear, sharp and feminine. He looked up and saw Crystal Haidt, standing a few feet away. Tall and slender, she looked terrific in a sharp, blue suit and a white blouse.

"She wouldn't be happy about it today, that's for sure."

"Can I sit?"

"The bench belongs to the city," he said, and motioned to the space next to him. She smoothed her skirt, sat down and crossed her legs. They were long and beautifully formed, running down to brilliant but court-appropriate black pumps.

"You did a good job. Jack admires you as a lawyer."

"Good to know," he said. "When is your surprise witness leaving town?" Crystal gave him a wan smile. Her teeth weren't showing, but she had lovely, sloping lips. Above them were light brown eyes and a perfectly shaped nose.

"Who, Andy's mom?"

"That's really not funny, Crystal."

"Lighten up, please. It's over. We all fought hard."

"It was traumatic, bringing her here. Probably for Holly, too, if she has any semblance of a heart left."

"You brought charges," Crystal said. "We answered them. And yes, she's gone already. Back to her mega-church. She didn't try to talk to your complainant or the sister, right?"

"No, but Kim was afraid she might try. She's mostly worried about Emily."

"Emily the sister or Emily the brand?"

"Jack's training you well."

"What's your point?"

"Your tactics were out of line," Alex said. "I'm not the type who'll smile in your face and then complain about you behind your back. You're hearing it from me. I'll tell Jack, too, when I get the chance."

"I can understand that," Crystal said, nodding and pursing her lips. "But what I think you're referring to is mostly the work of Bill Petrazzo, not us."

"Give me a break, it's your case."

"And Petrazzo came with it," she said. "With a few other people. What do you think, he works for us? Petrazzo is on loan to us, Alex. Jack will tell you the same thing. We don't know where Dunaway found him."

"Probably from some other rich creep," he said.

"Probably. But this is the reality of criminal litigation where the client is wealthy. Dunaway lost a few million when CIG separated from him, but he's still worth more than twenty, probably. He can afford things most people can't even dream of. The rich are different, in case you haven't noticed."

"I've been around money. I've seen it act better than that."

"Then you haven't seen it cornered," she said. Alex tried to think of a retort, but then gave up.

"It's a tough old world," he said finally. "My father was fond of saying that."

"He sounds like a wise man."

"He's mostly an asshole."

"You're just a barrel of laughs," she said, a bemused, almost bewildered look on her face. Then the face went flat. "Listen, watch out for Petrazzo, okay?"

"Petrazzo? Why?"

"He's not a nice guy, let's put it that way. And he thinks there's something about you he can exploit. That's what he does. But you didn't hear that from me."

"He played that card already," Alex said. "And I'm sure you know the details."

"He may not think he's played it out yet. It doesn't matter what happens today. Just watch out, that's all I'm saying."

"Why would you tell me this?" he asked. She held his gaze for a moment, her eyes moving around his face.

"Because you seem like a decent guy. Jack thinks so too, although he thinks you're a little sanctimonious. I see something else, though."

"Please, my girlfriend is a shrink. I don't need further analysis."

"She has her hands full, then. I know the type." She grinned again, and after a second, he returned it. A breeze blew a strand of hair into her face and she brushed it away, an angelic gesture with her ring and little finger.

"You made good arguments in there," he said. "You're good at this." He paused and stood up. "And thank you for what you said. I'd say good luck, but..."

"Gotcha," she said. He started to walk away, and then both of their phones went off. It was Evan, the judge's law clerk. The text was one word.

Verdict.

EIGHTY-EIGHT

"Members of the jury," Jude Lowe intoned, "I have your note stating that you've reached a verdict. Mr. Foreperson, please rise." The foreperson did so, an older man with a yarmulke and horn-rimmed glasses. "Has the jury reached a unanimous verdict?"

"We have Your Honor."

"As to count one, Attempted Rape in the First Degree. What is the jury's verdict?" Alex closed his eyes and held his breath.

"Guilty, Your Honor." A murmur spread through the courtroom. The word rang in Alex's ears. A mix of pride, intense relief and shock went through him. He heard the sound of something striking the defense table, not over-whelming but noticeable. It was Kevin, who had slapped his hand on the table and now had it balled up into a fist against his mouth. Jack was whispering to him with his hand on Kevin's shoulder.

"As to count two, Attempted Sexual Abuse in the First Degree. What is the jury's verdict?"

"Guilty, Your Honor." In his peripheral vision Alex could see Kevin sink into his chair and shake his head. There were three other counts, one for Sexual Abuse in the

Third Degree, and two for Assault in the Third Degree, the last two representing the two punches Kevin had thrown. The verdict was the same on all. Alex wanted to look back to where he knew Kim was seated, but he couldn't. Instead he kept his face neutral and his eyes forward as the judge polled the individual jurors at Jack's request. Then he stood, as everyone did, and nodded to the jurors as they were thanked and released.

Afterwards, Jack requested Kevin's bond be continued for sentencing, as Alex expected. There was, Jack insisted, a likelihood of reversal on appeal. The judge didn't even ask for a response from Alex. The defendant would be remanded to custody pending sentencing. With a last, silent pout, Kevin Dunaway allowed himself to be led by court officers through the rear door of the courtroom.

Now Alex did look back at Kim. Her eyes were fixed on the door Kevin had been walked out through. Her hands clutched the wooden railing that marked the perimeter of the well. Her eyes were dry but pained. Finally, they shifted to Alex, and seemed to brighten. She mouthed a 'thank you' and then allowed Judy to lead her out of the courtroom, a group of reporters following close behind.

EIGHTY-NINE

6:30 p.m.

"They came after me, too," Alex said, after leading Kim away from the courthouse a couple of blocks to a narrow street in Chinatown where he lit another cigarette. The air around them was damp after the earlier rain, heavy with the smell of frying meat and slowly rotting fish. "The defense team."

"You?" she asked. Around them, women argued with vendors in foreign dialects, and more men, including Alex, were smoking than not. "How?"

"That same investigator, the one who put Megan in front of you? He planted a guy to get close to my ex-wife. It's a long story, but they were hoping to gather information from her. Something that would have compromised me, I guess, to force me to drop the case."

"Oh," she said. "I'm sorry." She didn't say anything else, which Alex respected and was grateful for. He wanted her to know she wasn't alone in what she had gone through, but he didn't want to go into details either. As he suspected after working with her for a few months, Kim knew the value of privacy and where to leave things.

"Sometimes, they go after everyone in a case like this.

I asked Angie and Danny if they noticed anything out of the ordinary in their lives, but I don't think it got that far."

"Can they even do things like that?" she asked. Alex made a see-saw motion.

"Mostly, yeah, they can. At some point it can amount to witness tampering or some of kind of harassment, but it's almost impossible to prove. It's just how it is."

"You warned me," she said. "You tried to, anyway. I didn't see Megan coming. Not at all."

"Doesn't matter. In the end, you held steady. I couldn't be prouder of you, Kim."

"I didn't want to let you down. That meant more to me than winning."

"Did you tell the truth, when you were up there?"

"Yes. Every word."

"Then you didn't let me down. It would have been the same no matter what the jury decided."

"Kevin's lawyer wanted the jury to think I killed them," Kim said. "My sister and my father."

"He might have been insinuating it, yes, but I don't think that worked either."

"You know he could have asked," she said, looking down the block. Her eyes followed a bent-over Asian man pushing a cart full of brown and orange roots. "But he didn't. That's why I didn't have to lie."

"He didn't ask about what?"

"About what set off the explosion," she said, looking back to him. "Or who. I think he just wanted the jury to believe I set it up, somehow, so he implied that as much as he could."

"I think that's true," Alex said. "I was a little afraid of that as well, you know."

"Afraid of what? That I did it?"

"I didn't think you did it. But I knew it wasn't an accident."

"How?"

"You never used that word, for one thing. *Accident.*"

"Oh." She eyed him. "You noticed that?"

"At some point." He smiled at her. "It's part of the job."

"It was Kim," she said, exhaling. "She killed herself, my father and Lefty. She blew the house to bits. There was a chemical tank, a huge one, in the kitchen. She shot it with a handgun from just a few feet away."

"Was that what she told you she was going to do?"

"No. I saw her with the gun. She had sent me to Dolly's already, to grab Emily and get moving. But I went back for her, because I wanted her to come with us, and I had a bad feeling. I walked inside. That's when I saw her. She had a gun pointed at the tank. I had seen the gun before, it was a revolver. Kim got it during that period she had run away, and she showed me how it worked when she came back. My father and Lefty were standing there like two deer in headlights, watching her pointing it. But not at them-- at that tank. She turned and screamed for me to run. I made it to the middle of the yard before the house went up."

"Oh."

"She talked about doing it, grabbing some money from one of my father's stupid hiding places, then setting the tank off, somehow. She knew it would take the whole house out. And then we'd run and let them think we were all dead. But I didn't think she'd do what she did." Kim paused, cleared her throat and squeezed her eyes shut against the tears. "She did it for me. She did it so I could *be* her. So I could be Kim." She fished in her purse for some tissues, blew her nose and then seemed to wipe the sadness from her face. She took a deep breath and exhaled raggedly. To Alex, she looked too tired to cry anymore. "I've thought about it every single day of my life. There's no way I was worthy of that. She had a whole life ahead of her, too, and she gave it me. She was only eighteen."

"My guess is she knew you would take good care of Emily," Alex said. "That was part of her plan, too."

"Yeah, but I wanted it to be all of us." Her voice dropped to a whisper. "She was so strong."

"Well, maybe she thought she was strong in the moment, but that you'd be there to stay strong forever. I think she knew that about you, and she was right. Really, Kim, this case is a victory, but you should be proud no matter what. Go back to your life, now. You've earned it."

"You don't think anyone will come after me?" she asked. "For whatever I did when I was getting my life started with Emily?"

"No, I don't. But if you ever feel threatened, you know I'll help you, right?"

"Thank you. So, it's really over, huh?"

"For you, yes. It's over."

"What about you? You've got new cases, I guess?"

"Yeah, it never ends. Hang on one second, okay?" Angie was calling.

"What's your twenty?" she asked. "I'm with Danny. We've got Emily, she came down to see her sister. We found her at a hot dog cart. She's waiting for Kim to come out of the courthouse, but no one's seen you two."

"We went out a side door," Alex said. "Needed a break. We're on Mulberry, near Mosco, behind the park."

"We'll be there pronto."

"They're with Emily," Alex said to Kim once he'd hung up. "She came down to see you, I guess. They'll bring her by and give you both a ride home."

"I think Emily may want to walk around down here," Kim said, smiling to herself. "This is her kind of place." A minute or so later, Angie's unmarked car squeaked to a halt beside them. Danny stepped out and opened the back door for Emily.

"They got me a couple of hot dogs," she said, a broad smile on her face. She looked up and down the block. "Can we get dumplings and shit around here?"

"Pretty sure we can," Kim said, smiling back. She turned to Alex. "I don't have to come back for sentencing, right? Judy told me I could submit a statement, but that I didn't have to be there."

"Correct. Totally up to you."

"I'll let you handle it, then. I won't forget you, Alex Greco. I don't even know how to thank you." She looked beyond him to Angie and Danny. "All of you."

"Keep Emily happy and make millions of dollars," Alex said. "That'll make us even. My girlfriend might want a discount, though. She loves your facial scrub."

"Have her call me." She put out her hand for Alex to shake. Instead, he took it lightly and kissed it.

"Goodbye, Ms. Hadley."

"Goodbye, Alex." She held his gaze for a moment, then shifted it to Danny and Angie, now outside and leaning on the car in the bright afternoon sunshine. She waved and they nodded back.

"They gonna be okay on their own?" Danny asked as Alex walked over. Kim and Emily had fallen into step with each other away from them, headed east toward Mott Street.

"That's an understatement," Alex said. "Yeah, they're okay. But I'm going with you two. First bar you can think of."

"Amen to that, brother," Danny said. "Ang, you pick."

ACKNOWLEDGEMENTS

In creating this story, I remain in debt to Christina Carathanassis and Kristi Vannatter for crucial insights into the beauty industry, to Sue Horan and Rachel Singer of the Brooklyn District Attorney's Office Cold Case Unit for the latest technological input on DNA evidence, and always to the men and women of the New York City Police Department.

ABOUT THE AUTHOR

Roger Canaff is a widely known child protection and anti-violence against women advocate, legal expert, author, and public speaker. He has devoted his legal career to the eradication of violence against women and children, first as a prosecutor in historic Alexandria, Virginia, then as a Special Victims ADA in the Bronx, and as Deputy Chief of the New York State Attorney General's Office Sex Offender Management Unit. Most recently, he was employed as a U.S. Army civilian, serving as a Highly Qualified Expert training and advising military prosecutors on sexual assault and other special victims cases. With over 20 years' experience, he has prosecuted and consulted on cases involving sexual and physical abuse of children and adolescents, sexual assault against adults, and crimes against the elderly and persons with disabilities.

Mr. Canaff continues to provide training to attorneys, medical experts, law enforcement officers, victim advocates and the general public on all issues related to the investigation and prosecution of child abuse and sexual assault. He teaches law, comments on special victims issues for major networks, and is the author of three novels. He lives and works in New York City.

Thank you so much for reading Book 2 in the
Alex Greco Series!

If you've enjoyed this book, please consider leaving
a short review on Goodreads or your website of choice.
It would mean a lot to me.

Would you like to be the first to hear about
my latest releases and special promotions?
Please visit my website to sign up for my author newsletter.

www.rogercanaff.com

CPSIA information can be obtained
at www.ICGtesting.com
Printed in the USA
LVHW030538240320
651021LV00018B/2783